HER
ENEMY

BOOKS BY EMMA TALLON

HER ENEMY

EMMA TALLON

bookouture

Published by Bookouture in 2023

An imprint of Storyfire Ltd.
Carmelite House
50 Victoria Embankment
London EC4Y 0DZ

www.bookouture.com

ISBN: 978-1-83790-157-9
eBook ISBN: 978-1-83790-156-2

To Christian and Charlotte. You are the reason I breathe, my every motivation and the meaning to my life. Every word I ever write is for you.

PROLOGUE

She sat at the table, her head in her hands as she tried to process what was happening. Half an hour ago they'd finally been on the right track, and now here she sat with her whole world in tatters. She was never going to see her family again. And *worse*, they would forever look back over their memories of her with a feeling of sickness and betrayal. Looking back, she knew she could have avoided this if she'd just told them the truth, but she hadn't, and now she couldn't take it back.

He paced the hallway, speaking to someone on the phone in a low, urgent voice. He was arranging their transport out of here, over to the mainland. The idea of leaving her family, without so much as a goodbye, felt so wrong. She couldn't comprehend it. But she had no choice now. Her time was running out and soon *he* would come for her. Come to kill her. There was no other way. She had to leave, and it had to be now.

The call ended and he walked through the kitchen. 'Come on.' He grabbed her arm. 'They're en route to the pickup point. We need to drive over there now.' He paused. 'Are you up to this? Can you drive?'

'Yeah,' she said in a hollow voice. ''Course. Let's go.'

She stood up and walked through to the hallway, shrugging on her coat as he picked up both their bags. It was insane to think that those two small bags contained everything they would now possess in life. She lingered for just a second, then walked forward and opened the door.

'Goodbye,' Scarlet whispered, unsure who or what she was saying it to. And then she closed it, walking away from her life and her family for good.

ONE

Dry leaves rustled in the breeze as they chased each other in circles through the graveyard on the hill. There was no other noise here, apart from the occasional sobs of another visitor nearby. Luckily none were here today. It was just him.

Cillian stared down at the marble headstone before him. It was exactly one year to the day since his sister Ruby's body had been found at the bottom of an industrial oil tank. The coroner's report had stated she'd been dead for several weeks, though when they'd identified her body, she'd still looked exactly the same, as though no time had passed at all. The oil had preserved her body, they'd told him. It was one small mercy, he'd figured. Losing her had been hard enough; at least seeing her like that – still their Ruby, not just some rotting corpse wearing her clothes – was a better way to see her for the last time.

He could picture her now in the grey dismal coroners' room; her pale lifeless face had been so serene, so peaceful. It was an expression she'd never worn while she'd been alive. Ruby had never found her peace in this world, always moving with the chaos. Creating it when she couldn't find any to latch on to. The quiet had always been too much for her inner demons to cope with. Perhaps now she was dead they had set her free, and her weary soul could finally rest. He hoped so.

Cillian's vision blurred and the white marble swam before his eyes. He sniffed, looking away across the fields. The view was beautiful from this spot. It was why they'd chosen it. Fields and forest stretched out for miles, and the small village that the churchyard belonged to was tucked quietly away to one side. His mother, Lily, hadn't been able to bear her being buried in the city, where the bodies were all cramped together, surrounded by tall grey buildings and noisy polluted roads. He hadn't pointed out the irony of moving her away, in death, from the exact environment they all chose to live in.

He ran his thumb over the smooth surface of the bracelet he clutched inside his jacket pocket. It had been his last gift to his sister, on her last living birthday. A gold Tiffany bracelet holding a single ruby. A ruby for his Ruby. It had been a particularly extravagant gift, but it had been for more than just her birthday really. She'd been trying so hard that year, to earn her way back into the fold. It hadn't been easy for her, after years of choosing the needle over her family, but she'd finally turned a corner. He'd wanted her to know that he was proud of her, that he was rooting for her to succeed.

The memories cut painfully deep. Today was going to be a difficult day for the whole family. Or most of them at least. Lifting his chin, he clenched his chiselled jaw, and his gaze rested on the words etched into Ruby's gravestone.

In memory of Ruby Ann Drew
Beloved daughter, sister and niece.
Sleep now, angel.

There was no mention of a beloved cousin. A familiar

feeling of unrest bubbled under the surface as he thought about Scarlet.

There hadn't been much of an investigation into what had happened to Ruby. The oil tank had been in a large scrapyard and her jacket and some bedding had been found nearby. She'd clearly been hiding out there, and the police had put it down to an unfortunate accident. Not that they cared. To them Ruby was just another Drew. Another criminal off their hands. But Cillian wasn't as convinced that it was an accident. There was a reason Ruby had been hiding out in that scrapyard.

She and Scarlet had despised each other since childhood. They'd all assumed they'd grow out of it eventually, but instead it had grown into something much darker as they'd entered adulthood.

This hadn't been much of an issue before Ruby had returned and joined the family firm, but in such close proximity, the burning embers of their mutual hatred had flared into a roaring fire. In the end, Ruby had committed one of the biggest sins imaginable in their way of life. She'd set Scarlet up to be caught out by the police, aiming to get her sent to prison and ruin the life of Scarlet's then boyfriend in the process. Two vicious victories for the price of one.

But her plan hadn't worked out the way she'd hoped. Scarlet hadn't gone down and Ruby's actions had been exposed. Scarlet's fury had turned murderous, and Ruby had disappeared, taking two hundred and fifty grand from the family safe on her way out. Scarlet had tried to hunt her down, hellbent on revenge, but to the rest of the family's knowledge, she'd never found Ruby. None of them had. Cillian had searched for her himself, but Ruby had always been skilled at hiding when she didn't want to be found. The next time any of them had seen her, she'd been on a mortuary slab.

Cillian's thumb moved back and forth over the bracelet as he thought over it all. When Ruby was found, Scarlet had been adamant she'd had nothing to do with it. But something in the way she'd reacted was a little off. He'd accused her of lying, in his grief, desperate for an answer that made more sense. But Lily had commanded him to stop. She believed Scarlet and that was the end of it, she'd told them. The subject had never been discussed again.

These days, he and Scarlet worked closer than ever as their firm grew, but a sliver of suspicion still lurked at the back of his mind. On the one hand, he knew how much their family meant to Scarlet. As set on revenge as she was, it didn't make sense for her to have killed Ruby. She'd have punished her if she'd found her of course. Beaten her perhaps. That, the family would have had to forgive. Even in her most furious moments, Scarlet had always been careful and calculated in her actions, and killing Ruby would have had more consequence than reward for her.

But despite that, he couldn't forget the look in her eye when he'd accused her. There had been a flicker of something that didn't align with her words. What it was exactly, he wasn't sure. But it wasn't confidence or outrage, the look he'd expect from someone defending themselves after just being falsely accused of murder. It was something else. Something she'd quickly hidden.

After touching his fingertips to Ruby's headstone in good-bye, Cillian turned and walked back down the grassy hillside. As he neared his car, the engine started and the door was pushed open from the inside. He slipped into the passenger seat and unbuttoned his dark fitted suit jacket.

'Where to, boss?' the man next to him asked.

'The Hideout,' he replied, his tone low as the dark thoughts still circled his mind.

Scarlet would be there soon, waiting for him to arrive before they started their meeting. Anniversary or not, the businesses wouldn't sleep today, and their enemies wouldn't wait for them to mourn. Theirs was a harsh world, and there was no time for luxuries such as grief.

Still, perhaps it was a good thing they were so busy today. It was better to lose oneself in work than let grief pull you into its dark depths, in his opinion.

They worked well together, he and Scarlet. They were on the same wavelength, shared the same priorities and understood each other so well that at times they didn't even need to speak, a look or undertone often communicating more than enough. They'd always been close, he and his little cousin.

But, be that as it may, he thought, glancing back over his shoulder towards the graveyard before they turned the corner, it didn't matter how close they were, or how much he loved her. If he ever found out his suspicions were right and Scarlet *had* murdered Ruby – he'd kill her.

TWO

Scarlet ran a brush through her long dark hair and stared into the mirror at her dressing table. Her face had changed over the last year. Her grey-blue eyes stared back at her with a natural seriousness they'd not held before, and her high defined cheekbones now lent her an extra hardness, all softness gone from her face. Gone, perhaps, to the same place as the softness she used to have in her soul, she thought absently.

It was the anniversary of Ruby's body being found. A day she'd been dreading. The anniversary of Ruby's *actual* death had come and gone a couple of months before, but Scarlet was the only one who knew that date. The police had only been able to give her aunt a vague idea of when it could have been, due to the way the oil had preserved her body. So this was the first marked date for Lily and the twins, which meant it would be a hard one.

Scarlet placed the brush down on the dressing table and pinched her cheeks in the mirror, hoping it would give her pale skin some colour. It didn't. With a small sigh, she stood and picked her handbag up off the bed. Her knee-length fitted dress was simple and black, the colour tactfully chosen for today, and she smoothed the skirt as she left the bedroom and made her way downstairs.

'I've just put a pot on, if you want a coffee,' her mother, Cath, called out.

'Thanks,' Scarlet replied tiredly, entering the bright spacious kitchen. 'I think I probably need it on a drip today.' It had been another late one, the night before.

'Pot to vein? Might be a bit hot. Best stick to a cup,' Cath replied, handing her one.

She looked out of the kitchen windows at their long manicured garden. 'It'll be cold today,' she commented. 'Take your big coat, yeah? And your scarf.'

The corner of Scarlet's mouth hitched up in amusement. 'And make sure to eat the fruit before the chocolate bar in my lunchbox too, yeah?'

Cath narrowed her eyes at her playfully. 'Yeah, yeah, take the piss out of your old mum. Won't be laughing when you forget and end up snotty and miserable though, will ya? And anyway' – she turned back towards the garden with a warm expression – 'don't matter how old you get, you'll always be my baby.'

The warmth faded and she looked suddenly sombre. 'You with Lil today?'

'Not until later.' Scarlet sipped her coffee again and searched her mother's face, trying to gauge what she was thinking.

'She'll be a mess today,' Cath continued, her tone troubled. 'Maybe you should just...' She hesitated and trailed off.

Scarlet tensed. 'What? Maybe I should what?'

Cath grimaced. 'I think it'll be hard for her to see you today, that's all. Maybe you should steer clear. Or maybe not, I don't know.' She rubbed her forehead, looking stressed.

Scarlet felt her core turn cold. What did her mother mean

by that? She didn't know anything. *Did* she? She put her mug down on the breakfast bar, her expression neutral.

'And why would you think that?' she asked carefully.

'I just think seeing you today, an adult Drew daughter who ain't hers, might make her pain even harder to bear,' Cath said, a heavy sadness in her words. 'I know if it were the other way around, I'd find it hard to look at Ruby today. It would be a reminder that *my* daughter was gone, yet Lil's is still here. And, though I'm ashamed to admit it, I think I'd resent that.' She cast her eyes down and pressed her lips together.

Scarlet felt the coldness withdraw. Of course her mother didn't know anything. Why would she? Why would anyone? It had been over a year since Ruby had died in that tank. If anyone knew something, other than the three of them who'd been there, it would have come out by now.

'Maybe,' she replied. 'Or maybe not. Lil and I are close – we see each other every day. And surely having family around would be more of a comfort?'

'True. Maybe I'm just overthinking it.' She shrugged and turned to Scarlet with a smile. 'Ignore me, love. You're right. Forget I said anything.'

Scarlet nodded. Cath was right about one thing: Lily would be a mess today. And knowing her aunt the way she did, Scarlet imagined she'd deal with it by throwing herself into work.

'I need to get on.' She stood up and pecked her mother on the cheek. 'I'll see you later, yeah?'

'Yeah, 'course. Have a good day,' Cath replied, waving her off.

Scarlet walked out of the house and closed the door, glad to be done with the conversation about Ruby. Though it wouldn't be the last today. She unlocked the sleek black Mercedes, slipped into the driver's seat and closed her eyes. No matter how much time passed, she knew she'd never be free of her cousin. The memory of her at least. The memory and the guilt.

Forcing her eyes open, she pulled in a deep breath and turned the key in the ignition. The engine roared to life and she pulled forward off the drive.

No, she'd never be free of Ruby Drew. Ruby had made sure of that. Even in death her cousin still plagued her – and that was her cross to bear. One she'd accepted a long time ago. So today she would do exactly as expected. Be there with her family, nod at their fond memories and support them when their pain became too much to bear alone.

It was a small price to pay for a life in which Ruby could never again destroy anyone or anything; could never again wreak havoc or tear down all they held dear. It was nothing at all, really, in comparison to the overall peace her death had created. But even so, Scarlet would still be glad when the day was over and she could banish the dark shadow that would walk with them today, back to the box of memories that were hidden away. Because there was no room for the ghosts of the past here anymore. This world was for the living.

THREE

Scarlet pulled up outside the old industrial building and cast her eye across the large arch of small square windows. They'd called it The Hideout – a place that had started out as a sideline, nine months before, and had then become more successful than they'd ever anticipated. It had been Cillian's idea to open a bar and restaurant, and he'd taken the lead on the project, turning the place into something far more spectacular than the rest of them had imagined.

The downstairs area of the old industrial building housed the main bar and restaurant. The dark moody décor, along with the exposed brick walls and steel beams, was accentuated with low lighting and sleek furniture, creating an industrial yet luxury atmosphere. A long bar with seating away from the main restaurant allowed for customers to enjoy cocktails, and a resident DJ booth was tucked into a far corner, from which low chilled house beats were played every night. Almost overnight it had become a popular destination for dating couples and social media glamourites.

The floor above housed another, more exclusive bar, the main floor split into large booths with thick padded privacy walls, enterable through small open archways. Each booth was strategically designed so the conversations within wouldn't carry through the walls. It was the perfect set-up. Open plan and private all at the same time.

This was a membership-only area, with access closely guarded at the door. The membership itself was all above board – a paid-for service that ran through the books – but there was no criteria anywhere to be found for the average member of the public. Membership was granted personally by the Drews and only to those in their circles of the underworld. It had been wildly popular from the off – this new stylish space to conduct business, where they could speak freely and truly relax – and the crooks of the underworld had been quick to sign up. Because whilst there were other places that served those basic needs, there was nothing quite as stylish and upmarket as this. Cillian had created the perfect spot.

Scarlet stepped out of the car and made her way to the dark double front doors. She'd had the sneaking suspicion, when Cillian had initially approached his mother with this idea, that Lily had just agreed to it to keep him happy, as he'd been unusually restless in the months beforehand. Neither Cillian nor his twin brother Connor had been interested in taking the lead on projects before then, and though Scarlet would never say it out loud, she knew Lily hadn't trusted them to either.

The few times they'd gone off on a whim, away from the confines of Lily's carefully laid plans, they'd been reckless and had messed up on a colossal scale. But the success of The Hideout had changed things. Cillian had proven himself to be savvy and smart in ways they hadn't seen from him before. There had been a shift in the firm after that. Lily had started trusting him more, and to Scarlet's surprise, Cillian had stepped up to the challenge.

Her surprise hadn't been because she didn't have faith in him; she'd always known that Cillian was smart, but she'd expected him to grow bored and turn back to his usual side of the business. Because he and Connor had never been the plotters; they'd always been the doers – the ones who carried out whatever needed to be done, no matter how dark or hard. And they were good at it. Respected for it.

But Cillian hadn't lost interest in his new project. As the success of The Hideout grew, so did his desire to take on more. And this desire couldn't have come at a better time, in Scarlet's opinion. A year ago, Lily had told them, in no uncertain terms, that they needed to grow or they'd face professional extinction.

Lily, and Ronan, Scarlet's father, had built the firm from nothing to a successful and powerful entity, decades before. They hadn't been the largest or most powerful in London, but they hadn't been far down the ladder. They'd easily rivalled all the other medium-sized firms, holding their prime territory of East London, their reputation warding off any enemies watching for a chance to take them down. But things had changed over the years and those other firms had evolved and grown. Suddenly, although their businesses continued to be lucrative, they had found themselves significantly outnumbered, when faced with the firms they used to rival. And the gap between them and the smaller firms that had seemed so insignificant before suddenly hadn't been so wide.

Over the last year, they had actively grown, sought out potential and cultivated it. And Cillian had been integral to making it all work. Most of the men they'd taken on had come via him, in some way. From the boxing club, from the estates, people he'd come across on jobs – men who'd watched from the sidelines for years, hoping for a way in with the infamous Drews.

It hadn't been easy to let new people in at first. The action came with extra risks, and such openness didn't come naturally to any of them after years of keeping things tightly within the family. But it had been a matter of survival – and survival was something they excelled at.

Scarlet walked through the dark restaurant to the stairs that led up to the first floor. It was too early in the day for the place to be open, and the sharp taps of her heels echoed around the otherwise silent space.

At the top of the stairs, a young man stepped aside to let her pass and, once inside the room, Scarlet's sharp eyes quickly scanned the open archways into each booth until she found her waiting men. She tilted her head towards the back of the long room and they immediately followed her, waiting silently as she unlocked the door to the office.

They filed in, silently taking their seats on the low black leather chairs that curved in almost a full circle to face the wide desk that closed it. Scarlet checked her watch as she took the empty seat behind the desk. Cillian should have been here by now. This was his domain really. Most Drew offices were available for any of them to use as they needed, but they all had favourite boltholes, and this one was definitely Cillian's castle. The furniture, in style with the rest of the place, was chic and yet masculine. Oversized, yet minimalistic. The oddly contradicting styles fitted Cillian perfectly.

Scarlet looked around at the faces staring back at her expectantly. 'We might as well start. Anything urgent before we discuss plans for tomorrow?' she asked.

All but one man shook their heads. She watched him, Joe Tanner, catching the uncertainty in his expression. 'What is it?'

'I've heard whispers of outside bets being taken for our fights,' Joe replied. 'I ain't confirmed it yet, but I've heard it twice now, and...'

'And there's rarely smoke without fire,' Scarlet finished with a grim look. 'What did you hear exactly?'

'Someone training down the gym asked me if it was true we were allowing bets elsewhere, that they'd overheard someone talking about it at a pub. He said he'd been drunk and decided he'd probably misheard when I told him no.' Joe shrugged. 'I assumed he'd misheard too at first. But I was in the Black Bear last night and overheard someone tell his mate that his missus had been offered better odds elsewhere.'

Scarlet raised one dark perfectly arched eyebrow and cold anger flashed through her grey-blue eyes. 'Who were they?'

Joe shook his head. 'I half recognised his face but I ain't entirely sure. I'd have asked, but there were six of 'em and I was on me tod. And they got on the defensive when they realised I was listening, so I had to back off. Figured I'd chase it up today.'

Scarlet tilted her head to the side and let out a slow breath. 'Take Danny back with you. Ask around, find out who they are and where this information is coming from. No one takes bets for our fighters except us,' she said, her tone hard.

'Will do,' Joe replied.

'Anything else?' she asked, looking around.

There was a murmured chorus of *no*, and she nodded. 'Good. Then let's get down to the plans for tomorrow night. Most of the set-up has been taken care of, but—'

The door opened, and as Cillian walked in, her heart dropped at the unrest she saw behind his eyes. He was trying hard to conceal it, but he couldn't hide the effects of today from her. She'd known him too long. As his gaze met hers across the room, she forced a smile.

'Cillian,' she said, the casualness belying the wary turbulence she felt within, 'you're just in time.'

FOUR

Lily sat in one of the wrought-iron chairs at the bottom of the garden, her elbows resting on the hard unforgiving arms and her legs tightly crossed as she tried to ignore the cold that was creeping into her shins. She put her cigarette to her mouth and drew in a deep lungful of smoke. Usually, the familiarity of the action and the nicotine her body so craved would bring a little relief, but not tonight. Nothing would ever be strong enough to take the edge off this day.

She pulled the fleecy throw she'd grabbed on her way out of the house more tightly around her body and stared back at the warm lights of the house. The early evening November darkness enveloped her here, shielding her from view. She was far enough away that even if they looked out of the windows, they shouldn't see her.

Lily took another deep drag and blew back out, watching the long grey plume of smoke drift and curl upwards into the air, spreading thinner and thinner until it disappeared. That was exactly how she felt today. As if she had spread herself so thinly that she wasn't even really here anymore. As if she could disappear at any moment. If only it was that simple.

There was a clanging sound from inside the house, followed by a shriek and a muffled string of what sounded like expletives, from Cath, her sister-in-law. Lily laid her head back against the chair and looked up into the clear night sky to the stars. The orangey glow from the city made it so that it was never truly dark enough to see more than a couple of the really bright ones. The view would be beautiful from Ruby's grave though, out in the countryside where light pollution didn't ruin it. All the stars would be visible from there.

One hot tear escaped the corner of Lily's eye, and she wiped the trail away with the back of her hand. She sniffed, looking back down. Never in a million years had she thought she'd outlive one of her children. No mother ever did. Never had she thought she'd be sitting here grieving, unable to understand why God had chosen to take one of her babies before her. She'd begged Him many a time, as she kneeled in church week on week, to keep them safe. To help *her* keep them safe. And she wasn't a fool – she'd always understood the risks of their way of life. But that was why she'd always tried to keep them close. Keep them protected.

If it had been an enemy who'd come for her daughter, she could have put herself in their path. Fought them off or offered herself up in Ruby's place – and she'd have gladly done it. Because that was what motherhood was all about. Sacrifice. Putting your children's lives before your own. But she hadn't been given that chance. Ruby had been taken from her while she hadn't been there to protect her. Which meant she'd failed at the single most important job she'd ever had in this life.

The back door opened, flooding the patio with light for a moment, as someone stepped out. Lily watched as a figure made a steady beeline directly for her and exhaled slowly through her nose.

'Clearly I'm not as covert as I thought,' she said wryly,

taking a final drag on her cigarette before stubbing it out in the ashtray on the small table next to her.

Scarlet placed a tumbler of whisky on the table, then sat down on the matching chair the other side, pulling her coat over her chest with a shiver. 'Don't worry, no one else knows you're here. They all think you're upstairs.'

'Is that for me?' Lily asked.

Scarlet nodded.

Lily picked up the tumbler and downed the contents in one. The burn hit the back of her throat with a fiery intensity she knew was heightened by the cold outside. She closed her eyes, savouring it. Savouring the feel of something other than the cycle of failure and grief and guilt she'd been stuck in all day.

'You haven't just come out here to bring me whisky,' she observed, glancing at her niece.

'Mum slipped and dropped the lasagne all over the floor as she pulled it out of the oven,' Scarlet answered, as if this explained her continued presence.

'Ah.' Lily placed the empty glass back down on the table.

That did indeed explain Scarlet's strategic move out here. Cath would be raising hell right now. She'd made the lasagne from scratch for tonight. It was her go-to gesture of comfort within the family, whatever the weather. Caught a nasty cold? Cath made lasagne. Had a row with a partner? Cath made lasagne. Lost your daughter to a painful, lonely death...? She closed her eyes again, grief thumping her in the chest once more.

'I didn't search hard enough,' she muttered, finally letting some of the guilt slip out.

'What?' Scarlet asked.

Lily opened her eyes and turned to her. 'Ruby,' she said quietly. 'I should have been out there night and day, scouring the streets until I found her. I should have kept her safe.'

Scarlet let out a sound that was a mixture of confusion and

frustration as she sat back in her chair. Her dark hair fell to her waist, framing either side of her pale face, as she stared away into nothingness with a troubled expression. Lily knew she was trying to choose what to say carefully.

'Lil, it wouldn't have made a difference—' she began.

'It *would* have, Scarlet,' Lily cut her off firmly. 'She shouldn't have been there. I should have torn this city apart until I found her. And I didn't.' The truth cut even more painfully as she said it out loud. 'It was my responsibility to keep her safe, to be there for her, always. It was my *job*.' She shook her head sadly. 'The minute you become a mum, your reason to be here changes. Your centre of gravity changes. You ain't bound to this earth anymore; you're bound to *them*. And it don't matter what they do or how old they are, you're the *one* person who always has to have their back. But I dropped the ball.' Her voice cracked. 'And if I hadn't, she may well still be here. I failed her.' Her voice wobbled and she clamped her mouth shut, swallowing hard.

Scarlet shook her head. 'No, Lil, you didn't fail Ruby. You didn't drop the ball.' She sighed, her breath frosty and white in the air. 'You looked everywhere. We all did.'

Lily turned away, but Scarlet's hand gripped her arm, forcing her to look back round into her piercing grey-blue eyes. There was an intensity there, an earnest, serious intensity.

'Look, I may not know what it's like to be a mum, or the weight of that responsibility. But I *do* know that once a child becomes an adult, they have a responsibility to look after themselves too,' she said strongly. 'You're right, it *is* a mum's job to always be there, to be someone we can count on. And you're one of the best when it comes to that. But unless you plan on locking them up in a cage, you can't protect your adult children every second of the day. You're not a miracle worker.' Scarlet ran a hand back through her hair, stressed. 'You did everything you could, Lil. It wasn't your bad choice or lack of effort. Ruby *chose* to disappear, and then, for whatever reason, she chose to be in that scrapyard.' There was a small pause and she wiped a hand down her face. 'That was out of your hands. That was out of *anyone's* hands, other than hers.' Scarlet came to an abrupt stop and pursed her lips.

Lily shot her a look. Scarlet wouldn't go so far as to say it was Ruby's own fault and that was wise, because Lily wouldn't hear it. She *couldn't* hear it. Ruby's accident had been horrific. There was no way she would have intentionally put herself in that kind of danger.

'I know you mean well, Scar, but none of that matters,' she said, her mouth briefly flickering with a bitter smile. 'A mother's responsibility to her child goes beyond reason or logic. It ain't something I can really explain. You'll understand one day. You'd move mountains with your bare hands, do the impossible without even thinking about it, for your child. And all I had to do was find her. That was all I had to do...' She trailed off and her eyes dimmed.

Lily's pain rose up in a wave and crashed through her heart once again. It was a pain that resided in her permanently now, rolling acidly around the edges of the gaping black hole Ruby's death had left in her soul. Usually she was able to contain it, lock it away behind the distraction of work and the rest of her family. But today it raged through her head and her heart without mercy. It was all she could do to keep up the appearance of not breaking down under its weight. But appearances were important. Appearances still held strength when there was none to find anywhere else.

Lily straightened up and lifted her chin. 'I think I've had one too many of these whiskies – it's making me maudlin.' She pulled a tight smile. 'I'm fine. Is everything tied up for tomorrow? We haven't had a chance to catch up.'

'It's a hard day, today,' Scarlet offered, ignoring the subject change. 'It's natural that—'

'It's a Wednesday,' Lily snapped, standing up and folding the throw she'd wrapped around herself. She could no longer feel the cold. She was numb. 'Just another Wednesday. And tomorrow's a big day. Nothing can go wrong.'

Scarlet stood up too, but Lily held her stare levelly through the darkness. She didn't want to talk about Ruby with Scarlet. She didn't want to talk about Ruby with anyone really, but least of all her niece. Scarlet may not have had anything to do with Ruby's death, but she'd hated her. She'd wanted her gone – and while she had fair reason for wanting that, Lily couldn't share her pain with someone who was secretly glad. No matter how much Scarlet tried to hide it.

'Everything's ready,' Scarlet said dutifully. 'All the guests and suppliers are confirmed, Isla's set to coordinate everything, all that's left to do is meet tomorrow to go over the marks.'

'You're prepared?' Lily asked, turning to walk back towards the house.

Scarlet fell into step beside her. 'I'm prepared.'

'Good.' Lily reached the house and walked inside, her jawline hardening. 'We'll work out the plan and then burn the evidence. By the end of the night, we should have caught ourselves a nice rich mark. One that will never see us coming.'

FIVE

The next morning, far earlier than he'd have liked, Cillian pulled up outside his mother's house and stepped out of his car. Joe got out and leaned over the roof, catching his eye.

Cillian shook his head slightly. 'Stay here. I won't be long.'

Joe nodded and slipped back into his seat as Cillian walked up the front path.

The front door was unlocked, as expected, and Cillian followed the sound of voices through to the second lounge his mother used as an office-cum-comfortable meeting room. Scarlet was in one of the armchairs, partway through a low, urgent conversation with Isla, a petite blonde whose angelic, youthful appearance was at odds with the sharp intelligence and ruthlessness that had earned her a place in their inner circle almost two years earlier.

Before Isla, the Drews hadn't taken anyone from outside of the family into the firm since its creation, when Andy and George had joined the ranks. Still loyal to this day, they were perched on stools nearby, their expressions unreadable as they waited for the meeting to start. Lily sat opposite them, cigarette in hand, looking thoughtful as she stared down at something on her phone. Cillian nodded at Connor and took a seat beside him on the large sofa.

'I did open a great place to hold meetings just like these, you know,' he said sarcastically, the comment aimed at his mother. He pulled out a toothpick from his suit jacket pocket and placed it between his teeth, the same way he always did when the smell of smoke threatened to awaken his residual nicotine cravings.

'I've told you before,' Lily said quietly, her dark brown eyes piercing his, and her red lips pinching as she drew deeply on her cigarette. 'It's an ideal place for anyone else in the underworld, but we shall continue to keep our meetings private.' She blew out what was left of the smoke in her lungs. 'You've done a fantastic job of ensuring no one will be overheard, but people still have eyes.' She took another deep drag. 'We don't need anyone watching, noting who's there, wondering what we're plotting.'

Cillian looked away. The idea that anyone in their world would assume they weren't up to anything just because they hadn't physically seen them gather was ridiculous, in his opinion. The Drews had always been notorious, but even more so over the last year. People didn't need to see them together to know they were an active firm. But there was little point in arguing about it. Lily was still the head of the firm, and her decision was final.

'So, who's our target?' he asked. He shifted to face Scarlet and all eyes followed his.

'There are options,' Scarlet answered, a gleam in her eye.

She rifled through the folder on her lap and pulled a handful of papers from a plastic sleeve, then stood up and laid some of them out on the floor in the middle of the room, where they could all see. Cillian leaned forward to study them.

'It's been an unusually productive catch,' she continued. 'We actually have four potential marks.'

Cillian's eyebrows shot up in surprise and he glanced up at her. 'They're *all* marks? *Good* ones?'

Scarlet nodded. 'Different risk levels of course, and I have a favourite, but see what you all think.'

Cillian was impressed. The art heists were very lucrative when they could pull them off, but they were few and far between. They relied on Scarlet pulling in just the right type of mark, and the criteria meant that they were usually quite difficult to find. To have four viable marks to choose from was a first.

'I'll start with this guy, John Adams...' Scarlet started with the first picture and began to reel off all the information she had on each mark.

This particular type of con had been Scarlet's brainchild. Since childhood she'd been fascinated by fine art. She'd pored over books at home, taken all the related subjects at school and would spend hours upon hours roaming the halls of London's various art galleries.

Through chance and opportunity, they'd found themselves in a position to steal an already stolen Picasso, a couple of years before. It hadn't been the smoothest job but they'd got through it, and it had opened up a world of potential opportunities – ones that their skills were well suited for. From that job there had been an opportunity to pull another, and after that Scarlet had come up with an ingenious idea.

They'd bought Repton Boxing Club a year or so before. The club was important to them and to the local community – to the boys it had helped raise and the men who drew solace from within its walls – and so when an outside investor had threatened to tear it down and replace it with a block of flats, they'd saved it. The place had been a financial black hole ever since, its only saving grace the fact they could run illegal fights and make money on the bets. But Scarlet's new idea had turned the place into a small goldmine.

They'd opened up their own charity, using the boxing club as a front. With such a genuine cause to raise money for, the charity was completely legitimate. The club needed money to continue running and the charity donations went a long way. But behind closed doors there was a second set of books and a number of ulterior motives.

Fundraising events were run on a regular basis. They'd arranged several dinners and auctions, and now the upcoming ball. At these events, Lily syphoned in large amounts of their dirty cash to be laundered and paid back to them through sky-high salaries, taking the pressure off their smaller laundries. The genuine donations that came in all went to the club as intended, relieving the financial burden of the place too. It was a win-win situation, but as well as all that, it opened the doors to the social circles they needed to infiltrate to find the right kind of marks.

Cillian listened with interest as Scarlet finished outlining the first three potential marks. They all had their merits.

'... and then there's Tabitha Grey.' Scarlet's eyes twinkled as she looked around at them all. 'Forty-one, single, no relatives, she inherited a string of businesses including a family gold mine five years ago, when her parents died in a car crash.'

'A *gold* mine?' Connor asked.

'Yeah, in America. Her great-great-grandparents started mining their farmland after finding gold in the river. They struck – well – *gold*, and a lot of it. The family invested most of the money into other companies over the years – wisely, as it turns out. The mine is still going but it ain't producing much these days. She's inherited shares in a vineyard, a horse-breeding ranch, an engineering company...' Scarlet reeled them off.

'Sounds like a very busy woman,' Cillian cut in with a frown.

'Actually no. The family was involved in the running for a long time, but her parents were the first generation to take a step back and put directors or boards in place to run things. They weren't interested in hard work, by that point. They'd been born into more money than they could ever spend and just wanted to have fun.'

'How do you know all this?' Lily asked.

'She told me,' Scarlet replied. 'She's quite the chatty Cathy. Very lonely, I think.'

Cillian stared down at the picture. The woman was rather plain but not completely unattractive. Dark blonde hair curled under her jaw in a soft bob, and small blue eyes looked out from a round serious face. Surely that sort of money and the social status that came with it must mean she wasn't short of company?

'Why's she your favourite? What's she got?' Lily asked, taking a deep drag on her cigarette and looking down at the picture with a critical expression.

'I don't know exactly,' Scarlet answered. 'But there's something big in there. I met her at that arts dinner. She was one of the patrons, but when I started chatting in more detail about the pieces on display, she had no clue what I was talking about. Turns out her parents were the art lovers. They collected all sorts and put money into a lot of the museums and foundations in London. When they died, Tabitha just continued their work and goes to the functions because they're fun.'

'But how is she a viable mark?' Cillian asked. 'I see the potential, but all you have right now is a rich lonely woman who don't know jack about art.'

Scarlet smiled. 'A few glasses of wine and her life story later, she told me her parents' art collection was wasted on her. That in their big old house in Kensington there's a whole floor of priceless pieces she doesn't understand or appreciate. I asked her whether she'd ever thought about selling them, and in her drunken state she told me she'd love to, but there are certain ones she can't ever sell. She's worried that with her limited knowledge she'll mix them up and that *then* – in her own words – there would be *real* trouble.' She cocked an eyebrow at him and held his gaze.

'And you think that's because they're black market,' Cillian stated.

'They have to be. There's no other explanation. And from the picture Tabitha painted, they'd have been the type. Bored rich bastards who never worked and had more money than sense,' Scarlet replied. 'I want to go for her.'

There was a short silence and Cillian grimaced. If there *was* something there, it was a potentially great situation, but this was based on a lot of assumption. There were other options, safer ones. Cillian caught Lily's eye and saw his doubts mirrored there.

'If we did go for her and you're wrong, this will have been a serious waste of opportunity,' Lily said, giving Scarlet a hard stare. 'For all of us.'

Scarlet shook her head, holding her gaze confidently. 'I'm not. There's an incredible payload there and she doesn't have a clue.'

Connor made a quiet sound of unease and shifted in his seat. This was followed by another silence as everyone waited for Lily to speak. She eyed Scarlet with an unreadable expression.

'What sort of approach are you thinking?' she eventually asked.

'We give her what she wants. Attention, friendship,' Scarlet replied. 'She was all over me at the arts dinner, we swapped numbers, she's coming tonight because she's desperate for company. Let me spend time with her, then we tag team her with a bit of flattery and ply her with drinks all night until I get an invite to her house.'

'It's simple enough,' Cillian observed.

'Most of the best plans are,' Scarlet replied. '*But* it can't be an invite to see the art. It needs to be something else, so we keep her chatting until we see an in. Worst case I'll fake a night out around the area and invite her along, we'll do a set-up and get her so legless I need to help her home. Get in that way.'

'Then you'll find out what's there and what security there is,' Lily mused. 'As Cillian says, the initial stage seems simple enough. If there *is* something there and if the security is doable, it's ideal. But that's more ifs than I like.' She pursed her lips, still not quite convinced.

'These other three,' Cillian said, gesturing towards the other pictures on the floor, 'why don't we pick another and work two marks tonight?'

'No.' Lily's response was instant. 'We never work two at once – you know that. We all need to stay focused on one job at a time with things like this. It's safer.'

Cillian contemplated the options, his eyes drawn towards the first that Scarlet had outlined. 'John Adams. You say he has a couple of mid-range paintings and no security?'

'Yes,' Scarlet answered reluctantly. 'He's shown it off all over social media. They're in a large conservatory off the back of his house, and his lack of any security has become a public joke between people who know him.'

'Of the four, I like him better,' Cillian stated.

'But the prize is nothing compared to Tabitha,' she responded, glancing at Lily. 'It's easy, yes, but it's not the haul we could get with her.'

'*If* there's a haul to be had,' Cillian reminded her. He stood up and looked to his mother with a resolute expression, pointing down to the picture of John's face. 'He's a safer bet with a good outcome. It's not worth the risk of coming away with nothing. We could be chasing smoke for all we know, and then we've lost the opportunity to set up any of the others.'

'No.' Scarlet shook her head, moving to stand beside him. 'Come on – we can do better than that. Tabitha is the big prize here. I think we're letting ourselves down if we settle for John.'

'Well we can't work both,' Lily replied, casting her gaze between them both. 'So I guess one of you is going to be sorely disappointed.'

SIX

Lily watched Cillian and Scarlet as they faced each other and locked gazes. She took one last drag on her cigarette and stubbed it out in the crystal ashtray next to her. She was surprised at who was arguing each side. Usually it was Scarlet who erred on the side of caution and Cillian who dived straight for the biggest prize, no matter the details. Perhaps working as closely as they had over the last year had caused them to rub off on each other a little. Which wasn't necessarily a bad thing.

Scarlet spoke first, turning towards Lily with a look of determination. 'We're talking potentially millions of pounds' worth of paintings Tabitha can't report as stolen, if I'm right. Which I *know* I am.'

'*Potentially*,' Cillian stressed, once more. 'And let me ask you this, what sort of financial difference are we talking about, between those *potential* paintings and John Adams' ones?'

Lily's sharp eyes caught the slight change in the set of his jaw and the way his gaze focused in on Scarlet. This was what she privately called his chess face. The subtle expression he pulled when he was playing out a strategy.

'Millions!' Scarlet exclaimed. 'John's couple of paintings are only worth sixty, maybe eighty grand, on the black market. Plus, they'll be hot. They're legal, so he'll call it in as stolen. Tabitha wouldn't be able to report these. So no heat. And,' she quickly added, 'she's no Grace. There's no way in hell she has some sort of closet connections to chase after us with.' Scarlet drove her final point home with a confident flourish.

Grace had been their second mark. Their first too, not that they'd realised that at the time. They'd stolen an already stolen Picasso from her husband, only realising that his wife, Grace, was a black market art dealer when she hunted them down in an attempt to get it back. A vicious strategic war had ensued, in which both sides had been burned. They'd come out on top in the end, but no one wanted to repeat the situation again by stealing from the wrong person.

Cillian nodded slowly and then turned to Lily as he made his metaphorical move across the board. 'So I guess the real question is, *if* these potential paintings definitely are there, what are we then going to do with them?'

Scarlet opened her mouth to counter, then hesitated.

Checkmate. Lily thought.

'We still don't have a fence,' Cillian continued. 'We still have another painting worth silly money hidden in a vault because we ain't set up with the contacts or the accounts to make that level of sale on our own.' He shrugged. 'Sixty or eighty grand in the pocket is worth a lot more to us right now than millions we can't access.'

Lily looked at Scarlet. 'He has a point.'

From the first job, they'd hit a brick wall when it came to selling the paintings on. They'd made a contact in the upper eche- lons of the black market, only to find later that he'd been secretly working with Grace behind their back. It was a closed-off world that held no trust for newcomers and was hard to break into – much like their own – and they'd not yet found another way in.

Not that this deterred them of course. It was only a matter of time and perseverance. But Cillian was right. At the moment, they were not in a position to fence those kinds of paintings. And keeping hold of them for too long was an added risk they didn't need.

'Actually, I might have a plan for that,' Scarlet replied, lifting her chin.

'Oh?' Lily's eyebrows rose in surprise.

'Possibly anyway,' Scarlet added.

'Another *possible*,' Cillian muttered, running a hand back through his dark hair in irritation.

Lily ignored him, her interest piqued. 'Go on,' she urged her niece.

'At the event where I met Tabitha, there was this Italian guy lurking on the sidelines all night. Late forties, expensive suit, kept to himself mostly, seemed to appreciate the art but disappeared before I could speak to him,' Scarlet started.

'So you noticed some bloke because he dressed sharp and looked shy,' Cillian summed up dismissively. 'I ain't no expert but I wouldn't say that's out of place in the art world.'

'I noticed him because he looked like a con,' she replied sharply.

Scarlet's eyes flashed as she looked at Cillian. He held her gaze for a moment and then tilted his head in an offer to continue.

'He had the look about him,' she continued. 'And he was scanning.'

Lily nodded. She understood what Scarlet meant. There was a certain way people in their world assessed people and places. One they'd grown to recognise in others like them.

'I got the impression he was looking for someone who wasn't there.' She turned to pick up her folder and pulled out another sheet, which she handed to Lily.

Lily studied the enlarged picture of the tall attractive man in a suit walking down a busy road. He had smooth olive skin and his dark hair was speckled with grey.

'After he left, I asked around about him. His name is Matteo Oscuro.' Scarlet looked down. 'Those running the event didn't seem to like him too much. They told me his name and to steer clear. Apparently he's not someone good people go into business with. *The man's a crook*, one said to me. *Only in it for the money*.'

Lily felt a spark of interest ignite in her core and she sat up straighter, looking back down into Matteo's handsome face. 'And what have you found out since?'

'He lives in Italy but keeps an office here. His business is finding and importing or exporting artwork for private clients. Now, I know this doesn't necessarily mean he's on the black market, but that ain't exactly something you can just bowl up and ask outright, so George followed him around for a couple of days to see if there were any other signs.'

'And were there?' Lily asked.

Scarlet's eyes glinted and a smile spread across her face. 'There were. He mainly socialised while he was here. Lunches and cocktails and all that. But he popped to his office to meet a client. *This* client...' She pulled another sheet out of the folder and handed it to Lily.

It was of a pale man in his mid-thirties with a pot belly, a prematurely receding hairline and unhealthy pink rings under his eyes. Lily frowned and narrowed her gaze. The face was familiar, the image nudging at the edges of her memory.

'Where have I seen him before?' she asked.

'He's the husband of the woman we pulled that job with Grace on,' Scarlet answered. 'We never saw him in the flesh, but he was in all the pictures we had of her when we initially set up the plan.'

'Of course,' Lily breathed as the memory clicked into place.

'Which pretty much confirms it,' Scarlet continued

triumphantly. 'They were Grace's clients. Now she's gone, they'd have had to find another black market dealer. It can't just be coincidence.'

Cillian sat back down – a look of resignation on his face.

Lily rubbed the side of her index finger back and forth across her mouth as she weighed everything up.

John Adams was a safe bet. And as the saying went, a bird in the hand is worth two in the bush. But if this Matteo really was what he appeared to be... She took a deep breath and exhaled heavily, casting her gaze across the room.

'What do the rest of you think?' she asked. 'We'll all be in this grift; it's an equal risk for us all.'

There was a short silence and Lily felt irritation creep in. 'Come on – your mouths ain't glued shut.'

Connor spoke first. 'I'm with Cillian. It's a good set-up and we know what we're dealing with.'

He shared a look with his twin, conveying a message that only the two of them understood – part of an unspoken language between them that Lily had accepted many years ago she'd never be able to translate.

She turned expectantly to Isla.

Isla looked thoughtful and took a few seconds to decide. 'I don't think anyone chose this life because it was the easy route,' she said in her wide Mancunian accent. It had softened since she'd joined their firm, but it was still there, the contrast to theirs an ever-present reminder that she wasn't a true Londoner like the rest of them.

'I'd personally go for Tabitha,' she eventually said. 'Go hard or go home, right?'

'Or go hard and home empty-handed,' Cillian replied, his tone unimpressed.

Andy nodded. 'I'm with the boys on this one,' he said in a deep gravelly voice.

Not many people would get away with calling the twins

boys these days without it being seen as a slight. Her two muscular six-foot sons were very much fully grown men – hard men, who'd earned their stripes and a specific level of respect. But Andy and George had been by her side from the start, since the twins had been just babes in her arms. They'd earned the right to the odd casual term of endearment.

George looked at Scarlet and then to Lily with an expression that told her all she needed to know.

'Right,' she said quietly. It was a tie, three for three.

'She's got a knack, Lil,' he said, his craggy voice coloured with admiration. 'Her hunch about this Matteo bloke was bang on the money. I say we go for it. We've taken bigger chances before.'

Lily conceded with a small nod and then cast her gaze around the room. Everyone was watching tensely, waiting for her to decide which way they would go.

Her gaze rested on Scarlet and she felt a weight settle over her as she made her choice. 'We'll go for Tabitha.'

Scarlet had the good grace to swiftly hide her look of triumph. 'You won't regret it,' she said.

Lily stood up and stared at her, painfully aware of the added layer of tension this situation had created. 'I'd better not,' she said, her tone hardening. 'It's still a big risk.'

She met Cillian's eye and saw the neutral mask slip back over his face. She preferred him when he was angry and vocal. At least then she knew what was going on in that head of his.

They had worked hard over the last year to expand and climb up the underworld ladder and had done so as a strong, united firm. But Ruby's death had affected them all, and there had been a shift in the undercurrent between Scarlet and Cillian ever since. Whilst they still worked well together, there was also an unspoken guardedness between them and a quiet friction that occasionally reared its head. Unresolved and ignored by both, this friction crackled away under the surface, the sparks it created just waiting for a piece of kindling to be thrown in. And this could very well be that kindling, should Tabitha Grey's collection come to nothing.

'I know I'm right, Lil. Trust me,' Scarlet replied, holding her gaze confidently.

'You'd better be right,' Lily warned in a hard voice. 'And my trust in you is the only reason we're doing this.' With one last long look, she turned to leave. 'Do *not* make me regret that.'

SEVEN

Of all the London-born Irish ex-pats who'd made the move to the sunny shores of southern Spain, Finn Logan counted himself as one of the most savvy. *The* most savvy, if he was being completely honest. Most of the others who'd moved there over the years were now filling their days with siestas and sangria in the sun. Sitting on their backsides and waiting to grow old. And part of him didn't blame them. He enjoyed a drink and a sunbathe as much as the rest of them. His tanned leathery skin and sun-bleached hair – what was left of it anyway – was testament to that. But Finn hadn't allowed the change of scenery to stop him building on what he'd started so many years ago.

Walking across the busy transport hub towards the logistics office – a large portacabin set apart from the main building – Finn pulled a folded white handkerchief from his pocket and wiped his forehead, squinting up at the early afternoon sun. The door opened as he reached out for it, and a younger man stepped aside to let him in, before slipping out and closing it behind him.

'Christ,' Finn said as he refolded the hankie and placed it

back in his pocket. 'It's getting hotter every year now, I reckon.' He paused for a moment beside the aircon unit that was fitted into the window, allowing the cooler air to wash over him.

'Probably all that global warming shit they're always harping on about,' his brother Sean muttered in reply, not looking up from the paperwork he was studying with a frown.

'Let's see those new costings then,' Finn said, sitting down on a squeaky red office chair on the opposite side of the desk to Sean. 'What's the issue?'

Sean handed the papers over with a disgruntled huff. 'They're taking the fucking piss,' he informed his brother. 'Look at that.'

Finn frowned down at the papers and began to read through.

Like many of the other ex-pats in the area, the brothers' business back home hadn't been legitimate. They'd grown up in the shadow of London's underworld and, along with their other brother Cormac, they had carved out a place in its ranks for their family firm. The money had been good and they'd taken to the life like a duck to water. Over the following years they'd become so well established and had put down so many roots that they'd never even considered the possibility that they might not be there forever.

But one day their luck had changed. A deal had gone south and another firm had double-crossed them. Backed into a tight, inescapable corner, they'd been given only two options. They could give up their businesses and leave the country for a fresh start, or they could stay and have their darkest secrets exposed to the authorities. And so they'd packed up their families and moved to Spain. But that hadn't been the end of things.

As soon as they'd arrived, they'd set about rebuilding a new empire. Smart and resourceful, it hadn't taken them long to set up a thriving business, making connections and alliances through the underworld of southern Spain. As time had gone on, their families had settled into their new lives in the sun and the brothers had accepted they'd likely never move back. But that acceptance didn't mean they had forgiven or forgotten what had been done to them. Their need for vengeance had quietly simmered under the surface over the last decade, as they bided their time and worked towards the perfect revenge on the firm who'd taken their lives from them.

Anything worth having in this life takes time, their mum always used to tell them. And it was true, in Finn's opinion.

He frowned and tossed the papers into the bin beside the desk. 'They're having a fucking giraffe, ain't they?' he asked incredulously. 'That's almost a thirty per cent increase.'

A knock on the door interrupted Sean's reply, and they both turned to see who it was.

'Boss, the first of those trucks you wanted modified is finished,' said the man now leaning into the portacabin. 'You wanna take a look?'

'Yeah, show me.' Finn stood up and followed the man outside, Sean hot on his heels.

They entered the main warehouse and crossed the wide space to a parked truck with its back doors open. The man jumped up into the back and Finn followed, waiting as he pulled one of the wide floorboards up to reveal a hidden chamber underneath. Finn kneeled and unlatched the door, running his hands along the unyielding metal walls below.

'We've run it through all the checks – nothing shows up on the scanners and it's completely soundproof. All the extras you wanted inside are built in too,' the man confirmed.

Finn's eyes flickered around the space, mentally ticking everything off. 'Good,' he said. He dusted himself off as he jumped down. 'How long until they're all ready?'

'Two days, tops,' came the answer.

Finn and Sean exchanged a grim smile of anticipation. When they'd first heard word that the Drews were starting up their own logistics hub, they'd known it was an opportunity they couldn't miss. They'd quickly laid plans and set strategies into play, and now they were just days away from giving the Drews everything they were due. Everything they'd asked for. Finn wet his lips and nodded.

'Two days,' he repeated. 'So we'll leave here in three.'

'Then we can finally deliver our little surprise,' Sean added.

'I wouldn't call it little,' Finn replied. His gaze moved back towards the truck. 'But it certainly will be a surprise.' A cold smile spread across his face. 'One they'll never see coming.'

EIGHT

Scarlet glanced back over her shoulder as she moved quickly down the hall away from the ballroom into the kitchens. Steam rose from industrial pots, and pans sizzled over hot flames either side of the wide galley walkway. Chefs yelled urgent demands, and waiters rushed through, their trays laden with champagne. Scarlet pushed through the door at the other end and let it slowly shut behind her, muffling the chaos within.

Stepping back against the outside wall, she closed her eyes for a moment and exhaled some of the stress that was holding her together. All the suppliers had delivered – the lighting and décor were perfect, the caterers were in full swing, the string quartet was playing now and the band they'd booked for later were already chilling in a side room. Guests had begun arriving for the champagne reception, but there was no sign of Tabitha yet.

Scarlet slid her fingers down the side of her red satin ball-gown until they found the small opening hidden in a fold of the A-line skirt. She'd had pockets put in as an afterthought, not wanting to be burdened with a bag. And, in truth, so that she could hide her intentions at moments like these.

She pulled out a thin packet of slim menthol cigarettes, lit one and put it to her lips. As she pulled the warm minty smoke into her lungs, she savoured the way it eased her tension for a moment, then blew it out in a long thin plume, watching it drift away into the cold night air.

As it faded, she suddenly realised that she wasn't alone and she turned her head sharply. The man casually leaning on the corner of the same wall she was, a few feet away, wore an amused expression, and she tilted her head with a wry half-smile.

'How did you guess I was here?' she asked.

'Guess?' He laughed quietly, a deep rumbling laugh, and pushed away from the wall. 'I know your moves better than you think I do, Scarlet Drew.'

Benny James was a tall, handsome South Londoner of Nigerian descent, who worked for Lily's long-term love – and powerful ally to the firm – Ray Renshaw. Benny wasn't quite in Ray's inner circle, but he wasn't far off. In his mid-twenties, he hadn't been working for Ray for as long as many of his other men, but he was as loyal, hard and intelligent as they came, and it was clear Ray held him in high esteem. As did Scarlet.

He walked over to her until their bodies almost touched and looked down into her face. 'You know menthol doesn't actually mask the smell, right?' he asked. 'If you want to hide it' – he leaned down and kissed her slowly on the lips – 'you're going to have to do better than that.'

Scarlet bit her bottom lip as he pulled away. She smiled and flicked the cigarette away.

'You can't tell anyone,' she warned, slipping her arms around his sides and looking up at him. 'It's my dirty little secret.'

'*That's* your dirty little secret?' he asked with mock surprise. 'Christ, I need to work harder in the bedroom.'

She laughed and he grinned, wrapping his arms around her and pulling her closer.

Scarlet had been dating Benny for the last six months, after meeting on a job the two firms had partnered up on. He'd been the first person who'd made her really laugh since she'd lost her previous boyfriend, John, a year and a half ago, through one of Ruby's cruel games. She hadn't much felt like laughing after that. Her heart had been broken and the sun inside her soul had gone down and failed to reappear.

She'd picked herself up of course – the world didn't stop spinning for one broken heart – and she'd accepted that life would just be that bit darker and heavier now. But then, one day, Benny had come along. Over time, her burden had begun to feel a little lighter, and the sun had slowly reappeared. When he'd asked her out, she'd hesitated for only a second before accepting.

Benny stepped back and appraised her. 'Wow. You look stunning every day, but this' – he made a sound of appreciation – 'this is something else.'

'You don't scrub up too badly yourself,' Scarlet replied, straightening his bow tie. The well-tailored lines of his midnight-blue tux accentuated his athletic physique perfectly.

His smile faded and a crease formed on his brow. 'Why you hiding out here anyway? Something wrong?'

'No, just taking a breather,' she lied, her thoughts returning to Tabitha.

Benny studied her face for a moment then stepped away. 'I'd best get back.'

''Course. I'll see you in there,' she replied, shooting him a winning smile.

He disappeared back around the corner and Scarlet stared thoughtfully at the empty space he'd left behind.

They were close with Ray and his men these days. Closer than ever professionally. But they were still two separate firms and this con was Drew business. Benny wasn't stupid – he knew there were things going on tonight – but he also understood that it wasn't his concern. And that was the beauty of their relationship. They were playing the same game. There was no need to hide who they were from each other – which was refreshing after her past experiences.

The reminder of John sent a familiar stab through her gut, and she drew in a sharp breath, pushing his memory away. She knew she shouldn't still harbour feelings for another man, now that she was dating Benny. But it wasn't something she could help, even after all this time. What she and John had shared was something that she knew, even for her tender years, was a once-in-a-lifetime connection. The relationship had been doomed from the moment they met, and they'd both known it, but it still hadn't been enough to keep them apart. In the end, the only thing that *had* been strong enough to force them apart was the very love for each other that had drawn them together. He'd left to protect her – and she'd helped him leave to protect him.

Scarlet felt a vibration against her leg and reached into her other hidden pocket for her phone. She scanned the short message on the screen. It was from Cillian.

She's here.

She slipped the phone back into her pocket, then lifted her chin and reached up to touch the elegant chignon she pinned her dark hair into, checking it was still in place. It was showtime.

NINE

The string quartet filled the brightly lit ballroom with music, from the polished hardwood floor to the gilded plasterwork on the domed ceiling. People stood talking together in high-spirited tones as they prepared for an evening of opulent merriment. The gowns worn by the women were of every colour imaginable. Necks and wrists were shackled by impressive ropes of diamonds and precious stones, matched frosting on each set of ears. And as Scarlet glided through the room, for a moment she had to stifle the urge to laugh.

Because the whole thing was ridiculous. This was their ball, their function, but this wasn't their life. It wasn't even close. Several of the contacts she'd drawn in smiled as she passed, as if they were familiar. As if they were, on some level at least, the same. But they weren't. If only they knew.

If only they knew that this glittering façade had been put together by a bunch of East End working-class criminals, in order to commit financial fraud and run a con on one of their own, they'd be horrified. They weren't blind – they knew the Drews didn't have the same background and social standing. That was obvious in many ways, and they'd never tried to hide it. But these people had accepted the fact that for some reason or another, the Drews were wealthy. Wealthy enough to have been able to start a charity and throw the kind of parties they liked. And wealthy people liked other wealthy people. It was that simple. It was that shallow.

A petite woman with short, dark-blonde hair and a half-drunk glass of champagne in hand was walking towards her from the other side of the room, and Scarlet plastered on her most winning smile.

'Tabitha!' She leaned in to accept and reciprocate the kiss on each cheek. 'So good to see you again!'

'And you, darling,' Tabitha replied in a lazy upper-class drawl. 'Great venue choice. I was here last summer for a wedding.' She looked around with a small smile and then back to Scarlet. 'Love the dress. That colour really suits you. Scarlet by name, Scarlet by fashionable nature.'

She laughed at her own poor attempt of a joke, and Scarlet forced a smile of amusement.

'Yeah, that's me,' she said jovially.

Tabitha smoothed her free hand down her hips and preened. 'What do you think? I had this made especially for tonight. Designed it myself. Do you like it?'

'I love it,' Scarlet replied enthusiastically. 'You look amazing.'

It was a lie. The lavender colour washed her out and the high boat neckline accentuated the broadness of her shoulders; but Tabitha clearly felt good in it, which was the only thing that really mattered.

Tabitha's already thin lips thinned further as she gave Scarlet a smug smile. 'Yes, I do, don't I?' she said. She pulled a deep breath in through her nose as she cast a superior gaze around the room. 'I have a bit of a talent for designing, you see.' She shrugged as if modestly shrugging off someone else's praise. 'I don't know where it came from, but I can just naturally look at someone and know, instantly' – she clicked her fingers – 'exactly what suits them best. If I'd ever needed to work, I probably would have gone into fashion, you know.' She leaned into Scarlet and lowered her voice surreptitiously. 'And there are certainly a few here tonight who could have done with my assistance.' She waggled her eyebrows and gave Scarlet a conspiratorial look.

Scarlet bit the inside of her cheek hard and nodded. 'So have you been up to much since we last chatted?' she asked, changing the subject.

'No, not really,' Tabitha replied with a slightly regretful tone. 'My friend Samuel moved to Austria recently. We used to go out to dinner and for drinks together, but now...' She trailed off and took a sip of her champagne. 'Well, I just haven't found his replacement yet.'

Scarlet found herself feeling sorry for Tabitha. She'd been bang on the money before. The woman was lonely and desperate for company.

'Surely you have other friends in London?' she asked. 'Some girlfriends?'

Tabitha shook her head. 'No. I did spend some time with a group of ladies a while back, but I soon realised they weren't really for me.' She sniffed and raised her chin. 'Ghastly women really. Stupid and rude, they didn't listen to a *word* of advice and we didn't agree on anything. Better off without that nonsense.'

Scarlet had an inkling it may not have been an entirely one-sided story. 'Sounds awful,' she murmured.

Glancing across the room, she caught Lily's eye and made an almost imperceptible hand movement, to signal that she was getting somewhere.

'You have *no* idea,' Tabitha drawled. 'But it was always fine while Samuel was here. Until he fell for the Austrian hooker he moved away for anyway. I mean really...' She shook her head in distaste. 'I did *try* to warn him she was only after his money. She was an ER nurse for Christ's sake. Who'd want to keep doing *that* forever? Clearly, she'd do anything to get away from a life filled with blood and guts. But he wouldn't hear it.' She sighed.

Scarlet chose not to point out that the woman had probably chosen the career because she'd felt a calling to help people. 'Well, I'm no Samuel, but I'm free tomorrow night and I've been dying to try this new restaurant over your way, if you'd be up for joining me?' she said casually. 'I don't know if you've tried it; it's called—'

'Oh – my – *God*.' Tabitha grabbed Scarlet's arm, cutting her off dramatically.

'What?' Scarlet asked, alarmed.

'*Who* is *that*?' Tabitha asked. Her small blue eyes gleamed with interest as she stared at someone at the other end of the room, in the same way a starving predator might eye up its next meal.

Scarlet frowned across the room in the same direction and glanced back at Tabitha to check they were looking at the same person, before answering.

'Oh that's... He's no one important,' she said reluctantly.

'Importance is a matter of perception, Scarlet,' Tabitha replied, not looking away, her hand still gripping Scarlet's arm.

Scarlet tipped her head to the side in acceptance. 'Still... *really*?' she asked.

'Oh come on, you aren't blind – look at him! He's a stone-cold sex pot,' Tabitha continued with quiet excitement.

'Um...' Scarlet pressed her lips together in an attempt to keep her expression neutral as something in her stomach squirmed with discomfort.

'What's his name?' Tabitha pressed. 'You must know – you arranged the guest list.'

Scarlet exhaled a long, silent breath. 'I do,' she replied. 'He's a local actually. Trains at the club we're raising money for.'

Tabitha let out a low, almost evil chuckle. 'Even better,' she said with glee. 'A bit of roughage is always good for the system.'

Scarlet's eyes widened but she managed to keep her placid smile in place. 'So I hear. I think though, he's got—'

'Come on.' Tabitha suddenly darted forward and pulled Scarlet along with her. 'You can introduce us.'

With no other choice, Scarlet fell into step with the pushy woman and they made their way across the room together. Tabitha came to an abrupt stop directly in front of the man she'd taken such great interest in and then smiled expectantly at Scarlet.

The object of Tabitha's desire glanced at her blankly for a moment and then met Scarlet's gaze with a frowning half-smile of question. Barely able to hide her amusement, Scarlet smiled back and made the introductions.

'Tabitha, this is Cillian, one of the members of the boxing club we're here for tonight. Cillian, this is Tabitha—'

'Tabitha Grey,' she interrupted and thrust her hand into his. 'A benefactor,' she purred with what appeared to be an attempt at a smouldering look. 'It's so good to meet you. I couldn't help but notice you across the room.'

Cillian's hesitation was so slight that only Scarlet noticed. 'Thanks,' he said, still sounding a touch confused. 'You enjoying it so far?' he asked, shooting Scarlet another questioning look.

'I am,' Tabitha replied. 'Even more so now of course.'

Scarlet blinked and tried to get the conversation back on track as an awkward silence threatened. 'So, Cillian actually goes to the club most days, from what I understand. Which is why he's here tonight, being so emotionally invested—'

'Yes, that will be all,' Tabitha cut in sharply. She gave her a tight smile and made a slight shooing motion with her hand. 'We can take it from here. Thank you, Scarlet.'

Tabitha turned her back to her, and Scarlet's mouth dropped open at the rude dismissal. Cillian glanced over the woman's head at her with a look of consternation, then swiftly stepped into character, taking the change of events in his stride and taking Tabitha on with his most charming smile.

Utterly shocked and offended, Scarlet quickly pursed her lips to stop herself from responding the way she'd have liked, then turned and marched over to stand with her aunt. She let out a long hiss as she positioned herself to watch from across the room, the sting from the exchange not lessening with the distance.

Lily glanced at the pair and then back at Scarlet, one eyebrow hitched in question.

'Well,' Scarlet seethed under her breath as she shook her head, 'I can see why she doesn't have any friends.'

TEN

'Are you *fucking* kidding me?' Billie, Cillian's long-term live-in girlfriend returned to the dinner table and retook her seat between Scarlet and Lily, glaring across the room at the woman flirting outrageously with her man. 'She's still going? If this wasn't for the greater good, I'd have had her eyes out by now.'

Tabitha was now half draped over Cillian, across the room at another round dinner table, her arm resting on his broad shoulder.

Lily's mouth twitched in amusement. She liked Billie. In fact Billie was the only girlfriend either of her sons had *ever* had that she'd liked. And she understood the young woman's feelings. Love could incite far deeper anger than hatred ever could. She'd learned that the hard way.

She caught Ray's eye over the table, and as he purposely raked his eyes down the upper half of her body, she winked at him to let him know he could get a closer look later. His handsome, rugged face opened up in a wide, devilish smile, and she felt something stir inside her. He still did it for her, even after all these decades.

They weren't supposed to be on Ray's table, but after

Scarlet had hurriedly explained the unexpected turn of events, and that she'd not let on that Cillian was family, Lily had quickly changed the seating plan and had intercepted Billie, to ensure she didn't interrupt Tabitha and Cillian's conversation. Scarlet was almost as pissed off as Billie, after the woman had ditched her and treated her like the help. Neither were happy that Tabitha's clear interest in Cillian was now the main driver in tonight's plan, but they were both going to have to deal with it. This was business. And privately, Lily didn't think it was the worst idea. It would give Cillian a little more investment in this con and lessen the tense division in the ranks.

'Seriously, three courses down and the bitch is still looking at him like she ain't eaten for a month,' Billie spat, crossing her arms moodily.

Scarlet finally cracked a smile and reached across Lily for Billie's empty glass. 'Come on, Bills, let's pour you another drink,' she said.

'Listen, that man worships the ground you walk on,' Ray said. 'You ain't got anything to worry about.'

'Who said I was worried?' Billie asked. 'It ain't about that; I trust Cillian completely. But that don't mean I enjoy watching some stuck-up bint plastering herself all over him.' She took the refilled glass from Scarlet and downed it in one. 'Plus, this was supposed to be date night for us. *You* were supposed to be buttering her up' – she pointed at Scarlet – 'and *we* were supposed to be having a dance and a laugh over dinner.'

'Well, for the record, I'm as sorry as you are that it didn't work out that way,' Scarlet replied. 'I clearly just didn't have the abs for the job.'

There was a roar of laughter around the table from Ray, his men, Isla and even Cath. Cath clapped a hand over her mouth to try to stop it, but she'd had too much champagne to be successful.

'I'm sorry, love,' she managed as Billie gave her an accusing look. 'But even I have to agree with Scarlet here. She really doesn't have the balls to pull this one off.'

The laughter increased and Lily couldn't help but join in. Eventually even Billie grudgingly grinned.

'Anyway, I'd say these caterers were a hit,' Lily said, veering the conversation away from Tabitha and Cillian. 'Good choice, Scarlet.'

She afforded her niece a smile of approval and raised her glass for a toast. 'To a great evening and to all of you who helped make it what it is.' She extended her smile to Isla and Cath before clinking glasses with those in reach.

'And to the tables who spent so generously,' Scarlet added. She lowered her voice as her grey-blue eyes met Lily's. 'Especially tables sixteen to twenty.' Her red lips curled up in a brief smile of amusement, and Lily returned it.

'Especially those,' she agreed.

There were only fifteen tables tonight. The last four were fictional vessels through which they'd laundered a very large chunk of their illicit cash.

'You know what we should have done,' Cath said to Billie, who was once again glaring over at Tabitha and Cillian. 'Switched him out with Connor. She'd never have known.'

'That would have been a great idea, if he was here,' Billie replied glumly.

Cath reached over and squeezed her arm, dropping the subject.

Lily didn't comment. Connor was busy dealing with other pressing matters this evening. Not that she'd have swapped them out anyway, even if he wasn't. Despite their identical appearances, they were very different men, and the women they attracted only ever seemed to like one or the other. Something she'd found quite interesting over the years. If Tabitha was into Cillian, Connor wasn't going to cut it. And she needed to keep Tabitha's attention if they were going to get into that house.

Because Scarlet's offer of companionship clearly wasn't going to be enough.

Scarlet glanced at Lily. 'Where did Connor take him anyway?' she asked.

'The pub basement,' Lily answered, checking her watch. 'I was hoping he'd have got somewhere by now, but he hasn't messaged.'

'He will,' Scarlet replied confidently. 'He's never failed before.'

'True.'

Waiters appeared and began taking away the empty coffee cups from the tables, signalling that the dinner section of the evening was now over. Ray stood up and placed his napkin on the table, moving round to where Lily sat. She turned and breathed in his musky, woody aftershave as he leaned over the back of her chair, stifling the urge to reach up and run her hands over his chest.

'You ready to take me for another dance?' she asked.

'I'll have to take a rain check. I've gotta go. Something's come up,' he replied in his deep gravelly voice.

Lily ignored the pull of disappointment in her stomach and nodded. She understood. Changed plans, shady fires to put out at all times of the day and night, the endless strategic juggle of running an illegal firm. That was their life. Not dinners and dances.

'I'll catch you later then,' she replied, accepting the brief kiss of farewell.

As Ray walked away, Lily felt her phone vibrate and she quickly pulled it out of her clutch, her hope rising. But staring down at the words on the screen, that hope swiftly faded and her mood darkened.

'What?' Scarlet asked quietly. 'What is it?'

Lily clenched her jaw grimly for a moment before answering. 'It's Connor. We have a problem...'

ELEVEN

Connor pressed his head against one of the wooden support beams in the basement of the pub, taking a moment to catch his breath. He sniffed and wiped the sweat from his forehead, then placed his hands on his hips. The same sheen of sweat covered his partially bare chest and muscular arms as he stood in just the vest and tracksuit bottoms he'd donned for this task and would burn afterwards.

'Who's running it?' he asked in a tired voice.

The question was directed to a bloodied man tied to a wooden chair in the middle of the dimly lit basement. He was bent forward, almost doubled over, his head hanging low and a mess of floppy brown hair covering his face. The ropes that bound his wrists to the spindles on the back of the chair cut into his skin as the weight of his body pulled against them.

For a moment he didn't move, and Connor wondered if he'd passed out again, but then a low pained laugh rocked his beaten body. Connor exchanged a look of tired frustration with Joe, who quietly sat at the other side of the basement, waiting for instruction.

'Do you think I'm holding out for fun?' the man replied, spitting blood out to the side.

Connor walked over to an upturned metal beer barrel and leaned against it. 'I think you're an idiot, to be honest. That or a sadist. Because this ain't going to stop until you tell me what I need to know.'

'And I'm not gonna talk, so where does that leave us?' came the reply.

Connor stared at him, the anger inside him swelling. They'd been here for hours. After they'd grabbed him off the street and brought him back here, they'd started with a fairly standard beating. Most people on the other end of that sort of beating were smart enough to hand over the information quickly. Not many were stupid enough to draw it out. But this guy was one of the stupid ones.

Connor had stepped things up after a while, no longer taking care to leave bones intact. One of the man's hands was now a mangled mess, two front teeth were gone, one eye was swollen shut and blood covered his face from a broken nose and two nasty gashes. They'd waterboarded him for a while, and though he'd gasped and spluttered and suffered between each round, it still hadn't worked.

In his furious exasperation, Connor had beat him again mercilessly just now, slamming his fists into every inch of the man, over and over, until his energy was spent. And yet still he held on to the information Connor needed.

'You've been taking bets for our fights for months. Under-cutting our odds, stealing our customers – stealing our *business*,' Connor said with a deep snarl. 'We know you ain't the organ grinder. We know someone on the inside list is giving you the information and that they're running this. The only thing we *don't* know is who. So you need to tell me who that is. And you need to tell me *now*,' he pressed.

The man remained silent, and Connor snapped. 'Don't be

so *fucking* stupid. This ain't a crusade you can win. You're already in the shit because *no one* steals from us and gets away with it. But you don't have to suffer what I'm prepared to put you through to find out who's behind all this. All you've got to do is tell me the name and all of this stops.' He opened his arms wide and then dropped them back to his sides.

'I can't,' the man mumbled, spitting out another mouthful of blood to the side, spittle dripping from his swollen mouth. 'You don't understand. Nothing you do to me could be worse than what they'll do if I talk.'

Connor walked over and crouched down on his haunches in front of him, letting out a long, loud breath through his nose and pushing his hand back through his hair before he spoke.

'No, I don't think *you* understand,' he said in a level tone. 'You've got it completely the wrong way round.' He looked up into the man's half-open bloodshot eye. '*We're* the ones you need to be worried about. Because if you don't start talking, you ain't leaving this place with a soul still in that body.' He pulled an almost sympathetic grimace. 'And we're in no rush to make that quick.'

The man stared back at him, no expression on his bloody, swollen face. 'I've got all the time in the fucking world,' he said.

With an enraged growl, Connor stood up and swung his fist, smashing it into the cheekbone he knew was already broken, twice, in fast, vicious succession, before stepping away.

'Who is it?' he bellowed.

But there was no answer. The man had flopped forward once more, and when Connor grabbed him by the hair and lifted his head, his eyes were closed and his face had fallen slack.

'He's out again. For *fuck's* sake.'

He kicked out at an empty wooden crate and sent it flying, the wood snapping in two where his foot had connected with it.

He took a deep breath in then exhaled slowly as he tried to think. There had to be a way to get to this guy.

To break him.

The smallest of sounds came from the narrow arched hallway that led away from this main basement towards the stairs up to the pub above, and Connor sharply turned. To his surprise, he saw Ray leaning just inside against the brick wall, arms folded, watching the proceedings.

Connor's expression darkened. 'What the fuck are you doing here?'

TWELVE

Ray saw Connor's gaze flicker into the gloomy darkness of the hallway behind him.

'Where's Dan?' he asked with a flash of further annoyance.

Dan must have been the man Connor had left on guard outside, Ray decided.

'He's still there,' Ray replied, straightening up and walking into the room. 'I told him your mum had sent me to help out.'

He watched Connor's jaw tighten at this idea. Despite all they now knew about each other – or perhaps more realistically *because* of it – the tension between them was still strong.

Giving him a second to swallow the situation, Ray stepped forward and checked the man's face, the same way Connor had moments before. In his peripheral vision, he watched Connor catch Joe's eye and tilt his head. Joe immediately slid off the barrel he'd been perched on and left the basement.

Good, Ray thought. *Now we can talk properly*.

'You've certainly put him through his paces, haven't you?' Ray let the man's head drop to his chest again, listening as Joe's footsteps moved up the stairs. 'He'll be out for a while.'

The door squeaked open and then shut again, the soft click telling Ray they were now alone.

'Why did my mum send you?' Connor asked, cutting to the point.

'She didn't,' Ray replied, sitting down on the barrel Joe had just vacated. 'That's just what I told your doorman.'

Connor narrowed his eyes and shook his head with a sound of bitter amusement. 'Of course you did.'

Ray studied his son's face, secretly marvelling, as he did now and then, at the tell-tale signs he'd missed all these years. Both Cillian and Connor had their mother's deep brown eyes and her chiselled bone structure, but they had his thick, dark hair, strong brow and long eyelashes that any woman would be envious of, but which somehow just added to their look of brooding masculinity. They looked so much like he had, in his younger days.

Finding out the way he had, two years before, that Lily had lied about their parentage, had nearly killed him. Finding out that for all the years that he'd loved her, faithfully, loyally, giving up the chance of having a family of his own just to stay in her orbit, he'd had two living, breathing sons right in front of him. Two sons she'd kept from him for almost three decades.

He'd nearly killed her for that too, for that betrayal, and if she'd been anyone else on the planet, he would have. But she wasn't anyone else. She was his Lily. His one weakness. And though the path to getting back on good terms had been long and rocky, he'd forced himself to try and understand her reasons.

Now he was left in the odd limbo of trying to connect with two young men who'd spent their whole lives naturally not trusting him because he wasn't family – and who now trusted him even less because he *was*.

'What do you want, Ray?' Connor asked bluntly. 'Because I'm busy.'

'I don't think you are,' Ray said with a sarcastic smirk at the inert man in the chair. 'I wanted to congratulate you on the event tonight – you all did a smashing job,' he said casually.

Connor rolled his eyes. 'You came all the way down here to tell me that?'

'Yeah.' Ray shrugged. 'You weren't there and I didn't want to leave you out of my compliments.' He held Connor's stare, noticing the grim lock of his jaw and naked distrust in his eyes.

'Well you wasted your time. I didn't have anything to do with it.' Connor walked over to the side of the room and picked up his drink, gulping the liquid down thirstily.

He looked knackered, Ray observed. This kind of day could do that to a man.

'Oh right,' he said, feigning surprise. 'I just assumed as your brother was so involved...'

'He didn't do much set-up either,' Connor snapped, cutting Ray off.

'Yeah? He seemed to be at the centre of the job you're pulling off with the toff,' Ray replied, watching his expression. He didn't actually know what Lily was running, only that she was running *something* and that Cillian leading it up was an unexpected change of plan.

As expected, Connor tensed. 'What you on about?' he asked warily.

'The job with the woman at the ball,' Ray continued the bluff with a shrug. 'He's been running point all night. None of the others have gone near her. I assumed you knew, being his brother.' He let out a short laugh of amusement as the barb hit home. 'Ah, don't worry. I'm sure they planned to tell you at some point.'

'Obviously,' Connor said tersely. 'Seeing as we're a firm – one you ain't part of actually.' He glared at Ray, getting some of his fight back. 'So I don't see what it's got to do with you.'

Ray held his hands up in mock defeat. 'Nothing at all, just

shooting the breeze with ya. Plus, I wanted to talk to you about a deal I can get on some imported booze.'

'Why would you want to talk to me about that?' Connor asked.

Turning his attention back to the man in the chair, Connor pulled his face into view again and slapped it a couple of times. 'Oi, wake up, sunshine. We ain't finished here.' He let go and his head lolled silently back to his chest. 'Fuck's sake,' he hissed.

'For The Hideout,' Ray continued. 'For the bar. Would increase profit by a significant amount.'

'The Hideout's Cillian's,' Connor replied, still watching the figure in the chair.

'Oh.' Ray feigned surprise again. 'I thought that was both of you. My mistake.'

'Yeah, you make a lot of those.' Connor's tone was bored.

'Well, you know what they say. To err is human,' Ray replied good-naturedly. He waited a moment, then went in for the kill. 'So what are *you* doing when Cillian's busy leading the way on big jobs and running the bigger businesses?'

Connor's gaze immediately shot back to meet his, his expression hardening. 'So *that's* what this is,' he said. 'Alright, you want to know what I'm doing?'

He took a step towards Ray, pulling himself up to full height. 'When Cillian's too tied up with the newer business, I keep everything else going. I run the protections, organise the markets, pick up the earnings, sort out the men and the escorts, keep my ear to the network and beat up cunts like this.' He pointed back at the man in the chair. 'We all have our roles in a firm, Ray; you know that better than most, so don't try and play me like that.'

'I ain't playing ya,' Ray replied. 'But is that all you really want to do?'

'There's nothing wrong with what I do.' Connor was shouting now, Ray's words getting under his skin as intended.

'It's what I've always done and I'm fucking good at it, and what's more, I'm *respected* for it.'

Ray nodded. 'That's all true and I ain't saying otherwise,' he said placatingly. 'But Cillian's already moving up the ranks alongside your cousin, and it's well known that they'll be running the show one day.' He paused to let it sink in. 'You still going to be content doing this then?' He arched an eyebrow challengingly.

'Fuck off, Ray,' Connor spat, turning away with a tut.

'I've built a large firm over the last thirty years and I have a lot of loyal, hard-working men, but not one of 'em's blood,' Ray said sincerely. 'There ain't no next generation of Renshaws floating around south of the river; the only family I have – whether you like it or not – is you and your brother.'

Connor made a sound of frustration and ran his hand back through his hair, looking away. 'My answer's the same as all the other times you've said this. I'm not interested.'

'You should be,' Ray shot back, impatience now tinging his tone. 'Because you're already being left behind as the rest of them move up. And if you really *are* happy with that – happy with people wondering why your twin was good enough to be trusted with the running of the show when *you weren't* – then fine. You stay where you are.' He eyed Connor hard. 'You keep doing the heavy work and running round to the tune of your brother and your cousin as you grow old – but I promise you that if you do, one day you'll wake up and realise that ignoring this opportunity was a mistake. Because taking my offer and working up the ladder to take over from me one day ain't turning your back on your family. Staying where you are ain't the only way to add value to your firm.'

'You of all people should know I'd never do that to my mum,' Connor replied.

'Do what? Expand her empire?' Ray asked, exasperated. 'All this would do is *benefit* her. Connor, I've loved your mum since the day I first met her as a scrawny teenage street urchin.'

'Watch your mouth,' Connor snarled.

'It ain't an insult, it's the truth. We both worked our way up from nothing. And though I made some mistakes in my youth, I've spent decades making it up to her. I've spent decades paying for those mistakes too,' he added darkly. 'She means more to me than anyone and I'd give her anything. She could walk in tomorrow demanding the keys to my kingdom and I'd hand them over without a word. And she knows that.'

'But she don't *want* your kingdom,' Connor replied, meeting his eyes with a hard calmness. 'She has her own. One she built herself, for her family. That's all she's ever wanted, to give us something we can carry on. And you expect me to run off to join *you*?'

Ray sighed and shook his head. 'You're looking at this all wrong. It don't have to be one or the other. If Cillian and Scarlet took over your mum's firm and you took over mine one day, together you'd be the strongest criminal family this city's ever seen. Don't you see that? You could join the east and the south together as one. You'd be untouchable. This ain't me trying to take you away from your mum; I'm looking at the bigger picture – for all of you. Your mum would see it too.'

'Yeah?' Connor cocked an eyebrow. 'Then why've you not told her about these little chats we've been having, eh? Why've you not put this grand idea of yours to her?'

Ray closed his mouth, clamping it in a grim line. Connor had him there. The thing was, Lily *would* see it eventually, but she was a stubbornly independent and intrinsically defensive woman. Like Connor, initially she'd see this as some sort of attack on her close family unit. But it wasn't. He was being completely upfront about his intentions and she'd see that in time, if he could just get Connor on board before she could stop him. It was the best thing for all of them, in the long run. And *yes*, that included him. He would benefit from this arrangement too.

It had been something that had plagued Ray for years, the fact he had no one to pass the firm down to. He'd never married, never had children – or so he'd thought. He had no living siblings or nieces or nephews.

He'd long ago been forced to accept that Lily would never move into his orbit the way he wanted her to. They'd been together for the best part of thirty years, but she had always held him at arm's length and kept her day-to-day life completely independent of him. And so he'd been stuck in a strange limbo when it came to looking towards the future.

Several of his most trusted men had been by his side since the beginning, and he'd accepted a while ago that he'd probably have to leave the firm to them. They were competent and respected. They'd keep it running and make sure his legacy lived on. But it wasn't the same as leaving it to family. Passing it forward to your own blood.

After his shock and anger at the bombshell that Lily's two grown sons had been his all along had subsided, his hope had slowly been renewed. Sure, the twins were in their late twenties; they weren't youngsters he could mould – but Lily had raised them in this way of life already. They were already known and respected, already knew how things worked. He'd begun watching them both carefully and had quickly deduced that the clear leader of the two was Cillian.

It had been interesting, watching them so closely. He'd seen things no one else would ever likely notice. Though Ray doubted she meant to, Lily subconsciously favoured Cillian, when it came to dispersal of responsibilities. And though there seemed to be no great resentment, Connor was most definitely aware of it. It was partially why he'd focused his efforts on Connor.

Ray eyed him now, Connor's clear, direct gaze unmoving as

he waited for an answer. The corner of Ray's mouth hitched up in a wry smile. The younger man was more like him than he realised. No tolerance for bullshit, always shooting straight to the black-and-white core of any situation.

'You know why I ain't told your mum,' he said, deciding to be frank with him. 'She's so defensive she'd fight me before even thinking about it.'

Connor hitched an eyebrow.

'It's no insult, it's a skill that's kept her out of harm's way many a time over the years. But it's so ingrained she can't switch it off.'

Connor's expression relaxed slightly and he nodded, for once unable to disagree. 'Exactly, Ray.'

He broke away and checked the man in the chair again. He appeared to still be out cold.

Ray cast his eye over the unconscious man. 'He's a tough fucker, I'll give him that,' he said. 'Who is he anyway?'

'That's the problem,' Connor replied. 'No one seems to know. Which don't make any sense as he was front end for whoever's been running those bets on our matches.'

Ray frowned. 'No, that don't make sense at all.'

It was common knowledge that the Drews had discovered someone running bets on their illegal boxing matches. It had to be another firm because these matches were a closely guarded secret and attendance was strictly invite only. That certainly narrowed the suspect list down, and from the point at which they located their front man, it should have been simple. No firm would put a rookie at the front of that sort of operation. It would have to be someone they trusted, someone seasoned at this sort of job and who understood how to avoid or withstand the repercussions. Which meant they should have known this guy. They all kept up to date with the higher-ranking men within other firms. So the fact no one knew him was an oddity.

'I think you're going to need to change tactics,' Ray said,

eying the extent of the man's wounds. 'You know, ninety per cent of the time it works, and there's a beauty to it.'

'To what?' Connor asked, taking another drink.

'Being a blunt instrument,' Ray replied. 'It's how I made most of my way.' He shrugged. 'Hit 'em hard, double up where it hurts, never hesitate. They all come around when they realise that pain ain't gonna stop. But there's always the odd one that wants to hold out.' He moved off the barrel and walked in a slow circle around the man, studying him. 'You keep going, you'll just kill him.'

'No shit, Sherlock,' Connor muttered.

'What's holding him back I wonder?' Ray mused. There had to be more than meets the eye.

'Stupidity,' Connor replied impatiently.

'I'll help you get it out of him, if you want,' Ray offered, shuffling through some alternative options in his head.

'Nah, I'm good. This ain't your business.' The words were sharp. A warning.

Ray hid a smile. If he wasn't trying to recruit the little fucker, he'd be putting him in his place for all this disrespect by now. He hadn't got to where he was now to put up with men twenty years younger talking to him like this.

'It's an offer of help, not a hostile fucking takeover,' he replied instead, a hard edge to his words.

It seemed to be enough to remind Connor who he was, as the other man stared at him for a long moment before answering in a slightly less aggressive tone.

'It don't matter what it is. Like you said, these tactics ain't working. And as you just said, you're as blunt an instrument as I am.'

Ray opened his mouth to point out that this wasn't quite correct but then closed it again. Connor didn't want his help and he wasn't going to waste his time trying to convince him otherwise. Plus, that wasn't why he was here.

'Your choice,' he said with a shrug. 'Anyway, going back to your mum, we both know her natural reaction would be to defend against that kind of change. But that don't mean she's right. Now, I know you think you've come to a decision on this...'

Connor made a sound of derision. 'One I've told you about five times.'

'... but I'm going to keep asking until you make a better one,' Ray continued, not missing a beat. 'Because I'm right about this. If we do this, everyone benefits. And your mum *will* calm down, once she sees we're serious and that we're all still on the same side.'

A cold smile turned up the corners of Connor's mouth as he slipped his arms into his hoodie and zipped it up. 'You clearly don't know her as well as you think you do, if you think she'll calm down from that.'

'I know her better than anyone on the planet,' Ray answered confidently.

Connor was putting his keys and phone into his pocket and then picked up another phone and a wallet nearby. Ray glanced back at the bloody figure doubled over in the chair.

'Not giving up already, are ya?' he asked.

'No,' Connor replied darkly. 'I'm taking this to a much sharper instrument than either of us.'

He threw Ray one last glare as he moved into the dark hallway that led out of the basement.

Ray's mouth curled up into a ghost of a smile as he breathed her name. 'Lily.'

THIRTEEN

Scarlet put on her earrings and grinned in the mirror as Benny came up behind her and wrapped his arms around her middle, squeezing her close to him. She pressed herself back into his taut body, still warm from sleep, and closed her eyes as he buried his face into her long dark hair, kissing her neck.

'Come back to bed,' he moaned. 'Being up and dressed already at this time of the day is just indecent.'

Scarlet laughed and turned to face him. 'It's nearly ten,' she admonished. 'Some people would argue that it's indecent *not* being up and dressed by now.'

'Well they're fucking *wrong*,' Benny replied with such certainty she couldn't help but laugh.

'Go back to sleep if you want,' she said, kissing him lightly before unwinding herself from his arms. 'You don't have to go just because I need to.'

Benny screwed up his face. 'Nah, your mum's here.'

Scarlet shrugged. 'Don't walk around naked then.'

She reached into her wardrobe for the tailored suit jacket she favoured, to go with her white blouse and black cigarette trousers, ignoring his groan.

'This is why I prefer staying at my place,' he said. 'I don't have to think about these things.'

'I mean, walk around naked if you want,' Scarlet offered drily, moving in front of the mirror. 'But maybe just shout down to her first. You don't want to give her a heart attack.'

She cast her eye over herself critically. She was tired after the ball last night but luckily there were no rings under her eyes. Her dark hair hung in loose waves, and her rich red lipstick gave her face a bit of life. The only colour on her flawless skin was the light bronzer she'd applied to her high chiselled cheeks. *The Irish colouring*, her mother had always called it, her striking combination of raven hair, deep-blue eyes and the palest of pale skin.

'You like it at my place though, right?' Benny asked in a strange tone.

Scarlet turned to stand between his legs, where he'd sat back down on the bed, and looped her arms over his shoulders. She ran her fingers over the short springy curls at the back of his head and studied his handsome face with a smile.

''Course I do. What's up?' she asked.

They spent two or three nights together a week around their ever-changing work schedules, and more often than not, this was at Benny's flat, a large, stylish bachelor pad overlooking the river.

'Nothing's up,' he replied, running his hands up her hips and holding her slim waist. He bit his bottom lip with a smile for a moment. 'Just thinking how much I enjoy you being there.'

'Thanks,' Scarlet replied. 'We'll stay there tomorrow, OK? It was just easier coming back here last night with this meeting I've got coming up.'

'Sounds good. If you can get the night off, maybe we can even make it a date night in.' His brown eyes twinkled up at her.

Scarlet's mouth widened in a slow smile. 'You have a night off?'

'I might do,' he replied, pulling her closer. 'Just like I might put on some good music...'

'Oh yeah?' Scarlet's smile widened.

He kissed her stomach. 'And I might grill a couple of steaks with my special home-made marinade...'

'Oh, I do *love* your marinade...' She bit her lip as he pulled her lower and moved his kisses upwards.

'And I might even wear that little apron I know you like...'

Scarlet let out a low flirty gasp, pressing her body to his. 'With nothing else on underneath?' she whispered.

'Nothing,' he whispered back in her ear, before trailing kisses all down her neck.

Scarlet closed her eyes, enjoying the sensation for a few moments, until Benny tried to pull her back on the bed. Prising herself from his grip, she reluctantly stood up and moved away from him. He fell backward with a pained groan.

'I'm sorry,' Scarlet said with a laugh. 'I want to, but...'

'But you have a meeting,' Benny finished resignedly. 'I know.' He smiled at her. 'Go on – I'll be down in a sec.'

Scarlet smiled back. 'I'm definitely up for that date night if I can get off though.'

'Good. Just let me know.' Benny stood up and walked over to his clothes.

Leaving him to dress, Scarlet made her way downstairs and into the kitchen, where her mother sat reading a magazine in her dressing gown. Her *nice* dressing gown, that was. The one she wore when Benny was in the house, not the old comfy one she donned when it was just her and Scarlet.

Cath didn't look up, her eyes glued to the article she was reading as she spoke to her daughter. 'Apparently a mix of flooring in a house can weaken its energy, according to this feng shui guy. Proper bad.'

They both stared over to where the white quartz floor tiles that swept through the large airy kitchen met the darker grey ones in the hallway, at the wide squared opening between the two areas.

'But you're not even into feng shui,' Scarlet replied.

'Yeah, but this guy is in *Ideal Home*, Scarlet, so he must know a thing or two,' Cath said with a concerned glance back at the floor.

Scarlet frowned and walked over to her mother, taking the magazine from her hand and flipping to the front cover. 'Since when do you read *Ideal Home*?' she asked.

'I like to glance at it now and then,' Cath said defensively. She picked up a mug of tea from the breakfast table next to her and sipped it. 'Plus it was last month's issue and I was throwing it out at the salon.'

Scarlet gave her back the magazine and walked over to the coffee machine, pressing the on button and pulling everything she needed from the cupboard above. 'You don't need a magazine to tell you what to do – you've got great taste, Mum,' she said.

'Ahh, thanks, love,' Cath replied with a happy smile. 'It could do with a bit of a revamp in here though,' she added, looking around. 'We haven't changed anything in years. I've been thinking about redoing the lounge for a while actually.'

'Yeah?' Scarlet watched the coffee trickle through the machine into the first cardboard takeaway cup. She didn't have time to drink one here today.

'Yeah, the big sofa has had it. I keep restuffing it and fluffing it, but I feel like I'm flogging a dead horse at this point,' she replied, wrinkling her nose. 'Would be nice to get some new furniture and do it all up in there.'

'Good idea,' Scarlet replied, switching the cups and cursing under her breath as a drip of the hot coffee scalded her finger. She quickly sucked it until the sting eased.

Cath looked over in concern. 'You alright?'

'Yeah, fine.' She shook her hand in the air for a minute.

'You not stopping?' Cath asked, clocking the takeaway cups.

'No, got to meet Lil at the depot soon. In fact, should have left already really,' she added, checking the time.

'OK. Maybe tonight if you're not out we could sit and have a look at what we fancy doing with the lounge,' Cath suggested.

'Sure, sounds good,' she replied.

Cath flipped open the magazine again with a cheerful smile, and Scarlet watched her with a feeling of warmth. Since her father's death, it took a lot more to coax that smile out.

Benny jogged down the stairs, now fully dressed, aside from the bow tie, in last night's tux, and entered the kitchen. 'Morning, Mrs Drew,' he said, with his most charming smile.

Cath's smile widened; she liked Benny. 'Morning, love – though I've told you before, call me Cath.'

'Morning *Cath*,' he corrected himself. 'How is it that you look as fresh and beautiful as ever after all those drinks we had last night, eh?'

'Oh, stop it,' Cath said with a high tinkling giggle.

'Yeah... Stop it,' Scarlet repeated with a note of sarcastic disgust.

Cath tutted and shot her a withering look.

'What?' Benny asked, taking his coffee from Scarlet's outstretched hand and leaning back against the counter next to her. 'Your mum *is* beautiful. And you should be glad she looks so fine for her age, because that will be you in, what?' He winked at Cath teasingly. 'Five years?'

Cath giggled. 'Oh, you are a cheeky one.'

'Anyway, much as I hate to break this up,' Scarlet said with a roll of her eyes, 'I really do need to go.'

Benny looked at his watch. 'Yeah, me too. Catch you later Mrs D— *Cath*.' He shot her a smile and followed Scarlet to the door.

'See ya,' Cath called after them.

Scarlet grabbed her bag and car keys from the hallway, then made her way outside and closed the door behind them.

Benny stopped her on the top step for one last kiss. His deep brown eyes glinted with lust, and as Scarlet stared up at him, she couldn't help but feel herself respond.

She ran her hands up his arms and over his broad shoulders. 'You're a bad man,' she declared between kisses.

'The baddest,' he replied in a low growl before pulling away. 'But you are just gonna have to wait for tomorrow night.' He grinned and walked down the driveway to his car.

Shaking her head, Scarlet followed him, stopping beside hers. 'I'll catch you later.'

A white folded piece of paper stuck out from under her windscreen wipers, and she pulled it out with a frown.

'What's that?' Benny asked.

'Not sure, let's...' She opened it, and as she registered what was inside, she felt her insides turn to solid ice. Her stomach churned and her throat constricted, but somehow she managed to keep her reaction from her face.

She quickly refolded the paper, then swallowed hard and forced herself to speak. 'It's nothing.' She cleared her throat and opened the car door, shoving it into her handbag. 'Local window-cleaning company.'

'Ah, they do my nut in, these flyers on cars,' Benny replied, turning away from her to open his door. 'Catch you later.'

Scarlet waved him off, then slipped into her car and closed the door. All she could hear was the frantic pounding of her heart, and as Benny's tail lights disappeared from view, she pulled the note back out of her bag. Her hand shook slightly as she reopened it, the shock still coursing through her body.

There was just one line written inside. Seven very simple yet terrifying words, written neatly in black ink.

I know what you did to her.

FOURTEEN

The sharp ticking filled the otherwise silent car as Cillian waited to turn into the next road on his way out of London to the new depot they were in the process of setting up. The tension in the car was stifling, and as he glanced at the angry blonde in the passenger seat, he suddenly sighed.

'Are you going to keep this up all day?' he asked.

Billie glared at him, her bright blue eyes piercing into the side of his head as he focused back on the road. 'Yes, I bloody well am,' she snapped. 'All week most likely too. Maybe even longer. I mean really, what a stupid fucking question.'

Cillian held his free hand up in surrender. 'Alright, alright, calm down,' he replied quickly.

'*Calm down?*' she repeated incredulously, her temper clearly rising. 'You've got a nerve...'

'I didn't mean calm down about the whole situation, just here, within this specific conversation,' Cillian continued, raising his voice slightly.

Billie sniffed and looked away out of the passenger-side window. Cillian sighed again, this time silently. Of all the shit he'd had to deal with over the years – enemies, beatings, murder attempts – Billie's simmering temper was by far his least favourite.

She'd kept her cool last night, carefully distracted and managed by his mother through the several hours Tabitha Grey had draped herself all over him. But the moment they'd reached home, her feelings had erupted and they'd had a blazing row. Or rather, Billie had ended up having a blazing row *at* him. He hadn't been able to give her what she wanted, but neither could he disagree with her argument.

As she'd pointed out, rather loudly at the time, he'd feel exactly the same if the situation was the other way around. And it was true. If that were the case, he'd probably have told them to stuff whatever job it was where the sun didn't shine. But it wasn't that simple.

'I just don't understand why we can't switch you out with Connor from this point on,' Billie said, picking the conversation back up as though it hadn't been an entire night and half a morning – a morning through which she'd furiously ignored him – since they'd left off.

Cillian briefly closed his eyes with an internal groan. 'Would *you* date him?' he asked her bluntly.

'Obviously not – he's your twin brother and that's a completely different scenario,' she replied witheringly.

'No, if we hadn't met and you met him at a bar or on a dating site or something, would you date him?' Cillian pushed. 'Come on – think about it. As a totally unconnected individual, if you had a first date with him, would you go again? And it ain't a trick question. If it's a yes, that's fine,' he added. 'This is totally hypothetical.'

'Totally hypothetical?' she repeated, checking his face.

'Honestly,' Cillian said. 'Think about it.'

Billie chewed her bottom lip and stared at the road ahead for a few moments.

'Honestly? No, I don't think I would. And I ain't just saying that because he's your brother,' she added. 'But that's probably just because I *know* him—'

'It ain't because you know him,' Cillian said, interrupting her. 'We've had this our whole lives, every single time without fail.'

'What do you mean?' Billie asked, confused.

'We're identical in every way to look at, but there has not been one girl, *ever*, that has fancied us both,' he explained. They turned another corner and he sped up as the road ahead cleared. 'We tested it out a few times, years ago. Tried switching places to see if it was genuine. Same result every time.'

Billie pursed her lips and exhaled loudly through her nose. 'Well...' she said grudgingly. 'You do have completely different personalities.'

'Yep. Physically they can't tell the difference, but the moment we start talking, no matter how much we try to act like the other, they pick up on it. *That's* why my mum won't go for it. She knows.' He held his hands out in a helpless gesture. 'We need Tabitha to stay interested, just long enough for me to get inside and get the information we need for the job. After that, it's done with. You won't have to go through all this again. I promise you, Bills.'

He reached for her hand and squeezed it. She didn't pull away, but she still didn't look convinced.

'But how far are you going to end up going? She was practically humping your leg last night. What's she going to do when you take her on a date?'

'It's not a real date,' Cillian reminded her.

'Yeah, but she don't know that, does she?' Billie argued. 'Which means she'll think she's well in there. She won't stop at dry humping you this time, she'll be trying to stick her tongue down your throat and get you back to hers – and it won't be to view her bloody art collection!'

'Billie!' Cillian cried exasperatedly. 'I would never cheat on you – and certainly not with some posh fruit loop for a bit of cash. Christ, who do you think I am?'

He didn't know what else to say to her. He had to follow through with the new plan or it all would have been for nothing. Scarlet was burned now – there was no hope of her retaking the lead. Tabitha had scorned her more than once over the course of the evening and had made it clear she saw her only as a gateway to more interesting things.

They reached the depot and he pulled to a slow stop beside Lily's and Scarlet's cars, before rubbing his face with both hands, stressed. Billie had gone quiet, and as he pulled his hands away, he could see she was watching him, her expression calmer but still troubled.

'I know exactly who you are, Cillian,' she said seriously. 'And I trust you completely. But I don't know or trust *her*. And whether I trust you or not, I just don't fucking like it.'

Pursing her lips, Billie opened the car door, stepping out and slamming it behind her without another word.

FIFTEEN

It started raining just as Cillian and Billie walked into the main building of the brand new truck depot. Sharp, sporadic taps quickly gave way to a deafening onslaught that sounded like gravel being poured from a great height as it hammered down on the corrugated steel roof above them.

Lily noted Billie's tight expression and Cillian's grim frown. Clearly things weren't going well with the way the plan had changed. This was going to have to be managed carefully, otherwise *something* was going to be spilled, though whether it was blood or tears Lily couldn't quite guess yet.

Cillian glanced up at the roof as they reached the middle of the room where Lily and Scarlet stood waiting beside a trestle table. It was currently the only piece of furniture in there, and it was covered in plans and drawings and invoices all relating to the project. Lily followed her son's gaze with a grim smile.

'It won't be this loud once this place is kitted out apparently. It's because it's echoing,' she explained. 'Next week when the catwalks and internal walls are all fitted, it will be completely different in here.'

'Where's Connor?' Cillian asked.

'On his way. He needs to stop by the safe house first,' Lily said, her expression turning hard. 'Our new friend is still being settled in.'

'How long will he be?' Cillian asked, checking his watch. 'I need to get to The Hideout.'

'It doesn't matter,' Lily said dismissively. 'He doesn't need to be here to discuss the first part. Now, have you messaged her yet?'

Cillian held her gaze for a moment with a look that showed he'd rather be having any other conversation than this right now.

'Not yet,' he said.

Billie was silent beside him, but her clenched jaw and tight lips spoke volumes.

'Text her now. Tell her you want to see her tomorrow night. Or if not the night after. Let's get this moving quickly. We need to keep her warm,' Lily ordered.

Billie snorted at the use of words and crossed her arms, pacing away from them.

Lily squeezed her eyes for a moment. 'Billie, I think you should be in on this job,' she said suddenly.

'What?' The cry came from both Billie and Cillian in unison.

Scarlet seemed to tune in suddenly, pulled away from whatever thought had been distracting her, and did a double take, echoing the word just a second after them.

'Listen, I know you ain't in the game, and I'm not trying to recruit you,' Lily replied. She saw the look in Cillian's eye. 'I'm *not*,' she repeated strongly. 'The set-up you have worked for Cath and Ronan – he had a partnership with someone on the outside. It clearly works for you too and I'm not trying to change that – but if you're not on board here, Billie, it's going to cause problems,' she continued, a hard edge to her words as she stared down the younger woman.

'It won't,' Billie replied. 'I can't lie, I hate the idea, but I'd never try and scupper a job.'

'You might not think that now, but when you're sat at home twiddling your thumbs and letting your imagination run riot, things will look a lot different. Trust me,' Lily argued. 'No. You're better off here, in the thick of it. You'll know what's happening rather than waiting and imagining the worst. And it will keep you busy whilst he's... well, *busy*,' she added. 'I think it would be best. Plus, we need a lookout.'

She shot Cillian a loaded look and saw understanding dawn on his face. They didn't need a lookout. This was purely to keep Billie occupied and where Lily could keep an eye on her.

Cillian slowly nodded and turned to Billie. 'I think it's a good idea. But it's totally up to you.'

'OK,' Billie said, her voice more confident than Lily had expected. 'I'm in.' She lifted her chin and rejoined them, visibly relaxing. 'Yeah. Why not?'

'Good.' Lily gave her a small smile of approval. 'Now, Cillian, send that text and when she responds we'll work out the plan.'

Cillian pulled out his phone and began typing, and Lily turned her attention back to the table. The plans for the building they stood in were laid out from her previous meeting with the building company. She cast her eye over them once more, committing the dates they'd given her for the internal work to memory. They were nearly there now, and her nerves were on edge.

It had cost them an arm and a leg to build this structure and buy everything they needed to get it up and running as a business. After all the other developments they'd pushed forward with over the last year and a half, this had pretty much wiped them out, financially.

Two years ago she wouldn't have done it. She wouldn't have risked so much and spread the firm so thin just to expand in such a big way. Not when they already had a thriving business. But she'd been forced to realise that times were changing and all the other firms around them had been slowly growing in numbers and in strength. That had changed everything. Their world was too cut-throat to sit comfortably in their little corner of the city while they were slowly overshadowed by their peers.

Expansion, of course, came with its own risks. They were becoming more visible, not able to run as silently under the radar as they had before. But it was either that or eventually be taken over. And Lily had no intention of ever allowing that to happen.

Lily eyed the plans, feeling the tension twitch between her shoulders. She wouldn't rest easy until things were up and running smoothly. Probably not even then. They'd sunk too much money for it to fail. With the plans they had ahead of them, one mistake could cost all of them their freedom, their empire and everything else they'd worked for all these years.

'Sent,' Cillian said, slipping his phone back into his pocket.

'What's the play behind this place, Lil? It ain't just another laundry – it's too big for that,' Billie said, looking around the space with a thoughtful expression.

The corner of Lily's mouth lifted briefly. Billie was a smart girl. 'No, this won't be used for laundering. Being so close to the Dartford Tunnel, it's a perfect spot for trucks to stop off to be serviced and maintained, to be stored or switch loads. It will do well legitimately.'

Billie's clear blue eyes studied her for a moment. 'And?'

Lily grinned. 'And our own trucks will use it as a base to smuggle items in from the mainland. That's what will make the real money.' She pointed towards a door at the other end of the building. 'That wall keeps the last loading dock hidden from view on the inside. Once a truck backs in and that door is closed, no one can see anything. There's a false floor hiding stairs that lead to a basement, which runs under here about half the length of the building. Whatever comes across can be hidden there until it can be moved on.'

Billie's eyebrows shot up. 'That's a decent space. What you smuggling in, elephants?'

'All sorts really.' Lily hid a frown as she noticed Scarlet's attention was once again elsewhere. Her head had barely been in the room since she'd arrived, which wasn't like her at all. 'We'll take commissions to bring things over for other firms, which could mean anything, within reason. There's the odd exception of course.'

'What like?' Billie asked.

'People,' Cillian answered, pulling a toothpick out of his jacket pocket and placing it between his front teeth. 'We ain't getting tangled up in all that – it's too messy.'

'How?' she asked.

'Christ, you taken a job with the filth or something?' he replied jokingly.

'I'm just curious, that's all,' she replied with a shrug.

'Dead bodies, that's why,' Lily answered bluntly. 'We've come up against that issue before and it ain't pretty.'

The twins had pulled a truck heist a few years before and when they'd gone to unload it, they'd found a family had hidden in the back. Only a little girl and her newborn sibling had survived. They'd cleaned them up and dropped them off inside a hospital, where they'd be found and taken care of, whilst Ray had disposed of the bodies. That wasn't something any of them particularly wanted to repeat.

'Not just that though,' she continued, pushing the sad memory away. 'Trafficking is rife, which is just completely fucked up.' She shook her head with a grim expression. 'It ain't worth the risk of being involved in that. I like to sleep at night.'

'Drugs will be a no-no too, I'm guessing,' Billie commented.

Lily's breath caught in her throat as she drew it in, but she only hesitated for a fraction of a second. 'Actually no. We're allowing that.'

It had been a long and difficult discussion between them as to whether or not they'd agree to smuggling in drugs for the other firms. The Drews were the only criminal firm in London who had a hard policy against dealing in drugs. From a business point of view it was ridiculous. They had the set-up, the contacts, the territory – and it was one of the easiest and most lucrative illegal businesses going. Many years ago, Lily and Ronan had considered it, but when Ruby had started sliding down the slippery slope of addiction as a teenager, they'd decided against it, and had actively tried to keep it out of their territory as much as they could. Not that it had made much difference.

But Ruby was now gone, and with her Lily's reason for boycotting that particular business. And at the end of the day, as Cillian had pointed out in their discussion, business was business. And in their game a lot of it was gritty. They needed to remove emotion and think logically if this depot was going to thrive.

Lily swallowed and turned back to Billie. 'Other than people and animals, it's pretty much fair game. And as we're on that subject, I actually have something to discuss with you all.' Her brown eyes sparkled, coming back to life as she moved her focus to the potential new thread of business ahead of them. 'I've been reaching out to old contacts and friends who move stuff back and forth. There's been a fair amount of interest, but there's also been a possible opportunity come up. With something we haven't dealt in before. A market no one else seems to have cornered yet.'

Cillian frowned and tipped his head to the side in interest. 'What's that then?'

Lily paused as the door opened and Connor ducked in, his

suit jacket pulled up over his head as he tried, unsuccessfully, to stay dry. Shrugging it back down with a sigh of annoyance, he marched over.

'I'm fucking soaked,' he complained, casting his eyes around the inside of the building critically. 'Nice. When they starting the inside?'

'Next couple of days,' Lily replied. 'Once the catwalks are in—'

'No, no, no, don't leave us hanging,' Cillian interrupted. 'What are we looking at?'

'Eh?' Connor looked between his brother and mother, confused. 'What's going on?'

'OK. So, as we all know, in the UK self-defence is basically illegal,' Lily said, looking at them all in turn to make sure she had their full attention. 'We can't carry weapons of any kind. Knives, guns...'

'Bats without balls,' Cillian chipped in with a smirk.

'Exactly. Even with a bat, you need proof it's being carried for non-offensive reasons,' she agreed. 'But we live in a country where attacks are rife. The stats are sky-high for violence, rape, murder...' She reeled them off. 'And despite the fact that, generally, women are physically not as strong as men, meaning we're more easily overpowered, we ain't even legally allowed to carry anything for self-defensive. Which is fucking ridiculous.'

'It really is,' Scarlet murmured in agreement.

Connor opened his mouth as if to talk then shut it and scratched his head with a grim expression.

'Now, people still carry things like pens, hairspray, put their keys through their fingers, but that's all very close range. An attacker has to be pretty much on you for you to swipe a pen.'

'What you getting at?' Cillian asked, studying her face.

'Pepper spray is what I'm getting at,' Lily replied.

Cillian and Connor exchanged a frown. 'You're not serious?' Cillian asked.

'Here's something I'll bet you didn't know,' Lily continued. 'Being caught with a can of pepper spray in your possession here carries the same penalties as a gun.'

'*What?*' Scarlet exclaimed.

'You're kidding?' Billie's eyes widened in shock.

Cillian let out an incredulous snort. 'It can't do.'

'It does,' Lily responded with calm certainty.

She looked around at the sea of confused faces. It *was* a ridiculous notion, but it was also an opportunity – and because of the obscurity of the situation, no one in their world had seemed to realise it before now.

'*Pepper spray?*' Connor repeated in disbelief.

'It's an offensive weapon if used, even in self-defence. If you don't get caught with it and arrested before then, that is,' Lily confirmed.

'So what's the angle?' Scarlet asked.

'There are a lot of people out there, mainly women, who still want to carry one even knowing it's illegal. They'd rather get in trouble for using it than be raped or killed. What's putting a lot of them off is the risk of being caught with it. Now, it's legal in France, and unlike a lot of other countries who impose strict controls, trade is licence free.'

'You want to smuggle it in and sell it,' Cillian summarised flatly.

'Not exactly,' Lily replied. 'I have a contact in France who has started up a pepper-spray factory. He's only just starting to put out the feelers, and he's the first factory willing to open its doors to our world. The others are all straight. So what I'm proposing is that, firstly, we request full UK buying rights, so no one else can purchase from him. Make an offer so good he can't refuse.' She eyed them each in turn, pacing slowly up and down the side of the table. 'We buy in bulk and smuggle them in through here. We make sure the spray cans are generic, cans that could look like any small hairspray, then we run stickering to make it appear as if that's exactly what it is. We'll copy a big brand, make sure the differences are indistinguishable.'

'So even if a woman gets her bag searched, they won't suspect a thing,' Scarlet said, understanding dawning in her eyes. The understanding almost instantly folded into a frown and she exchanged a look with Cillian. 'We couldn't sell them through the markets though, surely? All it takes is one person to get caught and spill the beans, and we're done.'

'No, I wouldn't want to put that risk through our stalls,' Lily agreed. 'I'm thinking along the lines of selling in bulk to the other firms around the country. Firms we trust or with good-enough reputations to take a chance on doing business with. It could be a game changer.'

'What makes you think other firms will want in on this? It's new, it's random...' Cillian screwed up his face in uncertainty. 'I don't know. If *we* don't want to sell it ourselves, why would anyone else?'

'You're missing the bigger picture,' Lily replied. 'With anything like this, there's a market. It's something people want and it's something the idiots in power have made illegal. If we don't do it, someone else *will*, because people have a habit of getting what they want, one way or another. And any illegal product that goes out to the average Joe runs the same risks. Drugs, guns, fake readies – when the filth find any of that, they chase the source, but the firms who sell them have the right set-up to lead them to a dead end. Single-link sales chains.'

'I think it's a good idea,' Connor said quietly.

Lily turned to him and her brows lifted in surprise. It was unusual for the twins to have such different opinions on things like this. They usually stuck together.

'What?' Connor looked back at her, and a strange flash of challenge crossed his eyes.

'Nothing. I'm glad you're on board,' she replied, frowning as he looked away. Had she imagined that?

Connor shrugged. 'I just think if I was a woman walking alone at night, I'd want one.'

'Bit sexist,' Cillian joked.

'It's not though, is it?' Connor replied. 'Yeah, men too, maybe. But like Mum said, whether people like it or not, men are usually bigger and stronger than women. It's biology, not bigotry.'

'And, as we know, in any social construct, the weak are always preyed on by stronger opportunists,' Lily added. 'It's just the way of the world.'

Cillian inhaled deeply and raised his eyebrows with a conceding tilt of the head. 'You make a good point. I'm still not sold that we're going to get many takers though.'

'Maybe not at first,' Lily accepted. 'New ideas like this can be slow to take root. But once one firm takes, the next will and the next. It'll catch like wildfire and at *that* point' – she snapped her fingers – 'we'll be approached by every big firm in the whole damn country.' Her dark eyes twinkled with cold determination. 'And *that* is a power we've never even come close to before.'

The rain came to an abrupt stop, and all of them looked up to the roof.

'Well, apparently even God's listening now,' Cillian said wryly.

'I have a meeting set up with this contact in a couple of weeks,' Lily continued. 'Scarlet, you'll come with me. Connor, you need to pass this all on to Isla, get her to start looking into how we'll do the labelling. We'll talk again after the meeting.'

'What am I doing?' Cillian asked.

'You're focusing on Tabitha,' Lily reminded him. 'We can handle this without you for now.'

As if on cue, Cillian's phone beeped in his pocket. He pulled it out and glanced at the screen. Looking up into his mother's eyes, he nodded.

'It's her,' he confirmed with a cold, determined set of his jaw. 'We're on for tomorrow night.'

SIXTEEN

Scarlet strode through a narrow alley between two run-down blocks of flats in the middle of an estate that most outsiders wouldn't dare to enter even if their lives depended on it. The biting wind grew stronger and lifted her hair off her shoulders, forcing the dark tendrils to dance in the air behind her.

Her hand tightened around the note she held in her pocket, the words written there burning their vile poison into the walls of her mind just as much as her palm.

I know what you did to her.

There was no doubting what it meant. She'd thought about nothing else all day, desperately searching her mind for anything else it could possibly relate to, but there was nothing, no other possible scenario where those words could be relevant. It was about Ruby. But that just didn't make sense. There were only three people – still living at least – who knew what had happened that night. The three of them who'd been there, who'd worked together to try and save Ruby from her own murderous trap. And even if someone else had somehow seen them, it had been well over a year since Ruby had died. Why would they suddenly surface now? It just didn't add up.

Reaching the small electrical shop in the centre of the estate, Scarlet paused outside. She trusted Chain, the owner of this place and head of the gang who ran the estate. Ran it with the Drews' permission of course. This was still their territory. She and Chain had formed a natural alliance from the moment they'd met. Despite being from very different corners of the same underworld, they understood each other in a way that not many others did. They shared a darkness underneath the surface that subconsciously recognised its likeness. And over time, their bond had grown stronger than any bond Chain had with other members of her firm. He was loyal to her above the others, and in that respect he was unique. Most of their allies were loyal to Lily, some to Cillian, but Scarlet was the youngest of the family and had been the last to join, when most loyalties had already been divided and conquered. Chain was the exception. Unless that had changed?

Her hand wavered over the door handle for a second and then firmly she grabbed it. It hadn't changed. There were very few people Scarlet felt she could truly count on in this world, and Chain was one of them.

The bell above the door tinkled as she entered, and she carefully made her way down the narrow aisle to the counter at the other end of the shop. Chain knew she was here. She no longer had to wait for permission to enter the invisible boundary at the edge of the estate if she was alone, but one of his men would have texted to alert him of her arrival.

The door behind the counter opened and Scarlet looked up expecting to see him, but to her surprise she found it wasn't Chain who entered. A slim young woman wound herself around the door, closing it tightly behind her. She eyed Scarlet with a challenging expression.

Scarlet quickly deduced that this must be Chain's latest squeeze. The woman was beautiful, her golden-brown skin flawless, with high cheekbones and full perfect lips that any model would be envious of. Her large oval eyes were framed with kohl, adding a sultriness to her gaze as she stared Scarlet out. Leaning forward over the counter, she lifted one sharply arched brow.

'What do you want?' she asked, her tone exaggeratedly rude.

Scarlet narrowed her eyes. 'I'm here to see Chain,' she replied curtly. Who did this woman think she was talking to?

The woman smirked. 'Yeah, ain't you all,' she said. 'But this ain't a knockin' shop anymore, you hear me?' She stood up, staring down her nose at Scarlet.

'What did you just say to me?' Scarlet asked, her voice deadly low as her anger began to rise.

'You heard me, slag,' the woman answered. 'And you'll hear this too: I see you sniffing round these parts again, I'll pull your fucking hair out and drag your scrawny backside round these streets till you're bloody to the arsebone. You think you're the first girl tryin' a turn his head away from me, eh?'

Scarlet stepped forward, incensed. 'You stupid bitch,' she hissed. With everything she was already dealing with, she had no patience left for this. 'I should cut out your fucking tongue for that.'

The door flew open suddenly and Chain bowled in, hurriedly pulling a T-shirt over his head. 'What the fuck is this?' he demanded.

The woman crossed her arms and pointed at Scarlet. 'This bitch turned up, and—'

'*This bitch*?' he repeated, cutting her off in his anger. 'You idiot... You have no idea who this is, do you?'

'*What*?' she exclaimed, turning to him with a look of surprise. 'Chain, you—'

'Get the *fuck* out of here,' he yelled, grabbing her by the arm and propelling her, none too gently, back through the door. 'Go on, get dressed and fuck off back to yours.'

'But...' She looked genuinely scared now.

'That's Scarlet Drew you just cussed out,' Chain said, rounding on her in the hall. 'You're lucky she *hasn't* cut your fucking tongue out. Now go on. *Out.* Oh, but, Tash? Before you go...' He paused, leaning into her face menacingly. 'You ever come into my shop and speak on my behalf to anyone else again, I'll cut you myself.'

Scarlet felt her temper slowly subside as recognition and fear dawned in Tash's eyes. 'I-I'm sorry,' she stuttered, her voice devoid of the swagger and bravado it had held moments before. 'I didn't realise...'

'Out,' Chain roared.

Tash jumped and then slipped away out of sight without another word, and Chain turned back to the shop, running his hand back over his tight black buzz-cut curls.

'Man...' He shook his head, clearly irritated.

Scarlet gave him a half-smile of amusement. 'She can keep her tongue,' she said.

'I don't know, I think you should take it. Give me some peace,' he replied with a grin, and they both laughed.

'She seems quite set on you.' Scarlet leaned against the counter and rubbed her forehead tiredly.

'Nah, her time's coming to an end soon,' Chain replied with a shrug. 'Too much trouble.'

'Most partners are,' Scarlet said quietly.

'Trouble in paradise?' Chain asked with a grin.

Scarlet frowned. 'No. Things are fine with Benny, thanks. And that's not what I'm here to talk about.'

Chain sat down on the stool the other side of the counter. 'What's up?'

Scarlet exhaled heavily and pulled the note out of her pocket. 'This.' She slid it across towards him.

His grin faded as he read the words. 'You think it's about that night,' he said. A statement, not a question.

Scarlet nodded, feeling the weight of it wrap heavily around her shoulders like an iron cloak.

'It couldn't be anything else?' he checked.

She shook her head. 'I want it to be something else, I really do. But it's not. Can't be.'

Chain stared down at it and rubbed his hand back and forth over his chin as he thought it through. 'There was no one else there,' he said after a few moments. 'I checked. I was the last one to arrive, and I closed up that gate behind me, to make sure.'

'There must have been. Someone must have seen and followed you in,' she replied.

'Nah.' Chain shook his head, a dark cloud settling over his expression as his gaze locked onto hers. 'It was *her*. She's talked.'

SEVENTEEN

Jenny Ascough locked the outer door of the tiny village police station she worked in and began the short walk back to her small cottage.

It had taken her a while to adjust to the quiet and the slower pace out here in the country, but she'd settled in eventually. She'd learned to appreciate the benefits and the beauty of this very different way of life, but she still missed London. She would never have chosen to leave, under normal circumstances. But after all that had happened, it'd been the only way to put it behind her and the only way to hide herself from the very dangerous people who'd put her in that position in the first place.

Marching down the quiet country lane, she looked around with an easy smile. It was beautiful here. It was also getting dark already, she realised with surprise, despite the early hour. She pulled her woolly snood up over her mouth, but the sharp chill still bit at her cheeks. She'd have a hot chocolate to warm herself up, she decided. Maybe add a splash of Baileys. It was just what she needed. Something warm and sweet, plus her fluffy blanket and the new book that had arrived today – it was the perfect evening combination. Motivated by this thought, she upped her pace and turned down the narrow path towards her cottage.

She slowed as she spotted her elderly next-door neighbour outside, looking worried. 'Alright, Mrs Higgs?' she asked resignedly, already anticipating the answer.

'Oh, Jenny, thank goodness you're here,' came the serious, wavery reply. Mrs Higgs shuffled forward and grasped her forearm with a fearful glance over her shoulder towards her own yellow stone cottage. 'He's back,' she whispered. 'The man trying to kidnap my Arthur.'

Jenny patted the thin, age-mottled hand that gripped her and stifled a sigh. 'We've been over this, Mrs Higgs. No one's trying to take Arthur...'

'But they *are*!' Mrs Higgs insisted. 'They all want him, you know. I've seen the looks they give him.' She leaned in and whispered. 'They all want to *breed* with him. They want his handsome *genes*, Jenny.'

'Mrs Higgs...' She squeezed the old lady's hand. 'I promise you, your cat is as safe as any other around here.'

Mrs Higgs pulled back, affronted. 'My Arthur is *not* just *any* cat, Jenny, and I think you know that.' She sniffed and crossed her arms. 'He's a pedigree, you know.' She sniffed again, looking deeply unimpressed.

'I know he is,' Jenny said placatingly. 'And I'm sure you're the envy of the village, but no one is trying to take him.'

Mrs Higgs came into the station to report an attempted kidnapping of her beloved pet at least once a fortnight these days. Jenny had spent many a time searching her house and checking the garden when she seemed particularly perplexed, but there was never anyone there. The only thief in this particular case was old age, which was slowly stealing Mrs Higgs' marbles, one by one.

'They *are* though, Jenny. There was someone there – I saw

him clear as day go into your garden from the back,' Mrs Higgs insisted.

'Well, don't worry, I'm sure he's gone now,' Jenny replied, giving up. 'And Arthur's too clever to be caught anyway.' She pulled out her keys.

'He's *not* gone,' Mrs Higgs said with certainty. 'He's in your house now. Obviously got the wrong address. Good job you're a police officer – you can arrest the bugger.'

'Thanks for the heads-up,' she replied, finding her door key among the many others she had to hold for work.

Mrs Higgs shuffled off, and Jenny had no doubt she would be back to twitching the front-room curtains within moments. Twisting the key in the lock, she hesitated for a moment.

What if there really *had* been someone there this time? What if someone really *was* inside her house? But then she tutted and shook it off. The woman was barmy. They'd had this conversation a hundred times. It used to unsettle her. She'd started over here for good reason, and there were people she still feared would come looking for her one day. But over time she'd forced herself to relax. She'd been careful. She'd left no trail, deleted all social media, only met up with friends and family where they lived. She was safe here.

Jenny closed the door behind her, switched on the hallway lamp and took off her outerwear. She ruffled her fingers through her hair and checked herself over in the mirror. She didn't even look like the person who'd fled London, just over a year before. Her cropped bright-red hair was now shoulder length and back to its natural shade of brown. Her bright make-up and clothes had been replaced with more neutral colours and comfortable styles. She wasn't really sure why she'd changed so drastically. Her new style was more practical. Maybe it was that. Or maybe it was just that she'd lost her spark. She certainly wasn't the same person anymore.

Turning to the kitchen she filled the kettle and then picked up her new book with an eager smile. It was the latest steamy romance novel from one of her favourite authors.

'Well, this is certainly the most action I'm likely to see in *this* place,' she muttered wryly.

Kicking off her shoes, she flicked on the small storage heater she kept in the kitchen fireplace and sank down into one of the armchairs next to it, curling her feet underneath her.

As she opened the book, a small noise behind her suddenly sharpened her senses. As she started to turn her head, the sharp edge of a blade was pressed against her throat.

EIGHTEEN

Jenny's breath quickened and her heart thumped in horror. A hand gripped a fistful of her hair, yanking her back tight to the chair. A stifled sob escaped her lips as she opened them to talk, trying – not that successfully – to stay calm.

'Please,' she said, her voice cracking pitifully. 'Whatever you want just take it.'

She desperately held on to the hope that this was just a break-in. That whoever had the knife to her throat was only here to rob her. But as a cold, quiet laugh filled the air around her, her blood turned to ice.

Her heart seized in her chest, and she felt as though she was about to pass out from sheer dread as recognition kicked in. She'd know that laugh anywhere. It still haunted her nightmares. Her bottom lip quivered as she tried to find her voice. Eventually the words came out in a shaken whisper.

'What do you want?'

'What do I want?' came the silken response. 'I want *peace*. I want to go about my day without any unexpected surprises. Because unexpected surprises aren't always very nice, are they, Ascough?'

'I don't understand,' Jenny replied, her eyes darting around as she tried to work out what this was about.

'*Don't* you?' The voice was calm, the deadliness underneath only detectable by those who knew who they were dealing with.

A hot tear of panic rolled down Jenny's face, her mind working overtime. What had changed? What had happened? She'd thought she was safe here. She'd clearly been wrong.

'Please,' she begged, squeezing her eyes shut.

The hand loosened its grip and the knife slipped away from her throat, but she didn't dare move as the person holding it walked around the chair and into view.

The voice had been enough to reduce her to a quivering wreck, but as the tall, graceful figure, long dark hair and cold, hard face of the viper who ruined her life came into view, her heart dropped like a stone. It was the one person she'd hoped never to see again. The person she feared above anyone else.

Scarlet Drew.

Scarlet stared down at Jenny Ascough and a familiar ripple of irritation ran through her veins. Jenny had worked for John, back when he'd run a team at his station in London. She'd developed a crush on her boss, which had grown into something far deeper over time. Not that Scarlet had ever blamed her for that. John was a handsome, charismatic man, and a good person to boot. Someone it was all too easy to fall in love with. But that love had soon become a problem.

Jenny had been crushed when she'd discovered their secret relationship, and her heartbreak had evolved into an obsession with Scarlet, when John had disappeared. She'd stalked her, way beyond the boundaries of the law, consumed by the idea that they'd killed him or were holding him captive somewhere. In the end, it had taken Ruby's death to break the fixation.

She'd tracked Scarlet to the scrapyard that night and followed her in, watching from the shadows. She'd seen the showdown between the cousins and the trap that Ruby had laid for Scarlet. At the last moment, she'd called out, giving Scarlet just enough warning to jump out of the way as Ruby had rushed forward to shove her into the industrial vat of oil below. In her attempt to bring Scarlet down, Jenny had inadvertently saved her instead. The irony wasn't lost on either of them.

'I gave you one very simple, very clear warning, before you left London,' Scarlet said in a low, deadly tone. 'All you had to do was keep your mouth shut.'

'I *have*,' Jenny cried, the fear intensifying on her face as her gaze flickered between Scarlet's eyes and the long blade still pointed at her throat. 'I haven't said a word to anyone about that night.'

'Don't lie to me,' Scarlet growled, pushing the blade forward until the tip pressed into Jenny's throat.

Jenny whimpered and her eyes widened. 'I'm not lying to you,' she insisted. 'I've not told a soul and I've never wanted to. I never wanted to see you again. I just wanted to disappear and forget you ever existed, forget *all* of it, because meeting you *ruined* my life.' She sobbed and bowed her head.

Scarlet pulled the knife away and stepped back, regarding the broken woman carefully. Was this an act? This certainly wasn't the defiant spitfire of a woman who'd hounded her with such passion before. With a suspicious frown, Scarlet stepped back and sat down in the other armchair, leaning an elbow on the arm and resting her chin on her fist.

'What happened to you?' she asked, her tone detachedly curious as she studied the woman.

Jenny let out a short, humourless laugh. '*You*,' she replied. She rubbed the tears from her eyes tiredly.

'No.' Scarlet shook her head. 'I may be the reason you left London, but I don't mean that.' Her eyes roamed over the slumped shoulders, the lacklustre complexion and dull eyes. 'What happened to *you*?'

Jenny exhaled slowly. She was silent for a few moments and then shook her head. 'I don't know. It changed me.' She looked up and held Scarlet's gaze. 'I've always loved my job. With so much bad in the world, it felt good putting some of it right. Stopping bad things from happening, putting all the bad people away one by one. But when John disappeared...' Her voice faltered, and then she frowned, a flare of fighting spirit lighting her eyes. 'It was all just so *wrong*.'

Finally, Scarlet caught sight of the woman she'd known before.

'Then when everything happened with your cousin,' Jenny continued, the flare fading away, 'it made me realise that none of it matters.' She crinkled her nose. 'Everyone we catch, they're just a drop in the ocean. And we only see the surface. But that's nothing compared to what's underneath. I realised that, seeing your cousin, and you, and that gangster, Chain.' She shrugged defeatedly. 'It's deep and *endless*, and what we do doesn't make a blind bit of difference. All that effort, all we fight for – it's like rubbing anti-bac on a scratch, while the flesh of this world rots, en masse, from the infection under the skin.'

Scarlet didn't respond immediately. She twisted the handle of the blade in her hand, and the kitchen light glinted off it.

'The world *is* rotten,' she said eventually. 'To the fucking core. We're all fighting that, one way or another, in whatever ways are available to us. Perhaps you see now that the world isn't so black and white.'

'No,' Jenny whispered, shaking her head. The stubbornness had returned to her jaw this time. 'You aren't fighting it. You're part of the problem. All the illegal things you do and the dark secrets you keep, that's exactly what feeds it.'

Scarlet smiled, the action cold. She sat forward, closer to

Jenny. 'Well then I guess you're part of the problem too, aren't you?'

Jenny's pale cheeks flushed red and her eyes filled with hate. 'I only have these secrets because of you.'

'You have these secrets because you stalked me, *illegally*, and followed me into the scrapyard that night. No one asked you to.' Scarlet's gaze narrowed and she pointed the knife at Jenny's face. 'But you've been sharing those secrets and I want to know who with. And I suggest you think very carefully before you deny it, because someone knows. And whoever they are, they're threatening the safety of *all* of us.'

'*What?*' Jenny paled in shock, her eyes widening as she gasped out the word.

For a moment, her fear of Scarlet seemed to disappear in light of this new danger. She leaned forward, ignoring the knife and put her hands to her mouth, looking gravely worried.

'Scarlet, I don't know why you think I would, but I swear I haven't told a soul,' Jenny said strongly. 'Why *would* I? If *any* part of that came out, it would ruin what's left of my career and potentially cost me my freedom too. I'd lose the respect of my family, my friends...' She shook her head. 'I have no motive whatsoever to share that. And look around you' – she gestured with the sweep of an arm – 'even if I wanted to, who would I share it with? I'm single, I live alone, I work in a tiny village station.' She rubbed her temple and her gaze slipped back to the knife again as she suddenly seemed to remember the more immediate danger. 'Whoever leaked this, it's *not me*, Scarlet. I swear to you. What's happened? *Please tell me.*'

Scarlet studied Jenny's face. Her reaction to the news had been genuine. And she was scared. Truly scared. Jenny Ascough wasn't the culprit here.

'There was a note left on my car,' Scarlet said, her tone heavy. 'All it said was *I know what you did to her*.'

Jenny's worried expression grew deeper and a frown crinkled her forehead. 'But why now?' she asked, confused.

'Exactly,' Scarlet replied.

Jenny shook her head. 'None of us have reason to talk. It doesn't make sense. My life would be over, you'd lose your family. And Chain – I studied his file – he's known for keeping his cards close. He's done time instead of ratting before, refused every deal. He'd be the last person to talk.' Her eyes met Scarlet's warily. 'I imagine that's why you work with him.'

Scarlet cooled her gaze and didn't answer.

'So whoever sent that note must have been there that night,' Jenny continued slowly. 'But why wait all this time?'

Scarlet felt her control of the situation slip back out of reach, and frustration gripped her heart. Standing abruptly she leaned over Jenny's chair, glaring down at her, the knife inches from her throat once more. Jenny jumped back in alarm, her eyes widening with fear.

'If I find out you're lying,' Scarlet said in a low, deadly voice, 'if I find out you have any link whatsoever to this, the next time I come for you, you won't even see me coming.'

Jenny just swallowed and stared at her.

Reining in her emotions, Scarlet straightened up and rolled her shoulders in an attempt to ease the tension gathering there. She slipped the knife into her waistband and moved towards the hall.

'Wait,' Jenny called tentatively.

Scarlet paused and stared at her coldly.

'How did you find me?' she asked.

'I've known where you were from the day you left. Do you really think I'd be so stupid as to let you go without keeping tabs?' A hint of a smile played at the corner of her mouth for a moment. 'You've never been out of my reach, Ascough. And no matter where you go, you never will be.'

A new level of despair dawned in Jenny Ascough's eyes as, with one last, cold glare, Scarlet slipped away.

NINETEEN

Cillian pushed through the front door into The Hideout, and was hit by the loud buzz of busy tables and tantalising smells from the kitchen as they catered for the lunchtime rush. He made a beeline straight for the upper floor.

'Which booth?' he demanded as he passed the doorman at the top.

'Five,' he replied, nodding towards it.

Cillian walked over and entered, sitting down on the curved black leather bench opposite his brother. 'What you doing?' he asked with a frown.

'Having a drink,' Connor replied, mirroring his expression. 'What does it look like I'm doing?'

Connor put the glass to his mouth and downed the pale brown liquid in one. Cillian eyed the bottle next to him. It was already half empty.

'It's not even lunchtime,' Cillian said. 'Am I missing something? What's the celebration?'

Connor snorted. 'Celebration...' He shook his head.

Cillian's frown deepened in concern. 'OK, what's wrong?'

Connor poured another drink and turned the glass in his hand, staring down at it for a moment. 'Nothing,' he said. 'I'm fine. Just fancied a drink.'

He looked up at Cillian and smiled, seemingly calm and collected now. It would have fooled anyone else, even their mother. But Cillian had spent a lifetime staring into that same face in the mirror every day, so he knew that expression for what it really was. A mask. A lie to cover the fact Connor didn't want to talk about what was underneath.

For a few moments they sat in silence, and Cillian tapped his fingers on the table between them as he tried to work out what to say. Connor never usually hid things from him. They'd spent their life as two halves of one unit, a partnership against the world. Why would Connor shut him out?

'You still pissed off about that bloke who's been running the bets?' he asked.

Connor's brows rose momentarily in surprise.

'Joe told me.'

'Well he shouldn't have,' Connor replied, clearly annoyed. 'It ain't your concern. You've got bigger things to worry about.'

Was he annoyed Cillian hadn't been there with him? Is that what this was about?

'Oi,' he said sharply. 'It don't matter what I'm doing – if you needed me there, you should have called. I'd have come straight over.'

Connor laughed, no humour in the action. 'Right, because you could have done a better job. Or actually *done* the job perhaps. Well, you wouldn't have,' he continued defensively. 'There's nothing *you* would have done that I didn't, alright?'

'Woah!' Cillian pulled back and held his hands up in the air. 'What the fuck is *this*? That ain't what I was saying at all.' He studied Connor, alarmed now. 'Don't you dare put words like that in my mouth. Where's all this coming from?'

Connor looked away and rubbed his hand over the dark stubble on his cheek. 'I don't know. Ignore me. I'm just tired.'

'Right, well, to be honest, mate, I've already got a mental minefield to navigate, dating Billie,' Cillian said, exhaling loudly. 'I don't need you blowing up on me for random shit I haven't done as well, yeah?'

Connor grinned at that. 'That's married life for you, brother,' he joked.

Cillian grinned back and suddenly the tension was broken. 'Less of the marriage talk,' he warned. 'Birds have got sonar hearing when it comes to shit like that, I swear.'

The tension had gone and Cillian was glad, but the strange interaction still bothered him. Something had happened. But what?

'Join me for one?' Connor asked, tilting his glass upwards.

'Nah, I need my head clear for tonight. Got that dinner with Tabitha.' Cillian pulled a grim expression, filing his worries away to ponder another time.

'Oh, come on, it can't be that bad,' Connor replied. 'Dinner out with a rich bird who thinks you're the dog's bollocks? I'd take it any day.'

'It's not as fun as it sounds. Aside from the shit I get when I get back to Billie – which is fair enough,' he admitted, 'Tabitha bores the tits off me. I have to pretend to be interested in her pretentious drivel and still keep her at arm's length every time she throws herself at me, without seeming really bloody weird. It's harder than it sounds,' he added, seeing that Connor still appeared unconvinced. 'If I could get away with swapping you in, I would. But we both know the moment we open our mouths, people only go one way.'

Connor pulled a shrug-like expression. 'Oh well. Can't be helped.'

'What you gonna do about the bets bloke?' Cillian asked.

'Nothing,' Connor replied. 'Our tactics don't work on him.

He's unbreakable. He needs to be worked on by someone who's skilled at breaking the unbreakable.'

The corners of Cillian's mouth lifted in a grin. 'You gave him to Mum,' he surmised.

Connor nodded, his expression hard as he confirmed his brother's words. 'I gave him to Mum.'

TWENTY

Lily parked up on the side of the long residential street and walked on briskly for another few minutes until she reached the house she was looking for. Most of the unusually wide Victorian brick houses on each side had been turned into flats over the years, though some still remained unchanged. The house they'd bought here, a couple of years before, had been one of the few still intact. Or mostly intact at least.

Lily had had her eye on it for a while, and when, one day, the elderly owner had been left with no choice but to sell after the roof had partially caved in, Lily had swooped in quickly. Introducing herself and sharing a wonderfully detailed wish to turn it into her own family home, she'd charmed her way to a signed deal before her first cup of tea had grown cold.

The roof had been expensive, as had the damage to the floors and walls directly underneath, but it had been worth the expense. Not that it was the family home Lily had described to the old woman. These days it was used for a much darker purpose.

Walking up the black-and-white harlequin tiled path, Lily unlocked the heavy front door, glancing over her shoulder before walking in and shutting it behind her. Once inside, she paused by the large mirror above the sideboard and studied herself for a moment. Fine lines were beginning to whisper her age across her pale skin, and her tightly sprung curls weren't as bright a blonde as they used to be, as more and more greys subtly wove their way between the golden strands.

It was inevitable, she supposed. Time was the one thing that could never be cheated out of its prizes. Not that she had one foot in the grave just yet of course. At forty-eight she was still in her prime, but these changes served as a reminder that she wasn't as immortal as she'd felt in her younger days.

Moving to the kitchen, Lily made herself a cup of tea and stared out the window to the paved garden at the back, her eyes drawn to the weeds spreading up through the cracks. That was the trouble with small cracks. They may seem unimportant in the grand scheme of things, but unwelcome seeds always found a way to take root and grow, forcing the crack wider and wider until there was no going back. She made a mental note to bring some weedkiller round next time she was here.

Wrapping her hands around the warm mug of tea, Lily took it with her to the basement, carefully navigating the stairs down, in the dark. As she reached the bottom, she felt along the padded walls to the light switch and flicked it on. The basement flooded with light, and she made her way along the glass separation wall that created a narrow hallway that ran the length of the house and led into the open-plan area of the basement, through a door at the other end.

The man sitting slumped on the floor in the middle of the room, his arms chained behind him, around one of two wooden support posts that supported the structure, was yelling at the top of his lungs. The sound barely made it through the thick glass. It certainly wouldn't reach upstairs. That was the beauty of this place. Lily watched him for a moment before opening the door.

'*Help*! Someone, *help me*! Call the police! *Please*, can anyone hear me? *Help*!'

Lily glanced pointedly at the glass door before slowly closing it. 'You really think that's what's stopping people from hearing you?' she asked.

He fell silent and dropped his head back down to his chest, though whether that was due to her words or the fact he was just too exhausted to continue she wasn't sure. It was eerily quiet down here, quieter than any normal silence. Even the sharp taps of her stiletto heels didn't echo around the space the way they should have as she crossed the concrete floor to the armchair and coffee table set to one side.

'What is this place?' he muttered, his head still bowed.

Lily dropped her handbag to the floor and sat down. She sipped her tea before answering, looking around the space with appreciation.

'It's something special, isn't it? The lady who owned this place before was an opera singer, back in the day. For the last ten years of her career she would record here. Turned this basement into a studio. Opened up the space, soundproofed so the neighbours wouldn't be bothered, added muffler vents so it could stay ventilated without any noise escaping.' She eyed the dark-green padded panels that patterned the walls. 'There was a lovely thick carpet in here too, but as you can imagine, it's not so practical for us. Too much hassle to get the blood out. That was the first thing to go.'

She'd read about this basement in an article, years before. It had been a *see the inside of my home* piece and the basement was the reason Lily had set her sights on owning the house. It was the perfect place to hold a captive without worrying someone would hear or come across them – and unlike their other suitable locations, this was right in the heart of East London.

'If you're going to kill me, just get on with it,' the man said flatly. 'I'm tired of this and there's nothing more you can do to me.'

Lily's gaze moved over his broken body. His face was a mess of dried blood, swelling and bruises, his dark hair was matted and stuck to his forehead. His feet and hands were mangled, bones sticking out at all angles, and she could tell several other larger bones in his body were also broken. Connor had gone all out and yet, still, he hadn't even wavered.

'For someone so able to take such torture, it's surprising that you're so scared of your employers,' she said casually. 'Because the things is, I *am* going to kill you eventually,' she continued. 'And all this pain would have been for nothing. Surely you'd rather try and make a deal for your life?' Her question was met with stony silence, as she'd expected. 'No?' She feigned surprise and then took another slow sip of her tea. 'I imagine that's the Marines training, kicking in.'

The man's head lifted and the one eye he could still half open stared over at her for the first time since she'd entered the room. 'How do you know that?' he asked warily.

'Oh, I know a lot of things about you, Robert,' Lily replied, taking another sip. 'You might think whoever you're working for is dangerous and powerful, but I can assure you, you've not seen anything yet. You have no idea who you've pitted yourself against.'

Robert watched her, his gaze sharp now and every muscle he could still move tensed. He waited, not offering anything.

'Robert Holden. *Not* Brian Anderson, the name on your fake ID. You served twelve years in the Royal Marines 40 Commando, a highly skilled commando strike unit. So skilled they're the first unit to be deployed to any big crisis or threat around the world, I hear.' Lily pulled an impressed expression. 'Until eight years ago, when you were discharged for some reason. What that was, I have no idea. But since then, you've been freelancing wherever the pay takes you. You've taken hit jobs, recovery jobs, security detail – all off record of course. The pay isn't so good on the right side of the law, is it?' She took another sip of her tea and placed it down on the coffee table beside her. 'So I get it. You're hard. *Too* hard to be broken through physical pain.'

'And you haven't got anything else, lady,' Robert replied. 'So just get on with it. Stop wasting both our time.'

'Oh, but I do,' Lily replied, with a cold smile and a dark glint in her eye. 'You hid your tracks well. Most people wouldn't have found the details of your personal life. But I have a friend who specialises in getting information other people can't.'

Luck had been on her side with this one. When she'd shown her old friend Bill Hanlon Robert's fake ID, Bill already knew who he was. Another firm Bill occasionally worked for had engaged Robert's services a few years before. They'd wanted to know who they were dealing with and had asked Bill to look into him. Bill always kept meticulous records, and once someone was on his radar, he made sure to keep that record up to date in case he should need it again in the future. He'd kept tabs on Robert ever since that job and had gained more recent information that was of great value to Lily indeed.

Lily picked up her bag, then reached into it and pulled out a small, light blue crocheted bunny. She held it in her hand and straightened its ears before turning it around.

'This is lovely, isn't it? I bet whoever made it put heartfelt love into every stitch.'

She watched horror fill his expression, and his body jolted as he pulled himself up into a straighter position.

'Where'd you get that?' he spluttered.

'I think you know where I got it,' Lily taunted with a coy smile. 'Or rather *who* I got it from.'

He bucked now, trying his hardest to pull away from his restraints, but they didn't budge. Lily waited until he stopped trying, unfazed. Once she'd found out he was an ex-commando, she'd taken extra precautions to ensure he couldn't escape. Houdini himself wouldn't have been able to get out of the chains that held Robert now.

'If you've touched a hair on her head, I swear you'll not take another breath,' Robert yelled, his words full of fearful anger. 'Where is she?'

Lily smirked coldly. 'If you could stop me breathing – or stop me doing *anything* in fact – you would have done already. Empty threats don't get far with me. And as for where she is, hmm...' She pulled up the sleeve of her black turtleneck top and glanced at her watch. 'I'd say coming out of school right about now. Getting into that black VW Golf of her mum's to make the seven-minute drive back to their house. Which means in about twenty minutes, she'll be running back out, after getting changed, to play in the park across the green just outside the front door. Sasha clearly feels safe letting her out there, so close to the house where she can see her.' Lily watched Robert strain against his restraints once more at the sound of his ex-girl-friend's name. 'If only she knew how wrong she was.'

'She's a *child*,' he said, his chest moving up and down much faster, as for the first time since his ordeal began he finally started to panic. '*Please*. You have children, I know you do. You wouldn't hurt a little girl over money.'

'Wouldn't I?' Lily cocked an eyebrow and pulled out her phone. She set it down on the coffee table and kept her challenging gaze on his as she placed a call and put it on speaker.

Robert's breathing grew more rapid as his fear intensified. For three rings neither said a word, and then the call was answered.

'Yeah?' came the hard male voice.

'Are you there?' Lily asked.

'We're here. The car's just pulled up and they've gone inside.'

'Please...' Robert begged.

'She'll go in to change. Call me when she comes out to the park and then wait on my word before you take her,' Lily ordered in a hard voice.

'She's seven years old,' Robert cried.

'Yes, only seven. So light and weak,' Lily replied viciously, her cold eyes boring into his. 'You have just a few minutes to tell me what I want to know before I get that call, so I suggest you use them wisely.'

Tears began streaming down his blood-soaked cheeks. 'Do what you want to me but for fuck's sake leave her alone, she's just a *baby*,' he pleaded. 'Please...' A defeated sob escaped his lips.

Lily watched him for a moment. 'She's why you held out, isn't she?' she asked. 'Your Evie. They know about her too. They exploited your weakness the same way I'm doing now.'

A low groan escaped, but he didn't answer.

She nodded to herself slowly. 'I'm going to do something for you,' she continued. 'I'll make you a deal, one parent to another.'

He lifted his head slightly but kept his gaze trained on the ground as he listened.

'You have no choice but to tell me what I want to know, if you want no harm to come to your daughter. My men are poised and ready, and I can assure you there is nothing I won't do to get what I want.' Lily's voice turned hard and cold. 'You could call my bluff, but I assure you, you'd regret it. But if you tell me what I need to know, and if that checks out, I'll not only leave Evie alone, I'll also protect her and Sasha from the people you work for.'

Fresh tears rolled down Robert's cheeks as she cornered him, and she waited for him to make his choice. The silence stretched on for a minute or two and then suddenly the air was filled with the sound of her phone. Robert's head twisted towards her and she glanced down at the screen. It was the call. As she lifted her chin and moved her gaze to meet his, there was a subtle stand-off. His one open eye darted around as he tried to work out another way, and Lily reached over to answer the call.

'Yes?' she said, putting it on speakerphone once more.

'Evie's out in the park. She's wearing the red coat with the daisy on the pocket,' came the deep voice.

'No...' Robert uttered, his mouth dropping open.

'Only a few kids here, no sign of the mother. We're ready to grab her whenever you say.'

'OK,' Lily replied. 'Well, I don't seem to be getting anywhere here, so—'

'Wait!' Robert cried. 'No! I'll tell you. Please, just tell them not to touch her.'

Lily twisted her mouth and narrowed her eyes at him for a moment. 'Stand by for now.' She ended the call. 'I'd choose your next words wisely now, mate. And whatever you tell me had better be the God's honest truth, otherwise I won't just have them take her...' She reached into her handbag and pulled out a handgun and silencer, laying them on the coffee table beside her tea. 'I'll have them put a bullet in her mother's brain, and then hold that same gun to her head, to give you one last chance to tell me the *actual* truth.'

Robert cast his gaze to the floor, closing his eyes in pain for a moment. 'A couple years back, you pissed off another firm.'

'You're gonna have to be more specific than that,' Lily said flatly. 'We piss off a *lot* of people in our game. Keep talking.'

She stood up and crossed her arms, pacing slowly back and forth as she waited.

'Does the name Romano ring any bells?' Robert asked.

Lily let out a long hiss of air from the back of her throat as realisation dawned and the missing pieces of the puzzle fell into place. She closed her eyes briefly and then nodded with an expression of contempt.

'Mani Romano,' she said quietly. 'He's a sly old dog.'

'Yeah, well old dogs have hard bites. And he's aiming his

teeth at my daughter. You said you'd protect her if I told you,' Robert said urgently.

'And I will.' Lily turned to him, her expression genuine. 'You have my word. I'll make sure both Evie and Sasha are warned and out of harm's way. Do you have a safe house?'

Robert wasn't the first ex-marine she'd come across in this game. Most of them were smart enough and skilled enough to have set up a plan B in case everything went south.

'They know where to go,' he said guardedly. 'She just needs the warning.'

'Which is?' she asked.

He remained silent, a battle raging in his eye as he watched her.

'I can't help you if you don't tell me your go word,' she reminded him.

He exhaled slowly. 'Fine. Get this message to her. Word for word.' A ripple of grief flitted across his features. 'Ahab gave up the spear.'

'Consider it done,' she replied. 'She'll receive the warning before Mani is aware of anything.'

Turning on her heel, Lily walked away from Robert. She should have known it was Mani. He'd been smart. He'd left his revenge for long enough she'd almost forgotten he still had it in for them. And then he'd hired someone she couldn't trace back to his firm. It was clever. Or it would have been, had Connor and Joe not found Robert when they did.

They had come across him unexpectedly as he was leaving a crowded pub – no doubt taking more bets against their fights. There were no cameras around and, though it was busy, it was also dark and the people around were inebriated. They'd acted quickly, knocking Robert out from behind with a piece of pipe and pulling him into the car, without putting much thought into a plan. Their swiftness and spontaneity were the only reasons they'd been able to best him that night, she realised now.

Lily paced back towards him, careful not to come too close. Even as broken and as restrained as he was, she had no doubt he could still kill her if she got close enough. That was how deadly her catch was. He most likely *would* too, after all she'd just threatened. Which was the reason she could never let him leave this room.

'Who did you answer to?' she asked him.

'Emmanuel hired me, but his son Riccardo was running the play. I answered to him mostly,' Robert replied, no fight left in his voice.

'What about Luca?' Lily asked.

Luca was the one the twins had found sniffing around their clients, trying to steal business, a couple of years before. They'd beaten him and sent him off with a warning, but he'd come back with Riccardo and smashed in some windows with the threat that they planned to take over the Drews' turf. The twins had coordinated an attack on some of their businesses in retaliation, and then kidnapped Luca, returning him home only after he'd soiled himself, to ensure his future as a laughing stock throughout the underworld. Lily had put a stop to things there, knowing all too well that should they keep escalating, the price would become too steep for both firms.

'Luca follows Riccardo's lead. The men don't seem to respect him as much,' Robert told her.

'No, they wouldn't,' Lily murmured. 'My boys saw to that.'

Respect was a funny thing in a world like theirs. It meant everything, but the slightest thing could destroy it forever. To lose face like that showed the world that Luca was weak. And that, of course, had been the point. He'd have lost the respect of his men instantly. And some men could have recovered from that. If they were smart and hard and retaliated with the appropriate force to reinstate their image as someone not to be messed with. But Luca wasn't one of those men.

'How much have you taken?' Lily asked.

Robert let out a reluctant breath. 'So far, overall, maybe fifty grand.'

Lily's eyebrows shot up. 'You were certainly busy,' she said sharply.

Robert's gaze flickered towards her phone on the coffee table. 'Please,' he asked. 'Make the call. Tell them to back off. I've told you what you want to know.'

'We're not done just yet,' Lily replied. 'Tell me how it worked.' She sat down and leaned forward, watching him intently.

'A while back, someone started logging your odds from the fights. They got a pretty good overview of your fighters. I don't know who that was, before you ask.'

'That's fine – I do,' Lily replied.

The details of their fights were a closely guarded secret and the events were invite only, sent to all those within the under-world who the Drews were on good terms, or at least neutral ground, with. That had included the Romanos. Mani had attended a few but his son, Riccardo, had come every time.

'They knew they couldn't send out one of their own, or someone known to work with them, so they hired me. They'd never worked with me before, no one knew who I was and I'm good at keeping my head down. Or I *was* anyway,' he added bitterly.

Lily bit the inside of her cheek as she turned it over in her head. 'You would all have known it would come out eventually, so what was the plan down the road?'

'Call your men off,' Robert begged.

'Where was this headed?' she demanded.

He closed his one open eye and exhaled defeatedly. 'When the time was right, they wanted me to start being more visible, let you think you'd cornered me, then lead you into a trap.'

Lily's insides turned cold. 'Who exactly was to be led into this trap? Just me? The boys?'

Robert laid his head back against the post and looked at her tiredly. 'All of you,' he said. 'You, your sons, your niece. Any other men with you at the time.'

Lily swallowed, reeling. 'Who was to pull the trigger?' she asked calmly. 'You?'

'No,' Robert breathed. 'Emmanuel. That part was his.'

She nodded. 'Is there anything else I should know? Now is the time to say, because I'm not playing games.'

'I don't play with my daughter's life,' Robert growled. 'Not when I'm dealing with sadistic monsters like you. You're the lowest of the low, you know that?'

The corner of Lily's mouth twitched up in cold amusement. 'I've been called worse,' she replied.

Standing up, she smoothed the front of her skirt before picking up the gun and screwing the silencer to the end of the barrel.

'You understand it's nothing personal,' she said as she did this. 'We both know if I let you go, you'll kill me and my whole family.'

'After you threatened my *seven-year-old* daughter?' he spat through gritted teeth. 'You bet your fucking arse I would. I don't care what you do to me, but you'd better hold up your end of our deal.'

She turned to look at him and found him physically shaking with fury as he stared back at her. Checking the silencer was on tightly, she picked up the phone and dialled the same number on speakerphone once more.

'Boss,' came the gruff voice.

'Leave the girl. But stay nearby and watch that she gets in safely. She's under our protection now.'

Lily ended the call and placed the phone back on the table. 'For the record, I'm sorry you got pulled into this. This shouldn't have been your price to pay.'

Robert laid his head back against the post once more and lifted his chin proudly, staring at her unwaveringly.

Lily held his gaze as she lifted the gun and pointed it at his head, understanding that he wanted her to have to look him in the eyes as she did this. Knowing that he deserved that. Then with a slow exhale and a steady hand, she pulled the trigger.

TWENTY-ONE

George stared at his phone, pulled an expression of indifference, and then picked his pint up off the bar.

'What was that about?' Andy asked, gesturing towards the phone as he sat on the stool beside him. He'd entered the Black Bear pub as George had answered his last, rather short, call. 'We got to go somewhere?'

'Nah, we're good. That was just some bluff call for Lil. Something about a girl in a red coat.' He shrugged. 'I don't know what for. I just stuck to the script.' He took a long drink of his pint, savouring the cold bubbles as they washed over his tastebuds.

'Huh.' Andy caught the barman's attention. 'Pint please, mate. Whatever he's had. Wonder what she's up to,' he mused.

George snorted. '*I* don't. And *you* don't neither,' he warned. 'Whatever it was sounded nasty. And you know as well as I do...' He trailed off and raised one bushy eyebrow at his lifelong friend and colleague.

'If she don't tell us, we're better off not knowing,' Andy finished, raising both hands in acceptance.

'Exactly,' George said with a nod. 'Now come on, chill out and enjoy your pint. It's actually peaceful for once today.'

The pair fell into a companiable silence.

'You ever feel like we're getting too old for this?' Andy asked suddenly.

George frowned and sat up straighter. 'Speak for yourself – I ain't a day over thirty, me.'

Andy laughed. 'Yeah, twenty-five years ago maybe.'

Just then George's phone began to ring and they both stared down at the caller ID. George picked it on the second ring.

'Alright?'

He tilted the phone so Andy could hear, not able to put it on speaker right now. The Black Bear was a safe haven for criminals like them, but safe as it may be from the law, they didn't need other ears from the underworld listening in to their business.

'Alright. On our way.' He ended the call and looked grimly over at Andy. 'Well, I think we're both about to find out what Lil was up to after all.'

* * *

As the two men left and the door to the Black Bear swung closed behind them, Finn Logan smiled. He sipped his drink and pulled his flat cap a little lower. The Drews had no idea he was here yet, and he had no intention of letting them know, until the time was just right. His smile broadened as he thought of everything he had in store for them.

He imagined the moment in his head, mentally walking past their faces, one by one. And as he envisioned Scarlet's face, he began to quietly chuckle.

That girl truly had *no* idea what was coming.

TWENTY-TWO

Bright lights from streetlamps, passing cars and busy restaurant windows reflected off the rain-soaked tarmac of the busy Kensington road as Cillian jogged hurriedly towards the restaurant. He'd pulled the collar of his long, black woollen overcoat up over his neck, but it was no match against the large, fast raindrops that pelted down on him as though they had a personal vendetta.

Reaching the canopy outside the restaurant, Cillian stopped underneath it and placed his hands on his hips, turning to look back out into the rain as he caught his breath. He wiped the rain from his face and ran his hand back through his dark hair, trying to smooth it into place, then checked his watch. He was twenty-five minutes early, so he should at least have time to dry out a bit and have a drink before Tabitha arrived.

The warmth inside the restaurant hit his frozen face like a blast from a furnace, and he shrugged his soaked overcoat off as he reached the smiling host at the front desk.

'Good evening, sir, and welcome to Launceston Place. May I take your coat?'

'Sure,' Cillian replied, handing it over. 'I'm early, so...'

'That is no problem at all. May I please take your name?' the host asked.

'Mr Green,' Cillian said.

Tabitha had no idea he was related to Scarlet or Lily, so he'd donned the moniker for the duration of the grift.

'Ahh, Mr Green, your guest is already here. Let me show you to your table.'

Cillian's expression turned to one of surprise. She was early. He followed the host to the table and found Tabitha situated with an already half-empty glass of wine. *Very* early, he thought, making sure not to let his face betray how odd he found this. She only lived two minutes around the corner. She grinned up at him with excitement.

'Well, *hello*,' she said in her nasal upper-class drawl that he found teeth-achingly painful to listen to. 'Christ, you look as though you *swam* here!' Her voice rose several notes through her snorting laugh.

For some people it was nails on a chalkboard that dry-shaved their nerves. For him, it was Tabitha. Anything and everything about her.

'Hi.' He forced a smile and bent to kiss her cheek politely.

She twisted, attempting to move the kiss from cheek to mouth, but he outmanoeuvred her easily. Unbuttoning his suit jacket and retreating to his side of the table before she could do anything else, he moved his gaze purposefully to the host.

'I'll send someone over to get your drink order shortly,' she said, before nodding and moving away.

'Cheers.' Cillian turned reluctantly back to Tabitha, widening his fixed smile as if pleased to see her. 'Good to see you again,' he lied. 'You look beautiful, by the way.'

She blushed and blinked rapidly for a moment. 'Oh. Thank you.'

'No, really,' he insisted, flicking his gaze purposely to her lips and lingering there for a second before recatching her gaze.

'I don't know what it is – there's just something different about you tonight...' He bit his bottom lip. 'I like it.'

'Oh. Um...' She giggled and floundered, her earlier smug confidence gone as he caught her off kilter. 'I don't know what that could be. This is just my normal look really.'

'That's what it is,' Cillian said decisively. 'The dress and everything before, it was all very nice, but this...' He moved his gaze over her appreciatively. 'This is the real *you*. Much better.'

Tabitha's breath quickened and her pupils dilated as he deepened his gaze over the table, and his smile suddenly became more genuine. Not that it was a smile of warmth. It was the smile of a man who knew he was about to play the game and win.

He'd always found it horribly easy to charm women who'd already set their sights on him, the way Tabitha had. Before Billie – before he'd met the only woman who'd made him yearn for a deeper connection and want to be the best version of himself – he'd charmed his way into so many hearts on his quests to get into their beds, and he'd got the process down to a fine art.

'Great choice on the restaurant, by the way,' he said, continuing the flattery. 'It's exactly the kind of place I'd have picked.'

It wasn't. It was too stiff and quiet for his personal liking. But Tabitha had insisted on choosing the restaurant, in her standard bolshy way.

Tabitha gave him one of her tight-lipped, smug grins, pulling a loud breath in through her nose as she lifted her chin. 'Well, yes, I am a bit of a dab hand at picking the best places. You'll get used to that.'

God, I hope not, he thought.

'How refreshing,' he said smoothly. 'You're a woman who clearly knows what she likes.'

'I certainly am,' she purred. 'This is a regular favourite of mine, this restaurant. It was actually one of Princess Diana's favourite restaurants, back in the day, too,' she added with a superior look.

He nodded as if this was incredibly interesting.

The sommelier arrived and he ordered a drink, then waited while Tabitha chose them a bottle of wine.

'So tell me, Cillian,' she said, turning back to him as the sommelier retreated, 'how is the marketing game treating you this week?'

Cillian's alias, Mr Green, was a marketing consultant for a small tech start-up. He'd rambled on at the ball about code and apps and search-engine optimisation, stretching out his limited knowledge on the subjects, until her eyes had glassed over and she'd changed the subject.

'It's treating me well, thanks,' he enthused. 'Very well. Kicked off a new campaign for the latest app this week and getting some good results, so, you know... All good. Though there was a touch-and-go moment when the new guy was asked to create some fake props for the marketing shoot.' He creased his face up into an expression of amusement and shook his head. 'We had a good old laugh that day.' He laid the bait and waited, looking away with a half-smile as if enjoying his own private joke.

'Oh?' Curiosity glimmered in her eyes as he turned back to her. 'What happened?'

Leaning in towards her over the table, he carefully mirrored her stance, another standard tactic women never seemed to notice he adopted.

'The main theme for this campaign is *solid gold*,' he told her, 'and for the video shoot for the online ad, we needed a handful of gold nuggets.' He waved his hand in the air as though he was bored. 'Long story, not as interesting as it sounds. Anyway, obviously we couldn't get a handful of *actual* gold nuggets. Even if that wasn't ridiculous, we don't have the budget. So I tasked this guy with finding or creating some fake ones. Told him how many, the part it would play in the ad, sent him off.'

'Oh God, what happened?' Tabitha asked, picking up her wine glass and taking a sip.

Cillian reached for the stem of his own empty wine glass and twiddled it gently with his fingers, holding her gaze. 'Well, he tells me it's sorted, we move on to everything else and get ready for the shoot. Photographer turns up, actor turns up, we pull everything together, and this guy, he comes up to me and hands me – no word of a lie – a full cereal box of *Golden Nuggets*.'

Tabitha burst into a peal of laughter and Cillian pulled an expression of comedic exhaustion.

'You're *kidding*?' she asked.

'I wish I was,' Cillian replied. 'The bloke deadpan looked me in the eye and asked me what other types of gold nugget I thought there was.'

Tabitha guffawed and covered her mouth with her hand.

'Honestly, it was insane. The bloke had never seen a gold nugget before.' He rolled his eyes and shook his head. 'Well, I guess a lot of us haven't actually *seen* a gold nugget before, but you'd expect a grown man would at least know what one was, wouldn't you?'

'Of course,' Tabitha replied, still giggling slightly. 'You say a lot of *us*. Have you not seen one?'

Cillian shook his head. 'No, never seen gold in its natural form. Never had any cause to.'

'Oh how sad,' Tabitha drawled, looking at him with pity. 'You know...' She leaned in with a conspiratorial smile. 'I don't usually tell people outside of my social circles this, but my family's money actually came from gold.'

Cillian marvelled at the total obliviousness of the woman as the unfiltered words flowed from her mouth.

'You must keep that to yourself though. You're different,

obviously, but it's ghastly, when people who have never met someone like me before realise what I'm worth. You can practically *see* the pound signs light up in their eyes. Honestly, Cillian, these people who've never known real money can be truly vulgar.' She rolled her eyes and sighed. 'But anyway, as I was saying, our family fortune began with gold.'

Cillian watched her with a patient smile, waiting for her to walk into his conversational trap.

'A few generations ago we had a farm in the US and someone realised there was gold in the land. We mined it and then grew the operation as it began producing a healthy stream of gold. It's actually our other investments that are more lucrative these days, but we still do well enough from the mine too,' Tabitha informed him, rather self-importantly.

He couldn't help but grin every time she used the word *we*, as though she'd personally taken a pickaxe down the mines and brokered big deals herself.

'Impressive,' he murmured.

'Yes, it is rather,' she agreed, lifting her chin a little higher. 'Anyway, I have a box of raw nuggets from the mine at home. We used to bring one back with us every time we'd visit. Not that I've been for a while, I must admit. Life just gets so busy, you know?' She lifted her arms in a helpless shrug.

Sure. All these parties and dinners must take up so much time, he thought wryly.

'Absolutely,' he replied. 'You can't be everywhere at once.'

'Exactly. I'll have to show you my collection sometime. Then you can finally say you *have* been lucky enough to have seen a gold nugget yourself,' she offered in an exaggeratedly charitable tone.

Cillian watched her for a moment, weighing up exactly how bad his mother's wrath would be if he just slowly strangled Tabitha instead of seeing this through, then, reluctantly, he pushed this desire out of his mind and nodded.

'What a treat that would be,' he exclaimed a little too enthu-siastically. Refocusing on the end goal, he fixed her with a smouldering look and lowered his voice. 'Though I doubt it would be gold on my mind, if I'm alone with you, behind closed doors.'

Tabitha's blue eyes lit up once more and she put her hand to the side of her neck. 'I see,' she said, her excitement obvious.

'But for now, I'll settle for a drink,' Cillian said, purposely cutting the tension with a chirpier tone and moving his gaze away from her to the waiter coming towards them with their order.

'Oh. Yes. Right.' Tabitha was flustered, put off balance by the swift atmosphere changes, as he continued with his old pickup method.

Cillian smiled and thanked the waiter as he put the whisky down in front of him.

Tabitha stood up. 'Excuse me a moment, I must find the powder room.'

He waited until she disappeared from view and then dropped his smile, a cold steeliness settling in his eyes. '*Powder room...*' he muttered. 'Just call it a fucking toilet for fuck's sake. Unless you've got a few grams of Columbian marching fuel up your sleeve, I doubt you'll find any fucking powder in there.'

He took a deep breath and rolled his neck as he exhaled, trying to shake off the dark, jagged irritability Tabitha created within him. It didn't work. Everything about the woman was clawing under his skin in all the wrong ways.

He pulled out his phone and typed out a text to Scarlet, his jaw clenched in a hard line.

These paintings had better be worth it.

TWENTY-THREE

Two and a half hours and two bottles of wine later, Cillian finally got Tabitha out of the restaurant.

'It's stopped raining. That's a relief,' she said, looking up at him with an eager smile.

Cillian glanced up at the sky. 'Yeah. You live around here, don't you?' he asked, frowning as if he couldn't quite remember.

'I do, yes,' she replied, sounding hopeful. 'Just round the corner really. It's not far. Perhaps you'd like to walk me home?' The question was partnered with a flirty wiggle of the eyebrows and a coy smile.

'Of course,' Cillian replied smoothly, offering her his arm. 'I wouldn't be much of a gentleman if I didn't see you home safe now, would I?'

Tabitha took his arm and pulled him along in the direction of her home. 'I'm rather hoping you're *not* much of a gentleman,' she said with a low, dirty chuckle. 'That certainly wasn't the appeal.'

Cillian fought the urge to cringe. 'Actually, all jokes aside, I *am* a gentleman. I think it's important. Especially when it comes to people I genuinely like.' He gave her his most sincere gaze for a couple of seconds as they walked. 'And I like you. I think you're something special. Not for your fancy frocks, or because you have an exciting family history. That's all great, don't get me wrong – but I don't care about that kind of thing.' He stopped and gazed at her again, this time with more intensity. 'I care about what's at the very heart of a person. And *that's* where I think you're pretty special. You light up the room when you talk about the things that make you tick. You're intelligent and funny, and you have this softness that you try to hide, but it creeps out now and then, and that captivates me.'

Tabitha's beady eyes widened and her gaze deepened into his as she drank it all in. 'You have such incredible perception,' she said, awe in her tone. 'You're *so* right, but do you know something? Not many people actually notice those things about me.'

Cillian broke his gaze away before he betrayed himself. He masked the action by pretending to check the sky. 'We should get you home before the heavens open again. I wouldn't want you to catch a cold.'

'Yes, true,' she agreed seriously, taking his arm once more.

As she began to share her history of terrible colds, Cillian tuned her out and turned his thoughts to Billie. He bit his upper lip as he imagined what she'd have thought of his dating tactics. He'd never pulled them on her. He'd never wanted to. With her it had been different from the start. It had always been real and raw and bluntly honest, with all of the beauty and ugliness that came with. It was how he'd known that Billie was the one. Because he didn't just want the easy parts; he wanted *all* of her. All her flaws. All her bad days. And she wanted his.

He wondered how she was holding up right now. She'd be in a foul mood when he finally did get home. She'd want to know everything yet hate each detail he'd give her. She would most likely start an argument over something else, which they both knew wouldn't be about whatever that was. And whatever that argument was, he'd let her win it, he vowed. Because he knew that was how she worked. She'd need to shout and curse and throw her weight around, to dispel the storm inside, and then she'd be OK.

'... and that's when my mother *insisted* that I wear only woollen vests for the winter months. Which made sense. I don't know why the school don't insist on all students wearing them. Colds are no laughing matter for those of us who have delicate chests,' Tabitha droned on. 'It was a terrible time. My mother and I were *sure* it was pneumonia, but the useless doctor who saw us claimed it was just a cold.' She tutted. 'Stupid man clearly had *no* idea what he was talking about.'

'Clearly,' Cillian echoed, pulling his focus back to her as they came to a stop in front of a black wrought-iron gate. 'This you?'

He quickly cast his eye over the impressive, white four-storey house, noting partial cover of a large tree in the narrow space between the railing and the property front, and that the wide sash windows had discreet white security boxes in each inside corner of the glass.

'Yes, this is mine,' she replied proudly. 'She's beautiful, isn't she? My parents bought it back in the eighties from some socialite who lost her edge and couldn't keep up with the mortgage. Bad for her, good for us!' She snorted out a small laugh.

Cillian forced a laugh and turned to face her. 'Well I guess this is where I tell you goodnight.'

'Oh, no, don't go yet,' she insisted, alarmed. 'You *must* come and see the inside. Plus, I did promise you I'd show you those gold nuggets,' she reminded him.

'Ah, yes, you did,' he replied.

'I did,' Tabitha repeated in a low, quiet voice. She moved closer to him and wrapped her arms around his middle, looking up at him with clear intent.

Cillian fixed his hands on her upper arms and caressed

them, looking down into her eyes with deep intensity. Slowly, so slow the pace was almost glacial, he moved his head closer towards her. He felt the small thrill flush through her body and heard her breath quicken as he drew nearer, inch by inch. And as he got close enough to feel her breath on his skin, he suddenly moved his mouth towards her ear.

'I told you,' he whispered, 'I'm a gentleman.' He pulled back, watching her face fall and her body sag as her hopes collapsed. He squeezed her arms comfortingly and gave her a serious, earnest look. 'And that's important to me. Like I said, I actually like you. And I want to do this right.'

'You can still kiss me though,' she replied, a note of desperation in her tone.

He shook his head. 'No. I don't kiss on a first date. I'll kiss you the moment I know, without doubt, that we have something that's going to go somewhere. Because I'm the kind of person who believes in holding out for someone special.'

'But you've flirted with me *all night*,' she exclaimed, frustrated.

'Of course I have,' Cillian replied. 'I'm a gentleman, not a saint.'

'Oh *God*,' she suddenly blurted out in horror as something occurred to her. 'You don't believe in saving sex for marriage, do you?' She began to pull away and Cillian grasped her hands, cursing inwardly.

'No! *Christ* no,' he assured her with a laugh.

Appeased, she let him draw her back to him.

'But I don't just kiss anyone. It's all or nothing with me. So, if you want to kiss me, you're going to have to wait.' With this he gave her a cocky smile and pulled away.

Tabitha laughed. 'OK. Playing hard to get. I see how it is.' She held her smile, but it was still clear how unimpressed she was with this new development.

'Well, let me put it this way,' Cillian offered. 'Say you and I become a thing. Would you rather be with someone you know is choosy about who they invest time and affection with, or someone who kisses just anyone whenever they fancy it?' He raised an eyebrow and paused as she turned this over. 'I *like you*.' He pressed it home. 'And I *choose* to see *you* again, if you're up for a second date.'

Tabitha immediately brightened. 'Yes, I am up for it. Though I'm not promising I won't try to tempt you into kissing me next time.' Her eyes flickered up and down his body. 'And probably a lot more.' She sighed and unlocked the gate. 'OK, well... Thank you for a lovely evening.'

'Hey,' he said, stopping the gate with his hand as she moved to close it. 'I thought you'd invited me in for a tour? Or was that only if I stripped off for you, eh?' He cocked one eyebrow with an accusing smile.

Tabitha grinned. 'Well you would have got a much *better* tour,' she joked. 'Come on – I'll make us some coffee.' She turned and walked up the whitewashed stairs. 'Have you ever tried Black Ivory coffee before?'

'Don't think so,' Cillian replied, following her and subtly checking the street for security cameras.

It was a residential road so there were no public cameras, but he clocked high-quality personal CCTV on a few of the house fronts. Tabitha's included.

'Then you're in for a double treat tonight,' she replied. 'First time seeing real raw gold and your very own cup of the world's most expensive coffee. I only get the best, you see.'

Cillian turned to roll his eyes out of sight of her camera. 'Of course you do.'

She pulled her keys out of her handbag. 'Most people have no idea what they're talking about when it comes to the good stuff. In fact, most people believe the most expensive coffee in the world is Kopi Luwak. *Idiots*,' she added with a rude snort.

'Sure,' Cillian replied, bored.

'They think it's the best, because of the fermentation process the beans go through in the digestive tract of the Indonesian palm civets,' she continued. 'Strange little animals…'

'Sorry – what?' Cillian asked, suddenly turning to her with a frown.

She still had her back to him, trying to force a key into the door. 'I know. As if being digested and excreted by a bloody cat is going to make a difference!'

Cillian's eyes widened and his brows shot up. 'That's fucking ridiculous,' he blurted out, momentarily dropping his smooth act.

She didn't seem to notice. 'Isn't it?' she agreed.

Cillian shook his head and blew a long breath out through his cheeks, wondering at the sanity of people who paid stupid amounts of money to drink animal faeces.

'As *if* the stomach of a cat that small could be strong enough to change the physical make-up of a coffee bean. Oh, no, no, no…' She finally got the key in and turned it with a small noise of satisfaction. 'But that's why it's only two hundred pounds per kilo.'

'Clearly,' he said drily, feeling thankful that he wasn't about to be offered a cup of cat shit.

'The *real* deal, Black Ivory, is two *thousand* pounds per kilo,' she boasted. 'And that's because the beans go through the most *thorough* natural digestive refinement possible. None of this cat nonsense.'

Cillian tilted his head to the side, his frown returning. 'I don't follow. *Digestive*?'

'Yes, they're refined through Thai elephants,' she replied casually. 'They add the beans to their feed and collect them once through the system. Now *that's* a proper refinement – the acidity of the bean is totally transformed.'

Cillian's eyes widened. This nut bag paid two thousand

pounds a kilo to drink *elephant shit*? He was *not* drinking elephant shit.

Tabitha pushed open the door and walked inside. 'Do come in. Take your shoes off.'

Cillian did as she asked, looking around with appreciation. The décor in the grand hallway, and what he could see of the downstairs rooms, was light and tasteful. A perfect mix of contemporary style and period elegance that suited the building. If for nothing else, he had to give her credit for her styling skills.

'Hideous, I know,' she said conspiratorially. 'I haven't had time to re-do most of the house since my parents died, so this is their boring, outdated taste, not mine.' She rolled her eyes and made a gagging sound.

Or not, he thought flatly.

'Anyway, come through to the kitchen, I'll make us that coffee.'

Half an hour later, and with a cup of Fortnum & Mason's finest English breakfast tea in his hand after he'd firmly turned down her coffee, Cillian trailed after Tabitha as she gave him the grand tour. While she droned on about childhood memories and name-dropped various famous guests, Cillian made a mental map of the place.

It was even bigger than it looked from the outside, with a whole extra floor under the basement and a top floor that wasn't visible from the street. There was no way in through the back, much to his disappointment. No one ever covered the back with as much security as the front of their houses, so it was usually the easiest way in. But the stylish patio area, with the small square of perfectly manicured grass in the middle was sunk down below the house level, and was surrounded by tall walls and four other impenetrable garden set-ups.

He gathered pretty quickly that Tabitha's parents had been savvy when it came to security. The system was decent, if a touch outdated, and the doors and windows were sturdy. Despite all this though, there were a couple of things that had given him hope that the heist was viable.

The entire security system fed into one control room at the centre of the house. Tabitha didn't keep this locked. In fact, she'd shown him around it as if it were any other room in the house, and this had revealed two things. Firstly, that whoever had wired it in had been lazy, and had grouped all the feeds together with an adaptor before the main connection to the hard drive. This was something he could easily manipulate with very little time or effort. The second was that Tabitha clearly had no understanding of the importance of security at all. She didn't even keep the monitors switched on.

'Oh, yes, I keep them off,' she'd said, when he asked why the screens were black. 'It's still running, but I can't stand that blue glow around the doorway, you know? Makes you feel like there's a ghost or something in there.'

She'd have no idea if those screens were off. And her particular system was only internal. If it went off, there was no alert sent out to anyone.

'And this floor is the one I like to call the museum,' Tabitha said, finally taking him down to the lowest basement level.

She stopped in the doorway after flipping a couple of switches, and Cillian stepped inside, looking around with interest. There was only one internal wall down here, all the others knocked through to make one large gallery. The sculptures mounted on pedestals and the paintings on the wall all looked very impressive – not that he had a clue what he was looking at. But none of this drew his attention as much as the plain, unobtrusive door that led to the one space that was sectioned off. The white paint, clearly designed to make it blend into the wall, couldn't hide that the door was made of steel. Far too heavy duty for a simple internal door. Two keyholes sat under the handle too. This was where Scarlet's black-market paintings were. He was sure of it.

Not paying attention to what Tabitha was doing, Cillian made to move towards it, but she stopped him before he could take a full first step.

'No, wait! Just a second.'

It was then that he heard the tapping sound of a keypad behind him. He turned just as she closed the front flap, and annoyance flashed through him. He should have noticed it when he walked in. Casting his eye over the sleek black device, he realised that this wasn't part of the main security system. This was much more up to date.

'Why? Is that going to shoot darts at me or something?' he joked, gesturing towards it.

'No, but the alarm might deafen you,' she replied. 'There are laser sensors all over this floor which set off a ridiculously loud alarm and a security response unit.'

'A response unit?' he asked, his heart dropping.

'Yes, this feeds through to the security company. They get the alert and they're at the door within seven minutes. It's really rather efficient. My parents had it installed literally the week before they died,' Tabitha said.

She walked past him and gestured for him to follow. 'Come – I'll show you around.'

Cillian stared at the black box. He knew exactly what system this was and there was no way to manipulate it. It was impenetrable. His brain whirled as he tried to think of something, *anything*, that he could do to get around it, but there was nothing. It was over.

His mood darkened and anger began to bubble. The entire set-up had been a waste of time. And more than that, they'd thrown all the other, more viable marks out of play for *nothing*. Running both hands back through his dark hair, he tried to contain his fury. This was *exactly* what he'd said would happen. He'd warned them that it was too big a risk and he'd been right. It would be months before they had another opportunity to pull a job this big again. All that time and effort had come to nothing.

And *Scarlet* was to blame.

TWENTY-FOUR

Scarlet thrummed her fingers on the steering wheel of her parked car, her brow furrowed. There had been no one there that night. She was sure of it. The scrapyard was huge, taking up most of the space in the small industrial estate. Various businesses were run from the plain ugly prefab warehouses all around in the day, but they were devoid of any kind of luxury that would keep their inhabitants there beyond closing.

She spanned her gaze slowly across the buildings, searching for something she could have missed, but nothing new jumped out. She and Chain had both checked the area carefully that night. And before they'd got here, he'd had a watcher stationed who would have seen any other lurkers. The guy who'd followed Ruby to the scrapyard in the first place.

He'd left before Scarlet had even got out of her car – and according to Chain had gone straight on to a birthday knees-up, which he'd been able to verify from timestamps on the pictures that had made it to social media. Which took him off the suspect list. So how could anyone have been here?

She bit her bottom lip and felt the unease that had settled over her this morning vibrate through every cell in her body. It

had caught her off guard, the second note. She'd been so preoc-
cupied with the first one, she hadn't considered when or where
the next might appear. It had been tucked into the morning
paper that was wedged halfway through the letter box. When
she'd seen the scrapyard logo at the top of the flyer, she'd felt as
though all the oxygen had suddenly been sucked from the room,
leaving her unable to breathe.

'What's that, love?' her mother had asked, looking back at
her from the kitchen.

'Nothing,' she'd lied. 'Just a flyer.'

'In an envelope?' Cath had frowned.

'I know.' Scarlet had pretended to throw it away, then subtly
folded it into her bag. 'Random.'

'Honestly, some people really are just so irresponsible,'
Cath had declared, moving on to a rant about trees and recy-
cling and global warming.

Scarlet had forced herself to listen and nodded along over
their morning coffee, then she'd driven straight here. That had
been nearly two hours ago. She pulled the flyer out of her
handbag for the fourth time since she'd parked up and cast her
eyes over the royal blue printed lines. It was a sales flyer with a
tag line that had originally read:

Spare car and van parts for sale!

Except, someone had crossed out the words *spare car and
van parts* and had replaced them with *my silence is*.

Their silence was for sale. But *whose*? And why the cloak
and dagger if they wanted to blackmail her? If they expected
payment, they were going to have to reveal themselves
eventually.

Shoving the note back into her bag angrily, Scarlet
massaged her forehead. She had no idea what to do next. If
there was a trail, some crumbs to follow, she'd have hope. If

there was an enemy that could have been here that night, she'd have someone to focus on. But she had nothing. All she could do was sit and wait until whoever it was decided to let her in on the secret. *If* they let her in on it at all.

Pulling out her phone, she realised she had several missed calls. With a curse, she started the engine and pulled out into the road. Sitting here outside the scrapyard where Ruby died wasn't a good look. She didn't need anyone knowing she'd been here or they might start questioning why. Especially Cillian. Close as they were, things hadn't been the same between them since Ruby had been found. Despite moving past that initial period of questions and accusations, something had shifted. And it had never shifted back.

The phone rang again and she pulled a grim expression, her finger hovering over the screen of the car console as she debated whether to answer. The traffic lights ahead turned red and she decided against it.

Cillian could wait.

Reaching the pub, Scarlet nipped lightly up the stairs towards her office, scanning her messages and emails for anything important. She should have been here an hour ago, at least, to run the payroll for the charity, if she was going to get that wrapped up before the big weekly Sunday lunch.

She opened the door to her office and automatically reached for the light switch, but as she looked up, she realised with a start that there was someone already there, sitting behind her desk.

'Jesus Christ!' she exclaimed, her hand flying to her chest. 'Cillian. You scared the shit out of me.' She let out a short, relieved laugh and dropped her bag on the sideboard as she shrugged off her coat. 'What are you doing here?'

He didn't reply. His expression was thunderous, and a stab

of warning shot through her. She watched him warily, her smile dropping.

'What's wrong?' she asked.

'What's *wrong*,' he replied in a low, simmering tone, 'is that the job's a fucking bust.'

'*What?*' Scarlet crossed the room, frowning. She sat in the chair opposite him and leaned forward worriedly. 'How? What happened?'

'Exactly what I fucking warned you would happen,' he replied. 'She wasn't a viable mark from the off. You got greedy and lost sight of the rules and led the whole firm down the garden path on a fucking whim.'

His words were hard and the accusation instantly got her back up, but she gritted her teeth and stifled the urge to argue. Because she knew, deep down, that he was right.

'Where have you been anyway?' he demanded. 'I've been trying to get hold of you for hours. I even went by your house. Surely you've seen my calls?'

Scarlet's heart thumped hard against her chest as she quickly structured a viable story that didn't give away the fact she'd been sitting in her car, staring at the scrapyard where his sister had died.

'I popped to the factory first – I had to check something there for payroll,' she said in a dismissive tone. 'My phone was on silent; I was going to call you back when I got here.'

She rubbed her forehead, stressed, thinking back over all she knew about Tabitha, then shook her head.

'It can't be a write-off,' she said. 'It just can't. I *know* there's art there – she *told* me—'

'Oh, there's art,' Cillian replied, cutting her off. 'A whole fucking floor of it, underground. There's even a locked steel door off to the side that might as well have a sign on it with big red letters reading *the black market shit's in here*.'

'So...?'

'And it's all held in the loving embrace of the Catalon 500,' Cillian said.

Scarlet let out a groan and closed her eyes. The Catalon 500 was untouchable, with a high-tech failsafe, an owner code that changed every twelve hours and the most sensitive lasers on the planet. Even Bill Hanlon hadn't cracked it yet – and Bill could get past anything. She wiped a hand down the bottom half of her face and shook her head, lost for words.

'The entire floor is rigged,' Cillian continued. 'Only one way in and out, and no windows as it's underground.' His expression was still hard, his gaze boring into hers with silent, angry accusation.

Scarlet cringed. She'd fucked up – big time. Lily was going to be furious. 'You're right,' she said heavily. 'This is my fault. She was just such a big prize...'

'No, she was a big *possibility*,' he corrected. 'You didn't verify enough to confirm she was an *actual* prize. And as far as art goes, she isn't.'

Scarlet picked up on his choice of words. 'As far as *art* goes?' she repeated slowly.

Cillian lifted his chin and looked down at her, a glint in his eye. 'You're fucking lucky,' he said, his resentment still present but the hard edge beginning to wane. 'Because as it happens, I did come across something in that house that presented another opportunity. And I think it's one everyone's going to like...'

TWENTY-FIVE

Lily looked around the full table at the faces of all the people she loved – and all the people they loved – and allowed herself to feel a moment of warmth. Sundays had always been about celebrating family, being together once a week, without work or anything else getting in the way. Now the number of faces around the table had grown, but each one only served to remind her of the faces that were gone.

When Ronan – the brother she'd raised after they'd been orphaned as children and who'd been by her side every day since – had died, she'd thought she'd experienced the very worst depths of grief. But even that couldn't have prepared her for what she'd felt with Ruby. To have had to bury her own child in the cold ground, while she lived on, had been the most agonising pain she imagined any human could possibly go through and survive. And it never went away. It sat, cold and dark and heavy, inside her chest, every moment of the day.

The last time she'd seen Ruby had been just a normal day. Lily couldn't even remember what her last words to her had been. She should have told her that she loved her. She should have told her so many things. But now it was too late.

'Lil?'

Cath roused her from her thoughts, and she pulled in an energising breath, turning to her sister-in-law with a bright half-smile.

'You alright?' Cath's brow creased slightly.

'Yeah, sorry, million miles away,' Lily replied. 'What were you saying?' She picked up her wine and took a sip.

'I was saying that Scarlet and I are planning to redecorate the front room,' Cath repeated. 'New colours, new furniture, the lot.'

'About time – those sofas are so uncomfortable,' Lily replied, grinning to show Cath she was joking. Half-joking anyway. 'What colour you thinking?'

'Right now I'm leaning towards burned orange and gold,' Cath said excitedly.

Lily pulled an expression of mild disgust. 'Please tell me you're not getting orange carpet?'

Cath tutted. 'Honestly! You've never liked my carpets.' She raised her eyebrows at Lily accusingly. 'Even that lovely dusky rose coloured one I had when Scarlet was little. I *loved* that carpet. Till you went in and bloody turned it claret.' She rolled her eyes.

Connor frowned. 'I don't remember you having a red carpet.'

Lily and Cath shared a look and then laughed. Cillian chuckled and patted Connor on the back. Ray grinned, giving Benny a look that said he'd fill him in later, and Billie watched with an amused smile, clearly waiting for the story to unfold.

Scarlet remained silent, Lily noticed. Though she wasn't surprised. The memory of that night wasn't a pleasant one for her. Not for any of them, really, but for her it had been much worse. It actually wasn't a funny story at all, but Connor's misinterpretation had lightened things somewhat. He still looked completely flummoxed, so she put him out of his misery.

'We shouldn't laugh really,' she said, bringing the room back to a level of sensibility. 'Do you remember that night your uncle Ronan got hurt? Years ago. You were young, only been in the firm maybe a year. It was a rival firm, those brothers, do you remember? I can't recall their names now. They were going round claiming that half our territory was theirs. Tried to take us out. Almost succeeded with your uncle.'

She shared a grim look with Cath. It had been touch and go that night. Ronan had lost a lot of blood and they'd had to fix him up at home. The heat around them had become too high to risk the hospital. But her brother hadn't been the only person they'd had to deal with that night. When it had happened, Ronan had been quick enough to overpower his attacker and had dragged him back with him, with what strength he had left. And as Cath had sewn Ronan up with a sewing kit and a bottle of vodka in the kitchen, Lily had dealt with the rest.

'Christ, that really *was* years ago,' Cillian commented.

'Oh, we came to the house, didn't we? And...' Connor trailed off, his eyes darting to Scarlet as he suddenly remembered.

'It's OK,' she said, brushing it off. 'You don't have to pussy-foot around me.'

The room fell quiet as everyone who'd been there remembered the months of nightmares that had followed, for the youngest member of the family. Scarlet had been eight at the time, too young and innocent to know who her family really were yet. But the events of that night had changed that. She'd woken up and had crept to the stairs. Lily had eventually spotted her and tried soothing her with words of comfort, but she'd seen too much for her tender years, and it had haunted her for a long time.

'You came to the house,' Scarlet continued in a matter-of-fact tone, 'and you dealt with it. You saved my dad.' She cast the comment towards Lily with a small smile. 'Took out the bastard who tried to kill him. Which was exactly the right thing to do. You protected us like you always have.' She raised her glass towards Lily with a nod of respect. 'And I'm thankful that you did.'

There was a loaded pause as those who hadn't been there tried to work out what *wasn't* being said, and as those who had felt the weight of it.

'I wasn't thankful for what you did to my carpet,' Cath said wryly.

There was another eruption of laughter and the tension was broken. Even Scarlet laughed this time.

'My pride and bloody joy, that carpet was. Extra thick, imported, the best quality wool money could buy, and Lil goes and shoots someone on it. Honestly... You really couldn't have taken him elsewhere?' Cath asked her as the laughter continued.

'I really hated that carpet,' Lily admitted.

'She did,' Ray confirmed through chuckles of mirth. 'She even told me that afterwards. Called it the silver lining that she'd managed to get rid of it.'

'You never!' Cath gasped. Her jaw dropped in shock, and it was so comical that the entire table joined in with the laughter.

Lily gave her an apologetic shrug. 'I did you a favour. People were starting to confuse your house with the local nursing home.'

The laughter grew louder.

The banter continued, but Lily tuned it out, subtly watching Scarlet over the rim of her wine glass. The girl had been tense all day. And she'd caught several loaded looks between her and Cillian. Something was going on. But she doubted she'd find out what until the day was over. They tried not to talk too much shop at the Sunday lunch, for Cath and Billie's sake – and they didn't bring it up *at all* if Ray and Benny were there. Lily trusted Ray with her life, and let him in on a lot of things, but he was still the head of another firm. Knowledge was power. And she didn't need Ray Renshaw gaining any more power over her than he already had.

Noticing that the empty plates and platters had been that way for a while, Lily stood up and began to gather them.

'Here, I'll help,' Ray offered, following suit.

'No, me and Cillian will do it,' Billie said, walking round to Lily and taking the plates from her hands. 'It's our turn.'

'Is it?' Cillian asked, pulling a reluctant face.

'Yes,' Billie replied sharply. 'It is. Come on.'

Connor joined them without a word, and Lily hid an amused smile.

'Right, well, I'll go get the brandy then,' she said brightly. 'Who wants one?'

She walked through to the large second lounge at the back of the house, which she used as a study and informal meeting room, and made a beeline for the marble drinks trolley. The door opened again behind her, then Ray walked over and she smiled.

'Alright? Change your mind?'

'No, I still want one. Actually...' He leaned over and checked out one of the other bottles next to the crystal brandy decanter. 'I'll have a whisky.'

She nodded and passed him a whisky glass. He poured a measure and sipped it silently as she poured everyone else's.

'What is it?' she asked, not looking round.

'What?' he asked, with a tone of innocence.

'I've known you for too many years not to know when you want to say something, Ray,' she replied. 'So come on, spit it out.'

'OK,' he conceded. 'The boys. They alright?'

The gruffly spoken question caught Lily off guard. She placed the top back on the decanter slowly. They rarely spoke about her sons. Or technically *their* sons. He'd only found out he was their father a year and a half before. And he'd only calmed down about it enough to try and return to some sort of normality with her months later, when he'd learned of Ruby's death. Angry as he was, at the time, he'd come to her side and had held her in the darkness behind closed doors, while she'd fallen apart. She'd understood his fury and pain. But theirs was a complicated history and she'd had her reasons for hiding that knowledge at the time.

'They're fine,' she answered in a carefully even tone. 'Why do you ask?'

Ray shifted his weight and twisted his glass. 'Well, you know... They happy in their lives?'

Lily frowned and turned to him. 'What's going on? You dying or something?'

'Do I have to be dying to care about my sons?' he asked, a flash of dark frustration crossing his face. 'I might not have raised 'em, but they're still my flesh and blood. The only children I have.'

Lily watched him for a moment. 'They're fine,' she said gently. 'They're more than fine. They're doing well, they're happy and they're good men.'

'I know they're good men,' he said. 'They were raised by you.' The anger was gone. Or perhaps just contained, she wasn't ever fully sure. 'But are they really happy?'

This question raised her guard. 'What do you mean?' she frowned. 'Of course they are. They have everything they need. A loving family, money, freedom. Cillian's restaurant is thriving. He's really stepped up this last year, you know.' The pride shone through her voice. 'They've both always been hard grafters, but Cillian's really matured. He's stopped pulling the kind of hot-headed shit that used to keep me up at night. He's started thinking more strategically.'

'More like a leader,' Ray offered.

'Exactly,' Lily replied.

'And what about Connor?' he asked.

Lily's gaze narrowed. 'What *about* Connor?'

'You've been grooming Scarlet to take over one day, Cillian's put himself in the running now too. They'll make a great team, just like you and Ronan. But you know the saying, Lil, too many chefs...'

'What happens to this firm is *my* concern, not yours,' Lily snapped, cutting him off as she realised what he was saying. 'That future is a long way off yet, and the chips will fall where they fall.' She eyed him hard, her brown eyes glinting dangerously. 'What you seem to have forgotten – other than your place, when it comes to *my* firm – is that not everyone *wants* to be a leader. Everyone has their skillsets, and although the boys may look the same, they're very different people underneath.'

There was a long silence as they glared at each other. The tension in the room grew thick.

Ray pulled back first. 'Of course it's your firm,' he said. 'But they're *our* sons. And I won't make apologies for being curious about their futures.'

Lily reluctantly turned her head away and nodded. Whether she liked it or not, things weren't black and white anymore. And Ray was right – he had every right to ask those questions.

'Those boys mean everything to me, Ray, in a way that you can't understand. And I don't mean that because you weren't in their lives,' she added quickly. 'With the best will in the world, there are some things even the most dedicated dad don't get. When you're a mum, when they grow inside you, their souls become fused with yours. You feel every bit of their pain or happiness, every loss, every win, as deep as if it were happening to you.'

She picked up one of the brandies and knocked it back in one, savouring the sharp warmth.

'And that can fade, after they get their independence and

don't need you to wipe their arses anymore. But only if you don't figure out the new ways that they need you. Because they always *do*. Which is why I've worked so hard all these years to grow this firm. It was what the boys needed. *Still* need. A place they could rise up together and make their mark, with me there to keep them safe from themselves.' She eyed her empty glass and refilled it, feeling the stab in her chest that she knew was coming. She took a deep breath, forcing the next words out with difficulty. 'I didn't figure it out with Ruby.' The guilt spread through her, stinging viciously. 'Or rather I *did*, but I couldn't give her what she needed. A life of drug-induced escapism isn't something any mother can give a child.'

'Lil, you couldn't have—'

'Anyway, that's not the point,' Lily cut him off swiftly, not wanting to go any further down that path. 'The point I'm making is that everything I have ever done has been for my boys. *Our* boys,' she corrected. 'So you don't need to worry about them.'

Ray's jaw clenched and a strange look passed across his face, but he turned away before she could decipher it.

The door suddenly opened and they both turned to see Cath leaning around it.

'You starting up your own distillery or can we just use the bottle you got in here?' she asked.

'Here,' Lily said, picking up two of the glasses and handing them to Cath as she walked over. 'Take that out to Scarlet too.'

'Come on – let's head back to the others,' Ray said, picking up his whisky and following Cath.

Lily watched him as he moved away from her. What was going on in that head of his? She'd seen that look before, the one he'd just tried to hide. And although she wasn't sure what it had to do with her boys, she knew it meant trouble.

TWENTY-SIX

The front door finally closed behind Cath, and Cillian waited for Scarlet to rejoin them in the lounge. She walked in and sat on the sofa opposite him. He studied her. She was doing her best to hide it, but she was nervous. And rightly so. She'd messed up and had cost them all a *lot* of money.

A small part of him was quite enjoying the ironic role reversal. Historically it had been him and Connor who'd made the stupid moves, and Scarlet who Lily had relied on to help clean up the consequences. But this time *she* would fall from grace, and he would save the day.

Another part of him felt guilty for thinking about it like that. Scarlet was his cousin and they were a team. It shouldn't be about who did what, so long as they were all pulling together for the greater good of the firm.

But mainly he just felt angry that they'd wasted so much time and such a big opportunity. He was angry that he'd been forced to endure Tabitha's rude, ignorant company and her cringeworthy advances that had made his skin crawl. Keeping up the act had been harder than he'd thought it would be. Billie had suffered too, forced to accept something no partner should ever have to accept – and for what? It hadn't even been worth it. Or at least it wouldn't have been, if Tabitha hadn't pulled the stunt that she had, as he'd made his excuses to leave last night. In her desperation to keep him there, she'd revealed something he could actually use.

Lily lit a cigarette and rested back in her favourite armchair, crossing her legs and leaning to the side, propping her elbow on one of the hard arms. She pulled in a deep drag and narrowed her eyes slightly, flicking her gaze between him and Scarlet. From his left, he heard Connor sigh at the look on their mother's face. Cillian pulled a grim expression and sat back, waiting for whatever was to come.

Lily slowly cast her gaze around them all as she blew out a long plume of smoke. 'Well?' she asked. 'Who's going to enlighten me?'

Scarlet's grey-blue eyes met his. 'I fucked up,' she said simply.

'What do you mean you fucked up?' Lily asked, a deep frown immediately forming on her face.

Cillian watched his cousin's jaw tighten resolutely and her chin lifted up a notch.

'I mean I was wrong to push Tabitha as our choice of mark from the ball. The art is there, but it's unreachable.'

'What do you mean unreachable?' Lily demanded, her anger visibly rising. 'Cillian?' She turned to him with a sound of frustration.

'It's in a sub-basement with only one entry point, protected by the Catalan 500,' Cillian explained, sharing a look that told her he was just as unimpressed as she was.

'For fuck's *sake*,' Lily exclaimed loudly. She pinched the bridge of her nose and took a deep breath, her mouth closing into a hard line. When she spoke again, her words surprised all of them. 'This is my fault.'

'*What?*' Cillian and Scarlet both said at once, glancing at each other and then back to Lily.

It definitely *wasn't* his mother's fault.

'Lil, no, this is on me, not you,' Scarlet said strongly.

'No, it's not,' Lily argued, looking up at her with a hard expression. 'I allowed this ridiculous decision. I put aside all my years of hard-earned experience that told me to go the other way, to ensure we didn't waste our time, and I was wrong.'

She held Scarlet's gaze with a soul-shrivelling look of disappointment that Cillian knew all too well and was grateful he wasn't on the receiving end of, for once. He pulled a toothpick out of his pocket and put it between his teeth, waiting to see exactly how bad it was going to be.

Lily took another drag on her cigarette and then tapped it on the side of the ashtray. 'I let myself forget that you're not someone who understands all the intricacies and the delicate balances that need to be maintained to run jobs like these, to run a successful firm; you're a twenty-one-year-old *girl*.' Her heavy gaze intensified as she paused, then she looked away, taking in another deep lungful of smoke and releasing it slowly. 'I shouldn't have put so much faith in you.'

Her words were quiet and calm, but Scarlet flinched as though they'd physically burned her. 'Lil...' she said, the one syllable filled with hurt and surprise.

'No.' Lily shook her head, speaking sharply. 'I don't want to hear it. This is on me – it was my decision.' She looked Scarlet up and down. 'But it's one I will not be repeating. You have a lot to learn. More than I'd realised.'

Scarlet's pale cheeks grew red and for a moment Cillian wasn't sure whether she was going to explode or cry. Instead, she lifted her chin and swallowed. 'Lil, I admit this was a fuck-up, but—'

'There are no *buts*, Scarlet,' Lily bellowed, the unexpected explosion stopping Scarlet in her tracks. 'And like I said already,

I'm not interested in hearing it.' She eyed Scarlet with open fury now and her voice dropped back to a low, deadly calm. 'You can go now. The boys and I will discuss how we salvage this and we'll let you know the plan tomorrow.'

Scarlet's mouth dropped open, but as Lily glared at her, she quickly shut it, and a deathly silence filled the room.

Scarlet nodded, more to herself than to Lily. Standing up, she drew in a deep breath and walked out of the room without another word.

The tension remained in the room until they heard her car back off the drive.

Cillian twiddled the toothpick with his tongue, watching his mother, waiting for a sign that her anger was under enough control. Eventually she looked over, and he shifted his position.

'It's not a total loss,' he said levelly. 'I've got another plan that should still make all this worthwhile. It's not the millions we were hoping for, but it's not bad either.'

'Is this a Hail Mary plan because you're desperate not to walk away empty-handed or a genuinely viable plan?' she asked.

'It's a *very* viable plan.'

'Go on,' she ordered.

'After dinner I walked her back and got myself invited in, as planned. She gave me a tour of the house. After seeing that system around the art, I started making my excuses to leave, but she asked if she could show me something first. Something hidden in the office.' He saw Billie's mouth purse out of the corner of his eye. 'I agreed, hoping it might have been a favoured painting or something. She told me to wait outside for two minutes before going in, which I did, then when I opened the door, I found her stark bollock naked on the desk, wearing nothing but a diamond choker.'

'*What!*' Connor burst out laughing and slapped his leg, unable to contain himself. 'You jammy...' Catching Billie's furious expression, his words spluttered into an awkward, amused cough. 'Sorry, carry on.'

'Obviously I'd already told her I wasn't going to be doing anything on a first date, no kissing, *nothing*,' Cillian stressed, this part aimed at Billie. 'But she'd decided to pull out all the stops to change my mind.'

Connor chuckled quietly. 'Nice.'

'Not really,' Cillian replied tersely. 'After I managed to talk her back into her clothes' – *which hadn't been the easiest of tasks,* he added silently – 'she asked me to help unclasp her choker. I got her talking about it and about the other diamonds in the safe. I got a good look. There's quite a collection. A mix of jewellery and loose gems. All high-end. We're talking top-shelf shit.'

Lily's eyebrow kinked up in interest. 'How much we looking at?'

'I didn't want to ask too many questions but the woman's a natural bragger – she can't help herself. From what she said and what I saw, my guess is at least half a mill. Maybe more – it was hard to tell. But enough that it's worth it.'

Lily frowned. 'But how would we avoid the security system there any easier than in the basement?'

'See, that's the thing,' Cillian replied, leaning forward with a look of excitement. 'She's only got the Catalon 500 in the sub-basement. The rest of the house is still on an old crappy internal circuit system linked up to a security room in the centre of the house. She leaves it unlocked and keeps the screens off. The woman's a walking target. Scarlet was bang on about that part.'

'You'd be the first person she suspects after showing you last night. How do you intend to come out of this clean?' Lily asked.

'I meet up with her a couple more times – somewhere public,' he added quickly. 'But I'll pick her up each time.'

'You'll need another car,' Lily interjected.

He nodded. 'I'll lease something and then switch the plates.

The next time I see her, hopefully tomorrow, I'll spill something on her dress so she has to go change or something like that. Whoever wired the system up was lazy – they pulled all the wires into one adaptor, which leads into the main box with just *one* connection.'

'Jesus, they were practically begging for her to be done,' Connor commented.

'I know. I only need a minute to disable the connection. I can make it look like it just came loose on its own, leave it *almost* connected,' Cillian continued. 'She never checks it and nothing will seem out of place until they go to find the tapes after the job and see there haven't been any recordings for days. We leave it those few days, maybe a week. I'll see her again in between. Then the night we do this, I'll stay outside the house but ask her to go back in and put on the choker she wore last night. Tell her it's all I've been thinking about…'

'Oh, will you now,' Billie blurted out huffily. She rolled her eyes and held her hands up as Lily turned to look at her.

'Obviously that's just part of the play,' Cillian said pointedly. 'But it will ensure she goes into the safe while I'm outside and haven't entered for even a second. She'll see everything is as it should be, then she'll be with me all night. I won't be questioned as I won't have been near the safe or even in the house all evening, before or after the break-in.'

'Where are the cameras?' asked Lily. 'Won't they pick you up going into the security room?'

'No, they're only on the outside of the house and then one in the office. It's a bloody terrible set-up, honestly,' he answered.

'And the safe? What's the entry type?' she asked.

'Simple code and handle. And I have the code.' He grinned. 'Pretended to leave when she locked up – she didn't notice me watching from the door. Inside is the easy part. Outside is the main risk. There are a few houses with cameras that cover the front. They ain't close but they'll pick up basics. Whoever's on the inside team will need a full ID swap. Hair, weight, height if you can do that, the lot. Connor, you won't be able to come near this – it's too risky.'

Lily murmured her agreement. 'We can't have anyone spotting even a slight resemblance. And we'll need to have one of us in the new ID get-up hanging around the street beforehand, being picked up on cameras. We'll time that so it's totally out of sync with your visits, except one where whoever it is appears to clock you taking her out. You'll look totally oblivious of course.'

Lily squeezed her gaze as she ran through all the possible problems and loose ends. 'So we'll wait until you're gone, come into the street... What's your exit plan? I'm sure it's safe to assume you *don't* plan on dating her indefinitely.'

'I won't come in when we get back, will sort a phoney call with one of you that means I have to drop her and dash. That will keep me out of the line of fire for immediate questioning,' he replied.

'Until they check the tapes and see they stopped recording while you were in the house,' Lily pointed out.

'That's a wrinkle I still need to iron out,' Cillian admitted. 'Got any ideas?'

'You need some sort of pulley mechanism with a timer really, don't you?' Connor mused.

'That would mean leaving it in the house,' Lily warned with a frown.

'No, that's actually a good idea,' Cillian said, thinking it through. 'She really doesn't go in that room, and even if she did, there's no reason she'd find it. The wires are tucked away out of sight. How would we find something that does that though?'

Connor pulled out a cigarette and lit up, then rubbed his forehead before putting it to his lips for a deep drag. 'I could probably make it,' he said, breathing out the smoke between words. 'It's a simple enough idea. We'd need a dummy link with roughly the same weight and resistance to test it.'

'I can sort that.' Cillian nodded. 'You'd need to make it so it goes off four or five hours after I set it. That way the camera picks me up leaving and it'll go off in the early hours of the morning. I'll grab the device the next day and by the time they check it all out, there will be no doubt that it coming loose was just an unfortunate accident.'

Lily nodded. 'OK. Connor, fix something up. Cillian, try to convince her to invite a group of people over for something, in the next day or two.'

'How? *Who?* She has no mates,' he replied.

'Well then maybe that's your angle,' Lily suggested. 'Don't force it,' she added. 'But see if there's any chance. We need to try and add suspects to the situation. How are we getting in?'

'You'll need to pick the locks – there's two on the front. Basic barrels – won't take you long. I'll book something late night so there's less chance of people on the street. It's quiet anyway though.' Cillian bit down on his toothpick and took it out of his mouth. 'After it's all done, I'll give her a spiel about getting back with my ex.'

'A part I'm *more* than happy to play,' Billie added.

'I'll start mentioning that Billie – or rather Claire, as we'll call her for this – has been in touch asking to talk. Lay the seeds, so it looks like a genuine back track,' Cillian finished.

Lily's gaze slid over towards Billie, and Cillian could see the concern behind her carefully neutral expression.

'She won't actually come into play,' he assured her. 'It's just the back story.'

'OK.' Lily stood up. 'Work with each other to get this device made up quickly. We don't want to keep this going any more than it needs to.' She picked up her glass and walked out of the room.

The rest of them stood, but Cillian held Connor back with a hand until Billie had left the room.

'What is it?' Connor asked quietly, his dark brows

furrowing in concern. 'Is there something else? You worried about this job?'

Cillian turned to him with a grim expression. 'The job? No,' he said with a shake of his head. He glanced at the door, checking the others weren't about to reappear. 'It's Scarlet. Something's going on.'

'What do you mean?' Connor asked, confused.

'Something's off. She's been acting weird for days,' Cillian confided.

Connor shrugged. 'It's probably just this job. She knows you didn't want to do it.'

'That's what I thought too, until this morning,' Cillian replied. 'I couldn't reach her. Went to the house, Cath said she'd gone to run payroll. I ended up waiting in her office for an *hour* before she finally turned up.'

'Right, and?' Connor asked.

'*And,*' Cillian replied, wiping his hand down his face in an agitated movement, 'she told me she'd gone to the factory first, before coming to the pub. Except within that time I went and checked the factory. It was locked up. No one there, no cars. And when she finally did rock up, she drove in from the south.'

He held Connor's gaze and saw the surprise dawn. Connor's frown deepened and Cillian nodded slowly.

'Yeah,' he said heavily. 'She lied to me. And I want to know why. I want to know what the hell she's hiding.'

TWENTY-SEVEN

Scarlet pulled up on the side of the road just before her own and switched off the engine, plunging the car into silence. She pulled her fists back and slammed them viciously into her steering wheel, over and over, with all her strength, roaring cries of frustration escaping from somewhere deep within.

Reining herself in, she grasped the wheel and bent forward, resting her forehead on the cold hard leather. She closed her eyes and waited for her breath to calm.

She'd known Lily's reaction wasn't going to be pleasant, but she hadn't expected it to be that bad. She'd expected anger and blame, orders to fix it – *that* she could deal with. But this... Sitting up, Scarlet rested back, exhaling wearily as she stared down the dark, deserted road ahead.

That was what made Lily so dangerous. She didn't have to raise a finger, or even her voice, to destroy people. To an outsider, that conversation would have seemed like nothing. But Lily had just shifted the tables of power within the firm quite significantly. That short conversation had stripped Scarlet of all the respect and power she'd spent *years* earning. Within those few minutes, Scarlet had gone from being her aunt's right-hand woman – the second in command – to the very back of the line.

Sniffing, she wiped a hand down her face and turned to look at a streetlight across the road. She hadn't cared when Cillian had worked his way up to stand beside her. He'd earned it. It wasn't that she craved power over anyone else. But she'd worked so hard, sacrificed so much to be where she was. And to have Lily tear her down, label her as a naïve young fool and dismiss her from important meetings, was soul-destroying.

Realising the streetlight wasn't the only light bathing the tarmac, Scarlet glanced in her side mirror. A car had pulled up behind her, a few houses back. It idled, the headlights still on, pointing in her direction. She squeezed her gaze, trying to make out the make or model, but it was too dark.

A car had followed her in, she recalled, when she'd driven off the main road and into the quieter residential area. She hadn't paid it much attention. But now she thought about it, she was sure it hadn't passed her. She stared at it through the mirror. Someone was watching her.

She reached for her phone and then stopped, her hand hovering in mid-air. Who was she going to call? Who did she have who she could talk to about all of this? No one. Her closest family would become enemies if they found out the truth. The only person who knew was Chain, and she was hardly going to call him up like some pathetic damsel in distress. For once she was well and truly alone.

Placing her hand back on the wheel, she deliberated for a second, then started the engine. Maybe she was just being paranoid. She glanced down the road then pulled out and moved onwards, her gaze flicking straight back to the mirror. Her heart thudded as the car behind pulled out too.

She wasn't imagining it. He was definitely following her. She tried to think. Reaching her road, she glanced at her house in the distance and grimaced. If she pulled onto her drive, she'd be cornered. She slowed to a stop on the side of the road once more, but kept the engine on this time and one foot poised over the accelerator pedal. The car behind mirrored her movements again, snuffing out the last smidgen of doubt that had remained in her mind.

Seconds passed, the soft purr of the engine idling filling her ears as she debated what to do. She could easily lose him, but then she'd be no closer to finding out who it was. And it wasn't like time would help her gather any support. She'd be looking over her shoulder, just waiting for them to reappear. No, she couldn't live like that.

Unstrapping her seat belt, Scarlet reached over to the back footwell and grabbed the bat she kept there for emergencies. Testing her grip, she quickly opened the door and stepped out of the car before she could talk herself out of it. She glared at the car with as much confidence as she could muster, her heart beating painfully hard in her chest as she marched towards it, bat held low.

Drawing nearer, she lifted her chin defiantly and widened her arms in a questioning gesture. She wanted to shout out, demand to know who they were, but the last thing she needed was for a neighbour to wake up and the curtains to start twitching. The shape of the car was beginning to show more clearly, a few more seconds and she should be able to see what it was and who was in it, she realised.

But it seemed that whoever was inside also realised this at the same time, as suddenly there was a screech of spinning tyres and the car lurched forward.

Taken aback by the sudden move, Scarlet stopped still and tensed, ready to jump to the side if she needed to. For one long dreadful second, it seemed as though she might, but as she darted towards the pavement, the car steered away and raced off down the road.

Scarlet turned and ran after it for a few paces, trying to

catch some of the number plate, but she was too late and it was too dark.

'Fuck's *sake*,' she growled, throwing the bat down on the road as the tail lights disappeared around the corner. The hollow sound of wood bouncing on hard ground echoed around the empty street, and Scarlet let out an exasperated sigh, thoroughly shaken. She put her hands to her face. What fucked-up game was this person playing?

Things were getting out of hand. And that had been too close for comfort. Tomorrow she'd talk to Chain about stepping up the hunt for their new, faceless enemy.

When Scarlet finally reached the house, she was thankful to find her mother had gone to bed. She double locked the door and checked it twice. They'd always avoided home security cameras here. Her dad had never wanted them, warning that they could be used against them to discount alibis. But now she was beginning to wonder whether they should consider something.

She walked over to switch off the hallway lamp her mother had left on, then paused with a sinking heart as she clocked the white envelope propped against it. This one had her name on at least. Ripping it open, she stared down at the words as deep foreboding swept through her body.

It's nearly time to pay for all you took from me. Tuesday 10 a.m. Back where it all began. Come alone.

TWENTY-EIGHT

Lily stepped out of her car and the harsh winter wind hit her with force, whipping her curls back in fury and biting at her bare neck, but she didn't flinch. Instead she just stared across the green to a row of houses with a sombre expression. No children played in the park this afternoon, with the dark angry clouds racing above and the sporadic splatter of heavy raindrops as they threatened to unleash their wrath in full.

She opened the back passenger door and picked up a small holdall, slinging it over her shoulder. It was heavy but nowhere near as heavy as the weight she carried inside. She closed the door and walked down the long path that led to the houses, barely feeling the wild lashes of the wind as it raged around her.

It couldn't have ended any other way. Mani had made sure of that. She hadn't realised how deep his lust for revenge had been. Running bets on her fights had been bad enough – and stealing profit from their business that way *was* cause for a very violent and public response, yes. But if that had been the extent of it, things could have been dealt with in a less extreme manner.

Once she found out that Robert was one of the most highly

trained killers in the business though, and that he'd been tasked to kill her and her family, there had been no going back. Someone like that, especially one motivated by the kind of dark threat Mani had held over his head, would never leave a job unfinished. Really, his fate had been sealed the moment Mani had hired him. Because when it came to the survival of her family, Lily had always been prepared to do anything. Still, what she'd done to Robert before she'd ended his life didn't sit easy.

She'd suspected that whoever had hired Robert was threatening his daughter, after Connor had passed on all the man had endured and his unswayable resolution to take whatever torture they inflicted until he eventually died. This wasn't the Marines. These weren't political secrets he was protecting; it was an Italian gangster. There was no way that Mani's identity was more important to Robert than his own life. In fact, there was only one thing in this world Lily had *ever* found people would prioritise above their own survival. The one thing they were biologically wired to protect, beyond rhyme or reason.

That was when she'd known she'd have to fake the threat to Evie too, with the added promise of protection thrown in to sway him. She'd hated every second of it. It had gone against everything she believed in. They did a lot of bad things in their way of life, but it was pure evil to threaten a child. Not that her threat was ever real, but Robert had *thought* it real. And knowing that this was his last thought, his last fear, haunted her.

She made her way down the row of neat brick houses, each with the same three uniform square windows, and varying styles of cheap PVC front doors, until she reached the third from the end. Hesitating only a second, she rapped the scratched gold-painted knocker.

A large raindrop landed on her cheek and she looked up as another hit her forehead. As if a dam had opened, they suddenly began pelting down around her like small missiles. A woman in her early thirties, with dark hair pulled up in a clip, wearing a long blue cardigan over jeans and a T-shirt, opened the door and glanced up in alarm.

'*Gordon Bennett*, look at that weather! Er... Come in a minute,' she said awkwardly, left with no choice but to invite in the stranger practically drowning on her front step.

'Thanks,' Lily said gratefully, stepping inside. She looked down with regret at the puddle she was already creating in the narrow entranceway.

'Don't worry – it's just a bit of water,' the woman told her, wrapping her cardigan around herself and crossing her slim arms over her middle. 'Can I help you? I don't think we've met...' She squeezed her eyes as if trying to place Lily.

'We haven't,' Lily confirmed, pushing her soggy curls back off her face. 'You're Sasha.' It was a statement, rather than a question. 'I'm Lily, a friend of Robert's.' It was a necessary lie.

Sasha tensed as she became instantly alert. There was a small noise upstairs, and her body shifted to better block the stairwell. 'What kind of friend?' she asked, the earlier easiness gone from her voice.

Lily raised her hands. 'A *friend*,' she repeated gently. 'I'm no threat to you or Evie.' There was a silence as Sasha's eyes darted around her face. 'I'm just here to pass on a message and a package from Robert. That's all. Can we sit down?'

Sasha regarded her for another couple of seconds and then nodded. 'OK. Go through – we can sit in the kitchen. You're alone?' she suddenly asked, glancing back at the door.

'Just me.' Lily wandered into the lounge and pointed across the green through the grey sheets of rain. 'That's my car. No one else there.'

Sasha glanced out and then moved back to the door, double locking it. 'Evie,' she called up the stairs. 'Stay up there until I call you down, OK?'

A muffled agreement returned and Sasha closed the door to

the lounge, gesturing towards the kitchen diner at the back. Lily took a seat at a small wooden kitchen table, placing the holdall on the floor by her feet.

'Tea?' Sasha asked, eying her warily as she filled the kettle.

Lily shook her head. 'No. Thank you. I won't be staying long.'

'Suit yourself,' Sasha replied, pulling out a mug and popping in a tea bag. She turned and leaned back on the kitchen side, crossing her arms across her middle once more. 'How d'you know Rob?'

'Professionally,' Lily said, keeping it vague.

Sasha looked her up and down critically. 'Well you ain't a marine. So you're one of his newer clients.' She pursed her lips.

'Not a client. But we moved in the same circles,' Lily replied. It wasn't exactly a lie.

There was an awkward silence and Lily tried to decide how best to open up the conversation. There was never a good way to deliver this sort of news. A bright blue-and-orange painting on the fridge door caught her eye and she smiled. She remembered the days when her fridge had been covered as chaotically as Sasha's was.

'You have kids?' Sasha asked.

'Yeah. Mine are all grown up now though. I miss that.' She nodded towards the fridge. 'They never tell you how much you're gonna miss that, you know. The pictures. The sticky handprints all over the walls. The bits of Lego you find everywhere. You don't realise it till they're gone.'

A memory surfaced of her children all giggling over a pack of cheap bath toys, bubbles and water all over the floor, and her heart ached with grief. What she'd do to have one more day with them all like that. To have *any* day with Ruby again. Swallowing hard, she cleared her throat.

The kettle clicked and as Sasha turned to make her tea, Lily pulled herself together. By the time Sasha joined her at the table, she was fully composed.

'We try to make the most of Evie being young, Rob and I,' Sasha told her. 'When he's able to be here anyway,' she added wryly.

'You're together?' Lily asked, surprised.

'Sort of,' Sasha replied. 'It's complicated. He can't be here very often, but when he can, if *we* can, we enjoy what we have.' She shrugged. 'It is what it is. It works for us.'

Lily nodded. She could understand that probably better than most people.

'If he's sent you, he must be preparing to come home,' she said, her tone half hopeful, half unsure as she waited for Lily to confirm.

Lily felt the heaviness in her chest deepen as she looked across at the woman whose life she was about to destroy. 'Not exactly,' she said reluctantly.

'Oh, OK. Then what's the message?' Sasha asked, disappointment and confusion both clear in her expression.

'Sasha...' Robert's beaten, bloody face flashed through Lily's mind, his one open eye holding hers as she squeezed the trigger. She took a deep breath and forced herself to deliver his words as she'd promised. 'Ahab gave up the spear.'

Her words hit Sasha like a speeding train. Her skin paled and her mouth fell slack, her eyebrows knitting high as pain flooded her face. She deflated, her shoulders dropping as she slumped back in the chair.

'No,' she uttered, the word barely more than a pained whisper. 'No, he can't be.' She blinked, shaking her head. 'You must have it wrong. He can't be dead. Not *Rob*. He's as close to invincible as a mortal man can get, for God's sake; you *must* be wrong.' Tears began falling down her face, her eyes begging Lily to say it was all just a mistake.

Lily shook her head. 'I'm sorry,' she whispered. And she

was. More than Sasha would ever know. 'All I can tell you is that he asked me to deliver that message when he knew he wasn't going to make it. You two were the last thing he thought of. He wanted to make sure you were OK. That you were safe.'

Sasha's tears fell faster and her face crumpled. She leaned onto the table and shook her head wordlessly, then suddenly she paused with a horrified frown of realisation. 'Wait – that's the one that...' She looked up at Lily with fearful eyes. 'We're in danger.'

Lily nodded sadly. 'Yeah. You need to follow whatever protocol Robert put in place and you *must not* leave a trail.'

'*Jesus Christ*,' Sasha wailed, quickly clamping a hand over her mouth and glancing at the ceiling as she realised she'd been louder than she'd intended. 'How much time have we got?' she asked, her tone suddenly detached and focused.

Lily recognised the sudden shift well. Having Evie to protect would see Sasha through this. There was nothing stronger in the world than that instinct.

'Some. Not a lot,' she replied.

Whilst she would make sure they were safely away before approaching Mani, Lily couldn't guarantee he wouldn't follow through on his threats about Evie before then. For all he knew right now, Robert had just disappeared. He could easily assume the man had backed out of their arrangement. The sooner these two were out of Mani's reach, the better.

'Hours? Minutes?' Sasha asked.

'You need to be gone today,' Lily told her. 'As soon as you can. Don't waste any time.'

Sasha stood up quickly and darted over to the hob. She unhooked the grill from underneath the extractor hood and reached up into it, grappling for a moment before pulling down a small drawstring bag. She tipped out two passports and a few rolls of cash. It wasn't a small amount, Lily noted, but neither was it enough to compensate for having to start over in a whole new life.

Standing, she picked up the holdall from the floor and placed it on the table, unzipping it and pulling it open for Sasha to see. 'This is for you,' she said.

Sasha's eyes widened in shock at the sight of the bag *full* of neatly stacked banknotes. She glanced at her small collection of rolls and then back to the bag. 'Why is there so much?' she asked.

'It was Robert's,' Lily said simply. 'He'd have wanted it to go to you.'

The lie was much easier than the truth. The truth being that she owed his family this, now that she'd taken him from them.

'Payment for a big job.' Lily zipped it back up. 'It's yours. It will help you start over.'

Sasha nodded, the tears still silently streaming down her face. 'Thank you for coming,' she managed.

Lily looked away, the guilt almost overwhelming as the woman thanked her. 'I wish I hadn't needed to,' she answered. 'Just get out of here, OK? And whatever you do, Sasha, don't ever look back.'

TWENTY-NINE

Lily circled around the fiery sparks being sprayed from an angle grinder cutting in part of a catwalk and made a beeline for what would soon become one of the offices. The deafening clatter of metal on metal and the screeches and groans of heavy machinery filled the air, making it almost impossible to think. She paused, stepping her black stilettos neatly together as she waited for a forklift to cross her path.

'Mrs Drew? Mrs Drew!' the foreman shouted out to her but she ignored him, carrying onwards and checking her watch.

'Mrs *Drew*,' he called again, frustrated. He ran to catch her up and fell into step beside her. 'Please, if you're going to be here, you all need to be wearing protective equipment,' he pleaded.

'Why?' she asked, not turning to look at him.

'If something happened…'

'If something happened to me because I didn't wear a hard hat and steel toecaps, then that would be my own fault and I'd deal with it as such,' she replied. 'It's no problem of yours.'

'But Mrs Drew, it's technically *illegal* for you to be in here without the correct PPE on,' he stressed, as if trying to scare her.

A small smile played on her lips. 'Is that so?' she asked, looking at him with amusement. 'I'll tell you what...' She stopped and turned to him as she reached the new office door. 'If you're worried about getting in trouble, talk to your boss. I'm sure he'll put your mind at ease.'

She entered the office and promptly closed the door. Everyone was already inside, waiting. Connor and Cillian stood together, Isla was perched on the edge of her new desk and Scarlet leaned against the side wall, arms folded, her expression subdued.

'You get told off too?' Cillian asked with a smirk.

'It's not his fault – he doesn't know who we are. Jimmy only hired him recently,' she replied, taking the seat behind her desk. 'Listen, I need to run through something with you quickly, before we head out to the forecourt.' She rubbed her forehead. 'Those bets that were being run on the fights. It was the Italians. Mani and Riccardo Romano.'

Cillian let out a low hiss of air from the back of his throat and closed his eyes, as if kicking himself that he hadn't figured it out. Connor shook his head with a grim expression.

'Why?' Scarlet asked, annoyance and curiosity all over her face. She still had her arms folded tightly, Lily noticed.

'Apparently he was more upset over our dealings with Luca and their fish 'n' chip vans than we'd realised,' she replied. 'It was clever really, to leave it this long. And to hire someone from the outside. We're lucky things have gone the way they have or this could have ended very differently.'

'Luck ain't got nothing to do with it,' Cillian scoffed.

'Luck had *everything* to do with it this time,' Lily countered in a hard tone. 'The outsider he hired wasn't just someone looking to make a quick buck; he was an ex-marine. In fact he was one of the most *highly* trained marines going. You ever heard of Commando 40?' Blank expressions stared back at her. 'No, you wouldn't have, I guess. They're the elite. The ones the government send in when situations look impossible.' She looked at Connor. 'I wouldn't have let you go after him if I'd known that before. You were lucky you caught him by surprise that night.'

'Jesus,' Cillian said, looking at his brother with a frown.

Connor shrugged his eyebrows. 'Explains a lot.'

'What we doing about Mani?' Scarlet asked.

'Nothing yet,' Lily replied. 'We need to wait a week or so, keep this under out hats for now.'

'Why?' Cillian demanded.

'Because Mani had threatened to send a posse to hurt his daughter and girlfriend if he didn't deliver. Hurt or kill, I'm not sure which. Either way, enough that he was scared. I've warned them to leave, checked there's no one watching the house. They're going today, but I want to put some space and time between them and Mani's rage, when he finds out that we know.'

'What about the bloke?' Cillian asked.

'He's out of the picture,' Lily replied.

Cillian read the underlying detail and nodded. 'OK.'

Lily's phone buzzed and she checked the screen. 'We need to go. Ray's here.'

She stood up and led the way back out of the office, skirting down the side of the building and heading out through a side door to the forecourt beyond. Two cars were parked up just outside the large empty hangar Lily had had built for their own trucks to park securely in. It was currently empty, but it wouldn't be for long. They were due to be delivered by the company who'd fitted them out over in Spain, any moment.

Glancing into the empty cars, Lily continued into the hangar through the wide-open sliding doors. Ray stood in the middle looking around at the structure with an impressed smile. Benny and two of his other men stood with him.

It was quieter in here, the echo of their footsteps audible

over the sound of the works being carried out in the main building behind, and Ray turned at the sound of their approach.

'This is bigger than I thought it would be,' he commented. 'How many trucks you got coming?'

'Five to start,' she replied, looking around at the space. 'But I've left space for mechanical work and to expand. No point having to rebuild it down the line.'

'True,' he said. 'When will they be here?' He looked out through the open front expectantly.

'Any minute now,' Lily told him, her gaze following his. 'They texted not long ago to say they were close.'

Ray was officially their first customer, on the illegal side of the business. They would be running both sides of the coin with this venture, much like most of their other set-ups. They would sell their truck space to genuine clients, transporting goods back and forth across the Channel, then once they had schedules in place, they then offered those same routes to their off-book clients. The ones who would transport their hot goods in the secret compartments built in underneath the cargo beds.

'Your guy all set for the first run?' Cillian asked, his tone a touch brusque as he addressed the biological father he'd never wanted.

'It ain't a first run for us,' Ray replied with an amused smile.

Benny grinned and the small action visibly got Cillian's back up.

'I'm aware of that,' he replied with an icy frown. 'But *we* ain't dealt with him before. We want to make sure our trucks aren't gonna get held up that end, leaving our routes fucked about.'

There was a shift in the atmosphere at the coldness in his tone. Benny's smile dropped to a frown and the two other men looked to Ray for his reaction.

Lily stepped forward and shot Cillian a look that told him to back off. 'There won't be an issue,' she said calmly. She turned to Ray. 'Will there, Ray?' She lifted an eyebrow in subtle challenge.

He looked at her and chuckled under his breath. 'Like I said, this ain't their first run.' His gaze moved to Cillian and rested there a moment. 'Who's going on the first run from your end?'

'I will be,' Cillian replied. He pulled a toothpick out of his pocket and put it between his teeth, walking off a few paces to the side.

The roar of large engines caught Lily's attention and she turned to see her trucks pulling into the depot and heading for the hangar. They dropped back to the side of the entrance, and she smiled widely, excited by the sight of the gleaming red and white vehicles as they pulled in, one by one.

This was it, Lily thought, a thrill bubbling up from her core. This was the start of an enterprise that was going to take them up to the next level. They wouldn't just be playing in their own pond anymore – they were going international.

THIRTY

Scarlet watched her aunt's face light up and felt a moment of irritation flash through her. Lily's words, the anger and disappointment in her expression as she'd dismissed her the night before, played on a loop through her mind. Pulling her gaze away, she tried to subdue her rising resentment, but it was hard. She'd earned her position in the firm, and after all she'd done to add to it, she deserved a little bit of slack on the rare occasion she made the wrong choice. They were *all* human at the end of the day. No one was perfect. Yes, this had cost them money and time, but it hadn't threatened their future. It hadn't compromised their freedom or their relationship with another firm. In the grand scheme of things – especially compared to some of the stunts the twins had pulled over the years – it wasn't *that* much of a cock-up.

Yet Lily had treated her as if she were no more than a petulant child playing gangster and that really stuck in her throat. Scarlet hadn't joined up last week; she'd been an active member of the firm for three years. She'd given up *everything* to be here, had been propelled head first into the darkest side of their world and she'd *still* come out fighting. She'd been the brain behind some of their most lucrative ideas – including this one. Yes, Lily had been the one to put things into action and oversee everything; it was her project, but she wouldn't have even thought about it if Scarlet hadn't put it to her and outlined all the potential benefits.

She took a deep breath in, keeping her expression serene as all this raged inside. The trucks parked up and the engines were cut. Benny sidled over and slipped his arm around her waist, gently squeezing her into his side for a moment as they walked across the floor towards the nearest one.

'You OK?' he asked.

She looked up and saw the concerned question in his eyes. She nodded, forcing a smile. 'Yeah. Just tired.'

'Hmm.' He gave her a suspicious look, then winked and walked back over to Ray.

The door of the nearest truck opened and the driver paused to stretch on the top step. His gaze swept the group and then lingered on Scarlet for a few moments. A strange smile curled up the sides of his mouth, and she felt a sharp tingle of warning ripple over her skin. He broke away and jumped down, and she frowned, her unease growing.

'Finn Logan,' Lily said, stepping forward. 'It's been a long time since I last saw your face around these parts.'

The man chuckled and his piercing eyes moved over them all once more. 'It has indeed. Ten long years, to be exact.'

Lily nodded, and Scarlet moved to get a better view of her face. Was her aunt picking up on the strange undercurrent here too? Something was off with this guy.

'London hasn't been quite the same without you, I must admit,' Lily said with a tilted half-smile.

Scarlet watched her. There was definitely some sort of history underpinning their conversation, but Lily still seemed perfectly at ease. She clearly hadn't caught that look in his eye, as Scarlet had.

She thought back to the car that had followed her the night before and the three notes, currently hidden in the lining of her handbag. Her stomach flipped. Was it *him*? It seemed absurd that someone she'd never met, living in another country, could somehow know what went down that night. Yet nothing that *wasn't* absurd made any sense, so perhaps she shouldn't be so quick to rule it out.

'I'd have to agree with Lil on that one,' Ray said, stepping forward. 'London definitely ain't been the same without you running round causing havoc.' He grinned.

Scarlet's hands suddenly felt like blocks of ice. She clasped them together in an attempt to heat them, but it didn't help. Her mind raced as she tried to connect the dots – connect *something*, but she found herself mentally floundering. Nothing made any sense. *Shit*, she thought, pushing her useless, frantic wonderings aside. She was stuck.

Subtly moving her gaze over the group, her heart sank. He could just be using this meeting to taunt her. But this could also be the perfect place and time to reveal her secret, if that's what he intended. They were all here. And there was nowhere for her to hide.

'Well, I didn't have much choice, did I?' Finn replied to her aunt.

Finn's words were now barbed with a bitter edge, and Scarlet glanced at him sharply. What was behind *that* comment? The feeling of foreboding grew.

'No,' Lily replied, seemingly not put off by this. 'You didn't. But you survived. More than that, Finn, you've *thrived* over there. I don't think you looked this healthy a decade ago.'

Scarlet caught Benny watching her with a curious frown and quickly fixed her expression. He knew something was up. Like most people in their game, he relied on his instincts and could pick up on the slightest change. But this was one thing she needed him not to pick up on. If she had any chance of walking out of this meeting with her secrets intact, she didn't need him watching her too closely.

Finn laughed at Lily's words. 'Alright, Lil, watch yourself – I'm a married man.'

'*You* watch yourself, you old git,' Ray told him with mock aggression, then stepped forward and slapped Finn on the back with a laugh and the easiness of old friends. 'Come on then – you gonna show us these modifications or what?'

As Scarlet tried to figure out the situation between them all, Finn's eyes slipped back to hers. Once more the odd smile flashed briefly across his face, and with it something else. Her stomach flipped and she bit her top lip, trying to contain her rising panic as he looked away. It was about to happen. Whatever he had planned, it was happening now. She'd caught the unspoken promise – an excitement and anticipation that had practically glowed in his eyes just now, telling her. Taunting her. The small hairs all over her body prickled her skin, rising in silent alarm.

'I certainly am, Raymond,' Finn said, the excitement now seeping into his tone too. His gaze lingered on Scarlet and his smile widened. 'Come.' He gestured for them to follow him to the back of the truck. 'Come see what you've bought, Lil. It's everything you've paid for – and a little more too. In fact, rather a *lot* more. Do you like surprises, Lil?'

For the first time since Finn arrived, Scarlet finally saw Lily's expression grow wary. She hesitated for a half step, her shoulders tensing.

'Not really, Finn,' Lily said carefully, her sharp gaze darting around, briefly meeting Scarlet's and then resting on Finn's back. Her brows knitted into a small frown. 'What kind of surprise are we talking?'

'The kind of surprise you couldn't have predicted in a

million years, I'd like to bet.' Pausing ahead of them as he reached the back of the truck, he grinned. 'Come and find out.' And then he disappeared.

* * *

Lily stared after him and felt a cold trickle of unease run down her spine. Finn had been gone a long time. Ten years he'd been in Spain. She'd kept tabs on them, kept up with what they were doing, and from what she'd seen, they'd carved out a pretty great life over there. But he still seemed to be bitter about the past. She glanced at Ray, and when he met her gaze, she saw the same thoughts registered there.

She pursed her lips as they continued towards the back of the truck, her footsteps a little slower now. More cautious. Surprises were rarely a good thing in their way of life. She'd learned that a long time ago.

Eying the soft wall of the truck, she began to calculate how many men could fit into the back of one of these. Of *five* of these. Too many, she immediately told herself, pushing the pointless calculations aside. Each cargo bed was about eight metres long by two metres wide. A small army could be hidden in there.

A movement caused her to look over to the entrance of the hangar. Two of the other drivers were rolling the wide metal doors together, shutting them all in. A frisson of alarm ran through her body, awakening her natural survival instinct. Switching immediately to defence, she mentally assessed the building. The fire exits were too far away. It was completely open. Once those doors were closed, they were sitting ducks with no advantage.

'Cillian, Connor,' she said in a low, urgent voice.

They looked over and she nodded towards the doors with an expression of warning. They immediately peeled off towards the men and called out, but it was too late. The doors came to a close with a dull clang, and as the bar locked in, she felt two hands wrap around her upper arms from behind.

She jumped and swore under her breath. 'Jesus, Ray,' she said in a low tone of annoyance.

'What's the matter?' he murmured quietly, moving to stand beside her. 'Why you slowing up?' He eyed the door as the twins reached the two men keeping it shut. 'Surely you ain't getting jumpy? It's *Finn*. He can't open up the back with the hangar open for any Joe Blow to have a gander. What's the matter with you?' He frowned down at her.

'I don't know,' she replied quietly. 'But something's off. There's something else going on here.'

'Yeah, well, I agree with you there.' Ray glanced back over his shoulder. 'But it ain't with Finn.'

'What?' Lily looked up at him confused.

Ray tipped his head back towards Scarlet.

'Ah.' She pursed her lips. 'Don't worry about that. Family tiff.'

Ray shrugged as if to say it was none of his business, then gave her some space as they reached the end of the truck.

Lily's heart thumped against the wall of her chest as she slowed to a pause. Running a hand back and forth across her chin, trying to shake off the feeling of trepidation, she turned to face whatever this surprise was, at the same time as Ray.

There was no small army staring back at her. Not that she'd ever really expected there to be. Only Finn, with his bright blue eyes boring into hers. His face lit up with a very strange smile, but he didn't say anything for a moment, and her unease grew.

'Finn, what's going on?' she snapped.

'It was tough on us, you know,' he said, leaning against the side of the empty truck, looking down at her. 'Having our whole lives ripped out at the root, ten years ago.'

'Yet you've made an even better one,' Ray said, his voice

level as he eyed Finn a little harder now. 'In a way maybe it was meant to be. Wouldn't you say?'

'*Meant to be*? Ha!' Finn's expression turned bitter as he glared back at them both. 'We had a successful business, family homes, friends, the kids had good schools, we ruled turf that we'd *earned*, fair and square, here in the East End.'

Lily held his gaze. 'Well, that turf belongs to *us* now,' she said quietly. 'It's no longer under the rule of people who had no true rights to it in the first place.'

She lifted her chin proudly and they stared at each other for a long few moments. The silence stretched and became heavy. Lily's stare grew harder as she tried to work out where this was all going.

Slowly he stepped forward until he was right at the edge of the truck bed, looking down at her with an unreadable expression. 'You're right,' he said. 'It *is* yours now. And all three of us are forever grateful to you for that.'

Suddenly he grinned, the action shattering the earlier tension, and Lily smiled back, glad to see that her friend was back in the room.

'I'd have gladly handed it back to you, if they hadn't forced you to stay away,' she said, looking back over the years to the fierce battle she'd fought with the Italians over the Logan brothers' turf.

Mani had been as underhand back then as he was today, when it came to getting what he wanted. The Logan brothers hadn't been a large firm. Their territory was small, but their business was lucrative and one day Mani had decided he wanted it for himself. He'd played dirty, backing them into a corner and leaving them with no choice but to flee, if they valued their freedom.

Furious, Lily had fought back on their behalf. Ray had jumped in too, and together they'd pushed Mani out, warning him never to return or try to take over there again. They'd tried to get Finn and his brothers back, but Mani, in his bitterness, had made it clear that his threat still stood. He may not have been able to get what he wanted, but he'd promised that if they returned, he'd still ruin them. Left with no choice but to move on in Spain, the brothers had handed over the area to Lily, glad to at least see it in the hands of a friend rather than the clutches of an enemy.

'Why you bringing this up now anyway?' Lily asked.

'Because, old friend…' Finn said with a small private smile as he turned to start unlocking the false floor. 'We intend to repay a few debts on that front. Both to Mani, and to you.' The first hidden lock came loose and he pulled up a board.

Lily frowned. 'What do you mean?'

'Oh, in very different ways of course.'

The second lock clicked open and he looked back at her. Or rather past her, towards someone behind. Lily's frown deepened.

'Mani's gonna get what he's owed soon. And as for you. Well, obviously we owe you a lot more than this, but as a start, I thought I'd bring you a little present.'

The second board came up and Lily peered at what she could see of the door to the hidden compartment underneath. What the *hell* was in there?

'Something you never thought you'd see again.' Finn's eyes gleamed. 'Something Scarlet certainly never thought you'd see again.'

'*What?*' Lily asked, totally confused.

'Wait,' Scarlet said suddenly from behind her, panic clear in her tone. 'What are you doing?'

Lily turned to look at her, and her eyes narrowed. Scarlet was afraid. A sight none of them were particularly used to seeing. What did she have to be afraid of here?

'Giving you something you deserve, young lady,' Finn replied, grabbing the handle.

He pulled it to the side and yanked up the door. Scarlet stepped back two paces, breaking apart from the group as Connor and Cillian rejoined them.

'What's going on?' Cillian asked with a frown, looking from Scarlet, to Finn, to her.

'I don't know...' Lily said slowly, watching Scarlet closely.

'Scarlet?' Benny asked, moving towards her.

'Benny...' She backed up another step and then suddenly trailed off, her jaw dropping and her eyes widening.

Lily blinked, truly concerned now as her niece's pale face seemed to completely lose what little colour she naturally possessed. Scarlet swayed slightly and she took a step towards her, wondering if she was about to faint.

'Scarlet?' She reached out to her.

'Scarlet.' The quiet word was heavy with emotion, and it came from behind her, from inside the truck, but the voice wasn't Finn's.

Lily paused, her hand still mid-air, as the smooth baritone jogged a memory long since filed away. Scarlet's eyes lit up with a mixture of confusion and joy and fear, and Lily knew, even before she said his name, exactly who it was.

'John?' she whispered, every emotion poured into that one shaky word.

Lily turned, her eyes widening as they rested on the man they'd sent out of the country with a new identity nearly two years before. The man Scarlet had loved with all her heart. The man she still did, in the most private depths of her soul. How had this happened? Why was he here?

'Yeah,' he said, stepping forward into the light, his movements stiff after his time in the compartment. 'Surprise,' he said softly.

John's bright-green eyes drank Scarlet in, the love they'd

shared still burning brightly for all to see, and Lily's insides suddenly clenched in alarm as she remembered who else was here, witnessing this. Her eyes flew to Benny. His face had clouded over and his jaw clenched as he looked from one to the other. Lily looked back at Scarlet but she was still in shock.

Ray turned to face Benny, blocking his view and placing a hand on his arm. 'Listen, we should...'

Benny shook off his hand, stepping back, quiet anger radiating from every part of his body. 'No need for that, Ray,' he said, a bitter look on his face as he stared over Ray's shoulder towards his girlfriend. 'I'm out of here.'

His voice seemed to break Scarlet out of her state of shock and she turned towards him. 'Wait, Benny...'

'Nah, we're good,' he said, his tone hard and aggressive. 'It's all good.' He shook his head and glared at her. 'You've been acting tense for *days* and I've been wondering why, but now I *see*,' he said accusingly. 'Your *boyfriend* was en route.'

'No, Benny, it's not how you think,' Scarlet argued with a small frown. 'I had no—'

'Don't sweat it,' Benny insisted, his raised voice booming over hers. He backed away, his eyes burning into hers with an accusation of betrayal. 'You enjoy your *boy*, Scarlet Drew.' He paused, his expression contorting as he fought to control it. 'But I ain't staying to watch.' He turned away and marched out of the building.

'Benny!' Scarlet exclaimed.

But he didn't turn around. She stared after him worriedly, then glanced back at John. Her eyes darted back and forth, several times, and Lily could see how torn she was. But as Benny disappeared through the far fire exit, Scarlet remained where she was, an unconscious choice clearly made. She looked back to John, and as Lily watched their eyes connect, a shiver ran through her body.

Lily had no ill feeling towards John – he was a good man.

They'd had more than one reason to be thankful for him, in the past – but there was a reason they'd put him on that boat, two years before. And his presence back in their lives could only bring one thing. Trouble.

THIRTY-ONE

Scarlet stood outside the front of the safe house, her eyes trained on the far end of the long road. She was still in shock, still wondering if she was stuck in some twisted dream – but if she was, it was certainly a convincing one. John was *here*. In London. In her life. And she still had no idea how or why.

They hadn't talked yet. It had all been so sudden and she'd still been lost for words when Lily had taken control of the situation. Her aunt had greeted John and carried the expected small talk. Finn had assured her that John would stay out of the public eye while he was here, then claimed he hadn't been able to resist bringing him as a present for Scarlet.

This had been a confusing statement for them all. None of them understood yet how these people knew John and their history. John would stay in the hangar, he told them. Apparently he had all he needed in the secret truck compartment.

Lily had immediately offered to put John up somewhere more comfortable, and Scarlet was grateful to her for that. Not one to waste time, Lily had ordered the twins to escort everyone to their pub, then she'd asked John to follow her to her car. Scarlet had been about to argue, but Lily had cut her off, instructing her quietly to go ahead and buy all the essentials John would need and to meet her at the safe house. She'd felt her stomach pull into a knot of anxiety at the thought of walking away from him already, but she'd also realised it would be sensible to collect her thoughts before jumping straight into things. And so she'd simply nodded and left.

But now she was here, and Lily and John were nowhere to be seen. Where were they? Her anxiety was now gnawing through the bars of the cage she was trying so hard to contain it in. John was a fugitive. Yes, it had been two years, but his face was on every law enforcement system in the country. Facial recognition cameras were everywhere.

A sinking feeling suddenly filled her stomach and she paused her pacing, looking back over her shoulder to the end of the road again with fear in her grey-blue eyes. What if Lily had already sent him back? John was a threat. What if her aunt had sent her off to the shops to distract her, while she sorted out a way to get him back out of the country again? She couldn't cope with getting this close to John again, only to have him ripped away before she could even talk to him. She just *couldn't*.

As her thoughts spiralled, a black Mercedes suddenly pulled into the road and she heaved a deep sigh of relief.

'Thank God,' she muttered to herself.

The car stopped on the other side of the line of parked cars, and Scarlet's eyes met her aunt's through the passenger window. The back door opened and John stepped out with his hoodie pulled down as far as it could go over his face and sunglasses hiding his eyes. He kept his head down as he walked to the pavement and Scarlet moved to the car.

The window glided down and Lily handed her a set of keys. 'Here,' she said, glancing through the rear-view mirror. 'Take the spare off for John and keep the main set so you can come and go. He can stay here for now until...' She trailed off and closed her mouth.

Scarlet swallowed, the pain already clutching at her core. John would be leaving again, at some point. This was temporary. She nodded.

'I've given him a burner – take the number. He shouldn't leave the house unless it's absolutely necessary,' Lily warned. She lingered, looking at Scarlet with concern.

'It's fine,' Scarlet lied, seeing the unspoken words in her aunt's eyes. 'I'm fine. Don't worry.'

'OK.' Lily didn't sound convinced, but they both knew this wasn't the time or place to discuss it all. 'Scar, be careful what you say to Benny.'

Scarlet frowned. 'I know. I'll deal with it.'

She'd tried to call Benny on the way over here, several times, but he wasn't answering.

'What does he know about John?' Lily asked.

'He knows I loved him. That John is an ex who got into some trouble here and had to leave the country. He assumed he was one of us and I didn't correct him. I didn't lie; I just said I couldn't elaborate.'

Lily nodded. 'So he doesn't know he was one of them?'

'No,' Scarlet replied, shaking her head. 'He knows someone helped me off that charge, but he thinks it was a payroll plod. He doesn't know they're the same person.'

'Good. Keep it that way,' Lily ordered.

Scarlet felt the resentment flare up once more as she stared back at her aunt. 'I don't need to be told that, Lil,' she snapped coldly. 'I'm not an idiot.'

Lily's expression changed instantly to one that was a clear reminder of who Scarlet was talking to. Biting her tongue, Scarlet stepped back and looked away.

'You have a few hours before you're needed,' Lily said, her tone a touch sharp but otherwise ignoring Scarlet's response. 'Spend them wisely and then come back with your head in the game.'

The window closed and Lily drove off. Scarlet stared after her feeling angry and irritated. She needed to confront her aunt about the night before. She'd planned to do so today, but that had been before all this had happened. Turning back to the house, she pushed Lily from her mind and looked back to John.

'Come on,' she said, glancing down the street anxiously. 'Let's get you inside.'

Twenty minutes later, Scarlet waited in the lounge, anxiously chewing the end of one long red fingernail. She walked to the window and moved the closed curtains with her finger, looking furtively up and down the street. There was no one there of course. She turned away and walked around the room, waiting for John to appear after freshening up. She'd heard the shower turn off about five minutes before.

Reaching the mirror, she assessed her appearance one more time. Her black knee-length dress was flattering, her long raven hair hung soft and sleek around her shoulders, and her carefully applied make-up was still intact. She eyed her face, wondering if he'd find her changed. Wondering if he'd still find her attractive or see the extra hardness her life had added these past two years. Guilt set in then. She shouldn't care what he thought of her appearance – she was with Benny. Yet somehow she still did.

She heard the soft thuds of footfall on the stairs and quickly moved away from the mirror. The door opened and John entered wearing the white T-shirt and grey tracksuit bottoms she'd hurriedly bought from the supermarket just an hour before.

As she drank in the sight of him properly, she felt her heart lift and brighten, as though it was the sun rising into the sky. The smile that warmed her face refused to be dampened, despite her best efforts. And John stilled, stopping just inside the door, his dark hair tousled and wet from the shower, dripping onto his neck, as he stared back with a soft smile that said so much more than words ever could.

His green eyes stared piercingly into hers and something between them connected instantly, as though they'd never been apart. The connection pulled at her, like it was pulling her soul back home. As if it was reviving an energy she'd long forgotten had died. And even though she knew that allowing herself this moment was going to kill her again at some point, she let that warm glow of happiness and completion flow through every cell in her body anyway.

Scarlet could have stayed right there across the room from John for eternity. Not moving, not speaking, just standing there. Just *being*. But as she caressed his face with her eyes, she suddenly noticed a gash on the side of his forehead, running back into his hairline. Concern jolted through her, breaking her trance.

'Oh God, you're hurt!' She stepped forward. 'What happened?'

As she moved closer, she reached up towards it, but he grasped her hand.

'It's nothing,' he said. 'Honestly, it's...'

Their eyes met again and he trailed off. The touch of his hand on hers sent waves of electricity up her arm, and her heart ached with the familiarity of it, even after all this time.

'It was just a bumpy stretch of road. Somewhere around Montpellier, I think. I fell asleep, hadn't strapped in properly.'

He softly laughed the last few words, but his smile suddenly swam before her as Scarlet's eyes filled with tears. 'I'm so sorry,' she said, the words barely audible.

'*What?*' He frowned and pulled her to him, wrapping his arms around her tightly. 'No. *No*, Scarlet. Don't do that.' He kissed the top of her head as she sobbed into his chest, letting her guard down for the first time in years. 'Please don't do that. This isn't your fault. *None* of it is.'

'It is,' she argued through her tears. 'Everything you've been through, everything you've lost, is because of me. Oh *God*, John...'

'Shh-shh-shh, stop. Please, Scarlet.'

She breathed in the smell of his skin, still somehow the same, despite the years apart, the miles he'd travelled and the cheap supermarket shower gel he'd just used. She squeezed her eyes closed and controlled her breathing, and after a while he gently released her.

Scarlet stepped back and pulled herself up straight, turning away to the mirror. Mascara ringed her eyes and she smoothed this away with her fingers before turning back to John. He watched her with so much love and pity that she almost cried again, but she managed to hold it together.

'It's so good to see you,' she said simply.

He nodded and smiled sadly. 'How are you?' he asked.

Scarlet opened her mouth to tell him she was fine, to brush over the truth. But then she hesitated. She'd felt so alone, so isolated lately, holding all these secrets – carrying her burdens alone. John was the one person on earth who she could be fully truthful with. Who she could trust with anything, and know without question could handle it and would have her back.

'Things are a bit shit, to be honest,' she admitted with a half-hearted smile. 'And I'll tell you about that. But first I want to know how you're here. How did you end up with the *Logans*? How long are you staying? Is your life... is it good? Are you OK?' There were so many other questions she wanted to ask, but she paused there, giving him time to answer those first. She sat down on one of the two wide sofas.

John rubbed his forehead and pushed his hand back through his wet hair, then joined her, sitting the opposite end and twisting round to face her. 'That night we said goodbye... The boat hit the coast of Spain in the early hours. It was this little cove, middle of nowhere. The guy I'd gone with gave me a letter from the Tylers, with checkpoints and dates to turn up on. It said to keep going until someone met me with a package, which I did.'

He went quiet and Scarlet saw a small muscle in his cheek working back and forth.

'It was a new ID. A driving licence. I bought a cheap car and just started driving. I went to France for a bit and across to northern Italy. I found a couple of jobs that kept me going, waiting and bartending, but nothing long term. The problem was, I could only work cash in hand. I didn't have the credentials to go on the system. And I didn't want to use the money your aunt gave me until I could invest it into something that would provide an ongoing income. After a while, I found a place, this run-down building on a cliff overlooking the sea. It needed a lot of work, but it was cheap. I planned to buy it and open up a wine bar and lunch spot. Nothing fancy, simple but elegant. Light bites, local wine and a great view.' His green eyes turned wistful.

'What stopped you?' she asked, frowning.

'I had the money to buy it – enough to do the work and stock it too, if I was careful. But to buy property in Italy you need an Italian tax code and residence permit. And obviously I had neither.' John looked away. 'I'd been in the town a few months and had become friendly with a local café owner. They don't really have pubs there, just cafés with a bar that stay open late. I spent a lot of evenings there and it was often quiet, so we'd talk. He did most of the talking. I kept my story vague. Gave my fake name and claimed to be travelling around until I found somewhere I wanted to stay.'

Scarlet's heart ached as she thought about how lonely John must have been. Away from everyone he ever knew and loved, unable to tell any new people who he really was.

'We became friends. We'd drink together, talk about his life, my fake life. I told him about this place and he acted pleased for me. But I couldn't find a way around the laws. One day he asked me why I hadn't gone ahead.' John scratched his neck and shook his head with a tight expression. 'I didn't tell him, but I confided that I wasn't able to get a bank account or have my name on the papers. It was a risk even telling him that much, but I'd watched Giovanni do a few dodgy deals in the café before, so I knew he wasn't totally straight himself. My Italian is better than I'd let on, so he'd talked freely without realising I was listening. I was out of options, so I asked him whether he knew a way I could get around it. He offered to partner up with me. Told me if I fronted the cash and agreed on a fifty-fifty split, he'd put his name to it and do the payments through his accounts. It was daylight robbery, but what choice did I have? So I agreed. But that night I had second thoughts. It left me too vulnerable. I knew him better than anyone else, but still not well enough to put my whole future into his hands. I told him the next day that I didn't want to go ahead. He seemed pissed but then dropped it and that was that. The next night, while I was at the café drinking and talking with him, my room was broken into and the bag with all the money was taken.'

'*What?*' Scarlet exclaimed, covering her mouth with her hand.

John shrugged, looking tired now. 'There was nothing I could do. I confronted him and he claimed ignorance, then challenged me to go to the police. Which we both knew I couldn't do.' He sighed. 'I had a small stash that I kept elsewhere, just in case. I took that, packed up and drove back to Spain. After the money had gone, my options were limited to two. Either keep working crappy cash-in-hand jobs or embrace this life and make the best of it.'

He eyed her now. 'Back in my days on the force, a couple of my cases had crossed over into Spain and were taken over by

Interpol. They were linked to the organised crime network, so I'd studied the connections between firms and I still remembered a couple with friendly links to you.' He hesitated, seeing her eyebrows shoot up. 'Don't be surprised. They may not have the information to put you away, but they keep track of every connection they see.'

Scarlet tilted her head. 'I guess we should expect that. Anyway, go on,' she urged.

'Well, it was a long shot, but I figured if I found the right person and pled my case, I could maybe get a job. I have *some* skills, and if nothing else, I could at least prove myself loyal. I spent some time studying them first, but eventually I approached Finn, a couple of months ago. From what I gather, he checked me out with the Tylers, and when that came back OK, he told me I was in. Said he'd do anything for your aunt.'

'I wonder why the Tylers didn't tell us,' Scarlet said with a small frown.

John shrugged. 'I don't know. I *do* know that when your aunt contacted Finn a few weeks later about fitting the trucks, he decided to bring me along as a surprise. And I have to admit, I wasn't exactly sad at the prospect.' His face softened. 'In fact, it's all that's kept me going.'

Scarlet's heart leaped in her chest. She swallowed, trying to keep her thoughts on track. 'How long are you here for?' she asked.

John's eyes dropped from hers momentarily, but she still saw the regret. 'Only as long as they're here. A few days, a week... I'm not sure exactly.'

'Oh,' she replied simply.

'I'm sorry,' John said softly. 'I know this is hard. And maybe it was selfish, but I couldn't ignore this opportunity to see you just one more time.'

Scarlet shook her head. 'Don't apologise. I'd have done the same. Christ...' She let out a swift breath and glanced away. 'I'd have done *anything* to see you again. To see you're safe and OK and well. I had no idea you were technically so close.' There was a short silence as they looked at each other, taking in every detail.

'Have you met anyone?' Scarlet asked. The question seemed to jump out of her mouth before she had a chance to decide if she really wanted to know the answer.

'No,' John replied. 'I'm guessing that, er, well... the guy at the depot?'

Scarlet felt her cheeks warm with guilt, even though she knew the feeling was misplaced. 'Yes,' she said, looking down. 'Yeah, we um... just these last few months.'

It felt wrong, telling him this. Like it was a betrayal, after all he'd sacrificed for her. He'd lost everything and here she was with her life intact, moving on with the next guy.

'Don't,' John said.

She looked up questioningly.

'You sound like you feel guilty, but you shouldn't. It's been over a year and a half.' He ran his hand back through his dark hair again. 'I'll always love you, Scarlet. You may feel the same, I don't know, but what happened *happened*. We can't change that. This isn't the life I'd have chosen, but I wouldn't take back what we had. And I don't regret it. You know, love – *real* love – it...' He paused and exhaled heavily. 'I just want you to be safe and happy. Even if I don't get to be the one by your side. That's what matters to me.'

Scarlet's eyes filled with tears. 'I *do* feel the same. I've never stopped loving you,' she said shakily. 'And I will always feel guilty that you had to sacrifice so much. No matter what you say, that's never going to fade.' She sniffed and composed herself. 'I'm glad to hear you're with this firm. I don't know them; I actually thought that Finn was... Well, that doesn't matter. But I can tell my aunt holds them in high esteem. Ray too. That's a good sign. And now we know where you are, you can contact us. Anything you need is yours. Always.'

John nodded. 'I know. I'm OK though, really. Finn's a good guy. Well, if you're not looking at it from a legal viewpoint.' He grinned.

Scarlet made a short sound of amusement.

John studied her face. 'What were you about to say about Finn? You thought he was what?'

'I need to tell you something,' she said heavily. 'Something I haven't been able to tell anyone else. Not even my family. *Especially* my family.'

John sat upright, frowning deeply now. 'What is it? You can tell me anything.'

'I know,' Scarlet replied, meeting his gaze. 'It's a long story. A long nightmare really. And, as with so many of my nightmares, this one starts with Ruby...'

THIRTY-TWO

'OK, press it... *Now*.'

Cillian pressed the button and the cogs of Connor's home-made pulley contraption began to whirr, pulling the carefully placed strings in opposite directions. There was a moment of tension as they pulled taut and the cogs slowed, then suddenly the connection snapped apart and the last of the string wound around the cogs, bringing the action to a stop.

'Yes!' Connor threw his fists into the air in triumph.

'Bloody perfect,' Cillian replied. 'We'll run it a few more times with some extra resistance, just in case I've underestimated it, then we just need to sort out the timer.'

'I've got that.' Connor reached into a bag beside him and pulled something out. 'It's a mechanical timer. These are hours...' He pointed to the small dial. 'Once it's attached, I'll set it up so that it will run for four hours, then the handle will connect two wires to start the pulley.'

Cillian peered down at it. 'Genius. What will I need to do?'

'Nothing,' Connor replied. 'I'll set it up so all you have to do is attach it and pull out a stopper. Won't take longer than five seconds.'

'You're a legend,' Cillian declared.

They both turned at the sound of the front door opening. A second later, their mother and Isla marched into the room, arms full of various shopping bags.

'What's all that?' Cillian asked as they dumped the lot on the sofa on the opposite side of the coffee table they were currently testing Connor's creation on.

'The disguises,' Lily replied, glancing at the mess on her lounge table as she opened the first bag. 'Here.' She threw something to Isla.

'Thanks.' Isla took two other bags and then disappeared.

'Is that the thing to disconnect the security?' Lily asked, pulling a short black bobbed wig from another bag. She moved to a mirror and put it on, tucking her wild mane of tight blonde curls underneath with difficulty.

'Yeah, just testing it out,' Connor replied.

Lily turned and wiggled her eyebrows exaggeratedly. 'What do you think?'

'Eugh, no. Stick to blonde,' Cillian replied, shaking his head. 'You look bloody awful.'

Connor had to agree. Black straight hair didn't suit their mother in the slightest. He shook his head and pulled a face to match his brother's.

'Good,' Lily responded in a practical tone. 'It will throw them off completely then.'

Alone with his mother and brother, Ray's words suddenly came back to Connor unbidden, and he pushed them away, annoyed. *Fucking Ray*, he thought bitterly. The man was messing with his mind, screwing up perfectly normal moments for him. He frowned down at the mechanical timer in his hand, turning it over and over.

'What's up?' Cillian asked, noticing. 'You found a problem?'

Lily's attention was caught by this and she swivelled back around to look at him.

'No,' Connor replied. 'Just thinking about what I need to do, that's all.'

Lily nodded, satisfied, and took one last look in the mirror before ripping the wig off and throwing it back in the bag.

'Good stuff. I need a Jimmy Riddle – back in a sec.' Cillian pushed up off the sofa next to him and disappeared out into the hallway.

'You boys eaten?' Lily asked, looking at him with a hopeful expression.

'Nah,' Connor lied. 'We're starving.'

He and Cillian had made the joint decision years before to never admit they didn't need feeding when their mother asked. It was easier just to eat twice than to watch the disappointment on her face when she felt unneeded.

'Oh good,' she replied brightly, immediately making a beeline for the kitchen. 'I'll make us some food.'

The corner of Connor's mouth turned up in a fond smile as she disappeared, and he focused back in on his creation. As he leaned forward over the coffee table, Cillian's phone buzzed next to him. The screen lit up and, seeing Connor's identical face, it unlocked, opening the contents of the message on the phone's screen.

Connor's gaze slipped naturally towards the light and he immediately looked away, but as he registered the words on the screen, his eyes shot back. It was from some woman called Tiff. He read it properly this time and frowned.

I'll be free around 5.30. Let me know if you can come over then, if you can get away without Billie catching on.

Connor's jaw dropped. He glanced at the open double

doors into the hallway, half tempted to open the conversation. He thought Cillian loved Billie. As in *loved* loved Billie. As in would never cheat on her. And the realisation that this wasn't the case both shocked and saddened him, but what felt even worse was the fact his brother was clearly having an affair, and he hadn't confided in *him*. For their entire life they had shared every secret, every thought. So to find out Cillian was hiding something so huge from him felt like a physical blow to the chest.

As he reeled, Cillian sauntered back in, as though nothing was wrong. Connor quickly rubbed his eyes, faking a yawn to hide whatever his face was saying.

'Why you so tired?' Cillian asked, sitting down.

'Didn't get much sleep last night,' Connor muttered.

'Oh yeah?' Cillian replied with a cheeky grin. 'What's her name then?'

'There ain't any bird,' Connor replied, his tone sharper than he'd intended.

'Oh, come on,' Cillian cajoled, misreading his brother. 'Don't keep it to yourself – give me the juicy details! I'm off the market, remember? I need to live vicariously through you now.'

'Yeah, I know you do...' *You lying bastard*, he added mentally. 'But there really ain't anyone.'

Cillian picked up his phone and read the message on the screen, tilting his phone slightly so that Connor couldn't see it.

Connor watched the small smile play on his brother's lips as he tapped out a response.

Isla walked in and cleared her throat.

Glancing over at her, Connor's eyebrows shot up. She was wearing a black bomber jacket that looked older than she was, some oversized tracksuit bottoms and a pair of trainers. Her blonde hair was now covered by a long dark-red wig with a thick fringe, oversized gold hoops poked out from the sides, and the drastic smokey-eyed make-up had totally transformed her face. She twirled and then shot a smile at Connor.

'I'm heading out to hang around that street for a bit. Or rather *Starla* is. What do you think, Connor?' she asked with a giggle. 'Fit or what?'

Connor laughed. 'Well, it's certainly a good disguise. Wouldn't say fit though. The real Isla's got much more going for her than this Starla bird.'

'Oh.' Isla's cheeks flushed pink. 'Thanks, Connor.'

'No worries.'

He looked back to the timer, his mind still on Cillian's secret. He barely registered Isla leaving the room until Cillian nudged him.

'Hey, what you doing with that poor girl?' he asked.

'What?' Connor asked, confused.

Cillian rolled his eyes. 'For the love of God, Connor, surely you know she's got a huge crush on you?'

'What, *Isla*?' Connor asked, totally surprised.

'You really are as blind as a bat,' Cillian replied. 'She follows you round with puppy-dog eyes basically *begging* you to notice her. I can't believe you don't see it.'

'Stop it,' Connor replied, shoulder barging him. 'She ain't into me. I'd have noticed.'

'Yeah? OK. If you say so. I mean, you didn't notice when she styled her hair like Sandra's – the girl *you* follow round with puppy-dog eyes – or when she started doing her make-up the same way too. But yeah, I'm sure you'd have noticed if she liked you,' Cillian said, sarcastically.

Well I noticed when you hid a new fucking bird from me, you twat. Connor bit his lip as the sharp retort hovered on his tongue and there was a short silence.

'Hey, um, do me a favour, will ya?' Cillian asked suddenly. 'If Billie asks, can you tell her I was with you later this afternoon? Till about sevenish.'

Connor tensed. ''Course,' he said levelly. 'Where are you really?'

Lily passed the open doorway, glancing in with a smile before disappearing again.

'Ahh, I've just got some shopping to do. Getting something for her, but I want it to be a surprise.'

Yeah, I'll bet you do, Connor thought darkly.

'Yeah?' He turned to look at his brother challengingly. 'I actually need some more shirts. Let's go together.'

Cillian avoided his gaze. 'I'm not really going anywhere where they'll have shirts. Let's do that another time though, yeah?'

Connor nodded, turning away. 'Yeah, let's do that,' he replied flatly.

'Listen, while we're on our own...' Cillian turned his body towards Connor and leaned in. 'What do you make of John showing up like that?'

'What do you mean?'

'Do you think Scarlet knew?' Cillian's face grew troubled.

'No, that was genuine surprise,' Connor said. 'Though she was being pretty weird beforehand.'

'Yeah, I noticed that,' Cillian murmured. 'Something's really not right there. I can feel it. And we need to figure out what.'

Connor nodded. Scarlet *had* been acting suspiciously lately and even though she had seemed surprised, John turning up like this really was very odd timing.

'I'll keep watch on her, follow her about,' he offered. 'You're tied up with this job, but I have more time.'

'Good idea,' Cillian replied. 'I know she's family, but this is still business. We can't afford to be in the dark with each other here.'

'Yeah,' Connor said heavily, turning away with a grim expression. 'I completely agree.'

THIRTY-THREE

Scarlet pulled up in the small industrial estate just down the road from the scrapyard. It was early, not even eight o'clock. None of the small businesses were open yet, not even the scrapyard. Maybe by being here this early she'd catch whoever had been following her arriving. It still wouldn't give her an edge exactly, but at least she wouldn't be walking in blind.

She caught a movement in her peripheral vision and turned to see Chain walking out of the shadows of a nearby alley. He opened the passenger door and slipped into the seat beside her. She wasn't entirely surprised to see him here already. As he closed the door, she glanced at him, taking in his dark outfit and low-fronted cap. His thick gold chain still hung over his T-shirt, visible through the partly open zip of his thickly padded black puffer jacket.

Chain caught her glance, a smile curling up one side of his mouth as he looked back at her, a teasing glint in his dark-brown eyes. 'You checking me out, Scarlet Drew?' He rolled her name over his tongue, drawing the syllables out with the melodic undertones of the Caribbean roots that shone through his East End accent.

A corner of Scarlet's mouth hitched in amusement. 'You wish,' she retorted. She pulled one of the two takeaway coffees out of the cup holders between them and passed it to him.

'Mm.' Chain settled back in his seat, following her gaze to the front of the scrapyard. 'Maybe I do,' he mused.

They sat in companionable silence for a few moments, and Scarlet's face returned to the troubled expression she'd been wearing all morning.

'How long have you been here?' she asked.

'An hour or so,' he replied. 'No one's turned up. Not even the old man who runs the place.'

'He'll be here in a minute to open up. He sticks to his routine like clockwork,' Scarlet replied.

She picked up her coffee and forced herself to take a sip. She'd tossed and turned all night, worrying about what today would bring. Worrying about whether asking Chain to join her was a sensible idea or just a fast-track route to blowing this all up in her own face. The note sender had told her to come alone after all. But there was safety in numbers. Even a number as small as two.

'How's Tash?' Scarlet asked, trying to distract herself from her useless circling thoughts.

Chain made a dismissive sound. 'Gone,' he said firmly. 'Too much hassle. And far too self-important for a pretty little nobody off the estate. Girl acted like she thought she was the Queen of Sheba.'

Scarlet pulled a face of disapproval. 'Of all the things I'd pin on you, Chain, being the guy who wants to knock a girl for having confidence wasn't one of them. Pretty misogynistic really.'

'What did you say?' Chain turned and gave her a hard stare.

Scarlet raised her eyebrows and held it, challengingly. 'I said that's pretty misogynistic.'

There was a long, taut silence, then suddenly Chain nodded, his expression morphing to one of amusement.

'Those are fighting words, Drew. But I'll hear them from *you*,' he said. 'Because you've earned the right. Confidence wasn't the problem. I *like* feisty women. I'm no hater. But I ain't no gentleman either.' He shifted in his seat. 'I ain't gonna pretend she's a fucking princess and hang off her every word when she's just another lazy bitch looking for a free ride. I judge *all* people on the same three things. Whether they hustle in this life, whether they're smart and whether they're loyal. That's it. Now, she was hot. Might have even been loyal.' He shrugged. 'But she was stupid and lazy, and I don't have any respect for that.' He shook his head.

'Fair enough,' Scarlet replied.

'And don't get me wrong, it ain't about the money. My mum raised me and my brother alone, taking in other people's washing and ironing, and doing night shifts cleaning a factory, to keep us warm, clothed and fed. She never had two pennies to rub together by the end of each month, but we never went without. I have more respect for her than anyone. It ain't about the money,' he repeated quietly. 'It's about the mindset.'

Scarlet nodded. She could understand that.

'I didn't know you had a brother,' she remarked, taking another sip of her coffee.

'Yeah, well...' Chain's tone and expression darkened. 'Some things are best left unknown.'

Scarlet frowned at the odd remark, but she held her tongue. It was clearly a touchy subject.

Chain put his coffee down and rubbed his palms together slowly as he stared at the scrapyard. Alan had just ambled into view and was now unlocking the gates. The guard dogs inside jumped and barked in greeting.

'How much of a problem is *he* going to be?' Chain asked.

'None,' Scarlet replied, pulling her long dark hair to the side and placing a cool hand on the back of her neck.

The pressure of the situation was building up into a ball of anxiety inside her now. She wouldn't feel anxious at all if she just knew who she was about to face. She'd be able to focus her energy on finding a way out of this. But right now she was just stuck, waiting.

'He's in the know,' she continued.

'How deep?' Chain asked.

'My aunt goes to Alan for all sorts of odd jobs – he knows the score. Gets what we need, keeps his mouth shut and is always glad of the extra cash. If something happens today, I'll make sure he gets his due.' *If I can*, she added mentally.

She had no idea what was going to happen. This could be another trap for all she knew. In the same place Ruby had tried to trap her and lure her to her death before. The irony wasn't lost on her, if this *was* the case.

Chain bit his bottom lip and glanced over his shoulder. 'What if we get in ahead of them?' he said. 'Set ourselves up in the best position we can?'

'Go in now?' Scarlet frowned. 'We'd lose the advantage...'

'No, we wouldn't,' Chain replied. 'Think about it. When they arrive and we clock them, they'll clock us at the same time. That's no advantage.'

'But we still have the ability to get out of here if it looks like a set-up,' she reminded him.

Chain shook his head. 'This ain't a set-up. You don't believe that or we wouldn't be here.'

She tilted her head in grudging acceptance.

'If we go in, we can find the best place to be, which has an exit route. They don't know I'm here either. You can wait; I'll hide behind where they're likely to be. Then *we* have an advantage.'

Scarlet took another slow sip of her coffee and thought it over. Chain had a point.

'Let's just go have a look around; it's only just gone eight,' Chain urged. 'If we don't find a spot you're happy with, we can come back out.'

'OK,' Scarlet agreed. She exhaled heavily and then opened the door with a grim expression. 'Let's do this.'

THIRTY-FOUR

Sweeping her gaze cautiously around the open forecourt, Scarlet made her way inside through the tall wire gates. The two Dobermans that sat just outside the small hut where Alan spent most of his time lifted their heads as the two strangers entered their domain, but they didn't bark. They were too well trained for that. While the gates were open and Alan hadn't alerted them to any threat, other people were allowed to walk in.

Alan ambled out, peering over with a curious expression.

'Alright, Scarlet?' He greeted her in his slow easy way as she headed towards him. 'How you doing?'

'I'm good, thanks,' she lied with a quick smile. 'How are you?'

She glanced back out towards the road as a car drove past. It didn't stop.

'Oh, you know, ticking along.' Alan eyed Chain, who had walked on ahead and was now looking around. 'There something you two need help with?'

'Not just now,' Scarlet said, not sure how much to tell Alan just yet. Right now there was nothing to tell. 'We're meeting someone here in a bit. And Chain just thought he'd have a look around, see if there was anything... useful he might want.' It wasn't a complete lie.

Alan shrugged. 'Tell him to knock himself out.'

'Thanks.' Scarlet turned but Chain had disappeared towards the back. She took a deep breath and exhaled slowly. She hadn't been back here since the night it had all happened.

As if reading her mind, Alan said it out loud. 'I haven't seen you here since before your cousin was found.' He kicked at a stone on the rough ground. 'Bad business, all that.'

'Yeah,' Scarlet replied heavily. 'I'd better catch up with Chain or no doubt I'll lose him in this maze.' She lightened her words with a smile.

'Sure,' Alan replied. 'I'll walk with you. Was about to start my checks anyway.' He whistled at the dogs, and they trotted over as he and Scarlet began walking deeper into the scrapyard. 'How's your aunt doing?' he asked.

'She's alright,' Scarlet replied. 'She keeps busy. You know how she is.'

'I do,' Alan replied. 'And your cousins – they're all good?'

They passed a couple of paths that wound off around the towering walls of scrapped cars and parts, and Scarlet peered down them looking for signs of Chain. She continued walking straight, Alan keeping stride beside her.

'They're great,' she answered brightly.

Alan nodded and they fell into an easy silence as they continued. They were coming up to the first clearing she'd chased Ruby through, and the memory flashed through her mind.

It had been pitch-black, the tall walls of mangled metal throwing obscure shadows in the moonlight. She'd had a gun in her hand. She'd itched to pull the trigger and end Ruby's life there and then, but she hadn't. She'd held back for her family's sake. For Lily's sake.

The next clearing came into view, along with the grated metal steps at the other end that led up to the winding catwalk where Ruby had set her trap. Scarlet shivered as the memory played through her mind like a film she'd rather forget.

She'd chased her cousin, her anger growing with every beat of her trainers on the hard ground. She'd reached the clearing to see Ruby running up the steps and had shouted at her to stop. Her hand had risen, steady, despite the fact the rest of her body felt shaky with rage. She'd aimed the gun directly at the dark outline of her cousin as she moved closer. Ruby had taunted her, used her pain to bait her. Then at the last moment as Ruby ducked away around the twisting catwalk, she'd squeezed the trigger, and the sound of the shot had echoed around her as the bullet landed harmlessly in a mountain of metal.

Scarlet rubbed her forehead and looked around as they reached the middle of the clearing. Alan stopped at the same time she did, clearly waiting to see where she wanted to head next. She shot him an awkward smile.

'I'll have a wander around here, see if I can find him,' she said, hoping he'd take the hint and carry on to whatever checks it was he'd planned to do.

'Yeah, OK,' he said, scratching the back of his head and peering around at the edges of the clearing.

He lingered and Scarlet had to work to hide her impatience. They had no idea how long they had before the note sender arrived, and right now she had no idea where Chain was either. She needed to get on.

'Well anyway, it was nice to see you,' she said pointedly.

Alan nodded and squinted at something in the distance. 'You're very early today,' he remarked suddenly.

Scarlet blinked and then realised he probably wasn't used to seeing any of the Drews this early in the day. They weren't exactly morning people, the majority of their businesses keeping them occupied late into the nights.

'Yeah, well, I had a lot to do today, so thought I'd get a head start.' She glanced around at the various paths leading off from the clearing.

'You were supposed to be on your own too,' Alan replied, his words laced with meaning.

Scarlet's blood turned cold and she swung her head back to face him. He was staring directly at her now, the first time he'd held her gaze properly since they'd arrived.

'What did you just say?' she asked.

'You heard me,' he replied.

The two Dobermans seemed to pick up on the change in their master's tone and trotted over to sit each side of him, their attention sharp. Scarlet glanced at them and then looked back to Alan.

'It's you,' she stated flatly.

A hint of a smile pulled at one side of his thin lips. 'I thought you'd have worked that out by now. Smart girl like you.'

'You're one of our allies,' Scarlet said with a frown. 'Someone we've always trusted. I'd have assumed if you'd seen us that night, you'd have talked to me before now. It's been a year and a half – why now? And why like this?' *This didn't make any sense.*

'I wasn't going to say anything at first,' Alan admitted with a sniff. 'I don't like getting involved in other people's business. Gets messy. I'd told Ruby as much, when I let her sleep in that van. I didn't want nothing to do with your family issues.'

Something suddenly clicked in Scarlet's mind. 'And you didn't want us knowing you knew she was there, because then we'd know it was *you* who'd taken the money,' she said in amazement. She let out a breath of frustrated realisation.

Alan didn't answer for a moment, clearly deliberating whether or not to be truthful. Then he shrugged. 'Yeah, that too,' he admitted.

Scarlet shook her head and glared at him. Ruby had cleared

out the main family safe, after she'd destroyed John's life, and had then gone into hiding. After Ruby's body was found, the police had also found a makeshift bed and some items of clothing in an old lorry cab, here in the yard. But her rucksack and the money hadn't been found.

'Not that I'd ever admit that to your aunt of course,' Alan added.

'Then why admit it to me?' Scarlet asked, glancing over his shoulder furtively, still searching for Chain.

Alan noticed this and nodded to the side of the clearing. 'He's over there, hiding behind that old Ford, not behind me,' he said casually.

Clicking his finger at one of the dogs, he pointed in that direction. 'Jessie, *find*,' he ordered sharply.

Immediately the dog bounded off with a low growl, and a second later Chain hastily backed out from his hiding place, his arms in the air as Jessie barked and snapped at him warningly.

'Woah, woah, woah, easy, boy.' Chain made his way over, his cover blown. 'Call your fucking dog off,' he demanded as he reached Scarlet's side.

Alan ignored him, merely changing his command. 'Jessie, Lulu, *watch*.'

The other dog moved forward and stood before Scarlet, watching her with a distinctly less friendly demeanour than before. She felt her skin prickle with fear and took a long, slow breath to calm herself. Dogs could smell fear, she remembered. Her eyes narrowed coldly as she looked up at Alan.

'I admitted that to you because I've got something much worse to hold over your head,' he finally replied. 'A video of you murdering your own cousin. And this fella giving you a hand.' He gestured towards Chain.

'The *fuck* you talking about, old man?' Chain spat. 'You ain't got a clue. Not about that *or* who you're dealing with.'

Alan looked him up and down. 'Boy, I've worked with much

bigger gangsters than you, over more years than you've been alive. I know *exactly* who I'm dealing with. A Drew and someone so much further down the ladder that their name ain't known. So I'd shut me trap, if I were you. Unless you want Jessie here to shut it for you.'

He eyed Chain for a long few moments, and Scarlet could see the rage contorting his face, but he contained it. For now.

'What *are* you talking about?' Scarlet moved on, not bothering to take the sharp edge off her words. 'We didn't kill Ruby. We were trying to fucking save her.'

'*Save* her?' Alan repeated incredulously. 'You expect me to believe that when you found the cousin you'd been hunting for months and had told half of the underworld you were going to kill, you tried to save her?' He raised an eyebrow in exaggerated disbelief.

Scarlet hissed out a long, slow breath. '*Yes*, I was looking for Ruby. *Yes*, I wanted to kill her. But I'd promised my aunt that I wouldn't and I meant that.' She held his gaze, speaking calmly, willing him to see that she was telling the truth. 'When I found out she was here, I came to find her. I *planned* to beat the living shit out of her.' She felt Chain's eyes on her, but she kept hers trained on Alan. 'I was going to put her through more pain than I had ever put another living human through. But I *didn't* kill her.'

'No?' Alan asked. 'You didn't push her into that oil vat and then keep pushing her down until she drowned then?'

'No!' Scarlet exclaimed in frustration.

Lulu growled and let out a short warning bark, and Scarlet took another deep breath before she continued. 'No. I *didn't*. She lured me in here; *she* planned to kill *me*. She baited me and led me up there, then hid in a crevice, hoping I'd run on without seeing the gap above the vat, in the dark. I nearly went in...'

Scarlet closed her eyes for a second as the moment flashed through her mind with force.

She'd ducked past jagged bits of metal, almost blind in the darkness, just trying to keep up. Trying to get to Ruby. Debris tripped her, slowed her, but still she kept going, gun outstretched, murder in her heart – murder that she could never act on. It burned like a hot coal and forced her forward. But the footsteps ahead had stopped. She'd slowed, trying to listen, only seeing the dangerous gap just in time. She teetered on the edge, steadying herself and then looked down into the dark liquid, confused. Then someone called her name, a warning. Her instincts had forced her back against the side rails as she'd realised the danger. And then suddenly Ruby had catapulted past, arms outstretched, wild rage-filled eyes looking at her in horror as she twisted back around. But it was too late for her to change course – she'd put all her weight into the action. Ruby's fingers grasped for her top, but she was too far away. And then suddenly she was gone.

Scarlet swallowed, pushing the vividly dark memory away. 'Ruby rushed forward to push me, but I moved out of the way. She *fell* in. And I was trying to pull her *out*, not push her down.'

'Didn't look that way from where I was standing,' Alan replied.

'Where *were* you standing?' Scarlet shot the question back. 'Surely you could hear me asking Chain to help me get her out?'

'I couldn't hear what you were saying but I could see you well enough. And don't try to twist the story now, Scarlet, because I recorded everything. The minute I heard a gunshot, I started recording.' He raised his eyebrows at her accusingly. 'And before muscles here gets any ideas' – he nodded towards Chain – 'I've arranged a failsafe, in case anything happens to me.' He folded his arms and jutted out his chin. 'I get hurt or disappear, that video goes out.'

Scarlet closed her eyes with a sound of frustration. 'Alan, if you were that far away you couldn't hear us, then you can't honestly tell me you're *that* sure you've not got this wrong.'

Alan chuckled coldly under his breath. 'I don't buy it. And I doubt your aunt would either, considering how bloodthirsty you were for her daughter back then.' He eyed her, hard. 'So here's how it's going to go. Your new depot – I want a ten per cent share as a silent partner. Do that and your aunt will never see the video or hear what happened.'

'*What?*' Scarlet exclaimed. 'I can't do that. Even if I wanted to, Lil has the majority share and legal control. I physically *can't* arrange that.'

'Well I suggest you figure out a way around that – and quickly,' Alan replied.

Scarlet stared at him, her frown deepening. 'Why are you even going after it?' she asked. 'You got two hundred grand cash out of this already – why jeopardise a long-standing relationship with our firm for more?'

Alan snorted bitterly. 'Two hundred grand don't go far these days. I used it to buy my little two-bedroomed house, but it barely covered half the price. Still had to get a mortgage. But that aside, your little escapade cost me *dearly*.' He looked angry now. 'Do you know how much profit this place makes each year?'

Scarlet waited for the answer.

'*None*,' Alan spat. 'This place costs more to run than it brings in.' He looked around and shook his head. 'I don't even own the land, just the right to run my business here, and *that* costs me too. The only reason it was worth all my time and effort all these years was because I made out well from the *other* side of things. Your firm used to use me on the regular, for all sorts. But the day that vat had to be drained – and believe you me, I put that off for as *long* as possible – everything changed.' His eyes narrowed bitterly. 'I haven't made a penny from your firm since. Lil ain't even recommended me out the way she used to since either. I've lost almost all my income, because of *you*.'

Scarlet shook her head. 'I'm sorry for that, Alan, I really am, but this *wasn't* because of me. I *didn't* kill her. I didn't even want to be here. She did this to herself. *She* did this to *you*.'

'I ain't interested in which way you want to shift the blame. To be honest, I wasn't even interested in bringing all this up at first. Too much hassle, like I said. But *then* I learned about the depot and about all the new trucks. And do you know which straw broke the camel's back here, Scarlet?' He stepped nearer, a cold glint in his eyes. 'Finding out you'd had those trucks fitted out elsewhere. I know what you want in them; I ain't stupid. Before all your mess, your aunt would have brought them to *me*. That would have been *my* business. And here I am, struggling for no good reason on me tod instead.' He shook his head. 'Nah. I ain't having it anymore. I want compensating for what you took from me.'

Scarlet opened her mouth to speak, but he cut her off sharply and pointed a finger in her face. '*No*. Not another word. You *will* figure out how to get my name on that paperwork in the next forty-eight hours, or I *promise* you, your secrets will be shared for all to see. Starting with your cousins and your aunt.'

THIRTY-FIVE

Cillian's cheeks ached from the false smile he'd managed to keep up all evening, despite hating every second he'd had to waste with Tabitha. She hung off his arm as they walked back from the restaurant towards her house.

'... I do my part though, you know,' she said bravely, in that haughty nasal tone that grated on his brain like nails on a chalkboard. 'I mean, I used to have live-in staff, but they got so annoying and it was tiresome going through all the checks every time I had to rehire. These days I just have a part-time housekeeper. She comes late morning for a couple of hours each day, keeps things as they should be. But it does mean I have to put the bins out myself.' She shrugged with a sweet smile, as if being modest about doing something huge. 'Which is fine. I can push up my sleeves and muck in with the best of them.'

Cillian nodded, straining to keep his smile in place, and turned into her street. Keeping his eyes pointedly ahead, he scanned the area in his peripheral vision. A few houses down, on the other side of the street, a woman with short black hair, in a dark hooded tracksuit, leaned against a wall, smoking a cigarette. Flicking it away, she stood and wandered up the wide pavement.

Stopping outside Tabitha's house, Cillian turned his back to his mother and glanced up at the front door. Tabitha moved in front of him, wrapping her arms around his middle and pressing her body to his as she looked up into his face.

'Thanks for another fantastic evening,' she purred.

Cillian nodded. 'Thanks for the fantastic company,' he replied. 'It's really nice getting to know you properly.' He stared into her eyes intently, watching her pupils dilate in response to his smoulder. She began to lean up and he broke off, pulling away. 'I'll see you again soon.'

'Won't you come in?' Tabitha asked quickly. 'It's so early.'

'I'm not sure, Tabitha. Like I told you, I want to do this the right way. And I feel like you got the wrong idea the last time I came in...' He trailed off and then looked at her, reigniting the smoulder. 'I think you're something genuinely special.' He watched her preen. 'I've never met anyone like you before.' *That part was certainly the truth*, he thought wryly.

Frustration warred with giddiness in Tabitha's expression for a moment, so Cillian gently touched the back of his fingers to her cheek to tip the scales in the direction he wanted. She reached up and grasped his hand, staring back at him with all the starstruck blindness of a teenage girl.

'I really like you too,' she breathed. She bit her bottom lip. 'Look, come in. I promise not to try to tempt you this time. I shall keep all my clothes in place and my hands to myself,' she promised.

Cillian tilted his head and fixed her with a piercing stare. 'OK,' he agreed. 'But only as you've promised.' He gestured towards the door and then followed her up the steps. 'Because you're a lady – one of the things I greatly admire about you. And any lady worth her salt *never* breaks a promise.'

He hid a smile as a flash of annoyance crossed her face. He'd cornered her. *Finally*.

'Yes,' she said in a slightly disappointed voice. 'I am, yes.'

Cillian followed her into the house and through to the kitchen, waiting for her to discard her coat before he walked up behind her. He ran his hands lightly down the tops of her arms and heard her breath catch in her throat.

'This is a lovely dress.' He moved a hand up to her shoulder and then across to the top of the zip at the nape of her neck. She practically started panting as his fingers grazed her skin, and he had to bite both lips together in order not to laugh. 'Here, let me help you with the zip.' He pulled it down halfway, quickly and efficiently, then turned away, leaving her confused once again. 'Why don't you go up and get comfortable?' he suggested. 'I'll make you a coffee and then we can sit and talk.'

'Yes. Right.' She smoothed her hands down her sides. 'Thanks. I won't be long.'

'Take your time,' Cillian replied. 'Like you said, it's early. Let's just chill, yeah?'

'Chill. Yes. OK.' She turned, rather awkwardly, and walked out of the room.

Cillian switched on the coffee machine and pulled out two mugs, listening to her footsteps on the stairs. He grabbed a tea bag and quickly filled his mug from the boiling-water tap she had next to the sink. She was on the first floor already, about to move up to the second. He grabbed a spoon, careful not to make too much noise, and hastily swirled the tea bag around twice before dumping it in the bin. Moving closer to the hallway, he listened until he heard her climbing the second set of stairs then ran back, shoving the second mug under the coffee machine and glancing at the button. It wasn't green yet; the system was still warming up. With a grimace he left it and dashed back out to the hallway. Here he paused and tilted his head to listen, then as the door above clicked shut, he wasted no time.

Silently scaling the first set of stairs, he was careful to avoid the creaky seventh step he'd noted last time. He crossed the hall to the small security room, finding it unlocked and in darkness, as expected. He kneeled down and switched on his phone's torchlight, then followed the collection of wires to the simple connector that linked them to the main system.

'Gotcha,' he breathed.

He leaned the phone against the wall and pulled out Connor's contraption. It hadn't been easy hiding that in his pocket all night, but he'd managed to keep Tabitha on the other side of him for the most part. With steady hands, Cillian deftly attached each end, then pushed it back out of sight.

The sound of a door opening somewhere above caught him off guard and his head swivelled in alarm.

'Shit,' he hissed. That had been a lot quicker than he'd thought. He grabbed his phone and made to dart out, then suddenly remembered he hadn't unpinned the timer. '*Fuck!*' he silently exclaimed, dashing back. His heart hammered in his chest as he shone the light back over to the device. If she found him here, he was done. The job was done.

A creak sounded on the stairs above, and he quickly pulled the door shut. He listened intently, trying to work out how he could possibly spin this when she got downstairs and found that he wasn't there. Tabitha reached the first floor, the soft thuds of her footsteps passing the door. But instead of continuing down, she suddenly stopped.

Cillian held his breath, his stance tense as she hovered just feet away. Had he left some clue? She paced a couple of steps back towards him, until she stood directly outside the door. Cillian closed his eyes, his heart thumping hard now as he realised there was no viable excuse for him to be in here. And the device he'd planted wouldn't take long to find once her suspicion was raised. He wouldn't even have time to take it back off. This was bad. *Really* bad.

Tabitha suddenly tutted, the sound so close and clear that he was surprised she couldn't hear his internal panic. 'I always forget my damn phone,' she muttered.

Relief flooded through him and he quickly dived back to the device as she jogged up the stairs. He pulled out the pin and darted from the room, carefully closing the door, then pelted down the stairs as fast as he could without making any noise. He had just enough time to press the button on the coffee machine, shrug off his coat and fling it over the back of a bar stool before Tabitha appeared.

He turned to her, his expression relaxed, as though he'd been standing waiting for the coffee machine the whole time.

'That was quick,' he remarked, picking up her coffee from the machine as the last drips dropped into the mug. He handed it over with a smile and picked up his mug of rather unappealing weak black tea.

Tabitha noticed this and squinted at it. 'I thought you took milk and sugar?'

'I do usually,' Cillian replied, taking a sip of the pale bitter liquid. 'But I'm detoxing.'

'But you just had a whole bottle of wine with dinner,' she reminded him.

'Yeah, I'm not detoxing with alcohol – it's more of a gut thing.' He nodded seriously, holding her gaze. 'I read somewhere that black tea can rebalance your gut. It's good to have after a big meal.'

'I thought that was green tea?' Tabitha pressed.

Cillian shook his head. 'No, definitely black for the gut. Green tea I think is more for an all over balance of the system.' *What the hell was he saying?*

'If you say so,' she said, moving on. 'Anyway, let's go through to the lounge. I'm assuming cuddling is permitted?' She raised an eyebrow at him flirtily.

'Of course,' he replied, forcing a smile.

They moved to the lounge and Cillian quickly sent a one-letter text to Connor whilst Tabitha wasn't watching. It was the ten-minute countdown to his get-out-of-jail-free card.

Tabitha waited for him to sit down, then plonked herself next to him and backed into his side, taking the arm he'd laid across the back of the sofa and pulling it down over herself.

'So, you were saying about those bin men,' Cillian prompted resignedly, glancing over to the tall grandfather clock in the corner.

'Yes,' Tabitha replied with a deeply disapproving tone. 'Still, at least I know, this time. I had no *idea* when they changed days last time. That's the one benefit of being added to the annoying WhatsApp group with my neighbours, I suppose. They all tell each other this sort of stuff.'

Cillian's attention sharpened. 'WhatsApp group?' he asked. 'I didn't think you really knew your neighbours?'

'I don't really,' she replied. 'A couple of them don't live here, so their houses are empty most of the time. I used to know some of them, when my parents were alive, but over time they all moved away and new people moved in.' She shrugged. 'It was only because the new family at number four are trying to make friends that we got talking. The woman – Andrea her name is – added me to the group. She came knocking with a plate of home-made cookies. Eugh.' She snorted derisively. 'The woman is *clearly* new money. And *American* too. Casually invited me to pop round sometime for a drink. Ha!'

Cillian frowned, not following her train of thought. 'And you don't want to?' he asked.

'It's not an invite to make *friends*; it's an invite to *show off*,' she said, as if explaining something obvious. 'She'll no doubt have just decorated and wants all the neighbours to come and fawn all over her. Probably believes she has the nicest house on the street.' She sighed dramatically. 'No *thank* you. I can't go in there and pretend. Because I know full well that she actually has the *cheapest* house on the street. *Mine* is the most expensive. *Mine* is the nicest too. But then we're not new money.' She lifted her nose sniffily.

Cillian glanced down at the top of her head with a cold smile as she gave him the opportunity he'd been looking for. 'You're so right,' he said, grasping her hand. 'She's probably made a beeline for you, because she knows that too.'

'Exactly,' Tabitha replied. 'I know her type.'

Yeah, I'll bet you do, Cillian thought darkly. 'You know what you should do of course...' He trailed off and waited.

'What?'

'Get there first.' He gave her a smug, devilish smile as she turned to look up at him. 'Invite everyone on the WhatsApp group round *here*, before she invites you all there. Use Andrea's arrival to the street as an excuse. Put out some wine, a few snacks, get that sound system playing something atmospheric in the background...' He pointed to the set-up built into one wall.

'Oh, no. No, no,' she replied hurriedly, shaking her head. 'I have no interest in making friends with all these people.'

'Of course not,' Cillian agreed. 'But that's not what you'll be doing.'

'It isn't?'

'No. You're acting that way, but really you're just quietly showing them who the *real* Queen Bee is on this street. Let them in and they'll see for themselves. And you could show off all that stunning art you have locked away.'

'Mummy's art,' Tabitha said wistfully. 'She did used to love to share it.'

'See?' Cillian pressed. 'You can put this Andrea back in her place, show the group who they're lucky enough to have on there and make your mum proud all in one go.'

Tabitha thought about it. 'It *would* be good to remind people who they're living beside,' she said in a snootily smug tone. 'And to show Andrea that *class* is about a lot more than some cookies and new décor.'

Cillian refrained from pointing out that Tabitha's behaviour and treatment of people was anything but classy.

'You'll want to move quickly though,' he said. 'Send the text tonight and invite them round tomorrow. Make it sound casual.'

'Tomorrow? That's too soon; maybe in a few weeks—'

'In a few weeks, Andrea will already have them eating out the palm of her hand,' Cillian pushed, cutting her off. 'No, you need to get this in now.' She still looked unsure. 'Honestly, you'll regret it if you don't.'

'You'll be here too, won't you?' she asked.

'Of course,' he lied. He'd make his excuses at the last minute, so she couldn't back out.

'Well, OK then. Maybe a wine and cheese night. I'll bring out the good stuff from the cellar. Not that they deserve it or will have any clue what they're drinking of course.' She snickered. 'But it will show them just how out of their depth they are. Andrea especially. I imagine she probably counts a ten-dollar Napa Valley cab-sauv as the height of sophistication.'

Cillian glanced back at the clock. Connor should be ringing any second now. On cue, his phone began to vibrate in his pocket. He shifted Tabitha over slightly and pulled it out with an exaggerated frown.

'Sorry, I must get this.' He stood up and put it to his ear. 'Hello? Yes, that's me... What? You're joking! I told him the client needed it in *exactly* that shade. How much time do we have? Mmhm... Mmhm...' He sighed and pinched the bridge of his nose. 'Right. I'll be right over.'

'What's happening?' Tabitha asked, standing up and moving closer to him.

Cillian turned away, ignoring Connor's mumbled complaints that he was overdoing the bit. 'Just don't move, OK? I'm about twenty minutes away. Keep everything steady until I get there.' He clicked the call off and turned to Tabitha with a regretful expression. 'I'm sorry, I'm going to have to call it a night.'

'Oh, but *why*?' she whined. 'Surely whatever it is can wait until morning?'

'It really can't,' he said, walking through to the kitchen to grab his coat. 'This client has a huge event starting at 8 a.m., and this is integral. I'm sorry – I'll make it up to you another time.'

He moved back through the hallway to the front door, Tabitha scampering after him like a lost puppy.

'Wait, can't I come with you? Come see your work perhaps?' she asked.

Cillian gritted his teeth and then turned with an apologetic smile. 'Not really. I have to get there urgently.' He squeezed her upper arms and hugged her to him for a brief second. 'I'll call you tomorrow.'

Without waiting for her to answer, he opened the door and walked out. He jogged down the steps, and as he passed through the front gate onto the pavement, he almost collided with a pretty petite woman with dark wavy hair.

'Oh, I'm so sorry,' she said sincerely, looking up at him with big brown eyes. Her mouth was upturned in a natural smile, and he found himself liking her instantly.

'That's OK,' he replied. 'No harm done.'

'Oh good,' she replied.

It was then he noticed the American accent. This must be Andrea. She looked up and waved hello to Tabitha, who was still standing at the door scowling miserably, one hand clutching her fluffy dressing gown over her chest.

'Hey, Tabitha!' Andrea called up in an easy friendly voice. 'I was just coming over to see if you maybe wanted to join me for a drink this evening, but I see you have company, so...'

'Oh, no, I'm just leaving. Tabitha's free as a bird, aren't you?' Cillian called up to her.

She glared at him and he winked back at her, nodding towards Andrea.

'Well yes, technically I am,' she said grudgingly, 'but as you can see I'm not really dressed to leave the house.'

'That's OK – I brought the drink to you,' Andrea said with a light laugh. She pulled a bottle of wine out from her handbag. 'I was hoping to tempt you to a bit of a girls' night perhaps.'

Cillian glanced at the bottle and saw it was a Californian cab-sauv. He bit his lip and squeezed her arm.

'Good luck,' he said quietly then turned a beaming smile back to Tabitha. 'Tabitha has something she was going to talk to you about actually. An invite for tomorrow night. Anyway, gotta go – have fun, girls!' He winked at Tabitha once more and then turned away to his car, leaving a now very excited looking Andrea with a bitterly annoyed Tabitha.

His smile dropped and a dark brooding expression took over his face. That had been close tonight. But it was done, and that was what mattered. Now he just had to pray the device worked as it was supposed to. He also had to hope that he was right and Tabitha didn't randomly decide to check those monitors.

Getting in the car he'd leased for the job, he paused, staring back at the house for a moment. Then with a heavy sigh and tension lying heavily on his shoulders, he drove slowly out of the street, making sure the neighbours' cameras picked him up leaving the area.

THIRTY-SIX

Scarlet paced back and forth across the living room of the safe house. John sat on the sofa, his arms resting on his thighs and his hands clasped in front of him as he looked up at her with concern.

'I should have realised it was him – or *considered* it at least. I mean, no one else made any sense, but that yard is his *life*. Eugh.' She rubbed at her forehead. 'I'm such an *idiot*.'

'You're not an idiot,' John replied. 'He's been a loyal partner for years – you'd naturally assume you could count him out.'

'You can't assume anything in this game,' Scarlet replied, shaking her head. 'It was one of the first things Lil taught me. Trust *no one*. Not fully.'

'Cynical way to live,' John remarked.

'Only way to survive,' Scarlet countered. 'In our world anyway.'

'Listen, this isn't helping,' John said strongly. 'Scarlet, look at me.'

She turned and looked down into his bright-green eyes, feeling the pull of him even now.

'Beating yourself up or wearing a hole in that carpet isn't

going to solve any problems. We need to come up with a plan,' he said, sounding completely focused.

'We?' she asked. 'Look, I appreciate you want to help, but you're going in a few days. When the Logans leave, so do you.'

John stood up and walked over to her. He grasped her hands and squeezed them together between his. 'I'm not going *anywhere* until you're safe. Yes, I have to go at some point. I can't stay here – we know that. But my priority over anything else is protecting you. Because if I don't, then all we've been through was for nothing.'

Scarlet opened her mouth to reply but then shut it again, not sure what to say. There was a short silence between them.

'I'm not sure I'm going to get out of this one,' she said eventually.

'I'll do everything I can to help you figure this out. But if we don't and we run out of time, then how bad could the fallout get? I mean, you didn't kill her. They'll see the video and know you're telling the truth. They'll protect you still, right?'

Scarlet let out a silent, bitter laugh. 'No.' She shook her head and turned away. 'My family live to protect the family, but that means even against each other.' She looked back at him. 'And Ruby's death changed them. It changed all of us.' She sat down wearily on a nearby armchair. 'Even if they all believed me – which I'm not sure they would – Lil would never forgive me for covering it up. At best I'd be ostracised, sent away for good, left with nothing and no one. She'd never want to look at me again. She'd feel too betrayed. At worst, Cillian would kill me.'

'*Really?*' John asked. 'He and Connor were always so protective of you.'

'Of the *family*,' she corrected. 'There's a difference. Ruby was their sister. And for all her faults they loved her. Cillian especially.' She rubbed her forehead again, trying to dispel the tense ache there. 'He wouldn't let this go. Not now.'

John stared at her, his dark brows furrowing further. 'Then there's only one option, if we don't solve this.'

'What's that?' Scarlet asked.

'We leave and start afresh somewhere new,' John replied. 'Together.'

Scarlet hated herself for how quickly her heart leaped at his words. She was with Benny now. She was being completely unfair to him even being here, let alone talking about running away with John. But she had no other choice. She needed his help and his comfort. There was no one else on the planet she could freely talk to and not have to hide anything from.

'You need to put together a go bag,' John instructed. 'Leave it with me and we'll arrange a go word and a meeting place. If you text me that word, I'll take the bag and head there to meet you, straightaway. We can be out of London within an hour. Out of the country shortly after.'

'How?' Scarlet asked. 'The Logans won't protect me against my aunt – they go way back.'

'I have a backup route out of here,' John replied. 'The details don't matter, but just know I've got it handled. I wasn't going to fall in with a firm without exit options. I may not have grown up in your world, but I watched it for long enough to know how to protect myself.'

Scarlet nodded, the guilt at all she'd cost him hugging her core a little tighter at the reminder. 'OK, I'll sort the bag and drop it here. But...' She looked up at him, apology in her eyes.

'I know,' he said, reading her thoughts. 'The aim is to sort this so we don't get to that.' His carefully guarded pain shone out through his eyes for a moment. 'I want you to be happy and to be with your family more than I want you for myself,' he assured her. 'Don't worry. This is just a backup plan.'

'I know,' she replied. 'I just...' She trailed off.

'Why did he come back that night?' John asked, moving the conversation back to the issue at hand.

'Ruby had triggered a silent alarm apparently,' Scarlet told him. 'When she opened the gates. Some motion sensor near the front.' She shrugged and shook her head. 'He came back to check it out. He was looking around when he heard my gun go off, then he followed the sound and started recording.'

'OK. So you say he's got no family, is older – how old are we talking?' John asked.

'Somewhere around seventy, I'd guess,' Scarlet replied. 'I don't know exactly.'

'Tech savvy?' John pressed.

'Enough to take a video? Yes. Much more than that, no. He had a lot of contacts and was good with mechanics, but he was old school. Still bought his paper from the shop, hated the idea of social media. Even still uses the Yellow Pages to get numbers,' she recalled.

John nodded. 'Friends? Is he a social guy?'

'I couldn't say for sure. He's a grumpy old man who doesn't really like people on the whole. But that's not to say he doesn't have friends or isn't close with any neighbours.' She held her hands out and then dropped them helplessly. 'I really don't know any more about him than that.'

'The other guy, Chain, how much help could he be here?' John asked.

'He's invested in sorting this out, if that's what you mean,' Scarlet replied. 'If that video gets out, there's no best-case scenario for him. My cousins would end him.'

'Is he useful though?'

Scarlet nodded, thinking back over all the times she'd gone to Chain for his assistance on various jobs. 'He has a lot of skills. He runs the Eric and Treby.'

She watched John's eyebrows shoot up in surprise.

'I know,' she said. 'He's a tough nut. And a dangerous one. But we have a good relationship. He's had my back over the years and we respect each other. I trust him.'

John scratched the back of his neck, attempting to hide his disapproval as he exhaled slowly through his nose. 'OK. So Chain's on our side. Can he be strategic or is he as one level as the rest of those street gangs?'

Scarlet's eyebrows raised this time and her expression cooled.

'I don't mean people like you, Scarlet,' John said, holding his ground. 'I mean the kids on those estates whose only language is to attack first, think later. Most don't know any other way. And that's an attitude that's not going to help us here.'

'Chain isn't like that,' she replied with a curtness in her tone. 'And for the record, those kids are the loud, naïve base-level pawns that people higher up in the chain of command put into play to keep you lot busy and distracted, while they get on with the real business.'

She held his gaze with a challenge in her own, but he immediately broke off with a rueful smile. 'They aren't my lot anymore,' he said quietly.

The reminder immediately sent a shot of remorse through her chest and her lungs deflated. 'I'm sorry – you're the last person I should be aiming my stress at right now...'

'Don't worry. It would take more than that to upset me, Scarlet. But what *will* upset me is your life getting ruined. So we need to focus.' He looked back to her. 'OK. So you trust Chain and he can play the game. That's good. We have until the day after tomorrow, so here's what I think you should do first.' John ran both hands back through his dark hair, before placing them on his hips. 'Contact Alan tomorrow – tell him you've sorted it. Make up whatever story you need to.'

'What?' Scarlet frowned. 'John, that's—'

'A *lie*,' he said, cutting her off. 'One designed to draw him in. You make it convincing enough and stay cordial, and he'll relax. You need to simper a little. Take the loss with grace. Make out you're glad you can sort this out in a civilised way and that you can all move on from this. You need to tell him to meet you here tomorrow afternoon. Tell him the notary will be here, to oversee the signing of the paperwork.'

Scarlet thought it through and squeezed her eyes. 'And then?'

'You get him downstairs where your friend Chain and I will be waiting to grab him. We'll tie him up, take his phone and keys and start searching for this video and for who he's laid these failsafe plans with. From there we're going to have to just see what we find. It could be anything. But at least he won't be able to alert anyone.'

'Unless he has a timed check-in arranged,' Scarlet pointed out.

John considered it. 'It's a risk we'll have to take. Unless you have a better idea. But I don't think we have enough time to tread any lighter than that.'

Scarlet searched her brain for a better option, but John was right. They had to grab the bull by the horns and pray it didn't charge them into a wall.

'It's the only way,' she agreed.

She looked at her watch and cursed. 'Shit, I'm supposed to be at the pub. I need to go.' She stood up. 'I'll tell Chain the plan tonight, but, John...' She walked over to him. 'I can't tell him about you. I can't tell him you're here or who you are. He's not the type to leave a vague explanation alone. He'll dig and I don't know how deep his connections are.'

John searched her face. 'You're scared of him,' he said in surprise.

'No,' Scarlet said firmly. 'I'm not scared of him. But if he finds out who you are, he won't understand. A plod in the pocket is one thing, but one in the bed is quite another,' she said bluntly. 'It's not exactly accepted anywhere in our world, as you know, but with them it's an absolute taboo, and our alliance with the estate would be cut off. To claim the ground back would start a turf war, which would be dangerous and messy. Pointless bloodshed.' She bit the inside of her cheek, looking away. 'It's just safer that way.'

John clamped his jaw, clearly offended, but he nodded anyway. 'Fine. I'll disappear when needed. But let's just get this done, OK?' His voice was slightly gruff now, and Scarlet felt unhappiness wash over her.

'You know I never felt that way,' she reminded him.

'I know,' he replied, not looking at her. 'You'd better get going.'

Scarlet bit her lip and nodded. 'OK. I'll keep you updated.'

She moved to leave, but John stepped forward and grasped her hand. He wrapped his arms around her in a hug, kissing the top of her head, and she closed her eyes, allowing herself to enjoy the warm feeling of safety for just a moment before pulling free.

'I'll see you tomorrow,' she whispered, then turned and walked away.

As she got into her car and drove off down the street, Scarlet didn't notice the man standing in the shadows a few houses down, watching her. Just as she didn't notice when he got into his own car and began following her at a distance, where she wouldn't quite be able to read the number plate either.

THIRTY-SEVEN

Lily glanced at the clock once more with a frown as another round of raucous laughter exploded around her. It was getting really late and Scarlet was still nowhere to be seen. She looked across the pub to the seating area that Benny and a few of Ray's other men had taken over. Some of them were playing cards and chatting, but Benny sat back in the corner of the leather sofa with a face like a brewing storm.

She turned away and grimaced, pulling out her phone and typing out a text to her niece.

Where are you? Benny's here.

Slipping her phone away, she turned and picked up the two glasses of white wine she'd gone to the bar for and walked back over to where Cath stood with Ray and the three Logan brothers. She handed Cath one of the glasses and rejoined the conversation. For the second time in as many nights, she'd shut the place early and thrown a lock-in for the three firms. Hers, Rays and the Logans. It was so rare they got to enjoy the company of genuine old friends and she wanted to make the most of it. Plus, there was something she wanted to discuss with Finn that she hadn't had the chance to do the night before.

She joined in the jovial conversation for a few minutes and then turned to Cath, tipping her a signal.

'I actually don't fancy wine anymore, you know,' Cath declared. 'I need something else.'

'What you in the mood for then, Cathleen?' Ray asked, his spirits high.

'I really don't know. Take me to the bar and help me decide – I'm clearly too sloshed to do it meself.' She linked an arm through his and shot Lily a sly wink as she let him lead her back towards the bar.

'Ahh, Lil, I haven't laughed like this in far too long,' Finn said with a wide smile. 'What do we have to do to get you and Ray out to Spain? We've got some right interesting irons in the fire right now that you could jump in on.'

'That, Finn Logan, is a question there's no answer to. Nothing could tempt us away from this city – you know that. But I do have something else I wanted to discuss with you. All of you actually,' she replied, looking at them each in turn and lowering her voice. 'You mentioned you have something up your sleeve for Mani Romano.'

They looked at each other and quickly sobered up, glancing around to check who was listening in.

'We might do,' Cormac replied with a cagey grin.

'Well don't hide it from me,' Lily said. 'I want his neck almost as much as you do.'

'Really?' Finn asked, surprised. 'I thought you'd agreed a peace treaty after all that business with our territory was over?'

'We did,' Lily told him. 'And it worked well enough for a time. But a couple of years back we had some trouble. One of Mani's boys started trying his luck. We dealt with it. Or we thought we had. Shot back at their business and stripped the boy of his cred. After a bit of back and forth, I put a stop to it. I thought it was dealt with. But it wasn't.' Her expression darkened.

'And so?' Cormac asked.

'We found out he'd been running his own bets on our illegal fights. *Big* ones. And more than that, he'd hired an ex-commando to take us out once he decided he'd skimmed enough of our profits,' Lily said, her seething anger clear. 'Now we've dealt with all of that. Not that he knows it yet. But I want to take him down. In fact I want to take the whole firm off the map altogether.'

The three brothers all exchanged glances of surprise and intrigue.

'Now that certainly is interesting news,' Sean said quietly, studying her.

'I thought you might say that,' Lily replied. She saw Cath's signal out of the corner of her eye. 'This isn't the time or place. But we need to sit down and have a talk, when we can find the time. Just us,' she added meaningfully.

Finn nodded. 'Gotcha,' he murmured.

'Alright, boys?' Ray's gravelly voice boomed as he and Cath reached the small group. 'Christ, I've been away for five minutes and it's like it's turned from a knees-up to a funeral. You need to work on your game, Lil,' he joked.

'Oh, Lily was actually telling us about your last few games of poker, Ray,' Cormac piped up. 'We were just lost for words that you're so utterly shit.'

Sean, Finn and Cath laughed and the merriment returned. Lily grinned and Ray feigned offence.

'Listen, she *cheats*!' he exclaimed, pointing at Lily accusingly.

'I do not!' she denied vehemently.

'By God, you keep losing to your *woman*, man,' Cormac continued with mock disappointment. 'I mean have a little self-respect. There are three things a man should always be able to do better than his woman – play cards, drink whisky and box. And it doesn't sound like you're doing very well on any of those fronts.'

'He's really not,' Cath piped up, between laughs. She held her hands up in surrender as Ray gave her a look of betrayed accusation. 'What? It's true. I've seen Lil drink you under the table when the Laphroaig comes out – more than once – and you know it.'

Lily shrugged one shoulder with a casual look of acceptance. 'It's true.'

'You're killing my manhood here, woman,' Ray replied with a sigh.

She gave him a slow grin and he shot one back with a wink. Lily took a sip of her wine, enjoying this moment of fun and banter between old friends.

The door opened and she glanced over, looking to see which latecomer had finally turned up. To her relief – and slight concern too – it was Scarlet. Her face was drawn and her eyes were troubled, and Lily studied her, unnoticed, for a few seconds. Scarlet clocked Benny and her mask went up, smoothing over the raggedness underneath with a fixed neutral expression. He noticed her a second later, and as his face darkened, Lily prayed that things weren't about to turn sour.

Scarlet saw the storm behind Benny's eyes and felt her heart drop with guilt and worry. Looking around, she caught Lily watching her and nodded to her before walking over to Benny. He was sat on a sofa next to one of Ray's other men, opposite two more. They were playing cards, though Benny didn't seem to actually be involved.

'Hey,' she said. 'Can we talk?'

'Sure,' he replied, holding her gaze, a hard glint in his eye. 'Go ahead.'

The other men around the table all looked uneasily at each other and kept their heads down, their chatter now subdued. Scarlet looked at them and then back to Benny.

'I meant alone,' she said. 'We could go into my office, if you like. This is my pub after all.' The words were pointed. A barbed reminder of who she was and that she wasn't to be disrespected. She lifted her chin, looking down at him icily.

Benny's mouth twitched into a movement of grudging amusement. The man next to him stood up and nodded to Scarlet to show he was leaving, but Benny put a hand out to stop him.

'Nah, stay,' he insisted. There was a short silence as the man looked awkwardly between Scarlet and Benny, then over towards Ray. 'I'll go,' Benny continued.

The other man sat down, looking thankful that he didn't have to stay in the middle of their personal tiff, and Benny stood up, buttoning his suit jacket. He looked over to Ray and tilted his chin towards the door, signalling that he was popping outside. Ray nodded and continued his conversation on the other side of the busy pub.

Scarlet followed Benny outside, glad to be moving into the fresh air and the quiet darkness. They walked to the outdoor smoking area and Benny perched on the single bench there, looking up at her expectantly.

She stared at him for a moment, all her feelings for him flooding back in. 'Listen,' she said, pushing her long loose hair back off her face with both hands. 'I get why that blindsided you, in the depot. But I *really didn't know*,' she stressed. 'I had no clue he was coming. I didn't know he was rolling with the Logans, or even where he was on the planet before Finn opened that door.'

Benny's face remained sceptical and she sighed. 'I'm telling you the truth, and to be honest, I've never given you any reason to doubt me. So if you *do*, then we have a bigger problem here than John.'

'That's fair,' he said after a few moments.

Scarlet's hopes began to lift, but they were swiftly dashed.

'But the way you looked at him when you saw him up there is a whole other matter.'

She swallowed, mentally begging him not to ask her a question she didn't want to answer.

Benny studied her, his dark-brown eyes roaming her face. 'I can see there's still something there. I saw it then and can see it in your face now.'

He paused, perhaps waiting for her to deny it. She wasn't sure, but either way she remained silent.

'I don't know if that's feelings or just unfinished business, or what. But I can't sit here beside you while whatever that is is going on.'

Scarlet's heart beat out a painful protest at the way the conversation was going and some fight kicked in. 'Benny, I get that. I do. And I'm not asking you to do that. But I am going to tell you this.' She stepped closer and reached out to touch his face, her fingers running across his smooth skin. 'I'm mad about you.' Her words were soft. Gentle and raw. 'Genuinely. John was my first love, and I didn't think I would be able to truly love again, after that.' She swallowed again, trying to stem the emotions threatening to rise up her throat. 'But recently I've felt something completely new start to grow in my heart, with *you*. Something precious. And *real*. Something I think could lead to more happiness than I used to think possible.' She took a deep breath and exhaled slowly.

She wasn't used to being so open about such vulnerable feelings. Especially with people in their world. The silence stretched on and she closed her eyes, focusing on the cold wind that brushed across her face for a moment.

'I appreciate you telling me that, Scarlet,' Benny said quietly.

She opened her eyes to look at him. His anger seemed to have lessened now.

'You're not always an easy person to read, you know.'

She nodded. 'I know. It's what keeps me ahead in this game.'

Benny nodded back. 'That's true.' He exhaled heavily and looked away for a moment. 'Look. I think you know you mean the world to me. But I'm just a man, Scarlet, I ain't a saint. I can't sit here and smile while you deal with your past. So here's the thing.' He laced his fingers together and ran his tongue across his bottom lip, clearly finding this hard to say. 'I'm going to give you space. I'll be getting on with my life and you need to get on with yours. Deal with your shit. Finish your business and work out what you want and how you feel. And if what you want is me, *us*, then send him on his way and come back to me.' He eyed her steadily. 'But if you find it's more than that, then don't. *Don't* come back. Don't talk to me. Don't keep me around. Give me *that*.'

Scarlet felt her eyes well up with hot tears and blinked hard to dispel them. 'OK,' she managed. 'If that's what you want, I'll respect that.'

'This definitely ain't what I wanted, Scar,' he said quietly. 'But it's what I need.' He stood up and walked around her. 'Stay safe.'

He didn't go back into the pub; instead, he walked to his car. And Scarlet waited until she heard it turn out onto the road and speed off into the distance before she broke down in the darkness and cried.

THIRTY-EIGHT

Scarlet closed the door to the lounge and walked back into the large safe-house kitchen, checking the time. Only a minute had passed since she'd last checked. It was time. She wrung her hands together, noticing they were unusually clammy. The pressure of everything was getting to her.

Usually she was the one who stayed cool and collected in moments of stress. But then, usually she had the full force of the firm behind her too. She had her aunt in her ear, in her head, by her side. Her cousins had her back, and their men were ready and waiting to add support. But this time there was no powerful force behind her, no one to catch her if she fell. This time if she fell, she would lose everything.

Scarlet walked back into the hallway and checked herself one more time in the mirror. Would Alan fall for her charm or see straight through to the dark angle she was trying to hide? Her outfit was plain and light. She'd kept her make-up simple, just some winged eyeliner and lipstick, and some concealer to try and hide the dark rings around her eyes after yet another sleepless night. Her dark hair was loose and straight. She pulled this forward, then pushed it back, too nervous to stand still.

A knock sounded on the door and she tensed, staring at it for a moment before walking over. She took the time to fix her expression, and as she opened the door, she gave Alan a timid smile.

'Come in,' she said, opening it wider.

Alan hesitated, looking around the hallway warily and twisting the flat cap in his hand nervously. 'Who's here?' he asked.

'Just me and the lawyer,' Scarlet replied, keeping her voice light. 'Like I said.'

He still didn't move.

Scarlet gave him an apologetic look. 'Please, Alan. I really don't need my aunt finding out about this, and if someone sees you on the doorstep, I'm going to have questions to deal with.'

This seemed to register, and with a grunt of acceptance, he walked inside.

'Well, lead the way,' he said gruffly.

'Sure, follow me,' Scarlet replied. She walked across the hall towards the partly open door that led to the basement. 'He's in the lounge downstairs, waiting.'

'Downstairs?' Alan asked suspiciously. 'That's the basement, ain't it?'

'Yeah.' Scarlet turned and held his gaze with an open expression. 'The last owners changed things around, turned the basement into the main living area and the old lounge into another bedroom.'

Alan glanced at the door and then back to her, clearly unsure.

'Oh, where are my manners!' Scarlet touched her fingers to her head. 'You'll want a drink to bring down with you. I'm sure Mr Jenkins will probably want another by now too. He got here quite early.' She walked into the kitchen and pulled out three mugs from the cupboard. Without turning round, she called back to him, listening for the sound that told her he'd followed her in. 'Tea or coffee?'

The soft creak of the hallway floorboards sounded as he finally followed her in. 'Tea's fine. Milk, no sugar.'

She nodded and set about making the three teas.

'Jenkins – he's the lawyer, is he?'

'Yeah. The one sorting *this* out anyway,' she replied.

'What do you mean?' He was at the kitchen table now, taking a seat on one of the open chairs.

Scarlet turned around to face him. The first level of defence was down. 'Well, I couldn't exactly ask our main lawyer to sort this out.' She pulled a face. 'It wasn't easy, coming up with the angle, but I managed it. *Just.*' She gave him an accusing look now. It would have been suspicious if she hadn't.

Alan folded his arms. 'And what angle's that then?' he asked.

'Some of our companies own percentages of our other companies. It's a way of laundering money through different funnels.' She poured the water over the tea bags and stirred each serving. 'Jenkins is going to rework the paperwork to send the ownership of your ten per cent into one of my other limited companies. Lil's agreed on that, thinking that I'm then sending it on through a couple of our other outlets to help fund some of the streams I'm in charge of.' Scarlet squeezed each bag against the side of the cups then chucked them in the bin. 'Instead, once it's under the ownership of my first limited company, it will go over to a second, which is being set up today, and which *you* will be director of.' She poured the milk and added sugar to the other two teas. 'How you want to pay the money out to yourself is then your concern. Salary, dividends, whatever.'

It was all complete rubbish of course, but she needed to make it sound convincing, and she'd learned long ago that convincing someone of anything was all in the detail. She opened one of the cupboards, pulled out a tray and set the cups on it.

'How is that possible though?' Alan asked suspiciously. 'I didn't think you could transfer ownership in a chain like that, through limited companies. Money, yes, but a percentage of a company?' He scratched his neck. 'I can't see how that works.'

Scarlet shrugged. 'Ask Jenkins. He can explain it better than I can.'

Alan's eyes narrowed. 'You sure you're not just playing me, Scarlet?'

Scarlet's heart rate rose and she forced herself to meet his gaze with a frown. 'With something this serious hanging over my head?' she countered. '*No.*'

There was a silence and she could feel the tension rise in the room as Alan studied her closely. He *had* to trust her enough to follow her down to the basement. There were too many variables up here. Up here he could easily bolt and get out before she'd be able to stop him. He was an older man, but he wasn't unfit, and she wasn't confident that she could bet on her own strength against his. And even if that was no issue, they still didn't know what his security set-up was. If he had someone set up ready to drop the bomb on his word, there was every chance that person was currently listening in on an open call in his pocket. If he spooked, he could warn them and this would all be for nothing. But there was no signal down there. By the time he realised what was happening, the call would have ended. For these and many other possible reasons, she *had* to get him down there before she made her move. She took a deep breath and turned back to the cupboard, pulling out a plate and a packet of biscuits.

'It pissed me off, you asking for part of our business initially,' she said honestly. 'It really did. I was stood there thinking, *Who does this guy think he is? How can he possibly think he has a right to our hard-earned business this way?* But then the more I thought about it, the more I realised you had a point.' She opened the biscuits and placed several on the plate, adding this to the tray. 'I *didn't* kill Ruby. And that's the truth.' She looked over to him. 'But Ruby still died in your scrapyard, and that cost you a lot of business. For all her faults, Ruby was still a Drew. She was part of this firm and this family, and as such we owe you that debt.'

Alan nodded. 'You certainly do.'

'I'm not going to pretend I like how you went about getting it paid.' Scarlet studied him. 'But let's get this done. I just want it over with. And I want all copies of the video, names of anyone else you've told or shown it to and assurances that you'll take what you saw to your grave.'

'That's something you'll get *after* everything's signed and sealed,' he replied cagily.

Scarlet's eyes narrowed. 'And how do I know I can trust you?'

'You're just going to have to take that chance, I guess,' Alan replied, his confidence growing.

Scarlet eyed him, making herself look as though she was torn.

'I don't care about the ten per cent, Alan. I accept that's your due, but you need to know, that's *it*. There will be no more. OK?' She played out her part, showing vulnerability and worry.

He watched her, seeing everything he wanted to see, his sense of security growing. 'I'm a man of my word,' he claimed. 'Once I have what I asked for, you'll have what you want in return and we'll go our separate ways.'

'OK.' Scarlet gestured towards the hallway. 'Let's get this done then. Mr Jenkins has been waiting long enough.'

'After you,' Alan replied, standing up.

Scarlet carried the tray of tea and biscuits through the hallway and descended the stairs to the basement. Alan followed a few steps behind, and as she made her way carefully down each step, she strained to listen, making sure he didn't stop. Her head itched to turn and check, but she was terrified that if she did, he'd see the fear behind her eyes. They were so close.

He paused and a shock of terror fizzed through her body. She forced herself to make the next step, urging him to continue, but he didn't. Her eyes widened and her breathing quickened in panic as she tried to work out what to do.

'This is lovely workmanship,' he suddenly said.

Stemming the breath of relief, Scarlet turned with a curious smile. 'Mm?'

'The woodwork surrounding these stairs. Look at the joins.' Alan ran a hand along the edge of one of the steps behind him. 'That's been done with real love for the craft. Not your average set of stairs, these.'

'Yeah, I think the last owner spent quite a lot on the place,' Scarlet replied, turning back around and carrying on.

One step. Two. Still no movement. Three steps. Four. She turned and looked up at him expectantly. He was still looking at the wood. She hovered for a moment.

'Shall we...' She trailed off and waited, not wanting to sound too pushy.

'Oh, yeah.' Alan continued his descent.

Scarlet carried on, looking up to the heavens for a moment with a silent word of thanks. She passed through the door at the bottom and cast a furtive glance sideways without moving her head. Chain caught her eye and then moved his gaze to the doorway behind her, raising the bat high above his head.

Scarlet continued walking, making sure Alan's focus was still on her as she moved along the glass wall separating the hallway-sized area from the rest of the soundproof basement. There was a small end table a few metres in and she aimed for this.

'What's with the glass?' Alan asked behind her.

She placed the tray down, saved from answering by the dull crack of Chain's bat connecting with the back of Alan's head.

THIRTY-NINE

Scarlet sat down and took a sip of tea. Chain had dragged Alan in and was now securing him to one of the supporting pillars that stood in the middle of the room. The rope was a metre or so long, so Alan would be able to move around, to a degree.

They'd placed an old mattress and two buckets nearby, next to a few bottles of drinking water. As yet, Scarlet wasn't sure how long she'd need to keep him here, so it was partially set up for this reason, but it was also to scare him too. Perhaps once he realised how serious a situation this was, he'd start talking.

Chain wandered over and took the other seat, picking up his own tea. 'Thanks,' he said, lifting his cup with a nod.

'You're welcome,' she replied, taking another sip of her own and eying the phone in his other hand.

He handed it to her and she pressed the home screen button. It opened up immediately, no pin barring her way. She raised her eyebrows.

'Well that's a bonus,' she said quietly.

It was an older model iPhone and there weren't many apps downloaded. Other than the standard apps, the only ones Alan had were *Candy Crush* and *Solitaire*. She studied the screen, squeezing her gaze, then clicked through to photos and videos. There wasn't a lot on there. She scrolled through until eventually she came to the start of the camera roll. Her frown deepened.

'You got it?' Chain asked hopefully.

'No,' Scarlet said slowly. 'Hang on.'

She came out of photos and went through to messages, scrolling until she reached the bottom. She opened the first text and looked at the details. With a grim expression, she relocked the phone and chucked it onto the coffee table between them before closing her eyes and rubbing her forehead.

'The dates on the camera roll and texts all start a few days after that night,' she said heavily. 'This isn't the phone he took the video on.'

Chain cursed. 'OK. What now?'

Scarlet looked over at the inert Alan, lying peacefully on the mattress a few feet away. 'Now we get personal.'

FORTY

Lily looked across the room of tables filled with friends and acquaintances from throughout the underworld, all socialising and gambling, with drinks and cigars, relaxing freely in this space she'd created for just that purpose. Like so many of their other businesses, these gambling nights Lily held in the event space above the pub were not legal. They weren't regulated, there were no cameras, no paper trail and no proof. And it was a great earner, because it was true what they said – the house always wins. And this was *her* house.

She moved through the room as Andy and George, who quietly propped up the bar, kept a watchful eye. Cillian was here tonight too, though his attention seemed to be elsewhere. Every two minutes his phone was going off, and as he replied to each message and cut off each call, his expression was growing darker by the second.

Lily wandered over and stood next to him, staring out at the room. 'What's going on with you tonight? You and Billie having a fight or something?'

'That would be less hassle to deal with – and that's saying something,' Cillian replied, stressed. 'Nah, this is bloody

Tabitha. I swear to God, I could wring that woman's neck and *enjoy* it. Ugh...' He ended another call and slipped the phone into his pocket, shaking his head. 'She's got the neighbours round for her little drinks thing. Apparently more came than she'd thought.'

'That's a good thing. More suspects,' Lily replied.

'I know. But she's on my arse like a fly on shit about not being there. Which I'd ignore, if I didn't have to act like the lovestruck, doting boyfriend. So I'm fielding these texts with the biggest load of bollocks I've ever spouted in my life.'

Cillian closed his eyes with a sigh as another message pinged through.

'For *fuck's* sake,' he seethed, pulling the phone back out. 'Told her I'm out with a really important client, but she don't give a monkeys. Honestly, no wonder she ain't got anyone in her life, even with all that cash. No amount of money is worth putting up with *her*.'

Lily bit back a grin and squeezed his arm in support. 'Couple more days and it's over. Alright? Just keep reminding yourself.'

'Yeah, alright. You're chatting up the next one,' he joked.

Lily smiled and opened her mouth to reply, but then she froze, her smile fading. Two men walked into the room, looking around for an open spot on one of the tables.

'What the *fuck* are they doing here?' Cillian growled.

Lily stilled him with her hand, her eyes darting over to George and Andy, who had stood up and were waiting for her command. She gave them a subtle signal not to do anything and they both slowly sat down.

'*Don't* react,' she said in a low, urgent voice. 'Look away. They don't realise we know yet.'

'They fucking *will*,' Cillian replied vehemently.

'Yes, they *will*,' Lily assured him. 'But not yet. *The girl*,' she reminded him.

He swore under his breath but took a step back and turned his head away.

'They'll get what's coming to them,' she promised, her tone less urgent now Cillian was holding himself in check. 'But this isn't like last time. We're not just going to retaliate and force them back into line. This time we're taking out the whole firm.'

Cillian glanced at her, surprise in his expression. 'That's a big statement,' he said warily. 'They're a long-standing firm.'

'So are we,' Lily reminded him. 'Yet they were going to do the same to us. Once this job's finished, we'll talk about it. Until then, we need to carry on as if we're none the wiser. So get your game face on.'

Seeing Mani spot her, Lily smiled and moved across the room towards him and his son Riccardo. Mani said something to him as she walked over, and they both watched her, their expressions unreadable.

'Mani, Riccardo, it's so nice to see you.' She leaned in to Mani and they exchanged a kiss on each cheek, then she repeated this again with his son.

Riccardo smiled at her with all the charm and warmth of an old friend. 'It's so good to see you too,' he enthused. 'It's been too long.'

'Indeed it has,' she replied. 'And, Mani, how are things? Business and the family all well, I hope?'

'Can't complain,' Mani replied, his small, wrinkling eyes assessing her less subtly than she imagined he believed.

'Business is flourishing, and everyone is doing very well, thank you,' Riccardo said, taking over smoothly. 'My mother says to pass on her regards.'

Sure she does, Lily thought caustically. 'Please do pass mine back,' she said sweetly. 'And, Mani, it's great to see you're looking so well. I'd heard you were taken ill earlier in the year.' He'd had a heart attack, though this wasn't strictly public knowledge.

Mani grunted and batted this away with his hand as if inconsequential. 'Nothing wrong with me, Lil. I'm still tough as old boots. Takes more than the word of a few doctors to kill me.'

He held her gaze a moment too long, and Lily realised he was here to see what they knew. He knew his guy was missing and this was the first port of call. She smiled and touched his arm.

'I'm glad to hear it. There are too many old faces retiring or moving on. It's good to know you're not going anywhere soon,' she lied. 'Now let me find you a table. What are you feeling tonight? Poker? Roulette?'

'Blackjack,' Mani told her.

'Let's get you on the blackjack tables then. Please, follow me.' She turned and led them through the room, catching George's eye and calling out to him. 'Can you grab the El Dorado Special Reserve from downstairs – and two glasses?' She turned to Mani with a conspiratorial look. 'Now I remember how much you love a good quality rum, so I think you'll appreciate this. It's the twenty-one-year-old special reserve. And what a perfect reason to crack it open, eh? To share a tipple with old friends.'

She faced forward but watched them through the strategically placed mirrors on the edges of the room. The pair shared a look that very clearly showed they thought her oblivious. She narrowed her eyes at them hatefully.

Your time will come, Mani Romano. And much sooner than you think.

FORTY-ONE

John hadn't woken as Scarlet entered the master bedroom, or as she placed the tray of food carefully on the bedside table. She took a minute to just stare down at his sleeping form. He wore only his boxers, and as her eyes roamed his familiar body, her mind shot memory after memory at her with painful force. How many times had she watched him sleep like this, while lying next to him or in his arms? How many times had they staged a rebellion against the world and stayed in bed for the whole day, just to be with each other?

His dark hair was tousled, as though he'd also been up tossing and turning all night. This wasn't exactly the most stress-free trip for him. She gently sat down on the end of the bed, there being no chair, and he finally stirred. He pulled in a deep, reviving breath and stretched out, blinking his eyes open and searching for whatever had woken him. As he caught sight of her, his whole face, still relaxed from sleep, lit up.

Scarlet felt the pull of him, every cell in her body wanting to lean in to him. She knew if she did, he'd wrap her in his arms and pull her close, the same way he used to.

She swallowed and broke her gaze away to the breakfast

tray, trying to clear her head. 'I, um, I brought you up some breakfast.'

John looked over to the tray and then pulled himself upright and cleared his throat. 'Thanks. What time is it?'

'It's just before nine,' Scarlet confirmed. 'You don't need to get up yet, if you don't want. But I have some more information and I figured—'

'No, you're right.' John cut her off. 'We need to get on.' He rubbed his eyes, clearly still not fully awake.

'Here.' Scarlet stood up and passed him the mug of coffee. 'You wake up; I'll talk.'

'Deal,' John said, taking it from her and leaning over to grab a slice of toast.

'OK, so after we left yesterday, Chain took his keys and went to look around his house. He said at first it looked like a clean sweep. He looked everywhere, left no floorboard unturned. He said Alan doesn't have much in the house; he's pretty minimalistic, so it was pretty straightforward.'

'Did he find the phone?' John asked, taking another mouthful of toast.

'No, it's definitely not there,' Scarlet said tiredly. '*But* after he'd searched it all, he went back through and started searching for just anything that was out of place. And there was an old diary in one of the desk drawers from the year Ruby died.'

A spark of interest flashed across John's face. 'Go on,' he urged, taking a sip of coffee.

'They're work diaries – he always has one. He keeps times, customer names, parts, prices, all that kind of stuff. Always in black pen, everything uniform. But then on the date Ruby died, there are a load of numbers underneath all of that, in red pen. The *only* red pen in the whole diary.' Scarlet bit her bottom lip as her mind tried, for the hundredth time, to work out what they meant. 'That can't be coincidence.'

'Unlikely,' John said. 'Have you got a picture?'

'Yeah, here...' Scarlet pulled out her phone and passed it over.

'They seem completely random, no particular pattern,' he observed.

'I know,' Scarlet replied.

She'd studied the page for hours trying to figure it out, but she was no closer than she was when she first saw it. Down below all the neat little lines of information were just two last lines filled with numbers.

'It might not be anything, but it would be an extreme coincidence, like you say,' John mused. 'And also why else would he keep an old, out-of-date diary in his desk. It must be a code of some sort, relating to where he's keeping the phone.'

'How do we figure it out though?' Scarlet asked.

John took another deep gulp of coffee and then placed it down on the tray, swivelling his legs out of the bed.

'We interview him,' he said resolutely.

'*Interview* him?' she asked.

'Yeah. I didn't do as well as I did in the force for nothing, you know. I do have *some* skills.' He walked over to the pile of clothes on top of the drawers and began pulling them on. 'And if there's one thing I'm particularly good at, it's smoking someone out. So let's go and do just that.'

Fifteen minutes later, they were in the basement, staring at a bleary-eyed and angry Alan. He hadn't woken up before she'd had to leave the previous evening, so Scarlet had asked John to keep an eye on him through the night. He'd apparently woken at around midnight, and John had checked over his head before giving him some food and instructing him to get some sleep, but other than that he'd ignored the man's demands to be set free. Now his mood was still pretty much the same.

'Let me out of these ropes right now, you lying, scheming

little bitch,' he shouted. 'All that bollocks about your family and paying your debts – I tell you now, my girl, you're going to regret this. You're going to regret it very, *very* much indeed. 'Cause if you don't let me out of here, and I mean *right now*, my failsafe is going to kick into action. And you won't know what hit you,' he growled viciously.

Scarlet stared at him, her expression completely calm. Inside, her stomach was churning and her mind was on the verge of panic, but he didn't need to know that. She sat down on one of the armchairs, waiting for him to finish his ongoing rant. John, she noticed, was watching him carefully, noting his body language.

'You done?' she asked.

He narrowed his eyes at her and muttered something, but she ignored it.

'We know you haven't got the video on your phone, and we know the one you have now is the one you bought to replace the other one, the day you hid it. Now, I need to know where it is or who it's with, and I need to know that *now*.'

'Not on your fucking life,' he replied angrily. 'You think I'm stupid? You think I'd give up my one bit of leverage? You'd do me in a moment, same way you did your cousin. No, I ain't telling you *shit*. But it will all come out soon enough if you don't let me out of here and get back on with sorting out my dues.'

John stepped forward from the sidelines and took the other seat, leaning forward on his forearms as he began to speak.

'It's Alan, right?' he asked. 'I'm John.'

'You could be Elvis for all I care, mate. Unless you're about to help me get away from this psycho, you ain't nobody,' Alan yelled back.

'I'm right here, Alan,' John said calmly. 'There's no need to shout.'

'Oh fuck you,' Alan spat back.

There was a long silence as John stared him out and Scarlet waited, letting him take the lead.

'I don't think you have a video,' John said with confidence.

Alan snorted and shrugged with a cocky amusement, his slightly bloodshot eyes looking back at John with contempt. 'Think what you like, but you're wrong.'

John nodded. 'I don't think you've got a failsafe.'

'Ha!' The laugh was forced this time. He lifted his head and raised his eyebrows. 'Then you're an idiot. Who wouldn't have a failsafe in this situation, eh? Thinks he's so clever, don't he, eh, Scarlet?'

John nodded again. 'OK. How about this then... I think you *have* got the video.' He paused and watched Alan's face. 'But you *don't* have a failsafe set up. Instead, you've hidden it somewhere only you know, because you're an old miser who doesn't like or trust anyone, and you've written the details in code in an old diary that sits in your desk at home.'

Alan's face fell and the guilt that flooded his face was undeniable. He tried to bluster, but it was too late – he'd already betrayed himself. 'No, no, no, now you look here – you don't put words in *my* mouth. You don't know anything about how I conduct my business—'

'It's not your business though, is it?' John asked, cutting him off. 'No, it's you trying to blackmail someone else over something that's *their* business.'

Now Alan was angry again. 'That's exactly where you're wrong. Because it *is* my business. That's exactly what this is all about.'

'What's the code for?' John asked, ignoring him. Alan fell silent. 'The code. The numbers, what do they relate to?'

'I don't know what you're on about,' he said, the lie clear as day. 'And if I had a code, I'm sure I wouldn't tell *you*.'

Scarlet watched the proceedings, trying hard not to let her anxiety show in her expression. It wasn't easy. Every bone in her body was so tense right now, she was sure if she moved too quickly, she would snap. They were close to finding what they needed; she could feel it, but she also knew from experience that this didn't mean they were guaranteed the home run. There were still too many unknown variables, and every second Alan was here increased the risk those variables posed.

The two men had fallen silent, each now staring at the other. Alan's stance was alert and aggressive, John's thoughtful. After a few more moments, John stood up and indicated that she should do the same.

'Where you going?' Alan asked. 'Oi, you hear me? I said where you going?'

At the door, John turned to face him. 'There are three bottles of water next to you, and a day's worth of food left in the kitchen now. Once that's gone, nobody will be coming back to feed you or empty your bucket. From that point, if you don't tell us what we need to know, all you'll have are those ropes and these four soundproof walls. I suggest you have a little think before our next chat about whether or not you ever want to get out of here.'

John led the way out of the glass door, and Scarlet looked back at the panic on Alan's face as they walked past the glass wall towards the door that led out of the basement.

'Do you think that will work?' she asked.

'I'm honestly not sure. He's a tough one, but survival can be a pretty big motivator. We'll see.'

As they walked back up the stairs, John reached back and grabbed her hand. 'We'll get through this, Scarlet. One way or another, I'll keep you safe, I promise.'

FORTY-TWO

Scarlet walked back inside her house wearily and shut the door, kicking off her boots and walking through to the kitchen to make herself a coffee. She was exhausted.

The sound of a car pulling onto the drive hummed through as the coffee machine filled her cup, and keys jangled in the front door behind her as she took her first sip of the hot dark liquid. She turned expectantly, wondering where her mother had been. Cath wasn't due to work at the salon today, she knew that much.

To her surprise, her mother wasn't alone – Lily walked in after her. Annoyance cut through her like a sharp stone. Why was she here? They weren't meeting until this afternoon to go over the plan for tonight.

It had been decided only late last night that the plan was being brought forward. They had intended to leave it a few more days before they hit Tabitha's house, but apparently things were starting to get out of hand. Cillian was finding it too difficult to keep the woman at arm's length and Lily was worried about leaving the security system down for too long. Tabitha might be generally blasé about the whole thing, but that didn't mean she wouldn't decide to check it on a whim.

'Oh, you're back,' Cath said with a smile.

'Yeah, where you been?' Scarlet asked, taking another sip of her coffee. She noted that they both had takeaway cups in their hands so didn't bother offering them one.

'Dropped my car down the garage. You weren't here so Lil picked me up,' Cath told her, sitting down at the small kitchen table.

'Where did you go so early in the morning?' Lily asked, sitting opposite Cath. She watched Scarlet with sharp, curious eyes.

None of your business, Scarlet wanted to say. But she didn't, because Lily was still the head of this firm and as her boss needed to know where she was pretty much all of the time. There was no clock-off time in their line of work. They had to be ready for anything.

'I took John some food,' she answered.

Her aunt just nodded, as though she'd expected as much. Cath made a sympathetic sound and looked at her with a pitying expression. Scarlet looked away and sipped her drink again.

'How's he doing today?' Cath asked.

'Fine,' Scarlet answered, trying to sound casual.

Cath looked as though she had more to say on the subject, but then her phone rang and she pulled it out of her pocket. 'Oh, it's that feng shui master I messaged, Mr Dragon,' she said excitedly, standing up.

Scarlet and Lily exchanged a concerned frown.

'Mr *Dragon*?' Lily asked.

'You sure that's his name...?' Scarlet asked.

'Yes, shush!' Cath replied crossly, raising a silencing finger as she answered the call. 'Hello, Mr Dragon, thank you so much for call... Oh my apologies, is it *Master* Dragon?' Cath walked out of the kitchen. 'I know you're a... Oh, I see, my mistake. OK. *Dave*.'

Lily stifled a snort, and even Scarlet had to bite her lip as Cath disappeared off to talk to the man alone.

'What the hell is she up to now?' Lily asked, staring after her sister-in-law.

'Oh, she read some article about how feng shui affects the house,' Scarlet said, shaking her head.

'Oh Lord,' Lily groaned. 'I'm going to come home one night to all my furniture moved around, aren't I?'

'Probably,' Scarlet agreed.

She turned to look out the window, cutting their conversation short and cursed the fact her mother had left the room.

'Scarlet, we need to talk,' Lily said.

Scarlet closed her eyes for a moment. She didn't want to talk. Not right now at least. She had enough to deal with. But life rarely cared about what you wanted, she'd learned.

'What about?' she asked, turning around.

'You,' Lily replied. She squeezed her brown eyes slightly as she studied her. 'What's going on with you at the moment?'

'What do you mean?' Scarlet asked with a frown.

'There's something off about you. Something's bothering you and it's more than John,' Lily stated, cutting right to the point.

Scarlet raised her eyebrows. '*Other* than you tearing me down and demoting me on my own job, you mean?' she challenged.

There was a short silence, and Lily stared back at her with an unreadable expression.

'No, that's not it,' Lily mused. 'But that *is* something I wanted to talk to you about.' She sat back and took a sip from her takeaway coffee cup, watching Scarlet over the top.

'I was too hard on you the other night,' she admitted. 'You were careless and you fucked up. But it didn't cost us our freedom or cause us to lose face. I shouldn't have been so harsh.'

Scarlet stared back at her aunt, surprised. She hadn't expected an apology, even if she did deserve it. 'OK,' she accepted. 'I just don't understand why you went off like that. I've watched the boys do far worse and get off with far less,' she said frankly.

'I know,' Lily responded, tilting her head with a look of acceptance. 'And I know that must look to you like favouritism.'

'I don't care about favouritism, Lil; we're not in school here,' Scarlet said dismissively.

'Well, either way, it's not,' Lily said with a heavy sigh. She looked out of the window across the manicured lawn beyond. 'You got thrown into the deep end when you joined the firm. Most people would have drowned if they'd had to face all you did back then. But *you* didn't. You just took it all on the chin, worked out what you needed to do to get on top and then just *did it.*' Lily pulled a brief expression of surprised wonder. 'I'd never seen anything like it. You were tough, even though the life hadn't hardened you at that point.'

'I'd disagree with that,' Scarlet interjected. 'This life took my dad, remember.'

'And that *hurt* you,' Lily countered. 'But it didn't toughen you.' She cast her gaze over Scarlet's face. 'You look so much like him, you know. You have so much of him in you. And you have a lot of me too. Much more so than the boys.' She stood up and walked over to the bin, placing her empty cup inside. 'They're like Ray,' she admitted. 'Not that I'd ever tell them that of course.'

Scarlet had to smile at that as Lily shot her a conspiratorial look.

'Probably best,' she replied.

'Until recently I didn't think either of them had any interest in running things,' Lily continued. 'I won't be here forever, and this is a dangerous place to be if things aren't run properly. You know that.'

Scarlet nodded and waited for her aunt to continue. This was all true, but she still didn't see what it had to do with her.

'I've been training you up to take over since the day you stepped up,' Lily said frankly. 'And things have changed lately. Cillian is taking things more seriously, and if that continues, it will likely be the two of you. But *you* have to be the strong one. *You* have to lead.' Lily's tone was serious now, heavy with urgency. 'Your dad and I led together – and there were firms out there who thought he was the real voice here. But he wasn't. It was me. From the first day until his last.'

She paused and pushed her curls back, and they both looked away for a moment, thinking about Ronan.

'Every family is different, but in ours, it's *us* who've always been the strategists. You and me. Your dad, the boys, they're hard men, they're grafters. And they have their heads and hearts in the game, but they need direction. Even when they don't realise they're getting it. That's what you *must* do, when the time comes. But if you start to make mistakes like that now, if you become reckless in your decisions, Cillian isn't going to follow you,' Lily said with a grim expression. 'He *cannot* lose faith in you, Scarlet. Because the moment he stops trusting your lead and makes the big decisions without your input will be the moment everything we've built will begin to fall apart.'

Suddenly Scarlet could see the fear behind her aunt's anger. She nodded, the weight of that responsibility already feeling heavy on her shoulders.

'Now you see,' Lily said quietly. She studied Scarlet's face. 'It's a heavy cross to bear, but it's just the way this works. You must always make sure you're doing the right thing for the *whole* firm when you make a decision. Not just for you.'

'I know,' Scarlet replied. 'I will. I always do, Lil. I just messed up.'

Lily nodded then turned to pick up her bag. 'OK. Tell your mum I had to go, yeah?'

'Will do.'

'And, Scarlet?'

Scarlet looked over to see Lily staring back at her from the hallway.

'Whatever you're hiding from me, I suggest you deal with it. And *quickly*. Because if you don't, and this continues to distract you from what's important to this firm, I'm going to make it *my* business. And I promise you now, I'll deal with it in whatever way I need to to get your head back in the game.'

FORTY-THREE

Cillian got out of the car and pulled the collar of his long winter coat up around his neck. His breath clouded in front of him, curling like swirls of smoke before drifting away into the icy night air.

Looking up, he scanned the grey drifts in the sky, covering the moon and most of the stars. This was a good sign. There were streetlights dotted down the road, but the absence of bright moonlight would still help to dampen the detail that any home CCTV systems would pick up later.

He took a deep breath in and raised his face to the sky, closing his eyes as he exhaled and prayed for the patience to deal with the pompous whining monster that was Tabitha Grey. Lowering his face, he fixed his warm brown eyes on her house down the street. His chiselled jaw clenched determinedly and he strode forward with purpose.

This was it now. This was the last night he would have to endure Tabitha. Lily, Scarlet and Billie were set up ready to go in and pull the job as soon as he had her out of the way. It would be a quick in and out, and Isla was already hovering nearby in the getaway car, ready to whisk them away when they were done. Cillian had already been over this morning and taken the device back, and he'd quietly arranged some extra backup, just in case certain other elements didn't go to plan. Everything was set and ready to go.

Connor's creation had worked perfectly. The connection had been broken exactly as planned – hours after he'd left the house, so there would be no explanation other than an unfortunately timed loose connection coming apart – and Tabitha clearly hadn't checked it. He'd had to endure her rants and whining this morning about not turning up the night before, and he'd had to pretend to feel terrible and soothe her with the promise that tonight he'd give her a date she'd never forget. And it certainly *would* be a date she'd never forget, but not for the reasons she'd assume.

Slowing his pace as he neared the house, Cillian took his phone out of his pocket and put it to his ear, jogging up the steps two at a time. He knocked on the door and then turned and walked back down, pretending to be on a call when she answered.

'Yeah, no, the black-and-white one. That's what he wanted...' He turned and smiled, taking a couple of steps towards her and giving her an exaggeratedly appreciative glance. 'Yeah, that one.' He mouthed an apology then nodded his approval once more at her outfit.

As expected, she preened and gave him a smug smile. 'It's nice, I know,' she said. 'You like it then?'

He grinned and smiled, then tilted his head with a small frown. 'Yeah, sounds good. Er – hold on a sec, Dan, one sec...' He made a show of putting the phone to his chest while he stared up at her with a squint. 'You know what that's missing?'

'What?' she asked, looking down at herself in alarm.

'That choker you were wearing the other night. You know, the one you wore when, er...' He trailed off and raked his eyes down her body pointedly, with a mischievous grin. 'I quite liked that on you.'

Tabitha's eyes glittered with glee as he flirted with her. 'Well, perhaps I'll wear it then. Are you coming in?'

Cillian pointed to the phone with a grimace. 'I need to take this. I'll wait out here. We don't have long.' He raised the phone back to his ear and tapped his watch, then turned away as she disappeared back inside the house.

He kept up the pretence of the phone call for another few seconds, moving to lean on the low wall around the small front garden, then slipped the phone back into his pocket. The house next door's camera had picked up his approach and every moment since – something he was relying on to count him out of investigations later. He'd been careful not to let it catch a full frontal of his face, each time he'd been, so the police wouldn't recognise him, but it would show that he hadn't entered the house. And it would show Tabitha leaving, wearing the diamond choker from her safe, which at this point was absolutely fine.

Tabitha reappeared and Cillian turned with a smile, his eyes dropping to the inch-wide band of sparkling diamonds around her neck. 'Stunning,' he murmured.

'Yes, they are rather special,' Tabitha agreed. 'They were Mummy's. My father bought this choker for her on their honeymoon.'

'Oh yeah, the diamonds are nice too,' Cillian replied smoothly.

Tabitha giggled, letting out a little snort. 'Oh, you *are* funny,' she drawled. 'I imagine you've never seen diamonds of this level before.' The rude comment was delivered with an obliviously condescending tone. 'Not that you've ever had need to seek out good-quality diamonds. Not *yet* anyway.' She glanced up at him with a smile. 'And I mean, you don't find clarity like this in those cheap nasty little jewellery shops you'd pass the windows of on a high street. Not that there's anything wrong with those of course,' she added. 'I think it's a *good* thing that places like that make diamonds available to those less fortunate. It gives poor people something to work towards, doesn't it?'

Cillian bit his tongue and forced a smile.

Tabitha laced her arm through his and tried to lead him down the road. 'Anyway, let's go.'

Cillian stopped her. 'Wait, my car's this way,' he said, nodding over his shoulder.

'We aren't taking your car today,' Tabitha informed him.

Alarm bells began to ring in Cillian's head. 'I can't let you drive,' he countered. 'No, come on. You drink, I'll play the chauffer.' He tried to gently twist her round, but she wasn't budging.

'Now *that's* a game I wouldn't mind playing behind closed doors,' she said suggestively. 'But I *insist* on driving tonight. I brought out my favourite lady especially for the occasion.' Holding up her hand, she opened her fist and let the keys dangle down, the Porsche logo on the keyring glinting in the light from the streetlamp. 'Trust me, you'll want me to drive when you see what it is.'

Cillian exhaled loudly, stressed. He didn't like to be out of control, not at the most crucial point of the job. Tabitha pulled him along a few feet and then pointed to a small silver car nestled between two others on the side of the road.

'There she is. My little lady.'

Cillian opened his mouth to argue that it didn't feel gentlemanly to allow his date to drive but then paused as he saw the car. 'Is that... That's not a 1955 Porsche 550 Spyder... *is it?*' he asked. He walked over and bent down, moving his eyes over the smooth bodywork in wonder. 'It can't be.'

'It is. Our family has owned it from new. It was made especially for my grandfather,' Tabitha bragged.

'James Dean's cursed car. His *little bastard*,' Cillian

breathed. 'Wow.' He straightened up. 'I've never seen one in the flesh before.'

'Yes, that's right,' Tabitha replied. 'And I'm not surprised. Only ninety were made, and those that have survived all these years – and that have been looked after well enough to still run – are a very rare sight indeed.'

Cillian ran his hand reverently over the curved bodywork. 'She still looks as good as new.'

'That's because she's well looked after. Now come on.' Tabitha walked to the driver's door. 'I'll take you for a spin.'

Cillian hesitated for a fraction of a second, then opened the passenger-side door. This was a once-in-a-lifetime opportunity that he couldn't refuse.

Besides, he reasoned with himself as he slipped into the seat, *what harm could it do anyway?*

FORTY-FOUR

Lily frowned from the other end of the street as she watched the little old sportscar drive away. That hadn't been part of the plan, but so long as Cillian kept Tabitha busy, that was all that mattered. The tail lights disappeared as it rounded the corner, and thirty seconds later two figures appeared from that same direction. They walked together, one slim, scruffy girl with long red hair and an elderly lady with short grey curly hair, wrapped up in a large coat and shawl, using a walking stick as she hobbled along.

She waited until they were about the same distance away, then moved out from behind the bush, pushing her hands down deep into her awful purple tracksuit pockets. She glanced around furtively as she walked, careful not to move her head, but no one was around. It was *bitterly* cold. Her gloved fingers wrapped around the heat pads in her pockets. The last thing she needed were frozen fingers when there were locks to be picked.

The three women met at the front of Tabitha's house and climbed the steps in silence. Lily and Scarlet immediately got to work on the two locks, barring the view from the street as much as they could with their bodies.

'Go down and keep watch on the street, tell us if anyone's coming,' Lily whispered to Billie.

'Yes, right, 'course,' Billie replied awkwardly. She hurried back down the steps and set herself up beside the front gate. 'No one yet,' she whispered loudly.

Lily and Scarlet exchanged a loaded glance. They didn't need a lookout. They hadn't actually needed Billie at all. If anything, having an extra person only made them more noticeable. But including her had been the only way to distract her and keep her from going insane while Cillian pulled his part off.

'Good stuff,' Lily whispered back. 'Keep us updated.'

'I will,' Billie whispered back seriously.

Lily and Scarlet both hid their smiles. There was silence for a few seconds as they worked the locks, then Lily's finally clicked. She slipped her set of lock picks into her pocket and looked at the one Scarlet was still working on.

'How long?' she asked.

'I've nearly got it.' Scarlet twisted one of her picks and pulled a tight grimace as it turned without catching. 'Hang on.'

Lily shook her head. 'I still can't believe your father never took the time to teach you how to pick a lock as a kid,' she muttered. 'The boys could do it quicker than this at *twelve*.'

'Well, I guess he must have had it on the list next to teaching me how to ride a bike!' Scarlet hissed back sarcastically. 'He never did that either.' She rolled her eyes and reinserted the pins.

Lily took them from her and gently manoeuvred them into place with expert precision. 'Ahh, the bike saga. I remember all the excuses he made to get out of that one,' she murmured wryly.

'What do you mean?' Scarlet asked. 'It was just something we never got round to.'

Lily made a small sound of derision. 'No, he just let you

think that, because he was hiding the fact that *he* couldn't ride a bike.'

'*What?*' Scarlet frowned at her through the darkness. 'Don't be ridiculous. Any adult person can ride a bike.'

'Not your dad. Had the balance of a drunken fish on land, that one,' Lily replied wryly. The second lock clicked open and she pushed the door, gesturing inside. 'After you.' She held out Scarlet's lock picks.

Scarlet looked at them and pursed her mouth. 'I'm getting quicker,' she muttered defensively.

Lily just raised her eyebrows and nodded into the house. Scarlet walked ahead and Billie ran up the steps, heading in after her. With one more glance at the nearby visible windows, Lily slipped inside and locked the door behind them.

* * *

For the first time since they'd started this job, Cillian was genuinely enjoying himself. He'd dreamed about this car for years, knowing he'd likely never find out what it felt like to be in one – but now here he was.

The roar of the engine filled his ears and reverberated through his body as the car shot like a bullet down the dual carriageway. The cold air rushed through his hair and stung his face, but he didn't care. He'd never felt more alive. He just about heard Tabitha's carefree laugh over the noise of the wind and the engine, and then she leaned towards him, raising her voice.

'It's really something, isn't it?'

'It really is,' he agreed wholeheartedly.

He turned and smiled at her, the action full of true joy. In this particular moment, Tabitha didn't seem *completely* awful for once, and as he saw the same feeling of joy mirrored in her face, whilst he still didn't actually like her, he did feel his hatred towards her shrink a little.

But all too soon the moment passed and her look of joy turned to a concerned frown, and the car began to decelerate. She pulled into the slow lane and peered worriedly at the dials.

'What?' Cillian followed her gaze then looked back at her. 'What is it?'

'I don't know,' she replied. 'I'm losing power. That's not right.'

Cillian frowned. 'No, it's not.'

Tabitha bit her lip. 'She's OK if I stay at a low speed, but if I go faster than this, she's limping. Oh *God*.' She groaned. 'This can't be happening.'

'Where do you take it when it needs work?' he asked. It had to be a specialist place, for a car this special and valuable.

'They won't be open now,' Tabitha said, her face serious and tense. She scratched her chin, sitting up straighter in her seat. 'I'll have to take it home and get them to collect it in the morning.' She glanced in the mirror and took the turning she'd been about to pass.

'*What?*' Cillian asked, alarmed. 'We'll miss the show,' he blustered.

They couldn't turn back now – she'd walk straight into the middle of the heist.

'I'm sorry, but this is much more important than a comedy show, Cillian,' she said, annoyance in her tone now.

'You're right. Of course you are,' he said placatingly. 'But like you said, she's running fine at lower speeds and the garage can't see to it tonight. Why don't we just take it easy, go and enjoy the show and take her back later?'

Tabitha shook her head. 'I can't risk her not starting again. And I'd rather not keep her running any longer than necessary. I don't know *what* damage it's doing. No,' she said resolutely. 'I'm taking her back, we'll go grab the cover and then we'll head out again in your car. Worst-case scenario, we'll be twenty minutes late.'

'The cover? I think you're underestimating the time here. Let's drop her back and just jump straight in my car. We can sort the cover when we get back, yeah?' Cillian suggested, holding on to the small hope that he could keep her away from the house.

'No way!' Tabitha exclaimed. 'Do you really think she stayed in such good condition by me leaving her out on the street with no protection? I'd never do that. Besides, it's part of the insurance policy that if she's not in a secure unit, she has to be covered and the keys must be kept on my person or in the safe.'

'Well, that's OK – you have the keys. Where's the cover?' he asked.

'I put it away in one of the storage cupboards – look, don't worry about it,' she said dismissively. 'I'll be quick.'

'I was just going to offer to get it for you, that's all,' he replied. 'I'll sort the car; you can get warm in mine—'

'No,' Tabitha said, cutting him off firmly. She shot him an irritated frown. 'Listen, I know you mean well, but you won't know where to look and I am *very* particular about how I put it on. No one sorts out this car but me.' Her tone made it clear that it was no longer up for discussion.

Cillian stared at her, his mouth opening as he tried to think of some argument, but there was none. This car was more than a car – it was a valuable asset worth millions. No amount of smooth talk would convince her to change course on this. Mind reeling, he propped his elbow on the open side of the car and rested his head on his hand.

He was fucked. There was no way to warn them. On jobs like these, they all left their phones at home, in case their location was ever checked by the police in an investigation. The only person with a phone who was even relatively close to their location was Connor, but Cillian knew he was at least as far away as they were, if not further. He slipped his phone out of his pocket and sent him a quick text anyway, but he already knew it was futile. The reply was almost instantaneous, and his hopes didn't even have time to rise before he read the short answer.

Tabitha turned the car around and they steadily moved back towards her house. The clock was ticking now. They'd be there in just a few minutes and there was nothing he could do to stop it.

Cillian stared straight ahead, his entire body slowly turning to ice as he kicked himself for allowing her to drive, for allowing his own desires to come before the security of the job. What had begun as an incredible joyride had turned into a nightmare. What the hell had he been *thinking*, relinquishing his control on the most pivotal part of the night?

There was nothing he could do to warn his family to get out before they arrived. Not without acting suspiciously and showing his hand. And he *needed* to keep up this play. He needed to remain cool and free from any suspicion, in the hope that he could figure something out in the moment, and at the very least get them all out of this mess unscathed. But as the turning that led down towards her street came into view, his hope began to falter and his body flooded with dark, heavy dread.

FORTY-FIVE

Lily shone her small torch around the hallway and nodded appreciatively. 'She has good taste in décor at least,' she murmured.

'Actually, her parents did this,' Billie replied in a sharp matter-of-fact whisper. '*She* has no taste at all.' She pursed her lips.

Lily shrugged. 'She has good taste in men.'

Scarlet grinned, and Billie crossed her arms with a huff but tilted her head in grudging agreement all the same.

Watching her son's girlfriend simmer away in her ridiculous old-lady outfit was so comical that Lily couldn't help the small chuckle that escaped her lips. She crossed the hallway to Billie and put her arm around her shoulders.

'I know this is hard,' she said quietly, walking Billie forward with a squeeze, 'but this is the last night. It's nearly over. He adores you, you know that. And besides' – Lily stopped in front of the mirror and shone the light over her – 'why would he look elsewhere when he has *this* silver bomb-shell at home?'

The three of them let out a short burst of muted laughter,

and Billie's mood was officially lightened. Lily squeezed her once and then released her.

'Come on – let's get this done,' she said. She followed Scarlet silently through the hallway towards the office.

Billie took another look at herself and then followed, calling after them with an accusing whisper, 'Why did *I* get saddled with the old-lady wig, anyway?'

The office was easy enough to find, being on the ground floor and one of the only rooms that didn't flow through to the hallway in an open-plan manner. Scarlet opened the door and walked in first, looking around. Lily cast the torch over all the markers Cillian had talked them through.

'There's the bookcase,' Scarlet whispered, doing the same. 'And the Riviera painting.'

'And the abstract next to it that hides the front of the safe,' Lily added, homing in on it.

'And the big old wooden desk where that arrogant toffee-nosed troll got in her birthday suit for Cillian,' Billie added sarcastically under her breath.

Lily ignored her this time and headed for the painting. Scarlet took the torch and held it in place while Lily felt around the edges. Her fingers ran down the smooth grooves until finally she felt a small button. She pressed it, and with a small click the painting sprang away.

'There you are,' she breathed as the large black safe came into view.

'Should I be watching the door?' Billie whispered.

'Yes,' Scarlet replied over her shoulder.

'This one or the front one?' Billie asked.

A small flash of irritation crossed Scarlet's face, and Lily gave her a look that told her to have more patience. Neither of them wanted this distraction, but it was for the greater good of the job.

'This one's probably best,' Lily called back. 'We should keep close.' She didn't need Billie wandering off or touching anything she wasn't supposed to.

Scarlet tapped in the code Cillian had given them, and three green lights lit up, indicating it had worked. Lily's face opened up in pleasant surprise and she opened the door, eager to see what they were dealing with. So far this had been one of the easiest jobs they'd ever pulled. No one in the house, security systems down, plenty of time and no codes that had been changed last minute. *If only they could all run this smoothly*, she thought.

Scarlet shone the torch over the top shelf and let out a low whistle of amazement. 'Christ alive, now *that's* what you call a ring,' she breathed.

'Ooh, can I see?' Billie asked, hurrying over to peer in. 'Wow.'

They all stared for a moment at what was clearly the prize piece of the impressive jewellery collection. A ring sat high on a purpose-made stand right in the middle of the shelf, a gold band holding a single red teardrop stone almost the size of a two-pence piece. It glittered under the light, looking almost fluid as the facets danced.

'It's a Burmese Ruby,' Lily said quietly. 'I've seen them before but never this big. They're the most valuable rubies you can buy. You can tell them by the colour. I'd planned to buy one one day, for...' She trailed off, an instant stab of pain shooting through her heart.

It had been her plan to build a collection of rubies for Ruby to leave her, one day. A silly, fanciful idea really. Ruby wouldn't have wanted baubles anyway; she'd have much preferred the cash. Lily swallowed and took a step back. There was a subdued silence and she focused her gaze on the next shelf down.

'Anyway. Let's see what we're dealing with,' she said, her tone all business now.

Billie silently drifted back to her post at the door, and

Scarlet dutifully cast the light across the shelf. Four long, slim Perspex cases, two on each side, were filled with small, neatly stacked packets. Lily frowned and peered closer, clocking that the visible packets at the front showed an individual loose diamond sealed in with a details card. Picking up one of the boxes, she pulled off the lid and sifted through them. There were easily a hundred packets stacked together in each box, each holding at least one diamond, sometimes two.

'This is so much more than Cillian realised,' Lily told Scarlet quietly. 'This collection is insane. What are they doing with so many loose?'

'More money than they knew what to do with, I guess,' Scarlet replied.

Lily placed the box on the desk and lifted the second one out. The two on the other side weren't as full, and the emptiest box contained a velvet pouch. Curious, she opened this up, tipping some of the contents into her hand. A shower of loose diamonds poured out, glistening as she twisted them around under the light. Her frown deepened. Why were they all together like this when the others were so carefully and precisely documented? She looked up at Scarlet and saw the same confusion mirrored there.

'We'll figure that out later,' she said after a momentary pause. 'We need to get what we came for and get out of here. Billie?'

'Oh, yeah, sorry.' Billie opened her vast overcoat and pulled out a large drawstring bag, throwing it over to Scarlet. 'You know next time, I want to be the sexy redhead, OK?' she grumbled. 'This isn't a good look for me.'

'Sure,' Scarlet replied, handing Lily the torch and placing the first of the boxes into the bottom of the bag.

'Or maybe, like, sort of a punky pink-type wig. I think I'd suit that, you know. Always fancied trying it,' she continued, more to herself than anyone else.

Lily carefully dropped the diamonds back into the pouch and sealed it back in the box, her mind still circling the strange contrast. As she picked up the fourth box, her eye fell to the neat stack of paperwork beneath it and she leaned in with the torch to read the top page curiously.

'Guys?' Billie said, trying to get their attention.

Scarlet ignored her, too busy stacking the boxes of diamonds in a way that meant they wouldn't fall open. Lily barely heard her, too engrossed in the letter she'd found.

'*Guys?*' Billie's tone was sharper now.

'*Yes*, you can have a pink wig,' Scarlet replied, not bothering to look up.

'No, *guys*, someone's outside the front door,' Billie hissed urgently.

Lily looked up sharply. 'What?' she demanded.

'I can hear voices.' Billie leaned out again and then ducked back in with an expression of sheer horror. 'I think it's *them!*'

Lily and Scarlet stared at each other, their eyes wide with alarm, and then Lily looked around assessing the situation. The safe was wide open, two of the diamond boxes still sat on the desk and the others were in bags. There was no time to put everything back if they were right outside, and even if there was, they couldn't leave this room without being seen clearly from the front door. There wasn't even anywhere to hide.

The sound of the keys unlocking the door echoed through, and Billie ran over to stand beside them just as it opened. Billie drew in a sharp breath at the sound of Tabitha's voice, and Lily quickly grabbed her, holding a firm hand over her mouth to quieten her. She stared at the wide-open door of the office, her eyes darting back and forth as she tried to see a way out, but there wasn't one. In a few seconds, Tabitha would pass this door and see them standing here, frozen, in full view. They were trapped. Trapped and totally, royally, unequivocally fucked.

FORTY-SIX

'*Listen*, it can wait,' Cillian said, grabbing Tabitha's arm and pulling her back to him, twisting her round to face him as he did so.

'Cillian, it's just a comedy night,' she responded exasperatedly. 'Seriously, we'll go again if you're that worried about missing the start. But this is *important*.'

She turned again, pulling away, moving closer to the office by a few steps. Seeing that the door was wide open, Cillian felt a jolt of alarm race through him. Tabitha was just a few feet away from being able to see inside, and if they were in there, the game was up.

'It's not about the comedy night,' he exclaimed, grabbing her again, more strength in the action this time. He twisted her round again, taking a couple of steps forward himself to get a good grasp on her arms.

'Ow! Cillian, that hurt! What on earth has got into you?' Tabitha snapped, looking angry now. 'Let *go* of me please.'

Cillian's gaze flickered past her head into the office and his heart constricted as he saw them all there. His mother's eyes were wide with cold alarm and urgency. Her hand was over

Billie's mouth, who looked terrified beyond belief, and next to them Scarlet glared at him with horrified accusation. He caught this all quickly, careful not to let his gaze linger in front of Tabitha. He *had* to fix this. He *had* to get them out of there.

'I can't do that,' he replied, looking down at her with dark intensity as he tried to work out how to get her out of this hallway. He couldn't let her go to find the cover for the car. The second she turned around, this was all over.

'I said get *off* of me,' Tabitha shot back, shouting now.

'And I said I can't,' Cillian shouted back, his frustration and panic beginning to get the better of him now.

Lily's eyes widened in his peripheral vision, and her body tensed as she prepared for this all to blow up in their faces.

'*Why?*' Tabitha cried, totally confused.

'Because!' Cillian yelled, closing his eyes momentarily with a small growl of grim frustration.

There was only one way out of this now. Only one thing left that could sway her enough to lead her away and leave the path clear long enough for Lily to clear their tracks and get them all out of there. He *really* didn't want to do this, but he was left with no other choice. Taking a deep breath, he allowed his gaze to flicker one more time to his mother alongside a subtle hand gesture that communicated a warning.

'Because I can't take it anymore,' he continued, intensifying his gaze as he looked down into Tabitha's small, mean eyes. 'I can't wait another second.'

'I don't know what you're talking about, Cillian,' Tabitha responded, not immediately catching on, her mind elsewhere for once.

She made to turn away but he pulled her to him, pressing her body against his. He grasped the back of her neck and pulled her face to his aggressively, pure hatred fuelling the action, and then he kissed her with as much passion as he could force, cringing on the inside with self-loathing for what he *knew* this was doing to Billie. He closed his eyes, unable to look over to her now, knowing he wouldn't be able to cope with the pain and betrayal that he'd find in her eyes.

After a few seconds, he pulled away, and as Tabitha opened her eyes, he could see that her attention had been fully redirected back to him. Her breathing was ragged and her pupils were dilated. She wanted him. And giving her what she wanted, what he'd teased her with for so long, was the only thing strong enough to keep her attention away from her beloved car.

There was a flicker in her eyes as she remembered what she was supposed to be doing. He couldn't waste any more time. He leaned down to her face and showed her his darkest and most predatory expression. She immediately responded by pressing herself against him for more, but he held back, holding her chin between his thumb and forefinger.

'You have thirty seconds to start climbing those stairs so I can rip your clothes off and give you the night of your fucking life,' he growled. 'I won't tell you twice.'

'You don't need to,' she breathed.

She turned back towards the stairs, grabbing his hand to pull him along with her. Unable to stop himself, Cillian glanced up into the office. Lily stared back at him steadily, a sadness behind her hard eyes as she physically restrained Billie now with one strong arm, her other hand still gripped across her mouth. Billie shook, half struggling to get out, half sagging in defeat as tears streamed down her stricken face and across his mother's hand.

His heart shattered as he saw the raw pain he'd just inflicted. And then all too quickly the moment had passed, and they were no longer in view as Tabitha led him towards her bedroom, victorious.

FORTY-SEVEN

The first pink curls of daylight began to tint the dark sky just as Big Ben chimed to mark another passed half hour. Or perhaps it was a quarter. Billie had lost count of how many quarters and halves of hours she'd sat curled up on the raised base of Nelson's Column. Her whole body felt numb. Partly due to the half-empty bottle of apricot brandy wrapped in brown paper next to her. Mainly because of the cold. She didn't really care what the root cause was really. The numbness helped.

She sniffed, another tear falling from her exhausted eyes. She was amazed there were any left to fall. Surely they had to dry up at some point? Another one fell, the hot trail growing icy as soon as it fell off the edge of her face and into the fleece she'd tucked her knees up into below.

The last few minutes in Tabitha's house had been torture. She had no idea what Lily or Scarlet had said to her. She didn't remember much of the journey home either. The moment they'd gone and she'd finally been left alone, she'd changed her clothes and walked out. She couldn't bear to be there when he finally returned. When he walked in with the smell of that woman all over his skin. She couldn't listen to his excuses and the carefully crafted explanations. Not this time. She'd put up with a lot of things, but this wasn't going to be one of them.

Lily had urged her not to believe what she'd seen, telling her Cillian was good at making things look a certain way and then getting out of those situations. But he hadn't left that house last night. That much she knew for certain. When she'd left their flat, she'd walked, at first aimlessly, picking up the brandy from a corner shop at some point. Then she'd found herself back there, in that street. It had to have been a good couple of hours at that point, from the time they'd left, though she couldn't tell for certain. She'd left her phone at the flat, not wanting to give him even that access to her right now. But his car had still been there, and as she'd cast her heartbroken gaze up the front of Tabitha's house, she'd seen the dim light still shining through the drawn curtains of the second-floor window and had caught a glimpse of two shadows moving across the room.

She'd dropped to her knees and sobbed right there on the street before forcing herself to stand up and leave with the few scraps of dignity she still had left. From then it had all been a blur of shock and disbelief and pain and numbness. At some point she'd ended up here. It was a spot she used to visit with her dad when she was a little girl. When life had been simpler, and she'd had someone whose care and protection was unwavering and unconditional.

Reminded of all she'd lost when he'd died, several more hot tears escaped her sore eyes. She squeezed them shut for a moment before resting her head back against the cold grey stone miserably.

'I miss you, Dad,' she sobbed. 'I really, *really* miss you today.'

The wind picked up and its icy touch cooled her hot, aching eyes. She took a deep breath and exhaled, feeling a deep, dark emptiness inside her. She wondered if Cillian was still there, if he'd spent the whole night, slept beside her after he'd exhausted himself with her body. The thought of them together like that made her feel sick.

Making a sudden decision, she gently pushed her stiff legs out in front of her, ignoring the sharp complaints from each joint as they clicked and groaned after hours of being frozen in the same position. She shuffled forward to the edge of the stone base and after a small stretch, she dropped down to the pavement below. She stared down the road that led towards her home and the warm bed she ached to lie down in, then she turned resolutely and began walking in the opposite direction, a spark of flinty determination in her eyes. What they'd had was over. There was no avoiding that now. But she would have to face him at some point and she intended to have as many facts as she could gather, to help her through that. Which meant, right now, she needed to know if he was still there.

Twenty minutes later, Billie slowed her pace and walked through the alley that led to the end of Tabitha's road. There was a bush there that Lily had hidden in the night before, where she could watch the house unseen. The ideal viewpoint, Billie remembered her saying. Reaching the bush, she leaned back against the side wall and peered through the sparser branches.

Tabitha's house was in clear view, but annoyingly the space where Cillian had parked his car wasn't. She deliberated for a moment then pulled up her hood and stepped carefully out onto the pavement. It would take just a few moments to walk down the street far enough to see whether the car was still there. She'd be back here quickly enough. But just then, Tabitha's front door opened and Billie quickly darted back to her hiding spot.

Her heart thumped wildly in her chest as she craned her neck to see what was going on. There was a flash of dark clothing and then it disappeared again, as if whoever it belonged to was hovering just inside the door. A few seconds later, Cillian walked out, and her breath caught painfully in her throat. He turned back, still talking to Tabitha, his smile easy and wide. She wasn't close enough to hear what they were saying, but she didn't need to. She'd seen all that she needed to.

She sagged and her gaze dropped to the dark suit she'd helped him pick out the night before, and the pale-pink shirt she'd stupidly ironed for him like an idiot. The shirt was already crumpled again, several buttons open at the top. His thick dark hair, usually impeccably styled, stood out at all angles in shock, an obvious testament to his wild night. And though tears now blurred her vision, they didn't quite block out the sight of him pulling Tabitha to him and kissing her hungrily as he grabbed her backside.

Stumbling back until she hit the wall, Billie slid to the ground, one hand flying to her mouth and the other balling into a fist against her chest. Pitiful silent sobs racked her aching body, and as he turned his car around just feet away, oblivious to the fact she was there, she wondered how she was ever going to be able to face him.

FORTY-EIGHT

Cillian pulled up to his mother's house and checked his appearance in the mirror. He looked a state. Running his fingers through his thick dark hair, he tried to smooth it into some sort of acceptable state, but it didn't do much good. He desperately needed a shower, but that would have to wait. There were more pressing matters to attend to right now. Rubbing his eyes, he stifled a yawn and then got out of the car, glancing warily up and down the street before going into the house.

He shut the front door and glanced into the kitchen and lounge to see if any of the others were there. They weren't. Or not in those rooms at least.

'Mum?' he called, glancing up the stairs. It was still fairly early.

'In here,' she called, her voice coming from further back in the house.

Cillian walked through to the second living room and found her sitting behind the desk at the other end of the room. She was fully dressed and ready for the day already. She looked tense as she took a deep drag from the lit cigarette in her hand, the other arm crossed over her middle.

'Tell me you put it all back,' he demanded urgently, leaning heavily on the desk with both hands. He stared at her intently. 'Tell me you cleared all tracks.'

Lily didn't reply, holding his gaze with an unreadable expression for a few moments, before taking another drag and glancing down at a velvet pouch on the desk between them. As Cillian's gaze followed hers, his heart dropped and a stab of dread shot through his chest. He picked it up and opened it, pouring the contents out on the desk, then dropped the bag as if he'd been stung. He backed away, his hands flying to his head.

'What have you *done*?' he cried in horror, staring down at the pile of diamonds. He gripped fistfuls of his own hair, panic taking over. 'Mum, seriously, *what have you done*? I was *in the house*,' he yelled. 'When they question her, that's the first thing she'll tell them, that I was in the house with her *all night*. That I was there while she *slept*, that I had that *access*, Jesus *Christ!*'

He made a sound of exasperation and turned in a circle, unable to comprehend how his mother could do this to him. There was no way out of this for him now. If things had gone to plan and he hadn't entered the house, everything would have been fine. After Tabitha's little soiree with all the neighbours, there would have been a whole list of suspects to keep the police busy. On the neighbour's cam, they'd have eventually clocked the tracksuit-wearing girl with the black bob, her red-haired friend and the old lady who'd hung around the street, and the police would have been looking for those three women until the trail ran cold and it was all passed over to the insurance companies.

But things *hadn't* gone to plan. He'd had no choice but to go in and do what he did, to get the three of them out, and at that point Lily should have abandoned the job. No amount of money was worth the freedom of one of their own. But here she was, putting a bag of diamonds before the safety of her own son. Cillian just couldn't get his head around it.

'They won't *be* questioning her,' Lily replied, her voice perfectly calm. She stubbed her cigarette out in the ashtray beside her and picked up a pile of papers.

'What are you talking about?' Cillian asked angrily. 'Of *course* they will. She's hardly going to ignore all those diamonds suddenly going on the trot!'

'Oh, I think she will,' Lily replied, handing him the top piece of paper.

He snatched it from her and glanced at it. 'What is this?'

'It's a letter addressed to both her and her parents from a disgraced general in Sierra Leone.' Lily rested her head back on the high-backed chair and picked up one of the diamonds, rolling it between her fingers under the light from her desk lamp. It sparkled, sending shards of light shooting off in all directions. 'In it he thanks them for selling him a Swiss travel company for next to nothing and asks them to remain discreet about where they got the diamonds.'

He frowned down at the paper and then back up to his mother. 'I don't understand,' he admitted.

'All the diamonds in Tabitha's safe were very neatly organised and catalogued, but there were some set aside, including this bag, that didn't have any details attached. Under the categorised diamonds there was a full set of official papers. Under *these* ones was that letter.' Lily nodded towards it and then picked up another diamond. 'They're blood diamonds. No general makes the kind of money that could allow them to buy out a company of that size. He formed an agreement with Tabitha and her parents to officially buy the company for pennies to the pound, then paid them its real worth in unmarked diamonds.'

Cillian scanned the lines of the letter. 'How can you be sure? Wasn't the conflict over in Sierra Leone, like, twenty years ago?'

'Twenty-one, to be exact,' Lily replied. 'But blood diamonds are still circulating. A lot of the profiteers from that time hid their stashes away to be used later. Maybe he was waiting for the heat to die down, maybe he knew his days were numbered, I don't know. But they're blood diamonds. He's even suggested a specific jewellers in Hatton Garden where they should go to get them numbered and registered.'

Cillian's eyebrows rose and he read the letter again, sitting down in the chair opposite his mother. 'You said he was disgraced – how do you know that?'

'I looked him up this morning and read that he'd been arrested for war crimes about a year after that letter was dated.'

Cillian checked the date. It was from eight years before. He shook his head. 'Wow, I didn't think she had something like that in her.'

'She probably doesn't,' Lily replied. 'From what I've heard, her parents were the ones with the contacts and the black market streak. She's probably only included in the letter because her name was attached to the company he bought. Either way, if that letter was made public, she'd be looking at some serious prison time.'

'Which means she can't report them as stolen,' Cillian finished, finally seeing the overall picture.

'Exactly,' Lily said with a dark smile. 'Did you really think I'd ever put *you* in danger?' she asked, lifting one eyebrow. 'You're my *son*.'

Cillian let out a long breath and untensed his shoulders before slumping back in the chair and rubbing his eyes. 'No, of course not. I'm just exhausted; I'm not thinking straight.'

Lily pulled a grim expression and lit another cigarette, taking a deep drag and blowing out a long plume of smoke before she spoke again. 'Did you find her?'

He shook his head and looked away. 'Nah. I've checked

everywhere I could think of, but she don't want to be found right now.' The ache in his heart increased, throbbing painfully, and he clamped his jaw shut.

'Cillian...' Lily trailed off, and he looked back at her. She was frowning, a look of concern on her face. 'You need to find her.'

'I know that,' he replied tersely.

'No, I mean...' Lily squinted and hesitated for a moment. 'She's strong, your Billie. I always thought she'd weather anything. You know? I mean, she's not from our world but she's never batted an eyelid at anything that came with dating you. But last night...' Lily paused again and ran her hand down the lower half of her face, looking away awkwardly. 'Well, it broke her,' Lily said. There was an undertone of disbelief in her voice, as though she still couldn't quite believe it herself.

'What are you saying?' Cillian asked.

Lily shook her head. 'I don't know. I thought she'd be alright. I thought you'd be back soon after we'd left and that it would all be sorted by now. I wouldn't have left her if I'd realised...' She trailed off and pursed her lips.

Cillian closed his eyes as a wave of deep guilt flooded over him. 'What have I done?' he muttered.

'Don't focus on that,' Lily said quietly. 'Focus on what you can do *now*. Because you need to find her and make sure she doesn't do anything stupid.' Lily exhaled heavily through her nose and looked away, clearly uncomfortable now she'd said the words out loud.

Cillian's phone suddenly began to ring and he quickly pulled it out of his pocket, hoping against hope that it was Billie. But when he saw who it was, that hope died and his expression darkened. He flashed the screen towards his mother.

'Tabitha,' she noted. 'She's realised they're gone.'

'Probably only just putting that choker back,' Cillian said.

He silenced the call and put the phone back in his pocket, turning on his heel. 'Well she can fucking wait. I need to find Billie. That's all that matters now.'

FORTY-NINE

Scarlet paused on the pavement outside the safe house and looked around carefully. She couldn't shake the feeling she was being watched. She'd had that prickling feeling at the back of her neck for days, but every time she looked around, no one had been there. Shaking it off, she walked up the black-and-white flagstone path and went into the house.

John was waiting for her in the kitchen, sitting at the table and frowning down at his phone. He looked up as she entered and smiled, a gleam in his eyes. She dumped the bag of food she was carrying on the side and walked over.

'I think I might have worked out what those numbers are,' he said. 'Look at this.' He shifted over to the next seat and she sat down in the one he'd just vacated. 'I used the two lines as latitude and longitude and check this out.' He held the phone out towards her.

'It's a geographical location,' she said, kicking herself for not seeing it sooner. 'Of course it is.' She sighed and ran her hands back through her long dark hair. 'I'm such an idiot – why didn't I see that?'

'You're not an idiot,' John replied. 'The way the numbers

were laid out didn't make it obvious. And for something like this, it wasn't what I was expecting at all. But I suddenly realised I hadn't checked that possibility last night. And look' – he pointed to the screen – 'it's barely half an hour away from here.'

'Where *is* that?' Scarlet frowned at the screen. 'Are those trees?'

'Thorndon Country Park,' John replied, zooming out.

'That's a weird place to hide a phone, don't you think?' Scarlet looked up at him.

John shrugged. 'I've seen weirder. And I could be wrong but I think that's unlikely.'

'No, that has to be it,' Scarlet agreed. She stood up. 'I'll take his food down, then we'll eat. And after that, I'll head out there and take a look around.'

* * *

John watched her walk away into the hallway and hesitate before disappearing down the stairs. He could see the weight resting on her slim shoulders and it killed him that there was so little he could do to take it away from her. Scarlet had grown so much in the last two years. She'd grown even more beautiful, more powerful and more elegant than she'd been before. Something he hadn't thought possible.

But she'd also grown more afraid, more drawn and worried. She hid it well, on the whole, but not from him. He knew every inch of her body, every micro expression on her face, and he'd seen it there in her eyes. Under the shock and confusion when she'd first caught sight of him, there'd been a spark of relief. It had been the look of a tired soul that had never been so grateful to see its home, whether Scarlet had realised it or not. And *that* had been the moment he'd known she needed him.

Part of him – a very small, very selfish part – held on to the hope that Scarlet would have no choice but to run with the go bag. He could get her away from all of this and they could start again somewhere new. It wouldn't matter where or how – they could lose themselves in some small corner of the world and start again. Together. And they wouldn't have much, but they *would* have each other, with no boundaries keeping them apart. That would be enough – for him.

That small part of himself wasn't something he was proud of though, and he tried not to let himself think about that possibility. He had to focus on making her life safe *here*. Because that life wouldn't be enough for Scarlet.

John stood up, walked over to the kitchen sink and leaned on it for a moment, staring up into the cold blue sky. He hadn't realised how hard it was going to be, leaving her again. After two years apart, he'd assumed it would be easier, that it would feel maybe bittersweet at worst. But if anything, this time felt even harder.

A door opened behind him in the hallway and for a second John didn't move, caught up in his thoughts. But as it registered that the sound wasn't the hollow creak of the basement door but the heavier sweep of the front door, he twisted quickly.

'Alright, John?' asked a deep voice. The front door swung shut. 'How's things?'

'Connor,' John replied, his stomach tightening. 'What are you doing here?'

Shit.

FIFTY

Connor watched John with a suspicious stare and a shadow of a smile. 'Thought I'd just pop in, see how you're doing. Check you have everything you need.'

He noticed that the startled look John had tried to cover now morphed to one of wariness. This wasn't surprising. They'd never exactly got along while Scarlet and John had been an item.

'That's good of you,' John said levelly. 'I'm fine though. All sorted for now, thanks, mate.'

Connor's brows rose briefly in surprise. So he *was* going to play along. He pulled a shrug-like expression and nodded as he walked into the kitchen. 'Not the worst place to be confined to, is it, this place?'

He gestured around him as he spoke, noting the two unopened meal boxes on the side. That was clearly what had been in the bag he'd watched Scarlet come in with, but where was she now? The house was silent.

'Yeah, I've been in worse places,' John said lightly, forcing a smile. 'You'll have to thank your mum again for me.'

Connor shrugged. 'It's nothing. Was sitting here empty anyway.'

'I thought Scarlet had the only key to this place,' John remarked. 'Not that it's an issue; it's your property, I just hadn't realised you guys might be dropping in.'

Connor smirked and pulled his key out of his pocket. 'The only key Mum *knows* about, yeah. We had copies made ages ago.'

He wrapped his hand around it and shoved it back down into his pocket, studying John as the man turned away with a nod. The man was more than just uncomfortable, Connor realised. He was on edge.

'Where is my cousin anyway?' he asked.

John's eyes darted quickly back to Connor's face, his expression even more cagey now.

Connor pointed to the boxes with a frown. 'Well, I'm guessing they ain't both for you?'

'No, no, 'course not...'

John hesitated, and Connor's suspicion increased tenfold. There was definitely something more going on here than met the eye. But what?

As they stood there in silence, the door to the basement creaked open in the hallway and Connor saw the flicker of fear in John's eyes before he could conceal it. He turned to see Scarlet emerging with an empty takeout bag in her hand, and as she clocked him there in the kitchen, the same flicker of fear flashed across her face too.

'Connor! What are you doing here?' she asked, glancing at John and then back to him.

Connor's frown deepened and he walked out into the hallway, his eyes never leaving hers. 'What were you doing down *there*?' he asked.

Scarlet moved in front of him, the movement jittery. 'Nothing. I thought I heard something but I think it was the plumbing. You know what the pipes are like in these old houses.' She smiled at him but the expression was empty.

His eyes narrowed. 'You're lying to me,' he stated.

'No, seriously, there was a right grumbling in the walls,' John chimed in, walking over to join them. 'I asked Scarlet if she could take a look – thought she might know what it was.'

Connor noted the way John positioned himself between them.

'It's stopped now though, since we reset the boiler. Anyway, Connor just popped in to check everything was OK,' he said to Scarlet, before turning back to Connor with a polite smile. 'You staying for a coffee?'

John was talking smoothly now, his expression under control, but Scarlet was still rattled. Connor fixed her with a piercing stare and she tried to hold it, but eventually she faltered and he caught her desperation. Whatever she was hiding, it was *here*. And she was terrified of him finding it. Without warning, he stepped around her and flung open the door to the basement.

'Wait! Connor, *please*...' She grabbed his arm.

He flung her off with a determined shake of the head, jogging down the stairs. 'Nah, I don't think so. I wanna know what you're hiding.'

'Connor, you need to listen to her...' John called, but Connor was already gone.

Scarlet followed him down, trying to keep up and pull him back, but he was both bigger and stronger than her, and he had the advantage of being ahead.

'Connor, *please!*' she begged. '*Don't.*'

'Why, Scarlet?' he asked.

He could hear John following behind Scarlet, cursing quietly.

'I'm begging you,' Scarlet continued, her voice wobbling with sheer panic. 'Please go back upstairs.'

Reaching the bottom, Connor glanced back at her.

Scarlet looked genuinely scared. What the hell could get his cool, collected cousin *this* worked up?

She moved round him and stared at him, her eyes beseeching.

'Please,' she begged in a low voice. 'If you only ever do one more thing in this life for me, make it this. Turn around and come back upstairs.'

Searching her face, he slowly shook his head then took the final step into the room before reaching out and flicking on the light.

FIFTY-ONE

'Connor, wait, this isn't something that you need to be involved in.' John pushed past Scarlet and moved into Connor's line of sight.

Connor shoved him to the side, glaring at him dangerously and holding a finger out in warning. 'You get in my way again, your next bed will be six feet under.'

John held his hands up and backed off, frustration written all over his face. If he wasn't hiding out in their house, Connor knew he'd probably have fought back, but John knew very well that his hands were tied.

Connor turned and stared through the glass, his eyes widening in shock at the sight of the man chained to a post. Alan peered out at him with a confused frown, then opened his mouth and began to shout. The thick glass muffled his words, but it was clear enough already that he wasn't here by choice.

Utterly confused, he wiped a hand down over his mouth and looked at Scarlet. 'Why the fuck have you put Alan in there?' he asked.

Scarlet closed her eyes and shook her head. 'I can't tell you that,' she said, each word heavy and pained.

He eyed the set-up around Alan. She'd had him down here a while, judging by the mattress and buckets and supplies dotted around. He sighed. Clearly he wasn't going to get any answers standing here. Turning on his heel, he marched down the glass wall towards the door.

The moment he opened it, the muffled sound intensified to full-on shouts. Pleas for help dotted with insults hurled at his cousin. Connor walked over, already irritated by the pointless noise.

'Shut *up!*' he roared as he stopped a few feet away from the man.

The loud, angry demand was enough to shock him into silence, and Connor took a deep breath, exhaling slowly before he continued. 'You know, I really am having a bit of a day today,' he said frankly, pinching the bridge of his nose. 'And that's following a very late night in which I didn't get as much sleep as I'd have liked. So I'm going to ask you this question once and I want a straight fucking answer, without all the shouting. Do you understand?'

Alan nodded, his bright eyes watching Connor keenly, only darting away nervously when Scarlet and John walked through and followed Connor over.

'Good. I have no idea why you're here and my cousin apparently don't want to tell me...'

'Connor...' Scarlet tried to intervene, but he turned on her with a menacing growl.

'*No*. You won't answer me, so we're *done* chatting.'

'I'd be *more* than happy to tell you,' Alan said, licking his dry lips as his eyes darted from one to the other. 'Because this girl you call *family*—'

'You want to know why he's here?' Scarlet cut in suddenly, marching over to stand before Connor. '*Fine*. I'll tell you.' She took a deep breath in, lifting her gaze to Connor's with a mixture of fear and fire. 'Alan's here because he threatened to tell you that I killed Ruby.'

FIFTY-TWO

'*What?*' Connor stepped back from her with a look of sheer horror on his face.

Scarlet felt her throat constrict. This had all spiralled way out of control. Why was he even here? How had this happened? She took a step towards him, feeling a spear of pain shoot through her core as he looked at her in revulsion.

'I *didn't do it*,' she stressed, holding his gaze, pleading with him to see that she was telling the truth. 'I swear to you, Connor, on everything I hold dear, I did *not* kill her. I had no hand in it.'

'She *did*, and I've got *proof*!' Alan called from behind her.

'He has *nothing*,' Scarlet countered.

'Then why the fuck do you have him chained up in a basement?' Connor breathed, holding his hands to his head.

Scarlet exhaled through her nose, trying to calm her racing panic. 'Look, I *was* there that night, when she died. And I lied about that. I hid it because I didn't think any of you would believe the truth.'

Another groan escaped Connor's lips and he glared at her in

shock and betrayal. 'I can't believe this. I can't *fucking* believe this.' With a roar, he kicked one of the buckets across the basement. His chest rose and fell more prominently, and his eyes darted around as he reeled.

Scarlet reached out towards him, guilt flooding through her and mixing with the fear. 'Please, Connor, you *must* believe me.'

'How *can* I?' he shot back. 'How can I, Scarlet? Would *you* believe you?'

Scarlet swallowed, a tear running down her face. 'Ruby lured me there that night. She'd laid the trap for *me*. I was *angry*. And I won't lie, I *wanted* to catch her. I wanted to hurt her.'

Connor stared at her with such hatred and pain that several more tears welled up and fell down her cheeks.

'I wanted to make her pay for what she'd done to me. And to John' – she gestured towards him – 'but I *never* planned to kill her. I'd promised Lil I wouldn't and I'd *meant* it.'

'I saw her push your sister into that vat,' Alan spat. 'I even caught it on video. One I'll gladly share with you, if you get me out of here and away from this crazy murdering bitch.'

Scarlet turned on him, enraged. 'You know *full well* I didn't push her,' she screamed at him. 'Whatever you caught on video, if you even *did* catch anything on video, *that* wasn't it. So shut the *fuck* up, because you ain't in any position to be bartering right now.'

Grasping hold of her temper with difficulty, she turned back to Connor and held out her hands towards him. 'Connor, listen to me. I followed her into the scrapyard. I stupidly let her bait me...'

'No.' Connor shook his head. 'No, I can't hear this,' he breathed. All the colour had drained from his face and he stared at her now like he didn't even know who she was.

'Well, you have to,' Scarlet replied sharply. She swallowed hard. 'I ran up the catwalk after her. She was taunting me, pulling me in, but I was so angry I couldn't see it.' She closed her eyes as that night flashed back to her.

Raw pain and fury ran through her veins and the metal of the gun felt cold against her hand. The darkness wrapped around her like a cloak as she ran, no idea where she was, only knowing that Ruby was up ahead. Only caring about getting her revenge.

She forced her eyes back open. 'She'd always known how to press my buttons. But then it went quiet, and as I ran, I only saw the open vat just in time.' Another tear rolled down her face as she shook in anger at the unfairness of it all. 'I managed to stop just on the very edge and was trying to work out what it was when I heard someone shout out a warning. I stepped back and grabbed the railing, and then there she was.'

Connor shook his head and turned away.

'Please, Connor,' she begged miserably, 'you *have* to believe me.' She pressed her fingers into her eyes for a moment, a wave of sickness rolling around the bottom of her stomach when he didn't turn back. 'Ruby had hidden in a nook, ready to push me in if I didn't fall. She ran forward to do just that, but when I moved out of the way, *she* fell in instead. I had no idea she was there. I had no idea what was even *going on*. If I hadn't heard that warning, it would have been me.'

'You really expect me to believe that?' Connor spat in disbelief.

'It's the *truth*,' Scarlet insisted. She hesitated, wishing she could leave the others out of it but knowing that if any of them had a chance to get through this, she had to tell Connor everything. 'Ascough had followed me in. It was when she was watching my every move, after John left. She was the one who'd called out the warning.' She swallowed again. 'And Chain was there too.'

Connor let out a sharp bark of bitter amusement. 'Three of you?' he asked. 'There were *three* of you there when my sister died, and not one of you could save her or tell us?' His glare turned dark as he directed it at her.

'We *tried*,' Scarlet cried. 'I *swear* to you we tried. I tried to pull her out but she was too far down. Chain lowered me over and I grabbed her arms again and again...'

The pain on Connor's face broke through the last of her strength, and as guilt overwhelmed her, tears started to fall thick and fast down her face. 'The oil was too thick and slippery. Every time I got a grip on her she'd slip away again.'

One solitary tear rolled down Connor's face too, but he wiped it away angrily. 'If that was the truth, you should have told us. That was my *sister*.' His voice broke. 'That was my mum's *baby*.' He gave her a bitter stare. 'And you just *left* her there and let us find out when her body turned up *months* later. How could you do that to us? To your own *family*?'

'I was scared,' Scarlet sobbed, tears blurring her vision. 'I'd been so angry with her I didn't think you'd believe me.'

Connor shook his head, turning away from her and walking in a wide circle. 'If you'd come to us and told us back then, I probably would have done. But now... I don't know. It sounds more like you're just trying to cover your tracks.' His voice was full of devastation. 'I need to get out of here. I need to tell Mum.'

'No, Connor, please don't,' Scarlet begged. She tried to follow him as he walked out, but he shrugged her off roughly.

'*Don't*,' he warned. 'I can't do this.'

Scarlet fell back and watched him march away. A dark cackle filled the silence as Connor disappeared through the door to the stairs.

'Fucked yourself there, didn't ya?' Alan taunted. 'Should have given me what I asked for when you had the chance.'

Scarlet ignored him. He didn't matter anymore. Nothing did. She turned to John and saw the defeat mirrored there in his eyes. 'What do we do now?' she asked.

'Now we get the bags. And then we run.'

FIFTY-THREE

Billie stood outside their flat and put her ear to the door. There was silence within. She walked in, her tired eyes checking for him as she moved from room to room, but he wasn't there. Relaxing her tense shoulders, she collapsed on the bed, glad to finally be so exhausted that sleep should take her quickly.

But as she began to drift off, the jangle of keys being throwing onto the kitchen side jolted her awake. Her heart plummeted and she suddenly wished she'd just booked into a hotel instead of coming home, but it was too late for that now. She opened her eyes and saw him walk into the bedroom, worry and guilt written all over his face.

'Billie,' he said, relief filling the one word.

'No,' she replied, pushing herself up off the bed and away from him. She glared at him with all the hatred that had been building up through the hours since she'd seen him walk up the stairs with Tabitha. 'Don't you dare come near me.'

'Billie, please listen to me,' he begged, taking a few steps closer.

'*No*,' she cried, louder this time. 'I mean it.'

Glancing at the dressing table beside her, she grabbed a pair of scissors she'd left there the day before when she'd cut a loose thread from a new dress. Brandishing these in front of her, she glared at him.

'You come near me, so help me God, I'll stab you through the *fucking* heart,' she said, her voice shaking with emotion.

Cillian held his hands up and backed away, sitting down on the end of the bed and watching her warily. 'Alright, I won't come near you,' he said carefully. 'But you need to listen to me, Bills. I *know* it hurt you, seeing me kiss Tabitha, and I *hate* that I had to do that...'

'Ha!' Billie cried in disbelief. 'You are *unreal*. You're really trying to pull that with me? *It was just a kiss and it was all fake*,' she mocked.

'It *was*,' Cillian replied. 'I'm sorry, Billie. I would *never* cheat on you, not really. You're my absolute world. The one and only reason I did that was to save you from being caught and facing a potential prison sentence. There was no other way. And you can be angry with me, but I love you too much not to protect you. Whatever the cost.'

Billie stared at him, her insides curling up with molten fury. Her vision blurred as tears filled her eyes and she looked at him with disgust. 'How *dare* you sit there and lie to me, after all we've been through. Sleeping with her was bad enough,' she sobbed. 'You've broken my heart more than you could ever possibly understand doing that, but *lying* to me about it too?' She shook her head, unable to continue.

'*What?*' Cillian asked. 'No, Billie, I swear to you, I didn't touch her again after that kiss. Not *once*. Not in *any* way. I was out of there twenty minutes after you, and I filled those minutes with absolute bullshit excuses—'

'You *liar*,' she screamed, storming over and holding the sharp end of the scissors to his throat. 'I *saw* you. I went back to that house and I watched you leave this morning. I watched you *kiss* her and *grab* her, you heartless, selfish, *lying* piece of *shit*! How could you *treat* me like this? *How?*'

Cillian grabbed her arms, holding her tightly. 'You saw *Connor*,' he yelled back, his eyes wide and intense. 'Billie, for *God's sake*, I know I hurt you by kissing her and I'll spend my life making up for it, but I swear to you, the man you saw leave this morning was *Connor*.'

'You're lying,' she sobbed, a sliver of doubt seeping into her tone as she searched his face.

'I'm *not*,' he insisted. 'Bills, I've had him waiting in the wings the last couple of times, just in case I got cornered and had no way out of it. I didn't tell you because I didn't think it would ever really get that far. And last night wasn't planned; it all just changed so fast... Listen, Connor was on his way over to try and warn you to get out, but we were already too close; he was still a few minutes out.'

Billie lowered the scissors and started to listen. Cillian loosened his grip but kept a sharp eye on them.

'I realised that was the only way I'd get you out, and I knew I could switch him in as soon as he got there. After I got her upstairs, I told her I wanted her to have a really thorough shower. That bought me a few minutes. Connor still wasn't there when she got out, so I told her she needed to put on some lingerie and give me a show.'

Billie made a sound of disgust and pulled away, but he yanked her back. '*No*. I know it's hard, but you're gonna listen to me,' he snapped. 'Because we don't have secrets and I ain't about to start now. It was fucking horrible and not one thing about it was enjoyable for me. All I could think about was you, getting back home to *you*. When Connor arrived, I told her I was getting some ice. I ran down and let him in, we switched clothes and car keys, I caught him up and then *he* went upstairs and spent the night with her. By then all Tabitha cared about was the physical. Connor didn't need to talk or try to act like me

– he just gave her what she wanted. Gave her what I *never* would.'

Billie thought back to that morning and all she'd seen. It could have been Connor. She could tell them apart up close, but they were identical twins, so from a distance it was impossible. If Tabitha had only paid attention to his body, Connor *could* have pulled it off. After all, the woman had no idea Cillian even had a twin.

Cillian exhaled tiredly. 'I got home about half an hour after you did. But by then you'd gone, and you'd left your phone. You can check it if you want proof. There's a text on there from me asking you where you are, as soon as I got in. I spent the rest of the night trying to find you.'

Fresh tears began to run down Billie's face and she sobbed as relief flooded through her. 'For fuck's sake,' she managed to say before Cillian pulled her to him and held her tighter than he ever had before.

They remained there in that healing embrace for a long time. Eventually, after her tears had run dry and they'd reached a level of calm, he sniffed her hair with a small frown.

'You been on the brandy?' he asked.

Billie smiled tiredly. 'Yeah.' She untangled herself from his embrace and sat beside him, leaning her head on his shoulder. 'No secrets between us. Not ever, yeah?' she asked.

'There never has been. Well...' Cillian tilted his head to one side. 'Actually, I do have *one* more secret I've been hiding from you.'

Billie frowned. 'What?' she asked warily.

'I lied to you the other day. Told you I was with Connor when I wasn't,' he admitted, looking away.

'And where were you really?' she asked.

'Meeting another woman,' Cillian told her, standing up. He walked over to his drawers and rummaged around.

Billie felt her insides grow cold. '*What?* Why?' she managed to ask.

'She had something I wanted.' He closed the drawer slowly and walked back to stand in front of her. 'Or rather, she was helping me find something I wanted.'

His warm brown eyes held hers and his mouth curled up into a smile. Dropping down in front of her, he squeezed one of her hands in his.

'I was planning to do this in some fancy restaurant or with fireworks or something. I don't know – I hadn't got it entirely planned out,' he admitted. 'But after this week, sitting there in all those posh places and hating every minute, I realised it ain't about where we are. It's just about you and me, and the moment.'

Billie gasped as she finally caught on to what he was doing. Or what she thought he was doing.

'Are you...?' She trailed off, not wanting to be wrong and not wanting to ruin it if she wasn't.

'Billie Anne Archer,' Cillian said, opening his other hand and revealing a small blue Tiffany box, 'I love you so much more than I'm capable of explaining.' He opened the box.

Billie's hands flew to her face, covering her nose and mouth as she stared at the stunning emerald-cut diamond surrounded by a halo of delicate smaller ones set on a platinum ring. 'Oh my God, it's beautiful,' she breathed.

'You're my world. And I want to spend my life with you right here next to me. I want everything with you. The good and the bad, the easy and the hard.' He gazed into her eyes sincerely. 'And I want to spend the rest of my life trying to be the husband you deserve. So what do you think? Will you marry me?'

Billie's joy spilled over, and all she could manage for a few moments was a nod as happy tears washed away all the bad. 'Yes,' she managed as Cillian slipped the ring onto her finger. 'Yes, I will.'

FIFTY-FOUR

Scarlet sat at the kitchen table, her head in her hands as she tried to process what was happening. Half an hour ago they'd finally been on the right track; there had been some light at the end of the tunnel. Now here she sat with her whole world in tatters, about to go on the run with nothing but a large backpack. She was never going to see her family again. And *worse*, they were going to believe she'd killed her own cousin in cold blood. They would look back over their memories of her with a feeling of sickness and betrayal. And now there was nothing she could do about it. She could have avoided this if she'd just been brave enough to tell the truth when it had happened, but she hadn't been, and now she couldn't take it back.

John paced the hallway, speaking to someone on the phone in a low, urgent voice. He was arranging their transport out of here, over to the mainland. She would go ahead by plane, he'd told her. As she had her passport, it would be better for her to arrive legally. He would meet her on the other side.

The idea of leaving her family, of leaving her mother, without so much as a goodbye, felt so wrong. She couldn't comprehend it. But she had no choice now. Once Connor told them, Cillian would come for her. She knew that beyond a shadow of a doubt. Connor would rage and Lily would shut her out of both family and firm – but Cillian would kill her. He'd made it clear long ago that this would be the consequence of him ever finding out she had something to do with Ruby's death. And there would be no convincing him otherwise. Not now. He'd suspected her for too long; this would only serve to confirm his suspicions in full. So there was nothing else for it. She had to leave, and it had to be now.

She sipped her tea and worried about her mother. How would Cath cope? She'd barely survived Ronan's death, but she'd had Scarlet to still live for. Without Scarlet, she'd have no one. For a moment she considered taking her with them but immediately dismissed the idea. She couldn't put her mother through that.

John's call ended and he walked through to the kitchen. 'Come on,' he said, grabbing her arm. 'They're en route to the pickup point. We need to drive over there now.' He paused. 'Are you up to this? Can you drive?'

'Yeah,' she said in a hollow voice. ''Course. Let's go.'

She stood up and walked through to the hallway, shrugging on her coat as John pulled his hood forward and picked up both their bags. It was insane to think that those two small bags contained everything they would now possess in life. Lingering for just a second, Scarlet walked forward and opened the door.

'Goodbye,' she whispered, unsure who or what exactly she was saying it to.

John went ahead down the path as she locked up, then stopped abruptly when he reached the pavement. As she caught up, she followed his frowning gaze and saw what had stopped him in his tracks. There, leaning on the bonnet of her car, was Connor.

He looked at the bags and nodded slowly. 'Yeah, I thought you'd try to run,' he said quietly. 'But I can't let you do that.'

Scarlet's heart dropped and she felt an icy prickle of fear run up her spine.

John moved towards him and dropped the bags. 'I won't let you stop her,' he said in a low, menacing tone.

'I think you will actually,' Connor replied. He stepped away from the car, stopping just in front of her before looking away with a sad shake of his head. 'I was going to tell her, you know. Mum. I went over there with every intention of being honest. 'Cause she deserves to know what you did.' He glanced back at her accusingly. 'But when I got there, I found her looking at some old pictures. You know the ones she keeps in her desk drawer that she don't think we know about?'

Scarlet nodded, a lump forming in her throat.

'And she looked so tired,' he continued with a sigh. 'Grief does that to you, I suppose. And I couldn't do it. She's so strong, but getting through losing Ruby took pretty much all she had. She wouldn't be able to cope with losing you as well.' He stared at her, mistrust and pain in his eyes. 'I don't know what to believe, but I *do* know that this family can't survive any more loss.'

Scarlet felt hope dawn. 'So you aren't going to tell them?' she asked.

Connor shook his head. 'No.' He bit his lip. 'I don't like keeping this from Cillian. We don't do secrets. But I heard what he told you back then.' His dark eyes burned into hers, piercing right through to her soul. 'And I know he meant it. So for Mum's sake, I'm going to help you cover this up and then we never speak of it again.'

Scarlet nodded, tears welling up in her eyes. 'Thank you,' she whispered.

'Don't thank me yet. We still have a lot to do.' He picked up her bag. 'And you need to start by telling me exactly what Alan is blackmailing you for and how.'

FIFTY-FIVE

Hours later and under the cover of darkness, Scarlet kneeled down on the ground in the middle of a forest, shovelling earth and dead leaves and twigs aside, bit by bit with a small hand trowel. A low hoot nearby made her jump and she looked up at Connor in alarm.

'What was that?' she whispered.

'It's just an owl,' he replied. 'Come on – keep going.'

'This would go faster if we were both digging,' she pointed out.

'Your mess, your graft,' he replied dismissively, taking another drag on the cigarette he was smoking and turning around.

She couldn't argue with that. 'I'm a good foot down and haven't hit anything,' she told him, stabbing the trowel into the ground and scraping upwards over and over again. 'Are you sure this is definitely the place?'

'These are the coordinates you gave me,' Connor replied.

Just then, there was a metallic clang as the trowel hit something solid. She paused and hit the same spot again.

Connor turned back to her. 'Bingo,' he whispered.

Chucking the cigarette away from him, he kneeled down and helped her dig out the sides and eventually they pulled out a large rusting biscuit tin.

'Rookie,' Connor murmured.

Scarlet opened it up and shone her phone torch inside. There, in a plastic sandwich bag, lying beside the neatly wrapped charger lead, was Alan's old mobile phone. She held it up for Connor to see and he nodded.

'Come on – let's go,' he said gruffly.

Picking up the tin and the contents, Scarlet hurried after Connor and they made their way to the car.

'I know you don't want to talk about it,' she started.

'You're right – I don't,' he replied curtly.

'But if you can face it, I want you to watch this video.' She looked at him until he glanced back at her. 'You'll be able to see that I'm telling the truth. But it's up to you because if you watch it, you'll also see Ruby's last moments.'

Connor didn't answer her straightaway, and she could see the small muscle in the side of his cheek work back and forth as he clamped his jaw tightly. They walked in silence until they reached the car and, as Scarlet buckled her seat belt, he finally turned to her.

'I'm not watching the video,' he said. 'But I appreciate you asking me to.' He exhaled and stared ahead through the windscreen. 'I do believe you. I think I do anyway. And we'll move on from this like I promised. But right now, I can't forgive you for not telling us. That's going to take time, and I don't know how long.'

Scarlet nodded. 'I understand that.'

'Let's just get this back and work out whether or not it's been shared,' Connor said, changing the subject. 'And then we can decide what the hell we're going to do with Alan.'

FIFTY-SIX

The charging seemed to take forever, but eventually the screen lit up and there was a tense silence as John methodically went through all the apps and records still on there.

The video was there, exactly as Alan had said it would be, destroying any hope that the entire thing had been a bluff. Scarlet played it only once and looked away as Ruby fell, needing no reminder of that moment. Her memory was more than enough to have to live with.

Connor waited in the other room, only joining them after Scarlet informed him that the video had been deleted and that John had found no trace of it ever being copied or sent anywhere else. It seemed Alan had counted on this one device and one hiding place being enough to protect him while he blackmailed her.

'You're absolutely *sure* it ain't been sent out?' Connor asked. 'How can you tell? He could easily have deleted it.'

'There are ways of checking for deleted files,' John told him, looking down at the handset. 'I can't check the deeper levels without certain equipment, but I've checked as far as I can. Alan's a basic guy when it comes to this sort of thing, and from what I could see in the video data, it's never been sent, copied or uploaded anywhere. You see, every action leaves a data trail, and to delete that data trail requires a much more in-depth knowledge of things than most people have.'

'Yeah, alright, Steve Jobs, I don't need the ins and outs,' Connor replied snappily. 'I just need to know there ain't no one else lurking in the shadows.' He ran a hand through his hair, stressed. 'How can you be certain there's no one else in the know?'

'We aren't,' Scarlet replied grimly.

'I don't think there is,' John replied, looking at each of them in turn. 'It wouldn't make sense. He's bluffed his way through since the start, he's a classic loner and he's predictable. I'd bet my life on him working alone.'

'Would you bet mine?' Scarlet asked, watching him closely.

John looked at her, his serious bright-green eyes roaming her face for a moment. 'Yes,' he replied with certainty.

Scarlet nodded and looked at Connor. 'That's good enough for me.'

'It had better be,' he replied heavily.

Scarlet took a deep breath in and started to prepare herself for what had to happen next. It was time to pay the price for her sins. It was time to deal with Alan and bury her secret forever. She stood up and opened her mouth to speak, but Connor cut her off.

'Go home now, Scarlet.' He held her gaze levelly. 'I'll clean this up.'

'What? No,' she argued with a frown. 'My mess, my graft, remember?'

'Go home,' he repeated, his voice harder this time. 'I mean it. I have this covered.' He stood up and shrugged off his jacket, walking through to the hallway to hang it on the banister.

Scarlet looked to John, hoping for an ally, but he shook his head.

'Go,' he echoed. 'We've got this.'

Connor walked back in and the two men exchanged a look. Scarlet watched the unspoken arrangement settle between them and realised there was no point arguing. Connor's mind was made up, and apparently John had decided to help him.

'I'll get rid of the phone and charger,' she said, the situation not sitting well with her. They shouldn't be dealing with this. *She* should. 'I'll have my phone and I'll be on standby in case you need me.'

Connor looked up at her resolutely. 'We won't.'

* * *

Connor waited until the front door shut behind Scarlet and then turned to John. The other man was already waiting beside the basement door. 'You sure you can stomach this?' he asked.

John frowned. 'I was on the force for years. I'm used to dealing with dead bodies,' he said flatly, looking away.

'Yeah, but you've never been the one to create them before, have you?' Connor pointed out in a low voice.

John didn't answer, but his resigned expression told Connor all he needed to know. He nodded. 'Come on then,' he said grimly. 'Let's get this over with.'

'What do we need?' John asked.

Connor walked towards an unused room that was full of boxes. 'Behind the door there's a box marked sheets. Grab two.'

He waited for John to go ahead, then went to the kitchen and slipped one of the sharper knives into the back of his waistband. Following John into the store room, he unbuttoned his shirt cuffs and neatly folded them back up to his elbows, and as John grabbed the plastic sheets, he opened another box and pulled out two pairs of latex gloves, along with a black bin bag, which he folded up and slipped into his pocket.

'Here. Put these on,' he said, handing John a pair of the gloves.

John took them, hesitating for only a fraction of a second before pushing his fingers into one. Connor eyed him and for a moment felt a grudging spark of respect for the man, though for the life of him he still couldn't understand him.

'It's been nearly *two years*,' he said, his confusion clear in his tone. 'You weren't even together that long.'

John looked up at him, a whole world of emotions in his eyes. 'It doesn't matter,' he said calmly. 'You don't choose things like this.'

Connor shook his head and glanced back out to the hallway. 'You need to do everything *exactly* as I say. Do you understand?' He waited until John nodded. 'Alright, let's go.'

They walked down the stairs to the basement, and Connor felt a lump of regret settle in his stomach for what he was about to do. He'd known Alan for many years. As a kid, Alan had chased him out of the scrapyard many a time for playing on the stacks. As an adult, the man had helped him on all sorts of jobs. He'd always been a steadfast ally in the wings. But that had been before Ruby had died there. And before he'd tried to blackmail Scarlet.

They entered the large open space through the glass door, and Alan's weathered face brightened at the sight of him.

'Thank God you're back,' he said with feeling. 'Let me out and I'll take you to where I kept that video. You can show your mum, deal with that snake in the nest once and for all.'

Connor sighed. 'Stand up,' he ordered.

Alan did just that, slipping off the mattress and pulling himself upright awkwardly. He cricked his back and the joints popped loudly. 'Ooosh. That's what you get for getting old,' he said. 'Though sleeping down here hasn't helped. I'll be glad to get back to me bed.'

Connor pushed the mattress out of the way and pointed at

the floor where it had been. 'Lay the sheets there,' he instructed John.

John opened them up and did just that, overlapping them in just the right way without being told. Clearly he'd worked out how these things were done, from all the jobs he'd been on the other side of.

Alan frowned, his expression growing alarmed. 'Connor?' he asked. 'What you doing? I'm on *your* side, mate. 'Ere, listen to me, I'm the one trying to *protect* your family.'

'You're the one who just threatened my cousin and tried to blackmail her into signing over part of our business to you,' Connor replied in a hard tone.

His cold glare burned into Alan's eyes, and the man cowered back with an expression of fear. 'It weren't like that,' he said. 'I lost out because of what she did. I weren't trying to take *you* for anything, I just wanted what *she* owed me.'

'Scarlet don't owe you a damn thing,' Connor said resolutely. 'And if you take from her, you take from all of us.'

'I-I-you have to see the video, Connor,' Alan stuttered. 'Please, mate.'

His fear was visibly growing, and Connor sighed, saddened by the whole thing. 'I can do this the quick way or I can do this the painful way. Which one is down to you.'

Alan had crossed too many lines for this to end any other way, but for old times' sake, Connor didn't want to cause the man unnecessary pain. If he didn't struggle, he would make this as swift as possible. But Alan immediately began to quiver.

'No... N-n-no, no, no, *no*, please,' he begged, backing away. 'You can't mean that really, eh, Connor? No. No, no, I'm sure you can't.'

Alan's dark rheumy eyes darted around, and he suddenly looked about ten years older than his already advanced years. He crouched slightly and held his fists up in defence, shifting his weight from one foot to another in jittery movements. A dark patch appeared near the crotch of his trousers and grew, and Connor looked away with a grim expression. The man was terrified.

'No,' he said suddenly, his voice gentle. 'No, I don't really mean it, Alan.'

John's head swivelled round towards him, but Connor stayed him with a hand held out to indicate pause.

'I just wanted to give you a warning, that's all. You needed to understand that this can never happen again.'

Alan straightened up with a brittle laugh of relief. 'Oh thank God. I didn't fancy me chances fighting you, to be honest.' He looked down at his trousers with regret but didn't say anything about it. 'I knew you'd do the right thing.'

Connor nodded. 'Sometimes the right thing isn't always the most obvious course.'

'Quite right,' Alan agreed.

Connor motioned for him to step forward. 'Turn around, let me get those ropes off.'

'Yes,' Alan said with emphasis, doing just that. 'This one round me middle has been a right discomfort, believe you me.'

He turned around in front of Connor and waited expectantly.

Connor looked down at the sparse hair still covering the older man's head and the liver spots that were beginning to show on his skin and felt a desolate sense of pity for the way he'd wasted his life. Alan had never married or had a family. He'd never gone anywhere or had any adventures. The man had spent his whole life just sitting in that scrapyard, day in, day out, alone but for his dogs, taking whatever jobs paid him enough to exist in moderate comfort. And now he'd die here in this basement, unmissed and unnoticed. It was a sorry end to a sorry life.

'You see the knots alright?' Alan asked, glancing back.

'Yeah,' Connor said flatly. 'I see 'em. Stand straight.'

Connor pulled the knife out from his waistband, then in one swift movement he wrapped an arm tightly around the top of Alan's head, pulled it back and sliced his neck open.

There was a sickening gargling sound as Alan tried to breathe in and failed, instead filling his lungs with the blood that now poured from the wide gash. He struggled, his eyes bulging and arms flailing helplessly as Connor gently lowered him to the ground.

'It will be over in a minute,' Connor said quietly.

He waited as the struggles grew weaker and the rise and fall of his blood-filled chest slowed, until eventually it all came to a stop. Silence filled the room and he laid out Alan's body, placing it neatly in the middle of the plastic sheets before standing straight and stripping down to his boxers. Pulling the black bag out of his trouser pocket, he threw the bloodstained clothes inside.

John stepped forward without a word and began wrapping Alan's body in the plastic sheeting, carefully tucking each end and pulling it tight. Another trick he must have picked up from being on the other side of murders like these, Connor surmised.

'In another life you'd have made a pretty good criminal,' he remarked.

'In another life you'd probably have made a decent copper,' John replied. He cast a gaze over the wrapped body, a heaviness settling over his expression.

'Don't think about it,' Connor said quietly, understanding exactly what the man must be feeling. 'No one likes having to do things like this. But we do what needs to be done to survive and protect our own.' He tied a knot in the bag. 'Focus on that part.'

'I'm fine,' John replied. 'What are we doing with him?'

Connor glanced at the body and pulled a grim expression. 'I have an idea, but if we do it, you'll need to be careful to stick to everything I say.'

'OK,' John replied.

'First I need you to grab the gym bag out of my car,' Connor said, glancing down at his almost naked body. 'Then we need to make a call.'

'Who to?' John asked with a frown.

Connor met his gaze. 'Cillian.'

FIFTY-SEVEN

Cillian knocked on the door of Tabitha's house and it flew open within seconds. She glared at him furiously.

'You have a nerve, ignoring my calls after last night, you *really* do,' she seethed, stepping back and gesturing for him to go inside. She slammed the door once he was inside and then rounded on him. 'Did you really think I wouldn't notice, hm? *Did* you?'

'What, that I stole your diamonds?' Cillian asked unashamedly. 'No, not really.'

Tabitha made a sound of outrage and pulled back, putting a hand to her chest. 'The *audacity*,' she hissed. 'You're lucky I haven't yet called the police. I still have a lingering soft spot for you after last night, but I can assure you it will *not* last long. So you had better get those diamonds back to me *pronto*.'

Cillian looked down at her with open contempt, no longer bothering to hide his true feelings, and saw the confusion gather on her face. 'Few things,' he said curtly. 'Firstly, that wasn't me you slept with last night.'

'Oh *really*?' Tabitha drawled sarcastically. 'Who was *that* then, your twin?'

'Yes, actually. His name's Connor. I swapped places with him when I went to get the ice. And I did that because the thought of touching you makes me physically shrivel up and want to vomit,' he said scathingly. 'You are so ignorant, conceited, narcissistic and rotten to the core that I wouldn't fuck you if you were the last woman on earth.' He ignored the cry of shock as her jaw dropped. 'My brother, on the other hand, hasn't had the misfortune of getting to know you. And he's had a bit of a dry spell, so was happy to take me up on the offer.'

Cillian turned in a circle, admiring the décor of the hallway one last time. 'You have *terrible* taste, by the way. The only decent parts of this house and your life are the parts that were designed or cultivated by your parents and ancestors.'

'How *dare* you,' Tabitha raged, having found her voice. 'You jumped-up little nobody, you can't talk to me like this!'

'Oh, I can,' Cillian replied, turning to face her. 'And I *will*. Because actually, of the two of us, it's *you* who's the nobody, Tabitha. You have nothing. No value as a person, no one who loves you, nothing but this cold empty house and someone else's hard-earned money in the bank. You've not earned one single part of your life. Which makes the fact that you look down on everyone around you not just ignorant, but fucking *laughable*.'

'I don't have to listen to this,' she snapped. 'Get out of my house. And get my diamonds back to me in the next two hours or the next knock on your door will be from the police.'

'No, it won't,' he replied with confidence. 'You won't tell them a thing. Because if you do, I'll share that lovely personal letter with them, from your friend, the general, over in Sierra Leone.'

Tabitha's eyes widened and her face turned a worrying shade of purple, and for a moment Cillian wondered if she might actually explode.

'Get out,' she said in a deep shuddering voice. '*Get out!*' she screamed.

'Gladly,' Cillian replied with a smirk.

'You won't get away with this!' she screeched as he made his way back to the front door.

'Oh, but I will,' he said, pausing to look back at her one last time. 'In fact, I already have.'

He opened the door and walked out into the clear winter evening, then jogged down the steps feeling lighter than he had in a long time. And as the door slammed shut behind him and he heard her almighty screech of frustrated rage, he smiled.

Feeling the buzz of the phone in his pocket he pulled it out and checked the caller ID before answering.

'Alright, Casanova?' he said in a jovial tone, heading towards his car. 'I just left your girlfriend.' His smile swiftly dropped to a deep frown as he listened, and then his stride came to an abrupt stop. '*What* did you just say?'

FIFTY-EIGHT

Scarlet paced her room anxiously, and glanced at the clock on her bedside table. It was now three in the morning. She'd turned the lights out a few hours before, keeping up the pretence of normality for her mother, whilst privately screaming on the inside. It had been hours since she'd left Connor and John at the house and she still hadn't heard from them. She'd texted each of them an hour ago, but neither had read it or returned any message.

What if something had gone wrong? This was murder, they were carrying out, after all. Murder and then the disposal of a whole human body. And there were only two of them doing all that. She *knew* she should have stayed. This was her mess – she should have been taking the risks.

A sharp tap against her window made her jump and she darted straight over to it. Peering down, she saw a dark figure below in a hoodie, and she quickly opened up, leaning out to better see who it was. The figure pulled back the hood and she saw that it was John. With a deep sigh of relief, she pointed towards the back gate and closed the window back up. *Thank*

God, she thought, slipping out into the hall and giving her mother's closed door a quick glance before she crept downstairs.

John met her at the French doors at the back of the house and she let him in, leading him to the formal dining room they rarely used these days. Closing the door behind them she switched on the light and pulled out a chair, searching his face as he sat down beside her.

'I'm sorry – I couldn't text you,' he said, propping his elbow on the table and rubbing his eyes tiredly.

'What happened? Are you OK? Is Connor OK?' Scarlet asked, holding back the rest of the questions that threatened to tumble out with a bite to her bottom lip.

'We're OK. It's sorted. It's over,' he confirmed, reaching out for her hand and squeezing it.

Scarlet nodded. 'I'm so sorry,' she whispered. 'You should never have had to do that for me. You shouldn't have had to do that at *all*.'

'Don't,' John said, squeezing again. 'No one asked me to. I had to see with my own eyes that this was dealt with. That there's no more threat hanging over your head. And now I have.' He looked up at her, his green eyes possessing a hardness she hadn't seen there before. 'And I don't regret it. I did what I had to do.'

Scarlet swallowed, his last few words gripping her stomach. He suddenly sounded like one of *them*. He had that same look in his eye too. It sent a flood of cold guilt through her body. What had she done to him?

'There's something you need to know,' he continued, a heaviness to his words now.

'What is it?' she asked with a frown.

'Connor called Cillian. To the house,' he replied.

'*What*?' Scarlet stood up, shocked and alarmed. 'We need to leave. *Christ*, I can't believe he set me up like this!'

'He didn't.' John gripped her hips and pulled her back towards her chair. 'Scarlet, he didn't set you up.'

'What do you mean? I don't understand.'

'I mean he changed the story. Fixed the issue Cillian had with you once and for all,' John told her.

Scarlet sat down slowly, her frown deepening in confusion.

'We needed help,' John admitted. 'We would have managed, but an extra person helps on the disposal side of things. Connor came up with a story. Apparently Cillian's noticed you've been acting strange for a week or two. That's why Connor's been following you.'

'I *knew* I wasn't imagining it,' Scarlet muttered to herself.

'Connor told Cillian that it was because you'd figured out that it was Alan who'd murdered Ruby,' John continued. 'He said you'd found out Alan had bought his house and after digging around you'd worked out it was almost the exact amount that Ruby had taken from the safe. You'd put two and two together and had then spent the last two weeks following him and digging around for the truth.'

Scarlet nodded slowly. 'It's a good spin.'

'It is,' John agreed. 'It takes every ounce of suspicion off you, from then *and* recently. The story is that you found enough proof that you were certain and then you lured him to the house today to confront him. Connor arrived as you were having it out and you shared everything with him. You were hiding it until now because you didn't want to say until you were certain, didn't want to build hope if you were wrong.' He shifted in his chair and sat back. 'You'll need to speak to Connor first thing tomorrow and get the exact details. It's important that you keep it straight between you when either of you are talking to Cillian. Or anyone. *Really* important.'

John looked away but Scarlet still saw the detachment in his eyes before she even registered it in his words. 'You're not including yourself in that,' she stated flatly. There was a short silence and she felt her heart grow achingly heavy. 'When do you go?' she asked, no strength in her words.

'This was never meant to be more than a short visit,' he reminded her. 'It never *could* be anything more than that. Not with the target on my back.' He forced a pale smile. 'You're safe now, and you have a life here. A *good* one.' He tilted his head wryly. 'As good as it can be, on the wrong side of the law.'

Scarlet managed a smile, but the tears still welled up in her eyes anyway. John reached out and wiped the first one that fell, but the touch of his hand triggered several more and she reached up, pressing it to her cheek. 'I can't believe I'm having to say goodbye to you again,' she said, barely managing to get the words out.

'I know,' he whispered back, every emotion spilling out into his words. 'I love you so much, Scarlet. I never knew I could love someone as much as I love you. And it will kill me to walk away from you, but I *will*. Because it's for the best.'

Scarlet let out a sob as her heart broke jaggedly in two once more, and John leaned forward to wrap his arms around her. She buried her head in his chest.

'I love you too,' she whispered. 'And I think I always will.'

John buried his face in her neck and let out a groan of frustration and pain and then suddenly he pulled back, his mouth seeking hers as he abandoned his self-restraint. Scarlet met his kiss hungrily, feeling the explosion of pleasure and heartache combined as their lips finally connected. It felt like home and heaven and the forbidden fruit, all at once, and she savoured the feel of his soft warm lips, every past memory of them awakened.

But even as they sat there wrapped up in each other's arms, lost in that kiss, she also knew with complete certainty that this wasn't a new beginning or a bridge back to the path they'd once lost. This was a goodbye. Her tears rained down her face and mixed with his, and as their lips reluctantly parted, she rested her forehead on his, unable to force herself away from him just yet.

Eventually it was John who gently sat back, breaking the connection.

'No,' she uttered, but there was no conviction in the word. She knew this was over just as well as he did.

'Yes,' he whispered, grasping both of her hands in his and squeezing them for the last time. 'You won't see me again. Let this be our goodbye, Scarlet.' He looked into her eyes and held her stare for a moment. 'Let this be the last memory we have.'

She nodded, unable to speak for a moment. She cleared her throat and took in a deep breath, letting it out slowly as she tried to contain her emotions long enough to say goodbye properly. 'You know if you need anything...'

'I know. But I'll be OK,' he replied. He pushed his chair back and stood up. 'And if you need *me*, you must reach out. I know there were certain reasons for doing it this time, but don't try and deal with everything alone, Scarlet. Lean on your family. Let other people in.'

'I do,' she insisted.

'You don't,' he told her, giving her a piercing gaze. 'The only person you've leaned on since your dad died was *me*. You think you have to look after everyone, or keep worry away from them, or manage them – but you don't. Lean on *them* now and then. But if ever you can't again and you're in trouble, you can call on me. I'll be with the Logans.'

Scarlet nodded. 'Thanks.'

John cast his gaze over her face once last time with a deep sigh and then turned and walked back through the house to the French doors at the back. Scarlet followed him, her heart growing more painful with every step. It felt like sending him off at the docks, all over again. Nothing about this seemed easier.

Sliding the door open, John stepped through and turned

around to face her. 'I'm sorry if me being here has messed things up for you with that guy.'

Scarlet looked down and didn't answer.

'If he makes you happy and you have a future, I really do hope you can make it work.' He lifted her chin with his finger and caught her gaze with a look of sincerity. 'You have too much to give to waste your heart on me forever.'

Scarlet touched his hand and shook her head, her bottom lip threatening to wobble again. 'Not one second of loving you *has* ever, or *will* ever, be a waste. But the same goes for you. Find someone, John. Don't be alone. You deserve happiness.'

His face crumpled for a moment, but he just about managed to hold it together as he leaned forward and kissed her forehead.

She closed her eyes until he pulled away, then she followed his dark outline as he slipped down the side of the house. And then just like that, he was gone.

EPILOGUE

Several days later, after the shocking news about Alan killing Ruby for her money had swept through the family and most of the underworld, the family made their first united trip to Ruby's grave since the funeral. It wasn't a particular occasion, no birthday or sad anniversary, just a normal Tuesday afternoon. But for the first time in a long time there was a true harmony among them, and the static distance that had buzzed underneath the surface of Scarlet and Cillian's relationship since Ruby's body had been found, had finally disappeared.

The first time she'd seen him, after getting her story straight with Connor, they'd had a long talk and he'd apologised to her for the way he'd threatened her and kept her at arm's length. He'd also told her that he'd realised he'd been too harsh in his anger towards her, for making the wrong choice of mark in Tabitha. He'd admitted that the plan falling down the way it had had been his fault. That he'd strayed off the plan when she'd dangled his dream car in front of him. If it hadn't been for that, things would have run smoothly, but they were all human at the end of the day. And people sometimes made mistakes. It had been a big step in the right direction for the pair of them, and it had given Scarlet hope that they could run the firm in harmony together one day.

If anyone had noticed that Connor was especially quiet, they hadn't mentioned it. Scarlet was pointedly aware of it though, and every time she looked at him, she felt a spear of guilt stab through her, at the load she'd placed on his shoulders. He'd killed for her. Killed someone he'd known for many years. And though she knew he would shrug that off as his duty as her cousin, she also knew that wasn't the hardest part for him. The hardest part was having to hide the truth from his twin. They had shared absolutely everything their whole lives, from the egg they grew from to the cut of their suits and everything in between. They had *never* had secrets from each other. And it was her fault that, now, Connor did.

The family formed a semi-circle around Ruby's grave, and Scarlet fell in line between her mother and her aunt. The boys and Billie stood dutifully the other side of Lily, and they all waited as Lily stared down at her daughter's grave, her expression unreadable. Eventually she reached into her large handbag and pulled out a bottle of champagne and a packet of plastic flutes.

'Hand these around,' she instructed, passing the flutes to Scarlet.

Scarlet did so and Lily popped the cork, pouring them each a small plastic glass of ice-cold bubbles. The last flute she filled and placed on top of Ruby's headstone, before returning to her position in the centre of the family and raising hers into the air.

'I'd like us all to raise a toast, as a family – and Ruby, if you're wondering why I've included Billie in this meeting, you're about to find out why,' she added, aiming her words to the headstone in front of her, then she looked around at all their faces and smiled. 'To my son, the eldest by seven whole minutes, Cillian Drew, and his beautiful future wife Billie.'

'To Cillian and Billie,' the rest of them echoed, lifting their plastic flutes to toast over Ruby's grave.

'And to finally getting justice for you, my baby girl,' Lily added quietly as the rest of them sipped their champagne. 'Scarlet finally got the bastard. And your brothers sent him off to hell, where he belongs.' She lifted her flute again, this time just towards Ruby's headstone, then took a deep drink.

Scarlet tipped the glass back and downed the rest of it in one, casting her eyes to Ruby's headstone. She'd had no love for her cousin when she'd been alive. Though she'd had no hand in her death, it had been a relief and a blessing when she was finally gone. And though she knew she'd have to keep it to herself for the rest of her life, she secretly hoped Ruby had seen Alan's plan fail. She hoped she was raging from wherever she was watching from now. Because after all Ruby had taken from her, she deserved to feel that loss. Scarlet had finally closed the door on that chapter of her life and moved on. And Ruby would never get one over on her, or win against her in any way, ever again.

Connor shifted uneasily from one foot to the other, looking up at his mother with a strange expression of regretful anticipation, and Scarlet frowned, wondering what was going through his mind. He cleared his throat and fiddled with his plastic flute for a moment.

'As we're all here, it seems a fitting time to make another little announcement,' he said awkwardly.

'Oh?' Lily said, looking at him with a questioning expression.

'Yeah...' Connor glanced at Cillian, who seemed to be as in the dark as everyone else. 'A lot has changed lately. The business has grown and you've each opened up your different ventures. There's a solid team of men around now, so we're no longer so stretched.' He scratched his head and paused, clearly finding whatever he was trying to say difficult. 'And everyone's got their own lives, you know? You two are getting married...' He nudged Cillian with his arm and gave him a quick grin. 'And I couldn't be happier for you. I really couldn't. But I feel like I need something new to sink my teeth into too.'

Lily perked up and smiled at him. 'Yeah? What you got in mind? Let's hear it.'

'Well...'

He cast his gaze down and Lily's frown faltered as confusion flickered across her face. Scarlet exchanged a frown with Cillian. What was happening right now?

'I've actually decided I'm going to take a break from the main running of the firm for a bit,' he said.

Lily let out a short sound of surprised amusement. 'Yeah, alright then. Pull the other one,' she said. 'What you really thinking?'

'Well that's just it,' he replied. 'I'm serious.' There was a shocked silence. 'Ray's asked me to go over to learn how things work in his firm. Just for a while,' he added hurriedly. 'You know I'm not disappearing for good. But I think this could be a good thing, in the long run.'

Scarlet's jaw dropped and her head swivelled back towards Lily, much like everyone else's. Lily's pale face had gone totally white, her eyes wide with fury and her lips clamped so tightly they were just one long white line of stress.

'What did you say?' she asked, her low tone deadly.

Connor exhaled heavily. 'I said I'm going to work for Ray for a while.'

There was a long silence and Scarlet felt her mother shrink back next to her. She didn't blame her. She didn't particularly want to be here for this either. Sparks were going to fly and the aftermath wasn't going to be pretty.

Cillian shook his head as if shaking off an ugly thought, then turned to his twin with a look of complete disbelief. 'What are you *doing*?' he asked. 'We always said we'd never take him up on that.'

'*We*?' Lily questioned, her eyebrows rising so high they almost disappeared. 'What do you mean *we*? And *always*?'

Cillian turned back to her with a sigh. 'Look, we weren't going to tell you for exactly this reason, but Ray's been after one of us going over for a while.'

'Oh, has he now?'

Lily's most deadly tone was coming into play now, and Scarlet averted her gaze. There was no way she wanted any part in this.

'He has this idea that if one of us went over, we could unite the firms one day, rule it as one big super firm,' Cillian told her, looking back to his brother. 'But we said we weren't going to do it. Why did you change your mind? Why now?' He sounded as if he felt betrayed.

Connor looked away. 'I don't know. I just think it's time. And it's something for me. I'm still part of this family; I ain't going anywhere on that front and I really do think it would be a good move, for the long run.'

'This family...' Lily hissed, her temper rising. 'That's right, you're part of *this* family, *not* his. He has *no* right to you.'

'It ain't about rights,' Connor argued. 'And this ain't me going against you, Mum. This is just something I'm doing for myself. And I think it's for the best for all of us, long term.'

'You fool,' Lily said in a low voice. She shook her head and looked to the sky, letting out a bitter bark. 'All these years we've spent building this firm, and you just want to swan off to play house with *Ray*? The man you've *despised* your whole life? No. I don't think so. What's he got over you?' she demanded.

'Nothing!' Connor insisted, holding his hands out to the sides. 'I *want* to go.'

'I don't buy it,' Lily snapped.

'Well you need to,' he replied, his tone and expression resolute. 'Because I'm going.'

Something dark and dangerous flashed across Lily's face, and she glared at him for a few long moments as if she was about to say something. But at the last moment she turned and marched away without a word, heading to her car and then screeching off down the road.

'Shit,' Cath breathed, looking worried. 'Connor, what have you done?'

'What I need to, Aunt Cath,' he replied, meeting Scarlet's gaze for the first time since they'd arrived. 'It's just time for me to try something new. Spread my wings a bit.'

Scarlet saw it then. The real reason he was leaving. It was because of her. He couldn't be here looking into his mother's and brother's eyes every day, carrying around a secret of that magnitude. A crushing weight settled in her chest as her guilt rose tenfold. Just like so many other things the rest of them weren't aware of, this was her fault.

'Connor, we need to talk about this,' Cillian said, sounding concerned.

'Sure. But I ain't changing my mind,' he replied.

The group began to move away from the grave now Lily had gone, and Scarlet touched her mother's arm. 'I need to go do something. I'll catch you later, yeah?'

'Yeah, 'course, love,' Cath replied. 'Good luck.' She winked and Scarlet gave her a grateful smile as she walked away towards her car.

* * *

Scarlet hesitated outside Benny's flat, gathering her courage before knocking loudly. As she waited, she straightened her dress and smoothed her hair with her hands, suddenly self-conscious. Eventually he opened the door, and for a few seconds they both just stood there, watching each other with equally guarded and unreadable expressions.

'Can I come in?' she asked.

Benny stepped back. 'Sure.'

Scarlet walked in and followed Benny through to the living area. He sat down, still watching her carefully as she took a seat on one of the other sofas. He didn't speak, and she understood why. They had to be this guarded, in their way of life, to survive. It was a habit that so often spilled over into the protection of their hearts too.

'Listen, I came here to tell you that John's gone,' she said, cutting straight to the point.

'I'm sorry for your loss,' he said evenly.

'It's not a loss. He was never mine to lose. Or at least not this time,' she said.

'Did anything happen between you?' Benny asked.

'Yes,' she said honestly, holding his gaze. 'He kissed me. Just once, and as a goodbye, nothing more.'

He nodded again slowly, looking away out of the window for a few seconds. 'Is your business dealt with – is it over between you?'

'It really was nothing but a goodbye,' she reiterated. 'There's nothing going on and he's back out of my life. For good this time.'

It had been a painful realisation, but even as she'd agreed when John had told her to come to him if she needed, she'd known she would never take him up on the offer. Not ever. It was just too hard.

'I understand if all of this has been too much for you,' Scarlet continued, when Benny didn't respond. 'And if that's it, I'll respect that. But I wanted you to know that I meant what I said before. I loved John and he was a big part of my life. But that was over a long time ago and my heart beats for someone new now. For *you*.' She bit her bottom lip and stood up. 'I'm not going to beg for you to pick things back up with me. I'm just going to leave the ball in your court. What you do with it is up to you.'

Benny's eyebrows rose, but he still remained silent.

She cast her gaze over his smooth black skin and the well-defined muscles that the tight vest top he wore did nothing to hide, feeling the same physical pull towards him that she always had. Forcing herself to turn away, she shot him a parting smile and made her way back towards the front door.

'Hey,' he called, standing up and following her.

She stopped and turned back, her hope rising as he approached her.

'I'm picking up that ball,' he said simply.

As he gathered her in his arms, Scarlet wrapped hers around his neck and met his kiss with every ounce of warmth and passion she possessed.

* * *

Lily sat at her desk staring at the picture of Mani Romano on her wall, waiting for the phone to ring. A tendril of smoke wafted up from her lit cigarette, joining the cloud that lingered in the air above her. She took another drag and then a sip of the large whisky next to her as she narrowed her gaze and picked up one of the handful of darts next to her on the desk.

With expert precision, she launched it across the room, hitting the picture of Mani right in the centre of the forehead. The phone finally rang and she picked it up on the first ring, tapping her cigarette into the ashtray and leaning it there while she spoke.

'Finn, hi. All OK getting back? Good, good,' Lily said, listening to his reply. 'I'm glad. It was good to see you. Listen, we need a meeting to discuss this Romano plan. How soon can you get back to London?' She paused to listen. 'Perfect. The sooner the better.' She shot another dart at Mani's head, hitting the nose this time. 'That's ideal. Let me know the date once you've booked the flight and we'll get something arranged.' She picked up another dart and rolled it between her fingers. 'No, this will just be me. Ray will most definitely not be involved.' Her expression hardened. 'But don't worry about all that. Keep me updated and we'll talk soon.'

Ending the call, Lily took another sip of her whisky and narrowed her gaze at her target. This time, when she let the dart fly, she aimed for the second picture she'd pinned to the wall. A newer picture, right next to Mani. And, as with all the others, the dart hit exactly where she'd aimed it.

Right between Ray's eyes.

A LETTER FROM EMMA

Hello!

Thank you for reading *Her Enemy*, the latest book in the Drew series. If this is the first book of mine you've picked up, then welcome to the Drews! If you've been with me through this journey from the beginning, then welcome back, friend.

If you enjoyed *Her Enemy*, sign up here to be the first to find out what happens next for Lily and Scarlet. We won't share your details and you can unsubscribe at any time.

www.bookouture.com/emma-tallon

I think this book has been the hardest book I've ever written. Partly because life has thrown obstacle after obstacle at me, and after pushing back my deadlines time and again, it has still kept me up on more all-nighters than any author should pull in a lifetime of books, let alone one! It's also partly because there were a lot of powerful emotions coming through the storylines in this book. When writing any scene, as the author, I feel every single emotion that I'm writing, so with this one, especially with the Scarlet and John scenes, it's been quite an intense ride.

As always, I read every single review, message and comment that comes through my social pages or Amazon, and I love to find out what you loved or who you hated, what you want to see more of next time, etc., so please do keep those coming.

And now I need to go, as it's gone 2 a.m. while I'm writing this and I'm ready to crash.

Stay safe and happy.

Love always,

Emma X

 facebook.com/emmatallonofficial

 twitter.com/EmmaEsj

instagram.com/my.author.life

ACKNOWLEDGEMENTS

Firstly, I'd like to thank all of you, my lovely readers. I am so grateful to you for buying my books and for sticking with me through my series. It means a lot.

Secondly, I'd like to share some appreciation for my wonderful editor, Helen, who I'm sure I'm prematurely aging with all the stress I've put her through over the course of this particular book! Helen, you're amazing. Aside from being a wonderful person to work with, your patience and kindness has helped me through more than you know. Thanks for being you.

And lastly I'd like to thank two of my best friends in the world, Casey Kelleher and Victoria Jenkins. You two are my strength when I can't find any myself, you're the two people I can always be 100 per cent myself around and your friendship is something I genuinely treasure more than I can ever express with words. I feel so grateful to have you in my life. Please don't ever change.